NASH

KELLY FINLEY

Nash: Belles & Bratva Beasts, Book One

Kelly Finley

© 2025 Kelly Finley Publishing, LLC

Visit the author's website at kellyfinley.com

ISBN: 979-8-9890644-9-6 (eBook)

ISBN: 979-8-9916399-1-0 (paperback)

Interior Formatting by Kelly Finley

Cover design by Lori Jackson

Cover photo by Wander Aguiar :: Photography

Cover model: Aaron Gill

ALSO BY KELLY FINLEY

Belles & Bratva Beasts
Nash
Axel
Sire
Loch
Jace

Interconnected Books
Shameless Play
Shameless Game
Make Him
Tempt Her

The Six
Holiday For Six
Halloween For Six

After Him
With Him

CONTENT ADVISORY
WARNING: THERE ARE SPOILERS, TOO

This book contains a very spicy plot with swoony angst and witty snark set in an ex-mafia secret society. Congrats if this is your kind of romance.

It also contains topics readers may be sensitive to. If you have any questions about this list, please message me on my social media platforms @kellyfinleybooks (Instagram, TikTok, and Facebook).

- Touch her, and I'll kill you vibes (he does)
- Primal play. I mean, "beast" is in the subtitle
- She works at an adult shop ... so lots of sex toys
- Oh, she's earning a PhD in Sexuality (lots of lessons, too)
- A strong survivor of assault (no graphic descriptions)
- Age-gap love (He's 44. She's 30. Perfection)
- A taboo moment (She was 18. It's not what you think. You'll see)
- Detailed sex scenes that feature dirty talk, Daddy

kink, anal, cunnilingus fetish (you're welcome), a
swing, an audience ... okay, that's enough spoilers
- Still, he won't share her. Like, he's sociopathic
about it, but...
- There's a taboo initiation into a secret society
involving more than one, but only once ... okay ...
twice
- Kings who prove their love for their Queens (in
front of each other)
- They're brothers, too. But hell no. Never brother-
on-brother
- Adult toys to *sort of* torture (But the villain is an
a**hole. He deserves it)
- There might be an eye taken
- And some bloody fingers that play
- And a lethal golf club
- A plot surrounding human trafficking
- A badass woman who survived it and built an
empire of revenge
- References to parental neglect and abandonment
- Parental loss (not depicted)
- It's a book in a series about men who escaped the
mafia, so they're not big Bratva fans. Instead,
they're like the ex-mafia avengers

If this only got you excited, this book is for you.

PLAYLIST

Prologue
"Pretty Little Poison," Warren Zieders
Chapter 1
"Beast," Rob Bailey & The Hustle Standard, Busta Rhymes
Chapter 2
"Guys My Age," Hey Violet
Chapter 3
"Sports Car," Tate McRae
Chapter 6
"Guilty," BOBI ANDONOV
Chapter 7
"Older," Isabel LaRosa
Chapter 9
"Devil in a Dress," Teddy Swims

Chapter 47

"Certain Things," James Arthur, Chasing Grace

To all smutty readers
who deserve to be railed like queens

These dirty kings are for you

PROLOGUE

NASH

You know the saying, "Better the devil you know than the one you don't."

Oh, Vale knows me.

She just doesn't know I'm the devil.

Her merlot-colored lips sip a dollar draft beer, and I stare at them, obsessed, aroused, watching her lush lips part, swallowing the liquid before she licks them, satisfied.

Damn, what I want to do to her mouth.

It's wrong. Very wrong. She's my daughter's best friend, old enough to drink now but too young, too taboo for me to crave.

But I do.

I confess—I'm an evil man, but a good father.

But what's more evil than my desire for Vale Monroe and her tempting mouth is the man at the bar lurking behind her.

It takes one to know one—he's a predator.

Like me, he's watching, waiting ... *wanting*.

The girls slam their empty drinks down on the round cocktail table, high-five, and shout for another round. The bartender nods, reaching for fresh glasses to fill. Bass beats thump from the speakers, and voices fill the hot, humid air. Neon lights glow above the beach bar, and I lurk in a shadowed corner.

They don't know I'm here.

Talk about crashing your daughter's twenty-first birthday party; I won't do that to Alena. The smile on her face is what I live for.

But I'll kill for Vale Monroe.

And tonight, it seems I'll have to.

I watch as the evil piece of shit behind her palms a Benjamin into the bartender's hand before he deftly drops a pill into the foamy brew, swirling it with a lecherous smirk. Grabbing the innocent glass meant for my daughter beside it, he turns with two beers in hand, elbowing through his group of "bruhs."

"Bottoms up, my bitches." He slams the glasses down before them, his joke failing.

Alena rolls her eyes, hating him. Blair, Vale's twin, glares at him as Vale glances away.

Christ, there's that look again.

The one on her face that breaks my cold heart.

I've known Vale since she was thirteen; her stoic mask can't hide it from me. I see... No, I can *feel* her rage, her fear, her prison, trapped in a life with an ex-boyfriend obsessed with her.

It's disturbing.

But I get it. What man wouldn't be?

Vale's long, raven hair, twisted in two teasing braids, is intoxicating, her grey eyes mesmerizing, her skin alabaster in a town of tans and browns. Her gothic look doesn't belong on a Southern beach. She's different. She stands out on purpose. Like a red light warning you to stay away, she only draws men near.

Like me.

Like Chad, her ex.

Yes, I get the irony; I stalk Vale, too. I hate how I want her, feel proud that I've never touched her, and grieve how I never will. I relish her from afar because I'll never hurt her ... and I'll kill anyone who does.

Or *did*.

My daughter confided in me last week how Chad's stalking is hell for Vale, how she's scared and has every reason to be. Alena told me how Chad's violated Vale before. He was violent with her when they were dating years ago, and by the look in his eyes tonight and the drug he just snuck into Vale's drink, he plans on doing it again.

I gnash my teeth: *the fuck he will.*

Touch who I love and die.

Vale's friendship saved my daughter, and for that, I'll always love her.

But I never expected to want Vale, too, sharing the most erotic night of my life with her when she was only eighteen and I was thirty-two. It was a mistake I fantasize about every day.

Every night.

It fills me with shame.

And lust.

I swear Vale's the pretty poison I'd drink every drop of and offer my last breath. She's smart and a smartass. Sweet and snarky. Loving and aloof. Funny, but in pain. She's rare and every goddamn thing I want, and it sickens me how she's grown into a young woman I dream about, staining my sheets, my desire for her a nightmare.

Don't worry. I can hide it.

I'm hiding right in front of you. There. In the dark shadows that prickle your skin.

I have a syringe in my pocket with a special drug just for Chad, one he'll never wake from. I have a yacht, a lavish hearse to the perfect grave, the Atlantic Ocean. There will be no headstone for Chad because I always have a plan, and I never work alone.

I thirst for Chad's blood, but blood and bullets are evidence, and I'm no fool.

You only see me if I let you. If not, I blend in. I'm a regular guy. Leaning against a wooden pavilion pillar, my black golf shirt, khakis, and thick eyeglasses disguise who I am, what I'm capable of, and who I work with.

It's one of the six men I'm sworn to, waiting by the men's room for Chad.

As always, silently, we work together. It's a matter of time before we act.

Making people disappear is our specialty.

But before rapey Chad takes his last breath tonight for hurting what's mine, I'll tell him who it's for, who I love.

Vale will have her vengeance.

It's me.

Nash Allen.

VALE

"I'm not drinking dollar drafts," I mutter to Alena, "I'm chugging dread."

"I'd say I can't believe the dickhead is here," she replies, "but I do. It's typical Chad. He heard from Conner you'd be here, and like a fart, he reeks in the air around us."

Alena tries to make me laugh, so I fake a smile for her. I won't ruin her birthday.

I can't go anywhere in Charleston without my ex showing up, but *fuck him*. My stomach lurches when he's near, fear racing my heart just like that night years ago, but I'll never let his pathetic, preppy-ass see it. I won't give him the satisfaction.

I keep my back to him. I lift my chin and fake ignoring him.

I focus on my best friend and my twin sister, pounding down a Jägerbomb, and wince at the concoction. "You just wasted ten bucks to barf in ten minutes." I'm older by five minutes, so I'm the boss of her.

"Like you wasted ten bucks on that dress?" Blair, my mirror, smirks back. "You know, you look like Wednesday Addams, the aspiring pornstar version."

I glance down at my new look. I like it. It's intentional. It says, "Fuck me," but "Fuck you," too, because that's how I feel—complicated.

"I think it's cute," Alena defends me. She might as well be our sister, too. "It's hot and innocent at the same time. The double entendre is totally you."

"Thank you." I peck her cheek. "Now, murder my twin for me, please."

"Never. I'm an only child, and you two are my ride-or-dies."

Blair shakes her head at Alena, sighing, "Girl, I'm sorry because I don't understand."

Alena twists her face, confused.

"I don't understand," Blair huffs, "how you don't have a kitten litter of siblings because any pussy would kill to breed with your hot-ass father and his sexy seed."

"Jeez, Blair," I scoff, eyes wide.

"What?"

"That's Alena's dad! That's ick-factor level ten."

Blair shrugs. "That's me just saying what everyone else knows—Nash Allen is a god amongst DILFs. He's so zaddy with all that alpha sperm." She nudges Alena. "Didn't he like spawn you at fourteen?"

Yep, my twin's allergic to verbal filters.

Unfortunately, we share that DNA.

"My parents were sixteen when I was a whoops," Alena corrects her before she warns, "and I know how sex positivity runs in *your* family, how you're both sex gurus and all, but I'm positively begging you to never fuck my father. I'd die. I need best friends, not a new mom."

Blair rests her head on Alena's shoulder. "Don't worry," she assures. "I'm too busy fucking people my age first. It'll be years before I work my way into the forties, and *then* you can lock your daddy away from my prowling kitty."

They laugh as guilt stabs my heart.

A forbidden image by a pool. A taboo memory of a night years ago with Alena's dad. It floods my core with sudden heat.

I love Alena like she's my twin, too, but my secret feelings for her father run deep. I hate him, and I think I'm in love with him. It confuses me. It scares me.

Worse, it tempts me.

Nash Allen introduced me to desire, but I'll never act on it. Heck, I've never even touched the man because I'd never hurt Alena, but Blair is right.

Mr. Allen is a nuclear sex bomb. One touch from him would destroy my lonely world, and *yes, please.*

Break my cage open.

Wetting my thirst for everything I don't have, I sip my beer, searching the crowded bar with bodies pressed against bodies. In the sea of cold strangers ... I feel heat. Under the bright outdoor lights, I'm drawn to the shadows. Like someone's there for me, waiting, watching, and *loving me*.

But who am I kidding?

Love took a permanent vacation from my life years ago, and all that's left is sex, so I'm getting a PhD in it. I figure if I don't have one, I can at least be an expert in the other.

Besides, the only one watching *me* is a man I loathe, a criminal and a perv. The asshole.

I know he's behind me.

He's always watching me.

Claws: that's what they are. The people and memories that ambush you, piercing your skin and dragging your soul to its darkest depths. They leave you ripped open and praying you heal.

And I have. Mostly.

I hate Chad, but now I love myself more.

So, with my last gulp of beer, Alena joins me, and we high-five before signaling for another round. Minutes later, to my sickening surprise, Chad slams down two sloshing pints before us.

"Bottoms up, my *bitches*."

That word? From his mouth?

He sinks his claw in, and I glance away, fighting the instinct to murder and cry at the same time. The stench of his cologne brings it all back: how Chad hissed that slur in my ear, how he wouldn't stop, how it hurt. It's every reason I feel numb inside.

"Happy Birthday, Alena," Chad sneers with a threat dripping from his tone again, and I whip around.

"Get her pretty name out of your ugly mouth before I punch it out."

Chad stares at my threatening lips, his eyes swimming with evil delight, I don't know why, but this isn't about me.

I'd kill for Alena.

"Now, now, Vale." Chad looms. "Don't be jealous. I'll shove my cock back in *your* mouth, too."

My eyes narrow. "When I want to bite a Tic Tac again, I'll let you know. It'll be right around go-fuck-yourself o'clock."

"Yeah," Blair jumps in, "that'll be right around the time they find the cure for your little dick energy." She flips him off. "You're aware your Tesla Cybertruck is its first symptom?"

She knows. Alena does, too.

My secret lives with them and in Chad's dead blue-eyed stare. It's been locked on me since we were eighteen. I just wanted to go to my senior prom, but he turned it into my nightmare. That was five years ago, and I still can't wake up from it.

"Just leave us alone." Alena plays peacemaker. "Thanks for the beer and birthday wishes." She shoos. "Now, bye-bye, Chad."

"I'm not going anywhere." He presses into me. We're standing at a beach bar, but my sobbing memory is in the back seat of a Mercedes. "Right, Vale? Give me a kiss. You know it belongs to me."

I was too young and scared to do anything back then, and lately? I've tried filing stalking charges against him, but he's a corrupt judge's son. The law can't touch him. Nothing will stop him. Chad's everywhere I turn, even in my mind.

But I've grown since then. I'm stronger now.

Unfortunately, so has he, so I tell the guy behind him, "Conner, call off your dog. No one invited your Chihuahua and his pathetic micro pecker to the party."

I like Conner and the guys we went to high school with. We invited them to come tonight. They're like brothers to us, while Chad's a virus infecting our circle.

"Come on, bruh." Conner grabs Chad's shoulder. "Give her space. Go take a piss."

Chad steps back, eyeing me, while my twin snickers, "Need some tweezers to pull it out?"

I can't help it.

Blair makes me laugh as I absent-mindedly swig my beer. Beer that Chad brought to the table, but I don't focus on it. I glare defiantly at him. He looks so creepy, wearing his Aviator sunglasses like a headband as he watches me swallow before he sneers, acting pleased with himself before turning away and disappearing into the crowd.

For a moment, I'm relieved.

He's gone.

Then, dread floods my veins again because, like always, he'll be back to torment me. I'll never be free of him.

So, I get black-out drunk and don't remember the rest of the night.

But I can't forget; I can't stop wondering why...

I never saw Chad again.

CHAPTER ONE
NASH

Six years later

T‍HREE TIMES, A BLACK M‍ERCEDES HAS CREPT BY.

I've counted.

I always count.

They've done it over the past thirty minutes. They make it obvious they know I'm in here.

Watching them from the shadows of an arched window above Meeting Street, I unbutton my starched shirt. It reeks of perfume, sweat, and sex. Sex with seven men and one woman. The aroma is distinct. Taboo. Beastial.

And I savor it on rare occasions.

"We have friends." I give the intel.

"And we have a screamer," Axel replies.

He doesn't care. He knows we're covered. He reclines in a black leather executive chair behind his mahogany desk. The lamps in his law office are off. The light glowing from the dusk and gas lamps outside is enough to see how he's amused, and I'm annoyed.

We're done here.

I need to go home while the screams of the woman in the boardroom next door fill the otherwise empty office.

"He's cleaning her," I say, doing the same, wiping the sweat off my chest with my soiled shirt before tossing it aside. "He gets off on it."

"By the sound of it," Axel smirks, "so does she."

"She's barely twenty."

He shrugs. "She's his now; that makes her *ours,* too."

He makes it sound natural, and I shake my head.

Yes, it feels permanent now. I feel a bond after what we've done with her. I'll always protect her, too, but ... it's not natural.

Reaching into my cognac leather duffel resting on a side table, I grab a fresh, black golf shirt. Tugging it down my torso, I fasten the buttons at the top. The familiar strangle around my throat conceals me; I count on it, smoothing away wrinkles in my shirt before dropping my dress pants and kicking them away.

We never wear boxers or briefs for this. Our pants stay on while we drag our zippers down. So now my black Brooks Brothers trousers reek. Like a wolf, I can smell the seed of men and a woman's arousal on them; it's a maddening skill.

"We need a safer place for this," Axel says what I've warned for years.

Like tonight, our *meetings* get loud. Booming voices, raucous laughter, tell-tale creaking wood, screams of lust, and grunts like beasts; we sound like the animals we are.

It's risky. We can draw too much attention, and that's the last thing we want. We're trained to hide in plain sight.

"I think I found one," I say, sliding on the khakis I plucked from my bag; their neat front crease is not my style and exactly what I intend. Toeing on loafers I hate, I slide glasses from a case, pressing their thick, black frames over the bridge of my nose and securing the disguise.

"A place?" Axel asks. "Where?" He's skeptical. He knows every property in Charleston.

"The old Bonneau mansion."

Axel cocks a brow. "You mean Delta's, the sex shop?" He cocks a knowing grin, too. "Where you've been working for your *daughter's* best friend?"

Secrets don't exist between us. It's in his tone.

It's a bad idea. It's the best idea. It's genius, kind of like me.

"The books at Delta's are a mess," I reply. "Vale called me to fix them, and I'll have their audit done in a month, maybe two, and then I'm out, but there's a room on their third floor. It's private, protected, and very posh. It's perfect."

"No," Axel coldly commands. "Two of us already work there, and now *you*? That's too many targets in one location."

I gesture to the paneled, wooden door. The one not able to muffle the carnal feast in the next room. "Every time we meet, we run that risk. At least at Delta's, our meetings won't draw attention. They'll blend in, like us. But here? This is a respected law office where it sounds like a woman is being murdered in your boardroom."

"It sounds like a woman is *coming* in my boardroom." Axel chuckles. It's rare. "*Again*."

I growl, "He needs to hurry up. I'm going to be late."

I'm never late.

"She's finally his queen. Let him enjoy her."

We're waiting for them to finish. We're always the last to leave. Axel knows I have to check the locks three times when we do, or I won't sleep.

Leaning back in his chair, he admires my form, how my clothes hide my inked flesh but not my strength. We stay in shape. Our bodies are trained to perform together.

"It's time you find your queen, too," he says.

I wedge my dress shoes into my duffel before neatly

folding my soiled suit, laying it on top, and pressing it down, though I'll take it to the cleaners first thing in the morning.

"I know you heard me," he rumbles.

"You know I don't share." My snarl is low, and this fight is old.

"We're not sharing; we're *initiating*." To most, Axel is an attorney, and he's damn good, arguing, "It's our custom. It bonds us, protects *them*, and you know it's your turn." He tents his tattooed fingers. "And you know it'll be Alena's after that."

"You're *not* initiating my daughter," I sneer. "That's final and fatal if you do."

He nods. "Then find a vessel for her. Someone we'll symbolically initiate before she gets married. She'll need a second husband." Usually, ice slides through Axel's veins, but not about this, not about Alena. He offers, "It can be me."

I'm loyal to Axel and his family. I had none, and now they're mine. I've killed for them. They've killed for me. But this custom? This initiation of seven kings bound to seven queens. Of a second husband for each queen, each wife should the first husband die protecting her. One of us swears to claim her, protect her, and provide for their children.

It's an honor to be a second husband. It's ancient and admirable. It's also archaic and absolutely never going to happen.

Over dead bodies, it will, and they won't be mine.

Yes, my daughter needs protection. I agreed to let her marry. She'll be one of our queens, though she'll never know. She doesn't know who we are, what we do, and she'll never be initiated into our circle.

I don't care if they're like my brothers. I don't care if they'd sacrifice their lives to protect her. The thought of Axel as Alena's second husband makes it even worse. I see rage. I see death. I see blood, though he and I share none.

A double knock raps on his office door.

"I'm done." A deep voice grumbles, then a giggle tickles the air, calling out, "Goodnight, my kings."

Her tone sounds youthful with delight, though her voice rasps after hours of screaming orgasms.

It twitches my cock, I'm ashamed to admit.

My cock that was in her hungry mouth an hour ago.

She was begging for it. She was loving it. We *always* make sure they love it. Even the tests most don't pass, they're consensual. They're pleasing. They're taboo, which is my kink, but I couldn't do it. After all I did to her, when it was my turn, I couldn't come down her throat, though my hard dick ached to do it. Though her raven hair reminded me of *her*—my greatest shame, my greatest temptation—*Vale, my daughter's best friend.*

But our newest queen is twenty fucking years old. So, hell no. She's younger than my daughter, who will always feel like my little girl, though she's twenty-seven now.

"Goodnight, our queen." Axel shows her respect, calling toward the closed door.

The sound of the newlyweds' steps, leaving his law office, fills the air. The happy couple exits through the back entrance, as we will. It's private and secure, but still, I stand guard, surveying the window again, scanning for that black Mercedes.

I trust my instincts. I've earned them. *Shit's about to go south.* It makes me want to cancel tonight.

Alena's throwing a party where she'll announce her engagement. She thinks she's surprising me, but I'm always well aware.

Like now ... *something's wrong.*

The charming street below, with its oak trees draped in Spanish moss, bustles with innocent tourists taking leisurely strolls to dinner. They're none the wiser about Charleston,

South Carolina, ironically called "The Holy City." They don't know who or what evil hides in this sultry southern town by the sea.

It's more like ... what evil we control. Or stop. Or end.

"Nash." Axel breaks my concentration.

I turn, staring him down. I stare down decades devoted to my best friend and his family. I'd die for Axel. But he can't have my daughter.

He can't have his custom, either.

His glacial eyes bore into mine disguised behind fake glasses, my glare refusing, while his silently demands:

Claim your queen.

CHAPTER TWO
VALE

"Here it comes," Alena warns as I hold her long, tawny waves and she kneels, retching into the toilet, and *nope*.

Puke is my poison.

I lean over and hurl into the tub beside her.

"What were we thinking?" I sputter, turning on the water with my free hand, washing our stupidity away. "Red velvet cupcakes and spicy margaritas don't mix."

"But we're celebrating." Alena's happy voice echoes in the porcelain bowl, even as she flushes, "I'm getting married!"

"We should be tossing confetti tonight." I kneel beside her. "Not tossing our cookies."

"Cupcakes," she corrects with a laugh, plopping beside me.

We lean against the tub, her head resting on my shoulder. It's a familiar pose. Yeah, I have my twin, who I'm naturally close to, but Alena is my chosen family.

Hurt her, and I'll bludgeon you to death with a giant dildo.

"I think I failed the maid of honor test," I say, nudging my

Mary Jane against her high heel. "I'm pretty sure I'm not supposed to let you barf at your engagement party."

"I'm fine." She wedges into me. "When I'm sick, I only want you or my dad."

Alena's warmth is my rock, too. She lost her mom, and so did I. It's one of the hundreds of tears we've shared that's made us best friends since middle school.

And her dad?

Well ... I try not to think about Mr. Allen.

And it's a colossal failure.

Nash Allen is wired into my erotic system in ways I'll never confess. My nerves get tingly. My skin flushed. Heat blooms everywhere when I'm around him, even though he acts so cold to me now. I don't know what happened.

He's giving Antarctic vibes while my heart is serving a *What-The-Fuck?*

I don't get it. Someone help me understand.

Nash Allen is the kind of man who came to my college graduation because my father didn't. He and Alena gave me red tulips. They're my favorite.

He's the kind of man who made me a cheeseburger for breakfast after the worst night of my life. It's my happy meal. He had no idea what happened to me, but it's like, without a word, he knew I needed at least one man to care. To show me they don't all break your soul.

That's what drew me to him that night by the pool, but ever since then ... Nash is so cold he burns.

But then I look at him, and I'm like...

"He's really hot."

"It's okay; you can admit it." Alena laughs. "My fiancé is hot-as-fuck."

Sure, that's who I was talking about: her fiancé, not her father.

"Okay, yes. I have eyes, and he's perfect for you. It's like

Fate went to Build-A-Bear, but instead of a cuddly Teddy, it built you a sexy bear named Loch who wears a hot Forest Ranger outfit." Grinning, I elbow her. "He growls when he comes, doesn't he? Like an orgasmic grizzly in mating season."

Alena giggles, "Yeah, he does," her voice dropping to a giddy whisper. "I did that thing you told me to try. I was riding him so hot and hard until he was about to come, then I started going super slow, and he growled like a wild animal, but I told him it would intensify his orgasm, and it did. I swear he came for over a minute. It was so hot. I thought he was gonna have a heart attack."

"Did it work for you, too?" I ask. "Because I won't let you marry a beige flag in bed."

"Don't worry. He's perfect." Alena's shy. She was teased a lot in school, but she's not shy with me. Not about sex. It's my expertise. "Loch is my first love, and he'll be my last. We'll grow old together and—"

"Yes, but does he curl your toes? Does he make your thighs shake? Does he make you wanna be a dirty ho for him, or do I need to give him coloring books with arrows pointing to the clit?"

"Oh, he's found it." She nudges my ribs. "He says it's his now, that me and my pussy belong to him."

"Yay! I'm so proud." I squeeze her. "My sweet slut is marrying a savage."

"Maybe," her voice lilts, "at my wedding, one of his brothers will savage *you*." She pauses, leaning away. "Wait. Speaking of siblings, men, and savage sex ... Is Blair coming tonight?"

"Nope." I pop my lips. "She's home, having a pity-my-pussy party over an NFL quarterback. She can't stand love right now."

"And you? What if Loch has a brother who will cure you of hating love, too?"

"Doubtful." I tease, "Unless they're like him, all inked up and huge and hot as the devil's dildo."

I make her laugh, and she makes me care.

To most, I'm standoffish. I have my reasons, but not with Alena. We're close. I'm the manager of an exclusive sex shop because I refuse to finish my PhD in Sexuality Studies, and Alena is a forest ranger who geeks out on soil samples. We're opposites and perfectly paired best friends.

"I don't know what they're like," she replies. "I haven't met his family yet."

"Wait. What?" I turn to her. "You've been dating Loch for a year, and you're getting married in like two months, but you haven't met his *family* yet? What are they? Cloistered monks or serial killers? Because anyone else would have the manners to meet you. Hell, they should be here tonight."

"They're busy."

"That's sketch."

"Quit being protective. I'm all grown up and carry a sidearm now."

"You're trained to shoot dangerous animals in a national park, not inconsiderate assholes at brunch." I plead to her brown eyes, "Please tell me your dad's gonna meet them. He'd never let you marry into evil."

"Well," she hesitates, "my dad hasn't met th—"

"Alena?" A rough voice on the other side of the door jiggles the doorknob. It's Loch. "Are you okay? Can I come in?"

She scrambles to her feet. "Hang on." I join her. "We'll be out in a sec."

A sec turns into minutes of me fixing Alena's makeup, and her smoothing my long, black braids, praising me, "Only you can look like a sexy Wednesday Addams at an Isle of Palms party and make it look chic."

I glance down at my usual murderous, black minidress, matching thigh-highs with white bows, and my clunky Mary Janes. *Whoops.* As the maid of honor, I clash with her demure ivory cardigan, emerald sundress, and nude heels.

Yes, I love Alena, but I won't change my style for anyone. I can't. So, I gently nudge her toward the door and her waiting fiancé.

An hour later, the night is getting late, guests are leaving, and I've renewed my taste for spicy margaritas. I sip, watching Alena dance with her dad on the deck of his palatial beach house with stars twinkling above.

It's magical. It's sweet. Alena is so happy.

Mr. Allen waltzes her around, beaming at her. He won't stop being the perfect father. He won't stop looking so damn sexy doing it. And he won't stop making my fantasy hurt...

I wish a man would dance with me like that. Would love me like that. I wish it were ... him.

Whoops! Scratch that.

I'm a horrible person.

Ban me from best-friend status and maid-of-honor duties. All the years I've tried to stop them, I can't. These feelings for Mr. Allen erupt. They're my greatest guilt and darkest secret. They make me remember our night by this very pool and...

Suddenly, he glances up and busts me swooning. Shit, I'm probably drooling, too; it must be the tequila.

Why is he staring at me like that? Like he knows what I did that night?

He doesn't know. He can't *know.*

If you're the only one who knows your secret, it's safe. Right?

So why does he glare at me like he hates me?

There's no way he can know what I did, and it was years ago, so why is he such an asshole to me now? Why, when we work together, does he act like he doesn't care anymore?

I used to love that Mr. Allen cared.

I needed him to, even though I gave him shit about it. I complained that my tulips were wilted. That his burgers were dry. I was a teenage brat to him because I didn't know how else to hide my feelings for him.

Confession: I still do it. But now my brattiness has matured to snark.

Snark that masks how I love that Mr. Allen was the only man who cared for me like a father, but then again...

No.

That's not this scorching pull to him. That's not this ache in my chest. These feelings have always confused me, but I'm used to them.

Right?

So why, as he slices his stare away from me with such disgust, am I suddenly twisting my lips? Why am I biting them? Why are my nostrils flaring while tears bite at my eyes?

What the hell?

A stupid, hard lump chokes my throat, but I force a smile like nothing's wrong.

Because ... *nothing's wrong.*

It's right how Loch cuts in to dance with his fiancée as Mr. Allen pecks Alena's cheek. It's right how her father is a polite host, greeting his guests but ignoring me.

It's right how I'm standing alone. How no one dances with me. How people see me and walk the other way. I'm odd, I know. I dress this way on purpose.

If I can intimidate you, you can't hurt me.

So I focus on Alena, swept away in her fiancé's arms. They're perfect together. I watch them for minutes until she shyly waves at me. She's finally found the love she deserves, and a warm, fuzzy feeling, wanting romance and believing in love, showers me and...

Oh shit. I stagger. *I'm buzzing again.*

That's it. Too many emotions for one night.

I hug Alena goodbye. We make happy, teary, and tipsy plans to go dress shopping before I stagger out of the front door into the night.

CHAPTER THREE
VALE

THE BRINY BEACH AIR REVIVES ME AS I TAP ON MY PHONE, squinting to read it.

Focus, Vale. Focus.

"What are you doing?" A smoky voice asks from the shadows of the garage.

I whip around, shocked as darkness slices angles across a face until the gas lamp light reveals ... *it's Mr. Allen*, and like always, I suddenly fight for breath in his presence.

I hate it. I hate the effect he has on me. It's oddly arousing as I wave my phone. "Getting an Uber."

"I'll drive you home," he orders.

"I'm *finnne*." Did I just slur?

"No, you're not."

"*Yesssss*, I ammm." Yep, I got a margarita mouth.

"Vale," he sneers, "you're not getting into a stranger's car when you've been drinking."

"Okay, Boomer. That's what Ubers are for."

"I'm not a Boomer," I stumble a bit as he stalks my way, demanding, "and you'll do as I say."

Yes, this man is hot, but yes, he can be a royal asshole. He always does this. He always takes over whenever I hate to need him. He did it when I was a teenager, and he's done it every day since I called him to help me with a big accounting mess I made at my job, and now?

He fucks with my emotions. They shift from enamored to annoyed and...

Wait. Was he out here waiting for me to leave?

Who cares? I'm equally stubborn.

"You always forget; you're Alena's dad. Not. Mine."

"No. You're my ... my *guest*, and it's a Sunday night." He flicks his cigar into the sand. "It'll take an hour for an Uber to get here, and that's unacceptable." He jerks his chin toward a van parked in the garage. "Get in my car."

"You're not the boss of me," I sass back, suddenly sixteen again. "And it won't take an hour. It says it'll be here in..."

I check the app and roll my eyes.

"Uh-huh." He sounds amused, my pulse rising as he nears. "What does it say?"

"None of your business."

"My property." He casts shadows over me. "My business."

I snap my phone behind my back. "It says nothing."

"Your Uber app says the ETA is *nothing?*" He smirks. "What an abstract sense of time for such precise technology."

"Well," I huff, "I'll enjoy the night air."

"You'll enjoy standing in my driveway at midnight for over an hour?"

"Yep." I pop my lips, tipping my head back. *Whoops. Tequila.* I sway, searching the sky. "I can study the constellations. I'm looking for Orion."

"You're looking drunk."

"I'm not drunk!" Too quickly, I snap my stare back at him, and the world shifts on its axis. I stumble forward, and he's fast. He catches me in his arms.

His tan, smooth, beefy arms with muscles and veins

popping everywhere that I'm not supposed to notice, but fuck my life, I've memorized them. *He has a scar on his left forearm.* I've mapped it and his sexy face because that's the only flesh he exposes.

Even in black-rimmed geeky glasses, Nash Allen is hot. He's brooding. He's intense. He studies you like prey and smells like primal sex. Like he's an animal who just had it, though he acts too uptight to fuck.

For God's sake, the man fastens the top button of his snug, black golf shirt.

Who does that?

No one. It's against PGA rules.

Okay, it's not, but it should be. Because, on most, you look like a nerd doing it and not in a stylish way.

But on Nash Allen? He makes a tight golf shirt collar look as sexy as a BDSM choker. One he yanks as you kneel, wanting to serve him.

He steadies me, my breasts smashed against his chest before he shoves me away.

Glancing over my shoulder, he holds me at arm's length, his grip controlling as his eyes narrow, suddenly tracking something behind me before he growls, "Get in my car, Vale. *Now.*"

I'm sorry; not sorry. No man tells me what to do. "Did you eat asshole tonight because you sound like one?"

He raises a thick, dark brow. Intrigued. Irate. "The only ass I'll handle tonight is yours with a good spanking if you don't get in my fucking car right now."

And he always does *that,* too.

He orders you around, making your pride revolt while your pussy purrs. He plays whiplash with your emotions. His mindfuck, next-level. He doesn't give you a choice; he takes control.

Why can't he be nice and make me a cheeseburger again? Hell, I'd love his floppy tulips, too.

I barely drop my phone into my purse, letting him yank me by the arm. I barely climb into the passenger seat he promptly drops my ass into. I barely get a chance to protest before he's speeding out his driveway.

But now, trapped as his passenger ... I have all the time in the world to give him hell.

Why? Because Nash Allen has been ordering me around since I was thirteen, that's when I met his daughter, Alena.

At first, I liked it. My real dad didn't give a shit about me and my sister. So, I guess I liked Mr. Allen's overbearing protection, his unrelenting questions about my goals, and the pressure he put on me to succeed. Alena thrived under it, and I practically lived at their house, so Mr. Allen drove me, too.

But now?

Okay, he's literally driving me again, but he's not my father. Hell, Nash Allen works *for me* now. He's the accountant I hired for my employer.

He's a man so controlling that he does everything three times. Three times, he checks his math. Three times, he'll save a spreadsheet. Three times now, he checks his rearview mirror before suddenly stepping on the gas pedal, the inertia slamming me back into the passenger seat.

"You know,"—I huff—"if you want to drive like a bat out of hell, get a little sports car because you can't Tokyo Drift in your big, burgundy minivan."

He snickers, "Wanna bet?" as he starts flying down the quiet road with the dark ocean on our left and me, looking for cops who aren't around.

We're breaking every rule of the road, and usually, I'm a rebel. But now? Hell, no.

"This is a dad-car with duffel bags and golf clubs rolling in the back," I snap. "I bet your minivan wets lots of MILF panties, but I'm not impressed by speed. Slow down!"

"I'm not into fast MILFs." He stares ahead, making those thick glasses too sexy. "I'm in a new Honda Odyssey with a one hundred and twenty-nine horsepower, V6, three-point six-liter engine and—"

Fuck this. The speedometer reads eighty-one, physics works, and I'm scared. And when I'm scared, my mouth starts firing.

"I don't care if you're Lewis Hamilton rocking sexy braids, a nose piercing, and a Formula-One winning Mercedes. Yeah, he's hot. And I'm sure he fucks as fast and furious as he drives, but I can assure you, no man, sex, and *certainly* no burgundy minivan are worth dying for! Slow down!"

I grip my seat belt, glancing in my side-view mirror. Ironically, a dark Mercedes is following us, and ... *damn, they're close.*

"Sounds like you're having bad sex." He smirks. "Furious fucks are hot. Fast ones are not."

"We're racing over a three-mile bridge!" I shriek. "We can plunge to our death at any moment, and you have the nerve to lecture *me* about sex?"

"You brought it up."

"As an example."

"Oh, so you're *not* having fast and furious sex?"

"I have sex all the time!"

"Quantity," he swerves around a motorcycle not traveling at the speed of light like we are, "is not quality."

How is this happening? How did I go from a good buzz on a quiet night celebrating my best friend's engagement to racing down the road with her hot dad, lecturing me about my lousy sex life?

I'd be mortified, but death is imminent. It's impossible to care.

Besides, he can't know. No one knows how right he is.

His glance flicks to the rearview mirror. Three times. Again. Then, he slams the pedal down more.

"What are you doing?" I screech.

"Getting you home safely."

"Safely?" We reach the end of the bridge before he burns rubber on a left turn. "I'll arrive home in a pine box if you don't slow down!"

"Come on now." He pats my thigh. "I'd pay for a nicer coffin than that."

His sudden, warm touch thrills me, and if I live, I'm having a serious talk with my pussy. "Don't joke!"

"I'm dead serious."

"Don't say *dead*!" I grab the oh-shit handle, watching in horror. "Red light! Red light!"

"It's just a suggestion." He ignores it, blasting under it at Mach 5.

"No, this is just a one-way ticket to my grave." I howl, "Slow. The. Fuck. Down."

He's driving so fast, deftly weaving the van around cars, blasting through intersections, while the Mercedes behind us does the same. Other cars honk, angry at the deadly risk we impose, and I agree.

I can't look. I squeeze my eyes shut.

Who is this reckless man?

This isn't the uptight man I grew up with—the one who insisted on teaching me how to change a tire when I started to drive or taught Alena and me how to get out of choke-holds. He was obsessed with our safety, so when I went to college, I asked Mr. Allen to track my phone because, yeah, he was tough on me, but I always felt safe with him.

But now? He's scaring me, and not in the way I've felt for so many years. I'm used to the terror of wanting Nash Allen.

With one whiff of his cologne—leather and vanilla. With one look, my body wants him while my mind suffers so much guilt about it. *He's my best friend's dad.* I'd never betray Alena, though I ache for something I've never had.

Is it a father figure? Or is it more? I don't know, but he's the only man I've ever felt safe with.

Until now.

For minutes, I can't speak. I'm sweating. I'm scared. I'm going to throw up again. I fight tears, and I *don't* cry. I *won't* cry. Still, emotion floods my voice.

"Please, Mr. Allen, slow down," I quietly beg. "My mom died in a car crash."

Instantly, the engine stops revving high. He slows down. I feel him grab my hand, his warm touch brushing over my thigh again while he commands, "Vale, look at me."

I open my eyes. I obey. But when I turn to him...

What the...

I'm not looking at "Mr. Allen," the irritating man who practically raised me. The caring man who'd ask about my exams. The controlling man who thinks he's the boss of me. The uptight man who has to do almost everything three times. Or the cold man who ignores me now.

No. He's taken off his nerdy glasses. He's unbuttoned his collar. All the way.

Oh, my inked God, his tan pecs are covered in black designs. His light brown eyes are suddenly heated, foreign, and menacing while he swears, "I'll never hurt you, Vale, and I'll kill anyone who does."

I'm in awe.

In shock.

In love?

The Mercedes taps our bumper, and I scream, stunned out of my stupor, as he drops my hand and accelerates. Popping open his low center console, he pulls out a gun.

"Now," he orders, "for once in your life, Vale Monroe, don't give me hell. Do exactly as I say. Do you understand?"

It stammers over my lips, "Yes, sir."

"Good girl."

CHAPTER FOUR
NASH

Fuck, I thought I dropped this tail before I drove home. Fuck, they want blood. And fuck, now everything's burned. Locations. Cars. Businesses.

My daughter.

And the only other girl, I mean *woman*, I've cared about. Now, she's in danger, too.

Vale gapes, staring wide-eyed at me like she's seen a monster, and I am. She has no idea what I've done for my family and what I've done for her.

My Beretta rests in my lap while I use the Bluetooth in my van to start maneuvers. "Call Seven," I command.

"Yeah," a burly growl answers. There's no name on the screen. We use numbers.

"You're on speakerphone," I snarl. He'll understand. "We're burned. Secure her. *Now*."

"Copy." He hangs up.

"Call One," I command my technology. It rings, and Axel picks up. He doesn't speak. I do.

"You're on speakerphone, we're burned, and being followed."

Silence fills the air while I aim for the next bridge. The Ravenel Bridge. It's the third longest cable-stayed bridge in the Western Hemisphere and our only way to safety. I know what to do with the Mercedes chasing feet behind us.

"Who are you with?" Axel hopes I'll say "Alena." That I've secured her.

"Vale Monroe," I answer, and he's silent again, adding it up.

"Who is it?" He's asking about our friends, the ones I warned him about earlier.

"Same as your office. They followed me home."

I can't go into details. Details Vale can't know. It's for her own good.

"Your plan?" Axel asks. He'll call the others. They'll go to their second locations until we can get more intel.

"Lose this tail, drop this van, then secure my asset."

"Your *asset*?" Vale scoffs, but I whip my glare at her, and she rolls her eyes.

"Call when it's done," Axel replies, then hangs up.

"Your fucking *asset*?" Vale starts. "What in the hell is going on? Who's chasing us? Why do you have a gun, and why did it sound like you're best friends with Tony Soprano and Co.?"

"So, being a good girl. It's done?" I shake my head. "Should've known. I've had sneezes that lasted longer."

She doesn't answer. She studies my gun, then my face, my real one, ready for murder. "Oh my god," she sighs in shock, "you're mafia in a minivan."

"Mafia don't drive minivans," I assure her as I race up the ramp to the four wide lanes of the high bridge crossing the wide Cooper River.

Thankfully, it's one a.m. on a Monday morning. There are only a few other cars, and ours, being chased by a black Mercedes.

For a rare moment, Vale's silent.

Call the CIA. I found their next recruit. She's water-boarding my profile, interrogating my new image.

Then, because God hates me, Vale starts clapping. She's smart and quite proud of herself. She's figured it out, but unfortunately, she's also a snarky smartass when she's scared, and in the past, I adored it.

I'd piss her off for entertainment.

But not now.

"Let's all applaud," she says. "Let's show some warm Southern hospitality to the mafia in Charleston because *that's* why you drive a daddy minivan, not an I-got-a-little-dick sports car or a black SUV that screams felony offender. No, that'd be too obvious. And that's why you look like Poindexter when really ... you're a Dexter. You murder people. You're not a geeky accountant or an uptight dad. You're a hitman! You're a *made* man!"

I recheck the rear-view mirror. Then, I slide into the outside lane, preparing for my maneuver. I don't care that Vale's outed me. I'll deal with it later.

"Aren't you?" Or now, goddammit. "Aren't you mafia, Mr. Allen? Or some kind of organized crime because you have a gun, too many muscles, a sudden explosion of ink, and too much money to be—"

"I wish you were allergic to words."

"They're my weapons."

"Holster them." I accelerate, thankful for this engine. It's maxed out. "Better yet, silence them."

It's hard controlling the vehicle at this speed. We're going eighty-nine as Vale deadpans, "Twenty bucks says we die."

I can't help it. I fucking smile as I slow down.

"What are you doing?" she shrieks. "Don't listen to me! Don't slow down now! Don't let them—"

"Shut up, Vale!" I boom. *Here we go.*

I entice the Mercedes to pull up on my left as I press my

window down, racing over the bridge. I won't risk Vale. I won't shoot across her. Then, I grab my gun, thankful I'm a leftie, too, as the black Mercedes with its tinted windows appears, menacing and racing beside us, gunning its engine.

"Oh my god." Out of the corner of my eye, I clock Vale burying her face in her hands. She's losing it. "Oh my god, I'm gonna die."

"You're not gonna die."

"Yes, I am. I'm gonna die."

"I won't let you."

"News flash: you're still not the boss of me."

"Vale, I got this."

I steady the steering wheel with my right hand, the gun itching to fire in my left.

"No, you don't. You think you're in control, but we're going too fast, and there's too much speed and bullets and shit." She's rambling. "I'm gonna die on a fucking scary bridge, plunging into a cold, dark river below, drowning in an ugly-ass, preppy mafia minivan with a mean man." She's losing it. "And I've never even been in love or had a good kiss or even a legit orgasm. Lewis Hamilton will never know my greatness."

I can't reply. I can't process.

I wait for their tinted passenger window to lower, and as it does ... I aim my muzzle with its silencer and pull the trigger, unloading the clip.

The Mercedes swerves left, and I speed up. I don't know who I hit, but I watch in the rearview mirror as they lose control and crash into the side rails of the bridge.

For miles and minutes, Vale doesn't speak. She stares out of the front window as I drive north, with my gun resting on my lap.

I let my heart rate drop, my pulse calming. I make my

mind work, guessing who that was and knowing what to do next.

We're out of danger for now. It's clear. We're safe ... but then I glance over, and my heart starts racing again, facing a different threat.

In her panic, Vale hasn't noticed how her naughty black dress is bunched up, exposing her milky legs in those thigh-high stockings with little white bows. Then I let my glance linger over what I shouldn't and stifle my groan when I see what I've always wondered, obsessed about actually, and now I know...

Vale wears white cotton panties with a little red bow.

Oh, fuck. My teeth grab my bottom lip as I force my stare back to the road. In a moment like this, I should be focused on business, but I can't. I chew on guilt and lust, and yes, fear, too.

I'm not afraid to kill evil men. I'm not afraid to protect my family and the ones I love. I'm not afraid of my vow to six men and every dark and salacious ritual we perform that ensures it.

But what I've been afraid of ... ever since she was eighteen and I was thirty-two ... is that I crave Vale Monroe like I'm an evil, starving man.

CHAPTER FIVE
VALE

WE'VE CROSSED TO THE NORTH SIDE OF TOWN. IT'S nowhere near where I live, but I'm not speaking. Snark, terror, or the truth keeps flying from my mouth.

It's best kept shut.

For now.

Nash turns into a car dealership. Pressing a button on his rearview mirror, the security arms to the car lot swing open.

Once again, I'm shocked, but I don't utter a peep this time.

He pulls around to the service bay at the back, pressing another button on his mirror. The last bay door on the right rolls open, and lights flicker on when we pull in. Pressing the button again, the bay door closes behind us as he cuts off the engine.

The silence is awkward. The stillness is weird while he stares at my profile. "Since when do you shut up?"

I turn my face away. "I'm busy ignoring you."

"By all means." He chuckles. "Make that your full-time career."

Asshole.

I whip around.

"Does Alena know? Does she know her dad is really a murderous mafia dickhead with a rap sheet?"

"A dickhead? Yes. I grounded her so many times, I'm branded as such. And a rap sheet? Yes, she knows I have one. When she was a baby and I was seventeen, I landed in juvie for grand larceny. For stealing credit cards to pay for her diapers and food. I became a dad at sixteen and a dumbass thief to take care of her, but this..." he points between us, "she can't ever know about."

"What do you mean?" I point back and forth, too. "*This?* There is no *this*. Unless you mean the car chase, the murder, and the mafia part."

"Yes, I mean *us*, Vale."

"Us?" I lean toward him. Now that we're not gonna die— *yet*—I'm pissed. "Look here, Mr. Allen. My name's not Bonnie, and you're not Clyde. We're not in *this* together." He glares at me with stupid, sexy brown eyes. "And at least Clyde dressed in suits while you dress like you're getting a colonoscopy at a golf club. Like you shop at Uptight Dad's R' Us. Like you—"

"Are you done?"

I weave my neck. "I'm just getting started."

He narrows his eyes, his burning glare dropping to my lap, and I glance down.

Dammit.

My white panties are exposed, and I blush, feeling a throbbing tingle right where he's looking. Yanking my dress down, like I give a shit about modesty, I keep my pride. It's my other weapon because he needs to stop seducing me with his glare.

So, I lift my chin and glare back.

He grips the steering wheel so tight, veins pop on his

hand as he informs me, "You're right, Vale. We are just getting started because now, you're *mine*."

Laughter. Or lunacy. Or both bubble up my throat, and I erupt, "I'm sorry. What? *Yours?*" I nod. "Yeah, okay. That'll happen. I'll be possessed by a man like you can hold a fart in your hand."

"Fuck." He fights sudden laughter, throwing his scruffy chin up. "This isn't a joke."

"Yes, it is. Call Netflix. Because only in funny fiction will I *ever* belong to you."

"I mean, you're my responsibility now," he seethes, controlling his tone. "We're exposed. We've been burned, and until I'm certain who they are and that you're safe, you belong to me. You do as I say, go where I go, stay by my side, and shut up when I tell you to. Understand?"

I smirk. "*No comprendo.*"

He slams his fist on the center console. The plastic cracks, and I jump. "I'm fucking serious, Vale."

I try opening the door, yanking at the handle, but it won't budge. "What the hell?"

"Child locks." He seems sadistically pleased about it.

"I'm not a fucking child! I'm twenty-nine, and—"

"Then act like it. Appreciate the situation we're in."

"The situation you forced me into. It's not my fault you're a lying, controlling, criminal dickhead who thinks he's Clark Kent and sucks as an Uber driver. I'm giving you a one-star review!"

I keep zinging him, and he cracks a smile.

And you know what makes me even madder than a cat being baptized?

Nash Allen has a breathtaking smile.

It's rare. It's beautiful. It's bright. It reaches his eyes like a comet across the sky, and he goes from forty-something to a young golden god with tan skin and sexy, cropped, brown hair kissed by the sun. His beard is dark and neatly trimmed, framing his full lips that are almost pouty, but he'd never sulk.

No, apparently, he's brutal and menacing and covered in black ink...

And his eyes?

Call it.

The time of death on my resistance to him is right now. Because without his glasses on, which I guess are fake, I can see Nash's conflicted soul.

He's staring back at me, studying me like never before, and my cheeks blush. Something I've buried deep inside remembers him—the only man I've trusted—and desire licks at my sex. Because I swear, he can read my filthy mind, too.

It makes his teeth snare his bottom lip as he stares at mine. So, I force myself to speak. "What's our situation?"

He draws a long breath before answering, "Understand I can't give you details. It's for your safety. And understand that Alena doesn't know; she can *never* know, and it's for her safety, too."

My pulse triples. "Is she safe?"

"Yes. She has a guard."

"She does?" I've never seen one.

"Someone is secretly protecting her. I made sure of it. She's fine."

If it were anyone else, I wouldn't trust it. I'd risk my life to make sure Alena is safe. She's always been too sweet, and I've always been the bitch who protected her. When really? She saved me, too. I'd never trust anyone with her life except her father.

I know Nash was a deadbeat dad when she was born. He was sixteen, and so was Alena's mom. They were never really a couple and struggled as teen parents. Then, Nash got sent to juvie, leaving Alena's mom, Lainey, alone to raise her.

If it weren't for their landlord, Ms. Faye, Alena would've

ended up in the foster system. Lainey's mom threw her out. She had no other family, so Ms. Faye helped her. She's like Alena's grandmother now.

But when Nash got out of juvie, he got his shit together as a dad and got involved. He worked his way through college while Lainey joined the Army. When she was deployed, Nash was the full-time parent until Alena turned ten and Lainey was killed in Iraq.

Then Nash became her only parent.

A year later, I met Alena. She had lost her mom. She was grieving and quiet, and middle school was cruel. She was bullied, and I was a bitch who hated the bitches bullying her even more. So, my twin, Blair, and I took her under our wing, and we've been together ever since.

And as infuriating as I found her over-protective father to be—he never let Alena sleep at my house, so I always slept at theirs—Mr. Allen gave me funny feelings. I didn't understand them at thirteen.

Later, I realized precisely what they're called, and I've been scared ever since.

So, here goes my mouth again. She's aiming.

"What do we do now?" I ask. "Meet in the back room of a pizzeria and smoke cigars with a dozen made men and your Don? Wait. Are you a consigliere? Shouldn't you be fat and bald?"

"No one's Italian."

"Damn." My shoulders sag. "I love pizza."

His lips curl up. "I can work on the fat and bald part if you like."

"Since when is what I like part of this kidnapping?"

"You're not being kidnapped."

"You don't own a dictionary."

"I know what protection means."

"Oh, I get it. You're old *and* losing your hearing so let's press rewind on our convo. Quote..." I drop my voice, growling, "*You're mine now.*"

Again, humor hitches his lips, but his nostrils flare, fighting it.

"Careful," I warn, "when you fight your smile, your wrinkles get deeper."

And sexier.

He pauses before answering, "I'll take you home. I'll make sure it's safe. I'll stay with you, and tomo—"

"Stay? With *me*? In my old studio apartment with one bed, one loveseat you're way too tall to sleep on, and a kitchenette that collects dust? Are we freezing bras, too?"

"Keep. Your. Bra. *On.*"

He says that with a voice so thick with taboo tension, a fire tornado swirls in my core, and I poke the flames. "I sleep nude."

"You'll sleep in pajamas, and I'll sleep on the floor."

"Oh, okay, Father Allen." I chuckle. "Gird your monastic loins because I manage a sex shop, so my *pajamas*," I air quote, "are another woman's sexy lingerie."

"Vale." His tone drops so low, I bet his balls drop, too. "Keep. This. *Professional.*"

"I am *professional.*" I clip that last word. "I professionally manage the most exclusive sex shop in the South, wearing all their goods and testing all their toys to make sure they work and..."

He cocks an eyebrow. I don't think he meant to, and shit...

He heard me.

He remembers me confessing my deepest, darkest secrets that only escaped in my manic moment, thinking I was going to die, and I can't make him forget now.

It's true; I don't let anyone kiss me, I don't let anyone love me, and I've never had an orgasm with a partner. I can only do it alone and ... only when I think about that night by his pool.

File this under "I'm Screwed and Not in a Hot Way." And when I think about *that*?

"Fine," I huff. "I'll cut a hole in a bedsheet and wear it like a tent. Satisfied?"

"I'll take you to work," he proceeds. "I'll sit with you, etcetera. Your boss knows I'm helping you with the books, so the ruse can remain."

"The ruse? So what are you now? The Pope, Sherlock Holmes, and Al Capone all rolled up into a nerdy-looking, beefy golf pro?"

He leans forward.

I've pushed him too far; I can't help it; I use snark when I'm scared.

"No, Vale." His sexy lips snarl, and this time, he's not amused. "I'm the beast keeping you alive."

CHAPTER SIX
NASH

VALE IS UNCHARACTERISTICALLY QUIET WHILE I DITCH THE van and grab my Beretta before taking my duffel and black GO BAG from the back.

I signal for her to follow, and she does with venom in her eyes as I grab a set of keys to a new grey Accord from the garage wall of our dealership.

She's right. Only amateurs drive cars that scream "criminal."

We blend in. Our homes are in plain sight. Our aliases are boring. Our jobs, too. They allow us to infiltrate, connect with pillars in the community, and secure resources like this dealership under nameless LLCs, and more. We're every-where in this city, from churches to sex clubs, and we have enemies.

Enemies I've proudly earned.

I pull out of the car lot and turn, noting Vale pouting in the passenger seat, her arms hugging her waist.

"Are you hungry?"

"Am I human?"

I shake my head. *I've kidnapped a barracuda.* She won't stop snapping at me.

It's two a.m. as I pull into a drive-thru. I don't usually eat this shit, but I'm starving. I don't ask her; I order two quarter-pounders with cheese, and she looks surprised that I remembered.

"I've listened to you at work," I explain. "You still love cheeseburgers for lunch."

"What are you? Alexa?"

Silently, I hand her the brown paper bag.

"This is organic, right?" She unwraps her burger. "Farm to table grease?"

Good. She's got her snark and appetite back, so I take a huge bite. Usually, I have manners. And patience. And silence. It's part of my disguise, but around her, I feel like a teenager again.

Hungry. Angry. Horny. *Alive.*

I don't answer her. I drive down the highway, scarfing down my food and enjoying loud sips of Dr. Pepper while she does the same.

But then it happens. A bubble of carbonation erupts from my throat, and I burp, long and loud, before I wince, embarrassed because it's rude.

"Oh, good." She laughs. "He's not a beast. He's human again." Then she burps louder than me. "That was a ten," she praises herself with a smile.

And, fuck.

Don't do it. Don't smile back.

But, fuck. I do.

I feel dangerously unguarded around her when I'm already so exposed.

No one knows who I really am other than the kings and our few queens ... and yet, somehow, I'm tempted to let Vale see even more than they do. I'm tempted to let her see a man no one has known, not even myself.

But the temptation evaporates when I think of my daughter and their safety, hers and Vale's, as we drive down the blocks of historic Charleston.

Of course, I know where she lives.

Vale rents a unit on the third floor of a yellow, historic row house just two blocks from her work. Its narrow front faces a cobble-stoned street with long, open porches down the side.

I circle her block three times, scanning for threats, and I don't like it. Old homes like this are difficult to secure. The only good thing is it has a private, dedicated parking space, and Vale has a bicycle in it, so my car fits.

She turns to me. "Why are we at my place? Why aren't we going to one of your mafia safe houses? You call them 'safe' for a reason, right?"

"Nothing is safer than a secret, and that's what you and I are for now."

"So I have to hide you?"

"No, you have to let me protect you until I'm sure they won't come looking for you, too."

"How would they even know who I am?"

I pause, frustrated, before sharing my rationale, "They saw me outside my home, trying to get a beautiful young woman to shut her fucking mouth and get in my van. Fast forward to them wanting to know who the woman is so they'll explore my daughter's world. I've tried erasing her past, but there are high school yearbook photos with Alena hugging you in them. The damn things are online and a huge risk, and now it's a matter of time before they figure out who you are."

"Jeez, so much for being in the Glee Club." She looks around. "So what now?"

"I'll get my gear, and you'll stay behind me with your hand on my shoulder, letting me know you're there while I lead and make sure it's clear."

"Oh, it's clear." She huffs, "This is clearly hell."

No, it's normal dynamic entry tactics, but nothing is normal about feeling Vale's small, warm hand cup my shoulder like her life depends on it.

She's shaking. She's scared.

She hides it with sarcasm, making my pulse race faster than usual, my finger ready on the trigger.

I've cleared many locations, but not the studio apartment of a woman I shouldn't care this much about.

Once we climb two flights of exterior stairs. Once I unlock her door as she stays with me, squeezing my shoulder while I sweep the dark room. Once we're inside her one-room studio and I turn on a small lamp, making it glow by her bed, do I exhale.

I lock the door, checking it three times before I drag her loveseat in front of it.

Silently, she watches, resigned to the situation, before disappearing into her tiny bathroom.

I stare at its closed door, the only privacy she can find because her place is small, but it's charming. Old, polished hardwood floors. One exposed brick wall. The other walls are white plaster with framed prints of red tulips. There are two large windows with white sheers. A tiny but new white kitchenette. A ceiling fan lazily whirls above.

It's perfect for a single woman and the sparse furnishings are perfectly Vale.

A black, antique wrought iron bed, with its white comforter and piles of red velvet pillows, is centered on the brick wall. The loveseat, too, is red velvet, like an old Victorian settee. A gold-framed mirror is propped against the wall beside her bed, a lone antique dresser sitting beside it.

But the stacks of books circling the room get my attention. While water runs in her bathroom—she must be showering—I read some spines.

The History of Sexuality. The Ethical Slut. Come As You Are. Gender Outlaw. Sexing the Body. Whipping Girl. Fear of Flying. How To Piss Off Men. Sex, Sin, and Zen. The Hite Report. Sister Outsider. The Purity Myth. Promiscuities.

And on and on.

Tabs lace the pages with places she's marked in over two hundred books. Her organization isn't alphabetic; it's some order that only makes sense to her.

But what gets my attention is her silver laptop charging on her black nightstand and the three books stacked beside it.

A hardback of *The Kama Sutra*, a small paperback of *Tickle His Pickle* and the one I want to open the most, *She Comes First*.

I step closer to read its subtitle, "The Thinking Man's Guide to Pleasuring A Woman," and it stirs my cock.

It breaks my heart, too.

I can press rewind on our convo, as well. I heard what she said. I'll never forget it...

"I've never even been in love or had a good kiss or even a legit orgasm."

Why? How?

Is it because of what her ex-boyfriend did to her so long ago?

The thought of him now makes me gnash my teeth, my blood boiling, but he's gone. I glared into his dying eyes, said her name, and had a great, bloody day of making sure of it.

And it's possible it's his fault, but it seems she's moved on.

Vale's finishing her PhD in Sexuality Studies. She's supposed to be writing her dissertation because she's clearly well-read about it. She has no shame about sex.

I've watched her. I've heard her.

At Delta's, the adult store she manages, she offers customers suggestions and tips.

The other day, while auditing the store's taxes before the IRS does, I overheard her. She made a middle-aged man and woman laugh, suggesting they play with a Pickle Emojibator Personal Massager. It's what the couple needed. They needed to relax and explore the toys. They needed to find that spark again because it sure as hell sparked inside me.

Pride that Vale helped them. Happy they let her. Aroused how she gave the toy a ringing endorsement. There's only one way she knew it worked, and it flooded my mind, remembering how intoxicating she looks when she comes.

But she does it alone? She's never felt it with someone else?

How can a young woman as smart, beautiful, and sexual as Vale not know what true connection, true love feels like?

Then again, I'm guilty, too.

Sure, I can come with a woman, but I've never felt a connection. I've kissed plenty, but it was never love.

Maybe...

No...

Definitely, it's because, for so many years, I've felt connected to my daughter's best friend.

Guilt drops me onto her loveseat by the door. I drag my hand down my face as if I could wipe away the shame.

What have I gotten us into?

Vale's in my world now, and I'm in hers. We shared secrets tonight, but we can never share more. I can imagine the hurt in Alena's eyes if we ever do.

We can't.

We won't.

The click of the bathroom door opening lifts my troubled stare. Steam billows out before Vale appears, and a thousand bullets wouldn't hit me this hard.

She's naked and wrapped in a white towel, water droplets glistening on her alabaster skin. Her long raven hair falls like a silk sheet, free from its braids and trapping my stare.

I can't help it.

I never could.

The sight of Vale hardens my cock so fast; shame lashes my heart while she marches across the room, taunting, "Please avert your professionally, puritanical eyes, lest they burst into flames while, according to you, I must find something appropriately asinine to sleep in."

I clench my jaw and turn away, slamming my eyes closed because the thunder of my pulse is deafening. I don't need sights tempting me, too.

Drawers to her antique dresser open and slam shut.

"I can dress like a nun," she teases, "but it's a Bad Habit Nun costume and probably *not* what Father Allen had in mind. Oh, wait. I have a Sexy Chef Apron. Food's not your fetish, is it? Oh, and I have some virginal bridal nighties, too. They're safe because marriage turns you off, right? Since you've never done it. You'll never commit. Or—"

"Commit your fucking ass to that bed," I growl. "I don't care what you wear; just stop talking."

Stop driving me mad. Stop putting images in my mind. Stop making me want to toss you on that bed and show you how your sweet little pussy is the only food I crave.

"Fine," she huffs. "I'll compromise. A tank top and panties, it is."

Great. Raise a white flag, and my dick even higher.

Her tank tops and panties are my poison.

It's what Vale started to wear when she and Alena were in college, and they'd spend their holiday breaks together. They'd prance around my house in cute spirit wear from their colleges, and on my daughter, I worried Alena would catch a cold.

On Vale?

She looked so hot, I'd have to excuse myself. I'd have to commit my biggest shame in the shower, jerking off to the image of Vale's luscious tits and hard nipples under a thin, white Clemson tank top.

I keep my eyes closed, hearing her make a long production of settling herself into bed. Finally, when she clicks off the lamp, I open them.

"Here." In the moonlight glowing through the sheers over her windows, I see her toss a pillow onto the floor beside her bed. "And here." She throws a blanket beside it.

Shrouded in shadows, I can disguise the raging erection in my pants as I near her bed. I conceal it more, resting on my stomach. The wood floors are hard like me and what I need. They're brutally uncomfortable, matching how I feel inside.

Vale's only a few feet away, and I can smell her sandalwood shampoo. I can hear her breathing. It's shallow, like she's on edge with me here, and she's too close.

I won't sleep. I know it.

Once again, she's right.

This is clearly hell.

Heaven would be me climbing up onto her bed and making her feel every orgasmic pleasure she deserves. I wouldn't give her a choice; I'd make her come for me. It would get me off so much to do it. But hell would be the price I'd pay for it.

For minutes, our silence is heavy.

"Just tell me one detail." Then, her voice sounds so tender in the darkness. She doesn't wait for my permission; she asks, "You don't hurt innocent people, right? You don't traffic in women or girls or something like that?"

"No," I answer. "We kill the people who do."

CHAPTER SEVEN
VALE

I TOSS AND TURN ALL NIGHT, KNOWING NASH ISN'T sleeping either.

I can smell his sweet, leather cologne. I can hear his grunts and groans of discomfort, but of course, my horny mind translates them into sex sounds, and who can sleep all hot and bothered?

Finally, once dawn spills through the windows, I sit up and grab my laptop.

The clicking sound of my keyboard rouses the beast beside my bed.

"What are you writing?"

Great. Pile another fetish onto my horny pussy cart because Nash's deep voice sounds all raspy and sexy in the morning.

It's annoying. It's arousing.

"I'm not writing," I answer. "I'm checking the status of my burial plot. With you here, I'm seeing if it can be ready early."

He chuckles as he rises. "Find me one, too," he says, aiming for my bathroom, "because I'd take death over your mouth any day."

"You'd die and go to heaven in my mouth."

I blurt it before thinking, the innuendo making him stop in the doorway, the muscles across his back, even under his black shirt, obviously tensing.

"Do you have coffee?" he growls.

"Does the Pope have holy water?"

"Then answer my prayer and make me a cup."

"What will I get for making it?"

"The blessing to brew me more tomorrow," he replies before slamming the door.

Asshole.

I bet that word is hidden somewhere in the ink he hides, too. But this will be a long day, so I stomp across the studio and brew us a full carafe.

While he showers, I reach for one of my little black dresses, but ... I can't.

I know it tempts Nash and suddenly, tempting him is too tempting. I like that I get under his skin, that I arouse him, even slightly. He's a hot-blooded male. It's too easy.

But what would be hard, devastating actually, is if I give in to temptation, too. There'd be no going back, and Alena would read it all over us, the guilt undeniable.

I'd rather die than break her heart.

So, today, I break my naughty, gothic tradition. I still whip my hair into two braids, but then I slip on a vintage, white, mod miniskirt before I button on a tight, red cashmere sweater. Loyal to my Mary Janes, I wedge them on before checking the mirror above my dresser. My tube of Midnight Merlot calls next. Carefully, I paint my lips before swiping eyeliner on, creating thin, black batwings at the corner of my eyes before adding a little mascara.

There. That's as good as it gets, folks.

"Vale," Nash booms from my bathroom. "Bring me my GO BAG, the black one."

"Say, please."

"Now!"

"I don't speak Dickhead."

I giggle, loving this. I may need him for protection now, but who says I can't make him my entertainment, too?

"God. Fucking. Dammit, woman!"

He swings the door open and...

Holy towel snake and tattoos.

My jaw drops. Call a dentist. I cracked some teeth, too.

Why?

Look at him!

Nash Allen is all ink. Muscles. More ink. More muscles, then more ink with tan abs everywhere. Another huge tattoo, a skull with wings, spans the width of his Adonis belt, and I stare at it as his fist clutches his white towel that can't hide what's hanging huge under it.

He sees me staring right at it. I must look stupified, like a horny, mating doe in headlights, but he's too angry.

He storms across the room, fuming, "You gotta make everything hard, don't you?"

"Oh, *do I* make it hard?"

See? It's a disease. My smartassery can't be cured.

Ripping his bag open, he snarls, "Yeah, you make our lives hard when you're foolish like this. You play games when we need to play smart. We need to be on time, like normal, so no one knows, and I don't have time for this bullshit."

"Being polite isn't bullshit. It's respect. Speak to me with it if you want something done."

He pivots, holding his towel in one hand, his clean clothes fisted in the other. "What I want is to keep you alive without having to treat you like a goddamn snowflake."

My eyes narrow. "I can handle the heat."

"I know you can. I raised you that way, so fucking act like it."

"You *raised* me?" Disgust and rage barrel through my veins. "You're NOT my father. I never saw you that way, and I never will."

He shakes his head, his lips tensing. "And you're not my daughter. I never saw you that way, either. But I've known you too long, and I care too much. So, just shut up and do what I say."

I charge toward him. "Telling a woman to shut up is like turning your back on a tiger because every pussy will pounce and rip your fucking head off for doing it." I huff, "No wonder you're single."

I'm inches from him, able to smell my shampoo in his hair. Able to see ironically, how he has a snarling lion covering his right hulking pec and a raging tiger on his left one. They're like us, eye to eye and fighting over his heart.

"I'm not *single*," he growls, and my gasp is audible.

It's sudden jealousy and pain punching my heart.

I didn't know that. I don't want to imagine it, either. I don't want to hear how Nash has been secretly dating someone. How some woman has his heart because mine suddenly breaks at the thought.

All this time, Alena suspected her dad went somewhere with someone. You can't look like Nash does and not have a clowder of pussies trailing behind you. But Nash never brought women around Alena.

Or me. I'm shocked by how I feel, *that* I feel this for him, and it's overwhelming. Suddenly, I realize everything I believed about him was a lie, so I stagger back, hurt.

He reads my reaction, "I mean..." He reaches like he wants to grab me, but his hands are full. "I don't date. I don't commit. I'm loyal to something else."

My heart is relieved, but now, I'm confused. "Like what? A secret society of men covered in arrogance and ink?"

A grin tugs at his lush lips. "Something like that."

"So, you're in a gang of hot gay men?"

Please say yes. Then again ... please don't. I need a fighting chance.

"I'm not gay, either." He brushes past me. "And let's land the plane on this convo because I need coffee and to be on time."

IF YOU THINK MONDAYS ARE NOTORIOUSLY BAD, TRY suffering one with a pseudo-kidnapper who wets your panties, and a twin, trying to sober up from a one-night bender on dick and love.

Nash takes his usual place next to me at the front desk of Delta's. It's a huge, maple wood, antique Partner's desk made for two, but I may as well be solo.

He ignores me, his eyes glued to the desktop screen while his mouse scrolls through transactions.

This room used to be the front parlor, and this house used to be a mansion for French settlers.

Now, it's an exclusive adult store, and I'm its manager, over-qualified in all knowledge about sex and seriously sucking in all things math. That's why Nash has been here for two weeks. That's why he blends in now.

Somehow, I messed up the accounting software, and my boss, Stacey, said I could keep my job as long as I fixed it. So, I called the only accountant I knew—Nash Allen.

Little did I know that he also has deft skills in car chases, murder, kidnapping, and being a grumpy, sexy shithead in the morning.

But my twin outshines him today. Blair mopes in her fleece pajamas, slouched in an ivory wingback chair across the parlor.

Jace, our bouncer, sits on his stool by the front doors, feet away, trying to cheer her up, but she's committed to her misery over Beau Bronson.

I've indulged her pity party for months, but not today. "Blair, can you go restock the male masturbators? We got a new shipment in."

"We're fine." She rolls her eyes. "No one's masturbating on a Monday morning."

"Ahem." Nash shifts, clearing his throat before Jace laughs, declaring, "Clearly, you don't know men. It's the only way to start a week. Especially with the new Autoblow machines with AI. Damn, who needs a woman?"

Is that what Nash was doing in the shower? Jerking off? *Good god, that image is hot.* But if so, why is he still cranky this morning?

I don't know, but that makes two of us. "Exactly," I answer. "We keep selling out of them, so Blair, restock."

"Damn," she drags to her feet, "who died and made you the boss?"

"The owner," I snap, "who's alive and well and will be here soon, so I want those shelves restocked."

Blair glares, slowly clocking my new outfit. My bare, pale legs. Bright white skirt. Red, fuzzy sweater. She jeers, "You look like a tampon."

Nash snorts, Jace roars laughing, and I fire a rubber band at her tit.

"Ouch!" she shouts, rubbing her nipple.

"Just because you broke your heart and pussy on a big,

blue alien dick with a one-night stand doesn't mean you get to make the rest of us miserable for life."

"That was a secret, Vale!"

"All things are fair in monster cock sheaths and love, Blair!"

"You're such a bitch." She turns, storming toward our showroom.

"Yes, sister," I shout after her, "and so are you. So quit feeling sorry for your fucks and fight back. It's been months."

Jace watches Blair stomp up the grand wooden staircase. After a moment, his face bends. "Should I go check on her?"

"She's fine," I answer, opening the mail. "She needs to get mad to get over that man. I swear if I could, I'd kill Beau Bronson for breaking her heart, but he's too damn famous, and I heard the cheeseburgers suck in jail."

Silently, I sort through junk and bills as Nash clicks on the mouse, scrutinizing every transaction I entered last year.

"What's this?" He points to one.

"Oh." I read it. "That's our quarterly donation. Stacey donates thirty percent of our proceeds to a local women's shelter."

"Proceeds," he asks, "or *profit?*"

I hate this. I hate feeling dumb. "Proceeds," I snap over-confidently.

"Vale," he lowers his eyes behind those fake, nerdy glasses, "do you know the difference?"

"Yes."

"Tell me."

My sigh is long, my eyes rolling back like I'm losing consciousness. *I wish I could.* "Fine. Lecture me, please. I know you're dying to."

"No, it's my job," he answers coldly.

I snort, "Yeah, right, Don Corleone."

"Ahem."

Now, Jace clears his throat, which is weird because he usually stays out of the drama. I glance at him in his dark Armani suit, sitting stoic on his stool.

Raising a suspicious brow, I turn back to Nash, who leans in, mad and grumbling, "I'm *not* the godfather, and I'm *not* your father. I'm the accountant hired by you to tell you that proceeds don't account for cost. If a monster cock sheath costs you ten dollars to buy and you sell it for twenty, your *proceeds* are twenty dollars, but your *profit* is ten. You should be donating profits, or you will run your generous boss out of business."

Why does he have to look so damn hot teaching me? If he'd been my math professor, I would've majored in it. "Why, Mr. Allen, I get so wet when you talk cock sheaths and costs."

"*Vale.*" He glowers, "Professional. Remember?"

"Mr. Allen." I bat my lashes, pointing at my D-cups. "*Sex* professional. Remember?"

"Do I need to take a lunch break?" Jace interrupts us, and again, it's weird.

Usually, he's the sweet, silent, sexy mountain of muscle who sits by the door, not a meddling co-worker who gets all up in my hot mafia man business.

"We're fine," Nash clips, then cuts Jace a look I've never seen.

They were strangers until I introduced them two weeks ago. But now? They're speaking a secret language I can't translate.

"Just making sure." Jace spins the ring on his pinky before the bell rings. He checks the camera screen, then buzzes a customer in.

"Hi." A tall, blond man fidgets in the foyer. It's obvious he's new here. "I, uh. I heard about you guys and thought I'd come by."

Usually, Blair helps our customers, but she's upstairs, pining over NFL penis, so I jump to my feet.

"Sure." I stride across the room, extending my hand for a shake. "I'm Vale. I'm the manager. What can I help you with?"

The handsome man's cheeks blush instantly. Funny how sex toys do that to some. It's sweet, and I love my job. Giving advice, especially about sex, is my calling because I'm searching for help, too. I recognize the Peter Millar golf jersey he's wearing. "You play?" I ask, putting him at ease.

"Yeah," he answers, surprised. "You?"

"Used to."

His grin grows. "Why'd you stop?"

"My dad." His brows twist, confused, so I explain, "He's Duncan Monroe, and being his daughter in the sport made it go from fun to infuriating. I stopped competing in college."

"Duncan Monroe, the PGA Master, is *your* dad?"

"He's my dad and many others'."

I'm not joking. My dad's famous for his philandering, too. He's been married a hundred times, had a million girlfriends, too, and has a gazillion kids. That's an exaggeration but not by much, and Blair and I get the honor of being his first fuck-ups.

"So, the game is in your blood?" The guy admires, offering, "Maybe you'll play again someday."

"Maybe." I shrug. "But how can I help you today?"

Again, he blushes, but now we've bonded. He can tell me, "I want to buy a vibrator."

"For your girlfriend?"

He's not wearing a ring.

"No," the blush reaches his ears, "for a *future* girlfriend. I kind of want to be prepared. I read how they help, how many women can't, um, orgasm without them."

"You read right." I teach, "About seventy-five percent of women never reach orgasm from intercourse alone."

"So," he shuffles awkwardly, "what do you recommend?"

Tenderly, I smile. "I recommend a man like you because any woman would be lucky to have you." I gesture toward the stairs. "I'll show you some options that will surely satisfy her, trust me. I know."

He leads the way before I glance back and...

Who let the angel of death into the store? Nash is glaring at me. It's predatory. It's seething. It's warning me like I'm about to cheat when I'm just doing my job.

Oh, I get it, rolling my eyes at him.

He can be all morally grey and murder for a good cause, but I can't sell sex toys and satisfaction?

Whatever.

Thirty minutes later, I've sold Mr. Gorgeous Golfer a lipstick vibrator, a Satisfyer clit sucker, a vibrating cock ring, lots of lube, and a Deep Throat Pocket Pal for his lonely nights or eager partners. He leaves happy and horny as I turn to Nash.

Murder swims in his brown eyes. He opens his mouth to deliver more judgment than the Supreme Court, but I'm not here for it. "Don't do that."

"Do what?"

"That." I waggle my finger at his flared nostrils.

"What?"

"That." I poke his scruffy, cleft chin. "Don't scowl at me like I stole some saint's virginity. He wanted sex toys, so I sold him sex toys."

Nash leans over, seething so Jace can't hear, "He wanted *you.*"

"Don't speak so past tense." I raise a brow. "He Name-Dropped me, so we may have a future."

Confusion mixes with rage across his handsome face.

I'm about to explain the iPhone tech to him when Stacey, Delta's owner, trudges through the door. Ford, one of her husbands, enters behind her with his hand caressing the small of her back. It's a constant, sweet gesture between them, but today, they look distressed.

"Hey." I break from Nash's interrogation, focusing on my real boss. "Everything okay?"

"No," she sighs as Ford barks, "Yes!"

Stacey turns to him, pleading to his eyes, "Babe, it's *not* okay. You're worried and angry, just like me, but I need to talk about it. I can't hold every emotion in like you do."

"This is private," Ford grumbles.

"This is family." Stacey gestures to me and Jace.

So, Nash stands. He may be an asshole to me, but with others, his manners are impeccable. "I'll give you all a moment," he says. "I'll go to the deli and grab everyone lunch."

"Thank you," Stacey sighs.

"Thanks." Ford nods at him, but Nash isn't out the front door before Stacey bursts into a flood of tears and words.

"It's Hannah," she cries.

That's Ford's daughter and her stepdaughter, and I fear the worst. "Is she okay?"

"Yes," Stacey rushes, "I mean, no. She's being bribed. Someone is threatening to expose a relationship she had with a coach, which will ruin her chances with the WNBA draft, and she's devastated. We all are."

Brushing by Jace, Nash mumbles something to him. Jace nods.

And my suspicions skyrocket.

CHAPTER EIGHT
NASH

Winding my way along a crowded sidewalk, I aim for the nearest deli while I call Axel.

"All secure?"

"Yes," I answer. "I have my asset secured. Seven has his." I pause, shuffling around a street artist selling roses made of sweetgrass. "But I'm calling about Six."

"What about him?" Axel asks, sounding wary.

"The people trying to bribe him, do you know who they are?"

"We're working on it."

"Well, I think I found a lead, maybe a connection." The line inside the deli is long, but their service is fast. "Can you meet me at the Bonneau mansion in thirty?"

I won't say "Delta's," our location.

His chuckle is low. "And just how do you propose I introduce myself there?"

Axel hides under a pseudonym and an Americanized name, too. All of his brothers do. I'm the only one who doesn't have to worry about my real name.

"It's an adult store. Come as a customer," I smirk at the pun, "or come as you are."

"That's dangerous."

"No, it's an opportunity to help someone while we help ourselves."

He pauses, weighing the risks while I order six Shrimp Po' Boys before I speed this along.

"Listen, we need the room on their third floor, and it sounds like the owner and her husband need our help. Someone is bribing their daughter, and I have a hunch it's the same one bribing Six. It's not a risk; it's business."

"Not a risk? After last night?" He scolds, "You've lost your goddamn mind over Vale Monroe already."

"I'm in control and *won't* lose it," I growl. "Besides, we know who it was last night. You checked this morning, right?"

I have no doubt Axel has called our moles in the police department and the state department of transportation, too.

"Yes," he answers. "Daniel Ramirez was found dead, shot at the scene on the Ravenel bridge, but Claude Olan Turner the Fourth survived. He suffered a severe concussion and will be out of the hospital in a week. Maybe less."

"Fuck, I knew it," I mutter, paying the cashier.

Claude Olan Turner is fourth in the line of men into some dark crimes in this town. Unfortunately, he's inherited a fortune, too.

"It's like the myth." Axel warns, "Cut off one head; two more shall take its place."

"But now, there are seven of us and only one of him."

"Don't underestimate him."

"I don't. See you in twenty." I hang up, not giving Axel a chance to refuse before I grab our bag to go.

Minutes later, Delta's staff have turned the front parlor into a lunchroom. Even Blair, Vale's sullen sister, thanked me for the sandwiches.

"Is providing lunch included in your hourly rate?" Stacey jokes with me, but I can tell she's been crying.

She sits in her husband's lap. They struggle to eat their sandwiches, and I understand. Concern for your child will steal your appetite.

"With as much as Ms. Monroe has messed up your books?" I make Vale the butt of a joke. "Lunch is on me."

It lightens the mood just enough as the bell rings, and Five, I mean … *Jace*, opens the door.

"Welcome to Delta's," he greets the customer looming in the doorway.

"Is the owner here, please?"

"May I tell her who's inquiring?"

"Yes," the customer steps inside, towering just an inch short of Jace, "Michael Cummings. I'm a local real estate attorney and I have an offer to discuss with her, please."

"Uh, hi." Stacey rises from her husband's lap. "I'm Stacey James, the owner."

"Good afternoon, Ms. James." The customer enters the parlor, extending his hand to shake hers. "Michael Cummings." He notes our group gathered with sandwich wrappers open on Vale's desk. "Sorry to interrupt your lunch."

It takes everything I have not to smirk. I give Axel so much shit for his pseudonym. *Cummings.* It's loaded with puns, and yes, I've used them.

"It's okay," Stacey assures. "How can I help you today?"

But her husband eyes Axel. He's not buying what Axel is about to sell, but I know Axel will make an offer too sweet to refuse.

"May I speak with you," Axel nods toward Stacey, then Ford, "and your husband? Right? In private, please?"

"This is my wife's business. You speak directly to *her*." Ford rises. He's an imposing man. "I, nor our two husbands, tell her how to run it."

And he's a proud one, too.

"I respect you and your business, ma'am." Axel softens his tone, his glacial eyes addressing Stacey before he aims them at Ford. "But this is about family, too. It's about your daughter."

"Our daughter?" Ford sneers, whipping his glare around the room. "Who told you?"

Tension is rising, tempers, too, so I stand. "I did." I address him and Stacey. "I'm sorry. I couldn't help but overhear your situation before I left, and I have a daughter, too. I'd do anything to protect her, so I took the liberty of calling an associate I knew could help."

"You did *what?*" Vale mutters.

I glance down at her glaring eyes as Ford challenges Axel, "But you're a land lawyer. I've seen your shingle on Meeting Street—Cummings and Associates. How the hell can you help our daughter?"

"Yes, I have a practice, but I have family, too, sir," Axel answers him. "Please." He gestures to the stairs. "May we speak privately? I need to protect them, too."

Skepticism twists Ford's face, but he nods and agrees. He and Stacey follow Axel upstairs as the rest of us watch.

Once they're out of earshot, Blair sighs, "Fuck, that man just firehosed my panties."

"Finally." Jace chuckles. "She's alive again."

"Alive?" Vale hisses, turning to me, "No, I'm gonna kill you for calling that man, Mr. Orgasm of the Eyes Cummings, or whatever. You had no right to do that. You violated Stacey and Ford's privacy."

"No." I lower my voice. "I'm helping them."

"Helping them how?"

"Details, Ms. Monroe." I raise my brow at her. "Remember what I told you about those?"

CHAPTER NINE
NASH

I'M A MIRACLE WORKER. I'VE MANAGED TO PISS VALE Monroe off so much that she barely speaks to me for three days.

The silence is golden.

And amusing.

Because I know she's dying to say something snarky when I pick up another one of her books.

Last night, I read *Pussy: A Reclamation*. Quite informative. Very arousing. Because, yes, I imagined Vale's pussy the entire time. Tonight, I take her book and my spot on her loveseat while she sits on her bed, typing on her laptop.

After our days at Delta's, this has been our nights...

I cook. She cleans. I read. She fumes. I smirk. She snarls. It's domestic bliss.

So when I open her annotated copy of *Arousal: The Secret Logic of Sexual Fantasies*, she finally blows a gasket.

"Don't read that!"

"Why not?"

"Because," she huffs, "it's private."

Like a red cape to a bull, I wave the paperback. "It's published."

"It's mine."

I flutter the dozens of pastel tabs marking its pages. "Is someone shy about her sexual fantasies?"

She scoffs, "You couldn't handle my sexual fantasies."

It's instant. My cock stirs at her challenge. "Wanna bet?"

"Yes." She slams her laptop closed. "If I win, I'll ask, and you'll give me a mafia detail."

"And if you lose?"

"What do you want?"

Not to be a dumbass right now, who's so damn tempted to flirt with your fire, but days of your beautiful silence have weakened me.

It's cute how her ass shakes when she brushes her teeth. It's fascinating how she chews her bottom lip while she types. It's intoxicating how she slowly brushes her hair, how it falls like black silk down her back. It's sweet how she calls Alena, how they laugh and gossip. Then Vale hangs up and glares at me because she hates lying to her. I do, too.

"If I win," I answer, "you'll give me the silent treatment for another week."

She does it again. She glares. "That's not a fair wager."

"All's fair in sexual fantasies and details."

"Fine." She grins, sitting ramrod straight. "Stand up."

"What?"

"Stand up," she twirls her braid, biting her lip as her tone switches to sweet, slow, and seductive, "and if I can watch how I make your. Big. Thick. Long. Cock get so hard for me while I'm being a. Very. Bad. Girl. By confessing my. Dirtiest. Naughtiest. Filthiest. Fantasy to you, *Mr. Allen* ... I win." She licks her top lip. "Hint: It involves honey and my *ass*."

Holy fuck, I'm already hard. Rock hard. Her beauty. Her voice. Her tease. Her book is hiding my tenting trousers.

And she knows it.

She falls back on the bed, laughing. "Men are so easy. All it takes is an audible simulation of a classic fetish, of a 'bad girl being naughty for you,' and you're making pudding in your pants."

But I'm not laughing. I remember.

Her. My beautiful, bad girl.

I'm swollen, heavy and hard, and hanging on by a thread. That's all that's holding me back from enacting my ultimate fantasy, which is fucking the ever-living hell out of Vale's sweet pussy, then her sassy mouth, then her honeyed ass, before I start all over again.

My silence gets her attention. She sits up again. "What?" She teases, "Does my wet cat have your tongue?"

"You couldn't handle my tongue." I dare. I desire. "Wet would be where you'd start, and squirting all over my face would be where I'd end you. Over and over again."

It's another miracle. Vale's silent, her eyes wide.

She stops taunting and twirling her braid as her ribs heave, her breath deepening at my threat. Her little tank top can't hide the effect I have on her pearling nipples.

She stammers, "But, I... I can't co—"

"Oh," I snarl, "I'll *make* you come, Vale. So many times and for hours, I'll take my time and won't give up until you do. I'll give you more than what you need, what you can handle, and you'll take it like a good girl. You'll love it. You won't be able to walk the next day. You'll just lie there, satisfied and begging for more."

Her teeth grab her bottom lip. It starts to tremble. "Are you mocking me?"

"Never." My tone softens. "I'm making a *promise* to you."

Because I can't stop thinking about it. About her. About her secret and how I crave to help. I never knew she was suffering like this, and I can't lie on the floor beside her bed, listening to her huffs of frustration, knowing all I'd try for her, all I'd give her.

Honestly? I need it, too. Desire is one thing. Care another. To feel them both in one night shared with a woman? With Vale? It would be a first for me.

But I know what she survived, and I want to protect her too much. Even from myself. I'd never make the first move.

The tension is so thick between us; the only thing that's clear is how much we both want it. How much we want each other.

Her brows pinch as she barely whispers, "But... we *can't*... What about Alena?"

Suddenly, reality comes crashing down.

We can't. We shouldn't. And we won't.

But now, our sudden, forbidden exchange, her lonely secret, and my passionate promise make tears brim in her grey eyes before they spill down her ivory cheeks, and...

"Vale," I rise to comfort her, but her palm flies up, stopping me.

"Don't," she says. "Please don't hurt me with what I can't have. I'm used to it. I'll be fine."

I sit back down, my arms aching to hold her. "Is it really true?" I still can't believe it. "You've never had an orgasm?"

"Yeah," another tear slides down her cheek, but she jokes, "I won a contest, and the prize was not to be able to come during sex. Any sex. Unless it's with myself."

I gesture to her library. "Have you figured out why?"

"Yes." She gestures to her books, too. "They're why. They're in my head. I overthink when I'm with someone, and I can't get into a flow state."

"A flow state?"

"That's what some psychologists call it. When you stop thinking and judging and worrying and ... you just feel. You let your body take control."

"But alone you can do it?"

"Yeah." She shrugs. "I watch myself in that mirror." She points to the one by her bed. "And I use a toy or my fingers, and I can come almost every time."

"Why do you watch yourself?" It's so erotic, I'm obsessed.

"It's part of my therapy." She lifts her chin. "Because my pussy is beautiful, and it's mine, and at least I can give myself pleasure."

I want to tell her I know more. I know why she went to therapy. I know why she's safe now. Well, she was safe until I came back around.

"Why do you want to know so much?" she asks. "Why do you care about my sex life?"

I lean forward, resting my elbows on my knees. My dick deflated in the presence of her pain. I can't watch her suffer. "Because I care about you, and I care about your life, and I always have."

"Why?"

I shake my head. *She has no idea...*

"You saved Alena; you know that, right? Your friendship saved her life. I was so worried after her mother was killed. I took her to counselors and everything, but I always feared the worst until you came along. You were the first one to make her laugh after Lainey died."

Vale swipes away a tear.

Goddamn, I hate it when she cries. Her eyes look like smoky glass when she does. It's breathtaking, too.

"Do you ever miss her, too?" she asks.

"Yeah." I nod. "We became good friends, and as my daughter's mother, I loved Lainey. And it's been tough watching Alena become a woman without her. That's why you mean so much to her." I swallow. "To me."

"Alena saved me, too." She tucks her sexy braid behind her ear. "You both did. Growing up, it was me and my twin and our mom, always working hard to provide for us. I loved them, but I ached inside, feeling like I was missing something, and when I'd hang out with Alena at your house, I found it."

"Found what?"

Softly, she grins, not ashamed of her tears. "Home."

I roll my lips, swallowing the lump in my throat, confessing, "I always felt like you belonged with us, too."

She pauses, and I let her search my eyes.

If she looks deep enough, she'll find herself there. She'll find out how much I've felt for her ... for so many years.

"Why was it just the three of us?" she asks. "Why did you never find someone? It's been forever, and you're getting old, and you're really, really, really *not* hard to look at." Long pause. "At. All."

A grin hits my lips. "Forty-four is not old ... thanks and ... and it never felt right."

"Was it to honor Alena's mom? And Alena?"

"No, it's more complicated than that."

She tips her head. Her tears have stopped, but her snark hasn't returned. She's gentle ... and dammit, she's smart.

"It's complicated and has to do with that man, Michael Cummings, doesn't it?" she probes. "I could feel something between you two. You two and Jace. I'm right, aren't I?"

"Those are deadly questions, Vale. Quit asking them."

"Can I ask another question?"

"What did I *just* say?"

"I don't know. When it's not what I want to hear, I don't listen."

"Fuck." I chuckle, tossing my chin up. "What?"

"Will you sleep with me tonight?"

Now, I'm struck mute, her question racing my pulse. *Fuck. Will I sleep with my greatest temptation?*

"We won't do anything," she rushes. "We'll sleep with

pillows between us, but I swear, if I have to hear you grunt and groan like you're fucking my hardwood floors anymore, I'm going to scream. I can't sleep because you can't sleep, and yes, you're an asshole, but I've always cared for you, too. You fill some hole in my heart that I can't explain, so let's not try to, and finally, for the love of God, *sleep*."

I shake my head. "Your double bed isn't big enough for you, me, and a pile of pillows between us."

And the lust I feel for you, too? I can barely contain it.

"Fine," she says. "We'll sleep fully clothed and back-to-back, and if you snore, don't worry about your mafia enemies. I'll slit your throat myself."

We keep our promise. We sleep with clothes on, our backs barely touching, and it's hard because her bed dips in the middle where she usually sleeps.

"Nash?" she whispers.

"Yeah?" I rasp, ready. Worried. Wanting.

Tenderly, her foot brushes mine under the sheet. "What's this? Between *us*?"

Her skin is so soft, it's killing me. I stare into the darkness, the ache overwhelming and painful. "Something we can't have."

So, all night and for another week, I fight the gravity I feel to touch her.

But I can't fight the other gravity I feel, the one that's falling so goddamn in love with Vale.

CHAPTER TEN
VALE

It's got to be genetic. I swear there's DNA that makes verbal bullets shoot from your mouth, because Blair and I get in a girly gunfight today.

I've had it with her pity party. It's been almost four months since her Valentine's date killed her vagina. She doesn't go out like she used to. She doesn't smile. She's a real pill, and you'd think she'd be happy because she's writing her romance books when she's not being a pathetic pain.

But no. Today, she narrows her eyes, glaring at me as I sit at my desk.

Ready. Aim. Fire.

"What did you do to your hair?" she snipes.

I shoot back, "Can you fix your face so it doesn't look like you've sniffed a fart?"

"Can you fix your hair so it doesn't look like Exxon is your stylist?"

Jace snorts by the door. Nash taps his foot over mine under the desk, and I know I should be nice to her, but that hurt.

"What?" I touch my strands. "I'm wearing it down and straight. Is that a crime?"

"It is when it's all oily like that." She slumps in her usual chair. "When was the last time you washed it?"

I can't tell her how I'm afraid to take a shower. She can't know how I've slept next to Nash all week, and every morning when I wake up beside him, I'm all hot and aroused and agitated. So, when I take a shower, it's the only privacy I have from him, and I ache to touch myself and come, but now?

Now, I'm so damn flooded with emotions for Nash; coming at the thought of him feels like more than lust.

It's starting to feel like love between us, and that scares the hell out of me. It scares me how he smiles at me when I brush my teeth. It frightens me when I catch him grinning as I type. It terrifies me how he watches me brush my hair. How silently he makes me feel so beautiful. How I think he's beautiful, too. How he may be a beast, but he doesn't frighten me.

So, it's been a couple of days, and I thought dry shampoo and a whore's bath would suffice. But it doesn't under the scrutiny of my sister.

"It's been a minute," I answer her.

"It's been an eon, and *eww*." She grimaces. "You're gross."

So, I snap, "You know, your fleece pajamas are making a stench and a statement, too. They're giving 'I give up' vibes."

"Because I have."

"You can't give up on love, Blair. Not over one man."

"You have no idea because no man has ever loved you!"

The sting is instant. Tears bite at my eyes, and I look away.

"I'm sorry." She rushes to me. "I'm sorry." She kneels, yanking me into a hug. "I'm being a bitch, and I'm sorry. I've never been heartbroken like this, and I'm so sorry. I'm wrong. *I* love you. *Alena* loves you. And—"

"I love you."

I glance through my blurred vision at Jace, sitting on his stool by the door. Yes, he means it; it's in his blue eyes. Not in a brotherly way; it's more like a friend, but there's a little something between us. A little flirt. A little fun. That's all.

"Thanks," I mutter, feeling the heavy silence on my right. It's Nash, and he's the only one in the room not saying a word.

I think I know why. I feel the same way.

"I started my period today," Blair shares. "I'm bitchy and emotional as hell, and I'm sorry."

"Oh, shit."

Blair and I are synced up, and with all this Nash stuff going on, I forgot. But unlike Blair, my periods make me more than emotional. They make me sick.

"Do you have your Motrin?" Blair asks, smoothing my dirty hair. She knows what's coming for me. "I'll cover for you tomorrow, okay? And the next day. Just stay in bed, and it'll be over soon."

"*What* will be over soon?"

Wonderful. Now *Nash speaks?* Yes, please, let's all discuss my periods from hell.

"She has endometriosis," Blair answers. "Like she murders menstruation. Blood everywhere."

I close my eyes, dying inside. "Jeez, Blair."

"What?" she scoffs. "There's no period shaming here, and Mr. Allen has a daughter. Remember when Alena got her period at school? He was one of the cool parents who picked her up and kept her home a day."

"And you both were sweet to her," he answers. "Thanks for showing her how to ... uh—"

"How to put a tampon in?" Blair interrupts. "Yeah, we had it covered because some girls go for the wrong hole the first time and—"

"Blair. Just. *Stop*," I groan. "You're making this worse."

By the end of the day, it is worse. I take my birth control patch off, and my period hits me like a freight train. My core cramps, my stomach is sick, and my thighs ache. Then, I realize I'll have an audience for my massacre tonight, so I add to my agony by gently banging my head on the desk.

Nash whispers to me, "Let's go. Let's get you comfortable."

With my cheek smushed against the wood, I look at him and confess, "Comfortable is not on the itinerary for the next three days. This will be bad and bloody and so fucking embarrassing. Do you really have to witness my mortification?"

Blair is upstairs with customers. Jace is in the kitchen, scarfing down his third lunch, so we're free to talk.

"Yes." Nash takes off his glasses. Rubbing the bridge of his nose, he answers, "I don't like invading your privacy, but you're not safe. One of the men on the bridge survived. He just got out of the hospital, and he'll be coming for us."

"Us?" I pop up.

"Yes. He's going to go after everyone I care about. That puts you at risk and me by your side, protecting you."

"Oh, god," I groan, rolling my eyes. "Can't you just shoot him and get this over with? Or give me the gun. I'm cramping so bad all of humanity is in my crosshairs."

"If he comes around, yes, I'll take care of him, but he likes to hide, too."

"Where?"

"If we knew, he wouldn't be hiding."

"What does he do that's so bad?"

"The exact thing you feared *I* was doing, and if he gets a hold of you or Alena? I'll rescue you, don't worry. But when I catch him, I won't kill him. Death requires no imagination, and I'll get creative with his pain."

We're sharing the same fear: what would happen to me if I get kidnapped by his enemy?

"So, he'd ... *traffic* me?" It fills me with terror.

"To torture me, yes," Nash answers, "he'd torture you."

Sucking his teeth, for the first time, he truly looks like the beast he said he is. Like blood drips from his sudden fangs. His beauty turns dark, his eyes blank. Emotions can't find his face or heart. He looks dead inside, just like his ambitions for his prey.

I don't recognize him, but I recognize he's a serious threat. Who? Yeah, I mean both men.

It worsens the next twist in my gut, and I groan, feeling my pale face turn pallid. My pain suddenly makes the beast disappear. Nash brushes his hand over the small of my back. "I promise I'll give you privacy for this."

"But..." I can't believe I'm about to say this, "I don't want you to go. I mean, I like being kidnapped by you, not the Bridge Bastard."

Nash grins. "Yeah, you've made it clear that I annoy you with how amazing I am."

I grin back, even through wretched cramps. "And you thought kidnapping me was gonna turn out for you, but here we are. Me, about to send you to the store to buy two boxes of super-plus-plus tampons. How'd that turn out for you?"

He huffs a laugh. "Blood doesn't faze me."

Then he stops my breath. His fingers gently brush a greasy strand from my face. "Let's go," he soothes. "I got you covered."

Our routine is that Nash leaves first. He uses Delta's back exit and waits for me in the shadows of the blooming courtyard behind the house. A few minutes later, I leave, and he follows me home using the narrow, cobblestone alleys that snake behind the homes in Charleston's historic district.

But this evening, when I leave, Nash leads me to a black

RAM pickup truck, pulling up to the curb. When he opens the passenger door for me, I'm not surprised to see who's driving.

"I knew it!" I exclaim.

"Just get in." Jace sounds serious while Nash slides into the back seat of his double cab. I fasten my seatbelt, but my mouth is unrestrained.

"I knew it. You two and that Cummings guy work together. Like three peas in a mafia Avengers pod. Wait." I turn to Jace. "Does this mean Grant is, too?"

Grant is Jace's older brother and Delta's nighttime bouncer, and I swear they might as well be twins. They look and act alike, like big, beefy bouncers in Armani suits, so if one is mafia, both are.

"Listen, Nancy Drew," Jace warns, "we're not mafia, not like you think. But you're too smart and ask too many damn questions and see too much stuff for us not to tell you a few things because honestly, shit *will* go sideways soon, and you have to know who you can trust, and we'll have to protect you."

"And *you* need to protect *us* from your mouth," Nash adds from the backseat. "We're serious, Vale. No one can know. Not your sister. Not my daughter. Not your boss. No—"

"But," I ask, "isn't your Cummings guy renting the room on the third floor of Delta's now? How can Stacey *not* know who he is and who you are?"

"He's given Stacey a reason to trust him," Nash answers, "so she gives him a place for his meetings. Our meetings. No questions asked."

"Meetings?" I have no idea where we're going, but who cares? This makes no sense. "Who has meetings in an adult store?"

"Adults," Jace quips.

"Okay, smartass."

"Pot," Jace makes a fast left turn, "meet Kettle."

"So, do I go to your meetings now?" I'm excited. "Is there like a secret knock and a code word to get in? Am I in the not-mafia-mafia club, too?"

"Over dead bodies," Nash answers with so much ice in his voice, I shiver.

But I don't have a chance to ask more questions because Jace pulls into The Mercier Hotel's parking garage. Immediately, I figure it out—Nash got us a suite here so he could protect me while I can have some privacy.

It's so damn sweet; I can't speak as Nash grabs three duffels from Jace's cab before Jace drives away.

The elevator takes us from the garage to the grand lobby. We step out to find a crowd gathered by the hotel's front glass doors, and I see why.

Redix Dean and Daniel Pierce are here. They're not only Hollywood hotties but also in the most famous polycule in the world, and the paparazzi won't leave them alone. They stand with their wives, chatting with Luca Mercier, the hotel's owner, and his wife, Scarlett, as camera flashes pop outside.

I know them. They're friends with Stacey and loyal Delta's customers but I'd never divulge their proclivities.

I guess that's the discretion Nash says I require now, as he gently tugs my arm, not wanting us to be spotted.

Once we're on the gold elevator to our room, he reveals, "I went online today and read how hot baths can help with your symptoms. You don't have a tub at your place, so I—"

So, you're really melting my heart. I'm speechless, stunned, and staring up at him in awe.

"Look who's being the asshole now," he mutters, leaning over to kiss my strands. "And for the record, I think Exxon is doing a beautiful job with your hair, and it's cute when you dress like a tampon, and there *is* a man who cares way too much for you, and he's *not* your father."

I rest my head on his arm. "And he's *not* in the mafia, either."

"*Vale*," he warns.

"Okay, okay." I loop my arm over his. "Take me to a tub, please."

Blair said no man has ever loved me, and maybe that's true, even of our father.

But no man has ever swept me off my feet, literally, like Nash Allen does. Once the suite door locks behind us, he drops our bags and, in one deft move, carries me to a king-sized bed.

"Rest here," he says, "while I fill the tub."

No man has ever considered ordering lavender-scented salts from a hotel spa and having them sent to our suite so he could fill my bath with them.

No man has ever neatly placed a plush robe, a pile of towels, and a shot of tequila by a tub for me, either.

"I read you shouldn't drink alcohol," he says before leaving me in our suite's palatial spa bathroom, "but I know you like Casa Amigos and cheeseburgers. I'll order some for our room service while you relax."

Relax? No. I undress, then slowly ease my aching body into the soothing water while I drown in an even warmer feeling. It surrounds me, and I close my eyes.

I let a tear fall.

Yeah, no man has ever loved me, but I don't need love if I have Nash.

CHAPTER ELEVEN
VALE

NEATLY, NASH FOLDS OUR DIRTY CLOTHES, ONE PIECE AT A time, before packing them into our duffels.

I grin, sitting on the bed, watching his ritual, and get busted.

"What?" he asks.

"Nothing."

He raises a brow.

"By all means, move at a glacial pace," I answer. "I'll be a hundred by the time you're done, and I don't want to leave anyway."

"We can't stay forever."

"I really hate that word—*can't*."

"It's a contraction," he corrects me.

"It's a heartbreak," I confess softly, and he nods, looking away.

It suffocates us; everything we can't do. *Didn't do.*

Four days of luxury have passed, and all the spa baths and Nash's spoiling gave me the shortest period I've had in years. It's gone, and physically I feel great. But now we have to go. So, emotionally, I'm a hot mess.

I wish we could stay in The Mercier Hotel forever. Here, I see how my sister lost her heart to a man. It's a lavish escape from the world, and Nash has been perfect.

He watched movies with me. Although he hated my favorite horror flicks, he seemed content to sit beside me on the sofa. Probably because I wasn't talking.

He ordered massages for us in our room. Facials, too. The way he scowled in a green mud mask? The Grinch would be upstaged. I laughed so hard. "Say 'moisture.'" I tried to snap a pic of him, too, but he wouldn't let me.

He slept in the king-sized bed with me because I asked. Every time I think of what could happen to me if I get taken by his enemy, I don't want Nash to leave my side.

But we didn't do anything. He didn't make a move.

He can't.

It was just brief touches. Heavy sighs. Tender laughs. Quick kisses to my hair. Ugh! It was so goddamn sweet and innocent; we were like teenage virgins wearing purity rings and not adults who wanted to fuck in a hot frenzy of need.

We check out, and Jace drives us back to my apartment, which now feels even smaller.

Nash makes my second favorite dinner: lasagna. At least he satisfies my stomach. The man can cook.

While I wash the dishes, I side-eye him on the loveseat, reading my book, *She Comes First*.

My stomach flips. *Is he telling me something?*

It makes heat and tension fill every minute and molecule between us. I notice every lick of his lips. He lifts his glance, watching every subtle move I make. I catch how he adjusts himself, suspecting he's on the chapter about the cunnilinguist manifesto, and desire claws at my insides, wanting out, wanting him. Even in my shower, I can't escape it. I feel Nash everywhere, but I don't touch ... him or me.

I can't.

I know it will unlock something inside me, and I won't be the same. I know I'll suddenly be real, be in love, be lost forever to him, and everyone will see it.

I don't know how Nash is holding back because I'm not sure I can anymore. This is starting to hurt way more than it used to, and the cure to my pain sleeps right next to me.

But then I remember how it strengthens my resolve whenever Alena calls or texts. Or I'll hear how Nash softens his tone when she calls him. "Yes, sweetpea," is his answer to every wish she has for her wedding.

We can't.

He loves her. I love her. And if you've ever seen Alena's deep brown eyes when she cries, you'd never want to be the cause of her tears, either.

But I shed tears, too, because tonight, Nash emerges from my steamy bathroom wearing dark ink, tan muscles, black cotton pajama pants, and nothing else.

He's beautiful. So beautiful it's painful. I have to roll over; I have to turn away.

"Are you ready to return to the real world tomorrow?" he asks, lifting the covers as I turn off my lamp.

He settles into his spot on my bed, and I can feel his heat. Can he not feel this, too? How the air crackles between us. Is he not losing his mind? Because I am.

Why can't he be a horny beast when I need him to be? Why can't he just take over like he always does and end our torture? Why won't he make me do what we really want?

Why can't I have this man, the only one who's cared about me?

"The real world sucks," I whisper.

"Why do you say that?"

I hug my pillow. It's not enough. Tears bite at my eyes, choking my voice. "Just forget it."

"Vale?" He turns toward the center, toward me. I can feel

his every move, hear his every breath. "Vale." His fingertips brush down my bare arm. "What's wrong?"

His tenderness makes me cry even more. I stifle a sob. "You know what's wrong."

He withdraws his touch, and for too long, he's silent.

No. Did he fall asleep? Did he leave me feeling alone like this? Does he not care? Did he pick his daughter over us? I want him to. It's the right thing. I don't ever want to hurt Alena.

But ... I'm so tired of hurting, too. I'm tired of never feeling loved. I'm tired of—

"Will you let me fix what's wrong?" His voice sounds strained.

"We *can't*," I whisper.

"Will you let me try?"

"*You* can't."

"Oh, I will." I've never heard his voice sound so husky, either. "For one night, I'll show you what it feels like and—"

"But what if we get—"

"Shut up." He says it in the softest, sweetest, sexiest way. Pressing his hot, hard body against mine, I gasp at his erection, barely veiled by his pajama bottoms, urging against my backside. His sweet, leather aroma engulfs me, his lips steaming over my ear, demanding, "Get out of your head, Vale. It's time to let me inside instead."

It's not possible. I can't...

The sudden soft brush of Nash's fingertips over the curve of my waist while he ruts his hard cock against my cheeks makes shivers pulse through my body.

He presses closer, his nude concrete chest against my back. The room is dark. I have no sight or senses. Nothing but Nash's heat and touch barely thrilling my flesh.

His big hand slowly slides under my tank top, his warm palm skimming over my belly, making it quiver. He sighs, pressing his lips to my ear. "I've wanted to touch you for so long."

The pad of his thumb barely teases the swell of my breast, and I moan, my nipples tightening, anticipating.

"But you know that, don't you?" he asks, fondling my breast, palming its weight. "You know how long I've wanted you. You were eighteen, and I was thirty-two. Do you remember?"

"What?" I'm shocked. Confused. *He can't know.* I try twisting around, but he holds me too tight. I can't move.

"Shhh." His fingertip slowly traces around my puckered nipple, making arousal, like waves of warm oil, radiate down my body. "Don't overthink this. Just feel it." He starts rubbing my nipple, increasing his pressure, making me arch into his touch, my body quivering with lust. "Just remember that night by my pool because I do. I can't forget it. Every time I come, I think about it." He pinches my nipple. "I think about *you,* Vale."

"Oh, god," I moan at the rush of sensation, at his confession, at my guilt that he knows what I did.

"You were a very bad girl for me, weren't you?" He pinches even harder.

"Yes," I moan.

"And you liked it, didn't you? You liked being dirty for me?"

"Yes."

He grinds his granite length against my backside, his lips on my ear wetting my sex and memory, "You caught me, didn't you? You watched me jerk off by my pool."

I moan, my mind there with him, my body here with him now. With Nash reaching for my other breast, so I turn his way, just a bit, as he palms it, taunting, "What did you see, Vale?"

"I saw you." He tickles my right nipple, circling as it tightens, making me pant, "You were on a lounger. You had your pajamas pulled down."

"Black pajamas like these?" He grinds against me.

God, he's huge, and damn, he's hard.

"Yes. Yes, like those, and you sorta had your back to me, but I could see you and—"

"You saw my cock, didn't you?" He pinches my nipple. "You saw how hard I was. How I was stroking it? Tell the truth, dirty girl."

"Yes."

"What was in my hand, Vale?" He tugs my nipple, not letting go. He dry humps my ass, and I grind it back on him, moaning as he growls, "What was I being a filthy, fucking man about and jerking off with because I couldn't help myself? You drove me fucking insane for you."

This is so erotic. I've never been this wet in my life. *Get out of your head, Vale.* Just this memory. Just his words. Just his touch.

"My bikini. My bottoms. I left them outside to dry, and you were jerking off with them. Into them."

His lips press harder, hotter over my ear. "It was like I was fucking your pussy, wasn't it?"

"Yes," I pant, my nipples tingling, my cunt aching.

"And what did that make you do?" Brutally, he tugs my nipple so hard, I love it, crying out as he confesses, "Because I could see you, Vale. I was watching you in the mirror above the bar in the cabana. I could see what my lust for you made you do for *me*."

That's how! Oh my god, that's how he knows what I did, and I suddenly feel no shame about it. *He never hated me. He saw me. He wanted me and knew I wanted him, too.*

"I touched myself while I watched you."

"Yes, you did." His breath moves to my neck, his hand drifting down my belly. "You touched yourself ... like this."

Slowly, his hand glides under my panties, his fingertips sliding over my slick lips. "*Fuck*, my poison, you're so wet for me now." He does it again, drifting his fingertips over where I'm dying for him. The ache is excruciating. "Were you this wet that night?"

"No." I can't stand it. "Now, I want you even more." I reach, tugging my panties down.

"Leave them on," he growls. "Leave them around your thighs like yours were that night. Weren't they? You were so dirty for me. You pulled your panties down and stepped your thighs apart so you could do this..."

With the tip of his middle finger, he circles my clit, and I scream, "Nash, please!"

"But you couldn't scream that night, Vale, could you? Because you were being such a good girl for me." He keeps circling my ache, and I'm writhing, my breath panting for him. "You silently watched me stroke my cock for you, knowing that I wanted you, that I was imagining fucking you. I hated myself for it, but now, I don't. I'm gonna love making you scream for me."

He plunges two of his thick, long fingers inside my aching wet cunt, and I groan, my back arching, the need for him sweet agony. "Oh my god, don't stop," I beg.

"Look at me," he demands. "Open up for me."

By his heavy, heated tone, he means every part of me, my heart, too, and I obey. I turn, lying on my back for him, and open my eyes, but, "Nash, I—"

"It's too dark," he grumbles, "and I've waited too long to watch you come."

He slides his fingers out, and I gasp, needing him inside as he leans over, reaching across me to turn on the lamp. His inked pec, his hard nipple hovers over my lips, and I've studied men's erogenous zones, so I lift my lips, sucking it before flicking it with my tongue.

"Fuck, Vale," he groans, almost flinching, as a warm light floods the room. "Fuck, baby, don't make this about me right now. This is for you." He settles back beside me.

"Promise me," I beg. "Promise me I get to do this to you, too."

"Do what?" He props on his elbow, gazing down at me with the devil in his brown eyes as his heavenly fingers slide back inside my pussy. "This?"

"Yes," I groan, my eyes rolling, my hips too, lifting for more of him.

"You want to make me come with your hand? Like this?" His thumb circles my clit again, his two fingers slowly pumping inside.

"With my hand," I pant, opening my eyes. I stare up at him, swearing, "With my pussy, my mouth, my throat, my virgin ass. I'll make you come harder than you ever have before. You've never had a woman like me, one that's yours. That night was the first time I ever came, and now I can only come thinking about you."

His eyelids hood with lust, his lips parting. "Vale." His lips near mine. "Vale, goddamn, I want you. I always have."

He moves to kiss me, but I flinch. "I don't," I stammer. "I don't kiss on the lips. I can't ... It's just that—"

"Shh, it's okay." His lips brush over my jaw, nearing my ear. "Can I kiss you everywhere else?"

"Please."

"Are you mine?

"Yes," I sigh.

"Like here?"

When Nash's hot, hungry mouth claims my neck while his fingers thrust inside me, his thumb flicking my clit, it's a tsunami rising. Pleasure builds in my body, soaking my sex; I couldn't stop its force if I wanted to. It's coming, I can feel it. "Oh, god."

He lifts from my neck, his eyes locking to mine. He sees my edge; it's my torture; I always get trapped here. It's the cage I can't escape.

"Do you remember how I came for you, Vale?" But he takes over my mind. He's in it, not me, with his thumb strumming my clit. "Do you remember how hard I fucked your bikini in my fist? How I lifted my hips, thrusting and desperate like it was my cock pumping into your tight pussy? How I arched my back and said your name? How I came, shooting my cum all over my abs, grunting and in so much fucking pain for you?"

"Yes. Yes." My thighs shake. My lips, too.

"You came for me, Vale," he growls. "I watched you, fucking your pretty pussy with your hand. Your lips parted. Your thighs quaked. Your shoulders shook while you convulsed, coming so fucking hard watching me come that I spurted again. I couldn't stop coming for you either."

And I am now. "Oh, god." I thrash, but he bears down, his thumb igniting my clit. "Oh god, Nash, I'm coming."

He curls his fingers so hard inside my pussy, claiming my core, I can't escape him. I can't escape his control. I can't escape this pleasure. "Good girl," he coaxes, and I explode.

White light takes my vision. I buck so hard, groaning with the release, but he won't stop. I won't stop. Like a pleasure bomb that won't end, lighting every nerve inside me, my orgasm detonates down my body, spilling over his hand jerking inside me.

"Fuck, Vale," he sighs, "you're squirting, baby. You're squirting for me. Keep coming."

Another spasm racks my spine before my sight returns. It finds Nash, and I moan, feeling my sex clench, wanting him. I can't find my breath, my body shaking uncontrollably until he gently leaves my pussy empty, pulsing, dripping, and satisfied as warm, luscious quivers ripple through me.

"Oh my god," I sigh, full of awe. "Oh my god, Nash, you made me come."

The way he gazes down at me, everything we feel and fear, fills his loving eyes. *He's not a beast. Not with me.*

I can't help it. I start crying.

Happy tears.

CHAPTER TWELVE
NASH

VALE SMILES WITH TEARS STREAMING DOWN HER FLUSHED cheeks, and it breaks me open.

She's so beautiful.

Stop time. I don't want this moment to end. My urge to kiss her lips is so damn powerful, but I think I know why she doesn't kiss on the lips. I think I killed him.

What I'm willing to do for Vale? What I feel for her?

I love it, and I hate it at the same time. I feel like a saint and a sinner.

Our days and nights at the hotel were the happiest and hardest I've ever spent because I knew what she survived, so I waited for her to make a move. She didn't, neither did I, and it hurt like hell. When I heard her suffering over it like me again tonight, I couldn't take it anymore.

And here we are.

Me, feeling every emotion I shouldn't for her, and her, cupping my cheek as she tenderly confesses, "I hate you."

I nuzzle my nose against hers. "I hate you, too."

The weight of it feels too intense for us. Like we can't breathe because we don't know what's next, so I lift my dripping fingers to my mouth and taste her cum, making her grin before I smirk. "Your hatred is the best thing I've ever tasted."

She laughs. "Liar."

"I'll deceive about some things," I brush the back of my fingers over her cheek, "but never about this." I press my glistening digits to her lips, and she obeys. Gently, she sucks as I promise her, "This is our truth, Vale. It has been since that night, and it always will be."

I take my fingers out, and she asks, "You knew my secret all this time?"

"*Our* secret." I face her, our bodies wedged together.

"After that night and all through college," she says, "I thought you hated me. Even recently, you acted like you did."

"I hated that I wanted you. For that, I hated myself for a long time," I confess, playing with her silky raven hair. "I felt like a horrible man. But please know, I always cared for you, but it wasn't until you came back after your first month at college that I suddenly felt attracted to you.

"You'd grown so fast in so little time and weren't a girl anymore. You were suddenly a woman, and it scared the hell out of me because I couldn't fight it. Not that night. It was driving me insane, and I just needed some relief. I... I thought you were asleep."

Her fingertip traces over the tiger inked on my pec. Now, it will remind me of her.

"I kind of always wanted you," she confesses. "Like a crush teens get. It's innocent and safe. I always felt safe with you. You were always so stern and protective, like you wanted to put a chastity belt on me."

I laugh. "I did. I..." *Careful, she can't know this secret.* "I wanted to protect you because I meant what I said; I'll kill any man who hurts you."

It's so damn hard watching the trauma flash across her

stunning eyes, and I can't comfort her. I can't confess that I know about her ex.

Or what I did to him. *Gladly*.

"What happened that night by the pool?" she asks, moving past it. "I mean, for you?"

"I came home after a bad day. A bloody one, actually, and I saw you and Alena laughing and laying out. She was the same, but you'd changed. You looked mature in your black bikini, and it took my breath away. I couldn't stop thinking about you. God," I drag my hand down my face, "I felt like a horrible, horny man."

She laughs. "Then what's my excuse?"

I cock a brow.

"Because I felt horrible for being horny for you, too. From the time I was sixteen, you gave me pussy quivers."

I softly chuckle. "Pussy *what*?"

"Pussy quivers." *Damn, she's cute.* "You know that feeling you get between your legs that reminds you you're an animal, not someone who needs to renew their driver's license."

Laughter hits me. Jealousy, too. This is a stupid question. Of course, I ask, "Who else gives you pussy quivers?"

She smirks, making it last way too long, circling her fingertip over the lion on my chest. "That sounds like a detail to me," she teases.

"It sounds like the next thing that better come out of your sassy mouth."

She sticks her tongue out, and I grab it, making her shriek, then laugh. "Gaaah. Otaayy." I let go, and she says. "Only you! You're the pussy party of one in my pants."

I let that make my fucking day. Week. Year.

Life.

"What about you?" she volleys back. "Who else puts a tingle in your dingle?"

"Dingle? Poison, I'm way too big to dingle."

"Okay," she quips. "Who puts a big gong in your giant dong?"

I laugh, wrapping my arms around her. "Woman, you have a PhD in killing me."

"Then answer the doctor."

This is the part. The one that makes me regret everything and nothing. "I've never allowed myself to feel..." I press my forehead to hers, "this."

Softly, she asks, "Why not?"

"It's too dangerous. Too risky. It's a beast of a life, Vale. And if you ever see that side of me, you won't like him."

"You may be a beast, but you're a good father." Her fingertip traces over my heart. "I love how you love Alena."

The words sit on the tip of my tongue, but they're too dangerous. If I say them, I mean it forever. Vale would be mine forever.

"I love..." I swallow the rocks in my throat, "how you love her, too."

Suddenly, tears threaten her eyes. They're not happy; they're worried. "What are we going to do now?"

"Keep the biggest secret of our lives."

"Me?" Her brows shoot up. "You expect me and my AK-47 of a mouth not to fire? That feels impossible because I'm holding back a lot of ammo. All the sex secrets from Delta's. All your mafia stuff. All the Cummings, Jace, Grant, and your private meeting drama. And now this?" She grabs my chest, admitting, "Nash, I can't lie to Alena."

"You have to. It's for her safety."

"Okay." She props up on her elbows. "The secret about her dad-in-the-mafia part I get, but not us."

"Will you quit saying I'm in the mafia?"

"Aren't you?"

"Bratva." I blurt and immediately regret it.

Fuck! Lying next to Vale's almost naked body has me leaking like a sieve.

Her eyes get wide. "Bratva means Russian mafia."

"No, in Russian, it literally means 'brothers,' and that's what we are."

"Where have you been hiding all these siblings? I thought you and Alena had no family."

"No blood family." I sit up, scrubbing my beard. I need to escape Vale's gravity, or I'll sing like a canary.

"So…" she processes. "Jace and Grant and Michael Cummings, they're like your brothers?"

"We go way back. I owe them. They owe me. We're bonded for life."

"Are you Russian?"

"Half Scottish, half Spanish, and done with this conversation."

She flops back, falling silent.

That spells trouble.

I gaze down and see her overthinking everything.

"Vale," I warn, "I just told you more than I should. I know silence is a new concept for your mouth, but keep it shut because it also means safety. Because if that 'Bridge Bastard,' as we'll call him, ever gets his hands on you, he'll break every secret out of you, and your pain will kill me and kill Alena, too."

The severity registers across her eyes as she nods, studying me before they twinkle.

"Say, please," she taunts.

Damn, this woman.

I roll on top of her, my hands braced by her head. Slowly, I lower, aiming my mouth for the pulse in her neck. "Please." I kiss it, she sighs, and my dick stirs. "Shut." Gently, I kiss under her ear. "The." I nibble it. She giggles. "Fuck." I suck her earlobe, making her moan which makes me hard. "Up."

I'm about to devour every inch of her flesh, but she whispers, "I have another question."

Softly, I bang my forehead against hers. "Can you just *not* talk anymore?"

"But I have to know. I'll go crazy if I don't. I need this knowledge."

"I'm not answering Bratva questions either."

"Good, because it's a sex one." I raise a brow. "It's a two-parter, actually. One, do you jerk off every morning in the shower thinking about me, and two, do you think you can make me come again because I'm skeptical? That orgasm felt like Halley's comet, like it won't happen again in seventy-five years, and I'll be dead by then."

Kneeling, I rise. I straddle her, carefully tugging her tank top off, and tossing it on the floor.

Once I see her luscious breasts, I confess, "Fuck yes, I jerk off to you in the shower. Sometimes at work in the bathroom. Once in Jace's truck; don't tell him. Vale, I meant it. For twelve years, every time I come, I think of you."

I shift my body so I can take her panties off next. "Here's a three-part answer to keep you quiet." I lift them to my nose, inhaling what I did to her. "I used to guess the color of your panties, but now that I know you wear white cotton thongs with little red bows, that's all you'll wear for me. Only me. Understood?"

She nods, spreading her thighs, her pussy exposed. "Yes, Mr. Allen." It hoods my eyelids, the lust that crashes through me. "Now, answer my last question."

I tug my pajama bottoms down, exposing my cock as I kick them free. I'm so swollen with lust for her; it surprises us both. "You're not in charge tonight. This is."

"Oh my god," she sighs, her eyes taking in the size of what she does to me.

"I'm not going to fuck you, Vale. I swear, I'll lose my mind and our secret if I'm ever inside you. So, instead..." I crawl over her, needing to kiss her mouth, but I can't, so I demand, "You're going to fuck my face with your sweet pussy while I fuck your bed, and I won't come until I'm drinking yours."

"Let me taste you," she gasps. "Nash, let me taste you when you come."

I don't agree. Leaning down, I kiss, then bite her neck, fighting the urge to shred her apart until she's mine. "Time to lose control, Vale."

But I don't. This is for her.

I've been reading so much in her books about clitoral kisses, suction puckers, and coreplay; I'm about to earn a PhD in her sweet pussy.

I travel down her body, taking my first suck of her hard nipple, and she cups my head, holding me here, her back arching off the bed, her moans my reward for waiting so long.

For years, I've obsessed over what it would be like to suck her tits, and once I start, I don't want to stop. She makes my cock leak. She keeps arching for me, grabbing my hair and moaning when I tongue her nipples, crying out when I suck them. I reach down, barely tickling her clit as I do, and my name keeps filling her gasp.

I can't take anymore.

I rise, kneeling between her thighs. "Scoot up, baby, to the top of the bed." She obeys. "That's it. Now, hold your thighs back. Let me see you spread open for me."

She holds her knees, and I groan at the shameless sight of her unfolding, of her pink petals, her glistening opening, her swollen lips, her little puckered hole, and the sexy little trim of black hair she keeps groomed over her mound.

I stroke myself, my breath deepening, staring at her, at what I've desired for so long, and she surprises me, clenching her muscles, letting me see her swell before my eyes.

"Is this what you want, Mr. Allen?" She does it again, making me watch her opening pulse. "You want to see how wet my pussy gets for you? Come on. Take a little taste of me."

"Goddamn, you're my poison." I salivate. I've never been this thirsty before, wanting the taste of a woman so bad. I've never felt this dirty and deserving. This desire and determination.

I will make her come. I won't live without tasting her fall apart over my tongue.

I lie between her thighs, inhaling her and starting slow, steaming my lips gently over hers.

"Oh god, your beard," she gasps. "Oh god, Nash, it's so hot. I can feel it on my pussy."

I grin, barely lingering my tongue from her slick entrance, working my way up to her pearled clit. Gently, I kiss it, and it ignites her moans. I press down, holding her mound still while my tongue is a feather over her clit, my fingertip rimming her entrance. For minutes, every touch is light and teasing until I taste her honey. Until she's dripping, her breath telling me she needs more.

Much more.

Slowly, I slide my middle finger inside her, swirling my tongue over her clit at the same time, and her desperate moans drop into hungry groans. Her taste fills my mouth, making my hips grind, thrusting my hard cock into her mattress.

She tastes sweeter than I ever imagined. She's driving me fucking insane with this wet pussy.

Forever, I devour her, getting off on her smell, sounds, taste, and pleasure until it glosses my chin, until I need more, too.

"Look at me, Vale." I gaze up at her as she meets my stare. "Prop up on some pillows so you can watch."

She lets go of her legs to grab my pillow and hers while I lift her legs over my shoulders.

"Now do it," I demand. "Watch me eat your sweet pussy, and use your hips, putting it all over my face. Make me lick and suck you. Make me fuck you with my mouth. Don't let me breathe anything but *you*."

"Oh god," she sighs, sinking her hands into my hair while I let her guide me.

I slide two fingers inside her while I offer my tongue to serve her demanding clit. Fisting my hair, she controls me and her pleasure. She moves in small circles, then fast jerking motions while I lick, suck, and slurp, losing my mind to the salacious sounds of my spit, her arousal and moans mixing with mine.

Wedging my knees into her bed, the urge is too strong; I make the tempo of my tongue match the thrust of my hips, my cock rubbing against her sheets, imagining all the times she's fucked herself on them while thinking of me as her juice slides down my neck.

It makes me groan into her writhing sex. *She's wanted me as much as I've wanted her.* I put the urge to bite her, to have her, to literally eat Vale's pussy alive into my tongue, fluttering over her swollen clit.

"Oh fuck," she cries out, holding my head so tight and fucking my face with her pussy; her suffocation is my salvation. I want to dive into her. I need to thrust my hard cock so deep inside her; I make my fingers do it. I pump them hard, making Vale cry out, "Yes, Nash. Yes!"

My cock leaks. It swells, white heat building in my spine while I thrust my hard length against her bed, matching the rhythm of my fingers inside her swollen walls.

"Oh my, god," she sighs as I glance up at her hooded stare watching me. She can see my bare ass, how I'm fucking her bed while I eat her pussy.

"Now, be a good girl," I pant, "and make me come with your pussy on my face." I flutter my tongue over the clit. "Now, Vale, you got me so fucking close, too."

"Oh my god, Nash." Her thighs shake. "Oh, my god, you're getting off on this. On me. On eating my pussy."

I answer by puckering my lips and sucking her clit so hard Vale screams. With a hard curl of my fingers inside her, she bucks, coming with her legs around my neck. She could break it. *And I love it.* Her stream of pleasure fills my mouth as I moan into her pussy, letting her cum make me do the same.

Fuck, I've fantasized about eating her pussy for so long.

I hold her thighs, keeping her here, with my face buried in her tangy taste, her musky smell, her pulsing release while I find mine. While I pump my swollen cock so hard into her mattress and grunt, grunting again as I feel myself spill over her sheets, my tongue barely inside her where my cock aches to be. The sound of me coming with her pussy on my face makes her shudder. She comes again, pouring more of her sweet poison over my tongue.

With panting breath, a dripping cock, and a glistening face, I leave her pussy pulsing as I climb back up her beauty until we're nose to nose, mouth to mouth.

She stares in awe at me while I demand, "Lick your cum off my lips, Vale, and never doubt that I can make you do it again."

CHAPTER THIRTEEN
VALE

"Can I ask a question?"

I rest on Nash's chest, feeling it silently shake with laughter at the sentence that pops out of my mouth hourly.

His fingertips linger up and down my naked back. "Can I ever stop you?"

I grin, tracing over the fangs of the lion on his pec. Waiting. Annoying. Happy because eventually, he growls, "For the love of god, just ask."

"Why do you call me 'poison'? I get calling someone 'baby' or kinky names during sex, but poison is deadly and—"

"Because it kills me, Vale." He lifts my chin so our eyes meet. "It kills me to want you like this, to feel this way about you, knowing no one can ever know, and we can never really be together."

"We can keep it a secret, like you said."

"Not for long. They'll figure it out."

"They?"

His sigh is heavy.

"Do you mean Alena?"

"Yes," he answers. "Definitely her. And my ... brothers, so to speak."

"But Jace knows."

"He's the only one."

"Why would they care?"

"We care about someone when a brother cares about her. We make a vow to protect her, too."

"Um, Houston," I reply, "I fail to see a problem. You and a bunch of hot men who look like you, all tatted and jacked, caring enough to protect me? Feel free to convince me that's not every woman's fantasy."

A dark storm takes his eyes. He gets serious. Deadly serious. "You're too smart not to realize it's only fantasy in fiction. In real life, it's a gilded, barbed, and bloody cage, and you don't belong in it. I'll never allow it."

Resting my head back on his chest, I listen to his heartbeat. His lips softly graze my hair, his arms squeezing me tight. This intimate, tender side of Nash makes my throat tight, overwhelmed with emotions, but still, I whisper, "I kinda love your cage."

He whispers, "I kinda love holding you in it."

"I don't want to leave."

"I won't give you a choice."

For minutes, we don't speak. He holds me, and I hold him back. Finally, he's the one asking a question. "How do we do this?"

"Cherish it while it lasts?"

"Yes," his voice is deep and soft. "But I mean ... *this*." He wraps his leg over mine. "How do we sleep together tonight? I've never slept with a woman."

I giggle. I can't help it. "So you're a virgin with miraculous fingers and a transcendent tongue?"

He laughs, too. "Must be all those pussy books of yours I read."

"Are you serious?" I pop up, my hand braced against his granite pec. "You've never shook the sheets with a woman and then slept with her? Like *slept*?"

"Why would I?"

"Because, in the least, you were fucking exhausted. I mean ... got exhausted fucking, but at the most," I kiss his chest, "it's romantic, like a movie."

His fingertip traces over the bow in my lips. "I'm beginning to see that now."

It tickles. It makes me smile. "You need to stop making this go from an X-rated movie night to a G-rated one where I'm feeling all gooey inside."

Too late. I'm a goner. He smiles and slings sunshine everywhere.

"Then just answer me," he insists. "How do we sleep? Back to back as usual? Back to front? With your head on my chest?"

"Or your head on mine."

"Poison, I won't sleep with your breasts in my face."

"Fine." I lean over and click off the lamp before I suggest, "Let's just sleep like this." I nestle back into the spot that's mine now. I've claimed it. It's the one over his tiger while I caress his lion.

Silently, he holds me. His legs intertwine with mine, but then I remember, "I'm dress shopping with Alena tomorrow."

"Okay, shhh."

"But, what will I say?"

"Words. Lots of them, I'm sure."

"But, Nash.

"Vale," he softens his voice. "Shut up."

"But—"

"Shut up," he cups my head on his chest, his voice even softer, "and let me finally sleep with *my* woman."

Oh...

My heart flutters.

Okay.

"Now, this is Givenchy couture." The owner of the wedding boutique presents a stunning gown to Alena. "Ivory Alecon lace bodice, off-the-shoulder neckline…"

Alena looks so happy and beautiful in a blush silk robe as she considers dress number five.

"What do you think?" she asks me.

"I think you'll look beautiful in anything."

"I need my best friend right now," she says, "not my maid of honor. Where are your truth bullets when I need them? What do we think; should I wear ivory or white? Be honest."

Be honest?

I can't.

I'm squirming on this pink velvet bench in this exclusive bridal dressing room because Nash sits in the front reception area with Loch, Alena's fiancé.

One might think it odd that the bride's father and the groom are present, but nope, not when you're sort of not-mafia-mafia.

Nash is guarding me, and I guess Alena's bodyguard lurks somewhere outside the boutique, too.

I thought I could do this, especially after Nash's stern morning reminders that Alena can't find out. Talk about ruining my orgasmic glow. I don't get to have one because I'm too focused on lying to my best friend.

So, I dole out little truths. "Okay, honestly, I vote for the Vivienne Westwood so far because you smiled the most in it. You were slinging sunshine with that gorgeous face."

Just like your dad did in my bed last night.

After he made me come, then cry, then come again so hard that it ruined my life because now I know I can come with him, so I never want to let him go. Oh, and I'm in love with him, too.

Phew.

At least I can think the truth.

"Sorry, I'm late." A thick, sweet Southern voice breezes into the dressing room. "I had to get your favorite treat ever since you were a little girl, a Rainbow Row white chocolate bar. It pairs perfectly with champagne because, sweetie, this is a celebration!"

Ms. Faye glides across the room in her ivory Chanel boucle dress, wearing it with grace and grit while she carries a gift bag from a local chocolatier.

She pulls Alena into a big hug. She's like her grandmother—a gorgeous, hot grandma—and I worship her, too.

She not only protected Alena, giving her and her teenage mother an apartment rent-free, she babysat, too. She practically raised Alena, especially after her mom died.

Ms. Faye's like me—Alena's family now.

Those in the know also know that Ms. Faye owns the most exclusive, private sex club in Charleston. She's a legend. An icon. And yes, Alena knows about it and is forbidden to go, but I do.

Or did until Nash came around.

There, Ms. Faye rules her club with her dark hair in an elegant French twist and her piercing eyes, watching every member, making sure all follow her rules, though I've never seen her partake in the fun.

She's always dressed like high society, the ultimate hostess, but make no mistake. She rules with an iron fist. Men who break her rules pay a painful price.

"We're trying to decide," Alena updates her, "should I wear ivory or white?"

"Darlin'," Ms. Faye drawls, "you're a queen. Wear both."

Alena tries on two more white laced-with-ivory dresses while Faye and I sit together, sipping champagne. It makes me miss Blair, too, but I understand. Her heart can't handle this.

Mine barely can, and not because I'm excited for Alena. She'll make a beautiful, happy bride.

I can't handle the thought of ruining this for her. Of breaking her heart before her happiest day. Of killing our friendship when I need it, and she needs it too.

I can see the "Am I The Asshole?" Reddit thread about me now. The viral answer? Yes, you're the asshole maid-of-honor who ruined your best friend's wedding by fucking her father.

Not the claim to fame I'm going for.

"Now, then," Ms. Faye grins, nudging me, "just what kinda trouble have you gotten yourself into?"

I sputter my champagne, "I'm sorry. What?"

"Honey, I can tell when a cat has eaten a canary." She winks. "What's his name?"

Close your mouth, Vale.

"Oh, come on now." She laughs. "There are no secrets and shame in our secret, shameful world, so tell me. I haven't seen you at the club in weeks, and darlin', I can always tell when a lady has been laid properly. *Finally*, in your case."

"How... How did you know?"

Yes, I've fucked at Ms. Faye's club. Almost everyone does. I mean, you don't go to a sex club for the music.

She leans her rouge red lips toward my ear, whispering, "Every time a woman fakes an orgasm, a tiny part of my heart dies, and honey, I've watched you do it for years. So, congratulations. You glow."

I glow? How? I'm about five minutes from puking chunks of guilt and truth.

We don't have time to gossip more because Alena steps out in dress number seven. "I love this one," she beams, and Faye and I fight tears.

"Oh, my gosh, Alena, you look stunning." I rush to hug her.

"That's the one, sweetie," Ms. Faye agrees. "You look like a queen."

"But it's fifty thousand dollars," she worries. "I can't ask my dad to spend that kind of money."

"You just let me handle this." Faye winks. "Nash," she calls, "get your tail in here and tell your beautiful daughter she can have whatever she wants."

"She can." I hear Nash answer before he sweeps aside the white velvet curtain and stops dead in his tracks.

For the first time, I see tears well in his eyes at the sight of Alena, and I'm done. Nothing is more beautiful than a father crying at the sight of his child.

Tears spill down my cheeks while she tenderly asks, "Dad, what do you think?"

Nash swallows hard, his voice choked as he answers. "I feel like the luckiest father to have a beautiful daughter like you." He swallows again. "And your mother would agree."

"Oh, she's watching," Faye softly adds. "She's our angel."

Alena wipes her eyes, her cheeks hitched high in a smile. "But it's fifty thousand dollars, Dad. It's too expensive."

"It's priceless and yours," Nash answers. "You never let me spoil you, and since we can't have the wedding at our home because of the repairs, let me at least give you the dress, flowers, reception, and everything else you want."

Nash told Alena there was a major sewage leak in their house, and they had to evacuate. It requires months of plumbing repairs, and it's a shitty lie.

Since that night, he won't allow anyone to return to his home. Not until the Bridge Bastard is caught. Alena thinks he's staying at a hotel while he rents her a little apartment. He said he didn't want to crash at her new place while Loch was there.

When really? Nash has been crashing into me.

So, I cheered Alena on, getting her excited about her wedding at the Dunes Golf and River Club. A simple ceremony under the canopy of a vast oak tree dripping with Spanish moss by a Lowcountry river is very romantic. And it's what Nash wants, too.

"I can secure that location. We own it," he told me this morning. "So please help me get her excited about it."

"Alena, are you crying?" A gravel voice calls from the other side of the velvet curtain. "Are you okay, babygirl?"

"We're fine," she answers Loch. "But don't come in. I found my dress, and you can't see it."

My stare bounces from her, stunning and happy, to Nash, stoic with snarling lips.

What? Does he not like Loch, his future son-in-law? I don't know why. He's perfect, like made-to-order for Alena.

Or is it the "babygirl" nickname?

Yep, that's it. Because if I'm imagining Loch growling it in Alena's ear while he pulls her hair and she rides him hard ... so is Nash.

Okay, that's kinda funny.

I found Nash's Kryptonite. I'll have to give him hell about it later.

But later, after I have to make up a lie to Alena about why I can't come back to her new apartment and have a girls' night together, it's not funny.

Because I can't go without Nash's protection. All the while, Alena's at risk, and some secret bodyguard is protecting her, too. The whole thing sucks and makes me sick. So sick, I can't speak. When Nash and I return to my place, I flop on my bed, defeated.

"Since when do you not talk?" he asks, setting his Beretta on my nightstand.

"Since I have to lie to my best friend's beautiful face." I stare at the ceiling. "Let's kick this off. Go ahead. Ways we're going to break her heart."

"Her heart won't break because we'll never tell her."

I jolt up. "But I can't lie to her. I never have."

He pulls his shirt off, revealing his inked muscles, and yes, I can drool and be pissed at life at the same time.

"You can keep secrets, Vale. Me and you and the pool. You and your orgasm problem I fixed. All the kinks you know about your customers. And the—"

"Quit listening to me when I don't want you to."

"Too late," he barks. "It all is. We're in this until it ends."

"But how does it end?"

"It ends when we find our man unguarded. When we have a chance to strike. Until then, I protect you, and you keep your mouth closed."

"So once you catch and kill the Bridge Bastard, it's over?" I pause, my heart heavy as it sinks in. "*We're* over?"

He drops his pants, his sexy, black boxer briefs making this worse. "We have to be, and you know it."

He picks them up, neatly draping them over my loveseat's arm before sitting beside me on the bed.

But he doesn't hold me. He keeps a painful distance.

"Did you feel it today, too?" he asks, staring at the floor, not me. "Did you feel great, then sick with guilt about last night? About trying to hide it from Alena?"

"Yes," I admit. "I hated it."

"Me, too," he sighs. "When it was just my work, and she was a child, I felt no guilt about hiding it from her. The lie protected her. But now, she's an adult, and I've made tough decisions she can't know about, either. And I've made peace with it because it's the right thing to do. She's safe. She's happy. But she won't be if she ever finds out about us."

"What kind of decisions?"

"Details," he warns, not looking at me, not telling me the whole truth.

I have that nagging feeling there's so much Nash isn't telling me. I get not revealing names, crimes, and incriminating details about their operations.

Honestly, I don't want to know. But there's something more. A lot more.

It's that maddening feeling you get when you walk into a room; everyone knows the secret but you. Everyone is connected but you. You're on the outside, and they'll never let you in.

"Your details are real lady-boner killers," I mumble.

"It's probably safest that way. In fact," he turns to me, stoic and cold, "let's keep it that way tonight."

We sleep back-to-back, and tonight turns into three.

Part of me understands; I feel the same as Nash about Alena. Part of me grieves; I may never feel anything like I did with Nash.

CHAPTER FOURTEEN
NASH

If you think I'm furious and frustrated that I've made Vale off-limits to me again?

That I'm a fool to think I can have Vale by night, then hide it from my daughter the next day?

That I'm fighting the beast inside. The one that lies beside Vale in bed, my muscles tense and telling me to fuck her until we both scream for our lives. *For our love?*

I am, but she's taking it to the next level. Vale's not furious about it; she's ferocious. The worst part? She's even sexier with her claws out.

Like right now.

"It's not a business expense, Ms. Monroe."

"Look here, Poindexter." She points to the transaction on the screen. The one where she classified her purchase of a Bum Flick Vibrating Butt Plug as a business expense. "Testing the products we sell is a business expense."

"Personal items aren't expenses."

"How many times do I have to tell you? Sex isn't personal here; it's professional."

"Alright then." I lean back in my chair. "Let's audit."

"Let's not and say we did."

"Answer my questions like I'm the IRS because they *will* be coming."

She smirks. "It's our business to make sure they do."

"Exactly." I take off my fake glasses. I've had a headache for three days. They're not the cause. She is. "Did you test your product here, in your place of business?"

"Test a butt plug? While I'm paying our utility bills? No." She smirks. "Accounting turns me off."

Point on the board for her.

"Where did you test your product?"

Okay, now, I'm digging. I do and don't want to know, as she twists her lips.

"Where, Ms. Monroe, and was it during paid company time or on your personal time?"

She snaps, "Stacey doesn't pay me to go to the sex club and test a butt plug."

Point for me, and yep, I asked, and it was foolish.

My heart starts to pound. My pulse skyrockets. Reason feels optional. As if I won't kill now at the thought of anyone with Vale. Even me.

"So you went to another place of business, on your personal time, where you tested a very personal product with a..." I glance at the screen, reading the description more fully, "with a... with a fucking *remote?*" I seethe, "With another *person?*"

The tables turn. Now, Vale loves this because jealousy paints my face murderous.

"Yes, Mr. Allen." She leans in, lingering her fingertip over my clenched fist. "It's a vibrating butt plug that claims to feel like someone is flicking your A-spot or your prostate in three luscious speeds and seven sinful patterns. I needed to confirm the A-spot claim for my female customers, and man, did I ever, but as for prostates? Care to do a customer review for us?"

Damn, she rouses everything inside me.

Damn, I want some fucking heads to roll.

"*Who* played with your remote, Vale?"

Jace chuckles by the door. I swear that asshole pops popcorn on the daily for our tiffs. We make the Housewife series look as entertaining as paint drying.

"Details, Mr. Allen." She twirls her braid. "Remember our rule about those?"

I lean forward, grabbing her bare thigh, skimming my thumb over the inside of her leg. "If you don't tell me," I whisper, "you *will* be punished."

"How?" she taunts. "Are you going to make me eat my broccoli?"

Cute.

"No, I'll take all your toys away when we get home. I know you've been playing with them in the shower."

"Do you hear me?"

"Yes." My dick stirs. "I hear you moaning my name."

She arches her brow. "Then we're both being punished, aren't we?"

Yes, it is a punishment: her moaning my name, me grunting hers. Her poor shower. It's seen more action than Vegas for three nights.

The man in me knows we're fools to fight this. The least we can do is enjoy our time together.

The father in me knows I can never break my daughter's heart. At the bridal shop, the guilt was suffocating. I hide so much from Alena. But this secret of me with Vale? It feels like *the* lie that could break us all.

So, now we play this immature game because it's the only mature thing to do.

I'd rather fight with Vale than have nothing with her. I'm

alive with her. I see red over her. I'm ready to go another round with her.

I know she's had other partners, but not like me. I've slept with other women, but they weren't her. The thought of any man touching Vale after I finally have her makes me a very dangerous man.

"Am I interrupting?"

A familiar voice rips my raging focus away from her.

It's Axel. He's smirking. Jace let him in, and I didn't hear him enter the parlor. I was too jealous over Vale.

"Why yes, Mr. Cummings, you are," she replies, swatting my hand off her thigh. "I was just explaining to our accountant, Mr. Allen here, that my personal use of the butt plugs we sell is a legitimate business expense." She twists her braid, tilting her head. "Wouldn't you agree?"

"Achilles," he addresses me before nodding toward Vale, "meet your heel."

She smirks, happy for her little victory, but I'm not amused.

Goddammit!

This is one of the many things I've feared: Axel finding out about Vale. More specifically, that I want her more than my next breath.

"How can I help you today, Mr. Cummings?" she asks, completely unafraid, totally amused, and now in Axel's crosshairs.

"Don't mind me, Ms. Monroe," he answers. "I thought it polite to say hello before I check on my room upstairs. I had some things delivered late last night."

"Oh, I'm sorry," she answers. "I don't think they were delivered last night because I get notifications with videos from our security system whenever someone enters after hours."

Axel raises a brow. "You won't see me on your videos after hours, Ms. Monroe."

Vale does that Southern woman thing, smiling as she murders you with her glare. "As the manager of Delta's, Mr. Cummings, our security is my responsibility, and it stays *on* after-hours."

Smart woman. She guessed right.

We turn any security system off when we operate.

"No need." Axel keeps it cold and polite. "I have my own security. Therefore, Delta's is always safe, any hour, every day."

She seethes, "Is the owner aware?"

"Please, ask her yourself," he answers. "She's well aware. And per our lease agreement and as my personal cameras inside will surveil. No. One. Not even Delta's staff are permitted in my room at *any* hour." He smirks, slicing his eyes at me. "Unless invited, of course."

Yep, that pops her cork.

Vale jumps up. She's not playing his game.

Giving him her middle finger, she turns to me. "This? This rude asshole is your face man? The one who fronts your monkey business?"

Her giving Axel shit like she gives me is too good. I laugh. "Wise choice of words. Yes. He fronts our *monkey* business."

In his eyes, Axel's amused. "Careful with your choice of words, Ms. Monroe." But in his tone, he isn't.

Vale's standing too close to the truth. Literally. She's in his shadow.

But she doesn't care. She fires at close range.

"Careful?" She glares up at him. "I don't know what that means because you don't scare me. I just imagine you swimming with dolphins farting rainbows, and I'm not afraid of you. And you," she whips her aim at me, "why don't you take a lifetime supply of KISS MY ASS and plug it up yours." She smiles. "Remote included."

I'm stupefied, Axel's surprised, and Jace is laughing.

"Now," she sashays past Axel, "excuse me, when I'm mad, I masturbate with a *real* man. A Long Logan ten-inch dildo with balls is about to enjoy all my personal business."

With a side-eye, Axel admires what I've worshipped for years—Vale, swishing her ass in a plaid schoolgirl's miniskirt and white button-up barely containing her breasts. She's sexy, sassy, and smart, and she's been dressing like that for three days to torture me.

It works.

"Don't even think about it," I tell him.

"Oh, I'm not thinking." Axel turns back to me. "I *know* she's your queen."

CHAPTER FIFTEEN
VALE

THIS HOT BASTARD IS MAD ... AND FAST.

Leave it to him to ruin my dramatic exit by chasing me after we had another fight in the parlor at the end of the day.

Because I sure as hell will know what is in their "meeting" room on the third floor of the business I manage, and hell will freeze over before Nash tells me.

I firmly asked, and he flatly refused.

"You pick your men," I pointed at Jace, "over me?"

"There is no choice," Nash answered.

So, I threw my Long Logan ten-inch dildo at him. Side note: it gets my screaming endorsement. Then I stormed out the back door of Delta's.

But now he's following on my heels, twisting through the back, cobblestone alleys to my place, with palms and flowers blooming through iron gates.

Usually, I love our walks. They're kind of romantic.

But not today, Satan.

How dare he? Why won't he tell me? How dare Nash prioritize his "brothers" over me?

Would I do the same if Blair were involved? Well, that's not pertinent to this conversation.

Next question.

"Vale," he growls, taking two stairs at a time as I race up the ones outside my apartment. "Don't you dare enter without me clearing."

"Clear this." I've been using my middle finger a lot today.

But when I reach my apartment's white wooden door, it doesn't feel right. I've gotten so used to holding onto Nash's shoulder while he clears my place. I love feeling his tense muscles, his raised temperature, the wall of his hard body, and his dark gun protecting me.

It's instinct; I need him.

Besides, as I let him proceed and hold his right shoulder, it's the only thing keeping my fingers from gouging his eyeballs out.

"Clear," he says before he turns on my lamp. "And we need to talk."

"I'm sorry." I march toward my bathroom. "There must be a mouse in your pocket because there is no *we*. There's me, and then there's you and your Bratva brothers. Or wait, no, you're right, you are Bratva *beasts*."

"Listen to me!" he shouts, so I whip around in the doorway, angrily grabbing the door. "Do *not* provoke us. Don't *ever* go in that room."

"You know," I tilt my head, "they need to make doors so you only have to talk to the people you like. Oh, hang on. They do." I slam it in his face.

Dickhead.

Really beautiful, thick dickhead.

God, why does he have to be hung like a stallion? And even if he weren't, his fingers and tongue and that dirty, erotic mouth of his make my pussy want to call a cease-fire.

Just long enough for her to get a fix.

Then it's back to war.

Instead, I take a nice long shower. No, I don't get myself off because I'm too mad. But yes, I use all the hot water.

Wrapped in a white robe and turban, I leave the bathroom in a cloud of steam.

Nash is propped up on my bed, reading my annotated copy of *How To Piss Off Men*. When he sees me clock it, he asks, "Where'd you buy this? The Banshees R' Us Bookstore? I bet you're their best customer."

"I can't hear you." I storm across the room. "I stopped talking to you an hour ago."

"Send the memo to your moving lips."

"Okay, Boomer. No one writes memos anymore."

"No one, aka especially you, will enter that room on the third floor of Delta's, either."

"Uh-huh. I'm really known for doing what men say. Super reliable. Iron-clad guarantee. Don't you worry. I'll be a good little girl."

"I'll fucking make sure of it," he threatens before slowly rising and stripping naked, taunting me to watch, and I do. With a yawn.

So he smirks and disappears into the bathroom.

A few minutes later, I'm laughing my ass off because all I hear is, "God. Fucking. Dammit, Vale! This is cold!"

"Don't let it shrivel up and fall off," I shout back.

While he's in there, I grab my pillow and the blanket off the foot of my bed.

Still in my robe, I remove my towel turban and quickly comb the snarls out. Then I lie down and snuggle in for a good night's sleep on my loveseat.

Swinging the bathroom door open so hard that it slams against the wall, Nash emerges dripping with rage. So, why bother using a bath towel, either, when apparently, his dick is so raging hard it would only rip right through it?

You know that warning about poking a bear? Well, I provoked a beast.

Life goals.

"What are you doing?" he growls.

"Sleeping on my loveseat, Captain Obvious."

"The fuck you are."

He charges toward me, butterflies, fear, and lust soaring in my body. It's an intoxicating mix as he grabs me, lifting me. "We sleep together," he demands. "I don't care how bratty you are."

I punch his chest. I can't hurt him. But I need to make my pride proud, so I put up a decent fight. "I don't sleep with dicks!"

"Watch this." He tosses me on my bed. "Now, you're sleeping with a hard, angry one."

I bounce, landing on my back as he crawls over me, quickly grabbing my wrists to pin them over my head. "Get off me!" I scream.

"You either get a spanking, or you listen to me."

"Break out the paddle, big boy, because I never listen."

He smirks. "You just did."

"I'm not listening to you. You're too angry and hard. You can't be reasonable."

"Exactly," he growls, his brown eyes brimming with ire and heat. "I'm angry because I keep telling you I'll never hurt you, and I'll kill anyone who does, so don't make me do it. Don't make me hurt one of my brothers over you because I will. You ask me who I choose, but there is no choice. I pick you, Vale, every time, all the time."

"You have a funny way of showing it," I snap. "Why won't you tell me what's in that room? Why is it such a big secret?"

"Because I'm protecting you."

"From what?"

"From what we do in that room sometimes..." He licks his

lips, his knees wedging my thighs open. "Because it makes me hard. It makes *us* hard. We're like animals, and I don't want you around it."

"W-what?" I'm shocked, but my clit ignites, don't ask me why. She's such a slut. "What do you do in the room?"

"Something I'll never allow to be done to you."

"Do you hurt people? Do you hurt women?"

"Never. It's the opposite."

"What's the opposite? What do you do? Do you fu—"

"You're asking questions I'll never answer."

He glances down at his body planked over mine, at his hard cock aimed for my entrance, at my robe and thighs, falling open. Then he sees my nipples. They've tightened at the taboo he's hinting at. My ribs are heaving, wondering, wanting to know. I'm flushed and curious.

If it's with Nash, I want it. I want everything.

"You're getting aroused by it, too," he rasps, deeply surprised. "Aren't you?"

"Yes," I confess. "I'm not afraid if I'm with you. If I go in that room, what would you do to me?"

"Stop, Vale. It's not happening."

"But I—"

"But you won't keep your mouth shut, will you?"

"Never." I narrow my eyes, grinning, knowing how to wear him down and get what I want. "So why don't you put something big in it to make me shut up?"

I arch my back, rubbing my body against his. Lust drops his eyelids so fast because he's torn, so I rip him open.

"Please, Mr. Allen. Please let me suck your hard cock. I've fantasized about it for so long. I've been a bad girl so many times, touching myself while sucking on a dildo, imagining it's you fucking my throat. It makes me come, moaning your name."

"*Fuuucckkk*, poison," he growls. "Fuck, you kill me with that mouth."

"For once, you're right," I tease. "I'll take you to heaven with it."

He hesitates, so I reveal, "I had the remote, Nash. I played with the plug by myself and came alone that night, thinking of you. I always think of you so I can come."

I tug at him, guiding him to kneel, to straddle my face. By the heated look in his eyes, he can't resist. He's wanted this, too.

His length curves, heavy and long, his tip hanging over my lips. He stares down at me, watching as I gently kiss it.

"Shit," he hisses. "Shit, poison, this is going to kill me."

"Have you fantasized, too, Mr. Allen?" I ask between kisses that go from soft to firm, sliding my slick, puckered lips over his glistening tip. "Have you imagined fucking my dirty mouth with your thick cock?"

"Yes," he confesses as I lick his frenulum, the sensitive spot where his head connects to his shaft. "All the goddamn time."

I grin, knowing every technique to blow his mind, cock, and world, and I want to. I want to give Nash the pleasure he's given me. I want him to surrender to me as much as I have to him.

So, I lick him, flattening my tongue and teasing him while he stares down at me, anticipating, needing me to take him into my mouth. His eyes narrow. His lips part. I could tease and torture him all night, but he wants this too much.

He laces his hand through my hair while I lick his tip. "That's enough teasing, Vale." Tugging hard at my strands, he demands, "Now be a good girl and suck my cock while I fuck all the bratty little words out of your mouth."

God, I want to say it. My kink is on the tip of my tongue, but what if it's not his? What if I freak him out?

Then again, his eyes look lost in lust. His cock is rock hard, his breath heavy, his grip on my hair so controlling, so hungry for me.

He's wanted me as much as I've wanted him. Maybe just like this...

"Yes, Daddy," I sigh, taking the risk before slowly sliding my lips over his swollen tip and locking my eyes on his, watching his reaction to my kink as I plunge my mouth down his thick shaft.

"*Fuucckkk yes*, Vale!" He almost roars, the veins in his neck straining while he cups my head on the pillow. "Yes, be such a dirty girl for your daddy now. Yes, suck me. Suck me, baby."

It's our kink unleashed. It makes moans crawl up my throat as he starts fucking it, but he's not forcing me. No, every muscle on his body, straddling mine, is tense with restraint.

This is so powerful between us. It could overwhelm us if we let it, and I love it. I wrap my hand around his swollen base, and we find a maddening tempo. Me, bobbing my head, moaning and teasing him with tongue techniques while my hands pump, and him, gently thrusting his cock into my mouth.

"Goddamn," he mutters. "Goddamn, Vale, you're good at this." He shudders when I lick his slit. "So fucking good."

I want more. I want it all. I want all of Nash's secrets, all of his life, all of his heart, so I take as much of him as I can until my throat gently gags on his mass. I grab his thighs, my fingernails digging into his firm ass cheeks, so he can't move. He has to let me do this, choking on him while I stare up at him, my tearing eyes swearing how much I love his cock in my mouth.

"Fuck, Vale." He marvels, "Fuck, how can you take so much of me?"

I pull off; my spit webbed from my lips to his tip.

"Because you belong to me, don't you? Just as much as I belong to you."

"Yes, yes," he pants as I go back to sucking him. He keeps saying it, over and over, and with my name, his praise driving me harder.

Giving Nash pleasure is making me wet. I ache for him, but I want to share more, so I carefully cup his balls. He moans like he likes it, but I'm brave. I want this for us, so I move my fingertip, massaging his perineum, and his moans drop deeper. I indulge him for minutes, lavishing him before I slowly move my fingertip to tease his ass.

"Fuck." He stops thrusting into my mouth.

I circle his ass. "Do you like this?"

"I've never let anyone do it," he confesses.

"Will you let me?" I keep circling and teasing, but my heart is sincere; I want to give this to him. "Will you share a first with me like I shared with you?"

He's so powerful and vulnerable at the same time, gazing down at me, his thumb brushing my cheek. "Yes," he mutters, "yes, you can have me, Vale."

I put my fingers in my mouth until they're dripping before I return, circling and teasing his ass while I suck his tip, my other hand fisting his shaft.

My pussy clenches, hearing his deep gasps and grunts; he's loving it. So slowly, I enter him, watching his mouth gape, watching him give me something no one else has had. His surrender. His pleasure. His trust.

When I curl my middle finger inside him, rubbing his soft fleshy spot, his corded thighs, straining over me, start to shake. "Vale," is all he can grunt as I take him; I claim him; I give him pleasure like he's never felt, and his eyes roll back.

Fisting my hair, his hand shakes, too. "Fuck." He grunts, "Fuck, Vale, you're making me come so hard," and I moan for it, my mouth full of him, wanting every drop he gives me.

I've never seen Nash's face while he comes, and it's beautiful, primal, and raw how his veins pop, his sinews strain, his muscles twitch. He groans, thrusting and watching me, his body clenching around my finger curling inside him while I don't stop giving him this pleasure until his cum spills over my lips.

Gently, I pull out, licking my lips clean as I gaze up at him, and he gazes back. His chest heaves, finding his breath as he lowers his mouth so close to mine like he wants to kiss me, like he wants to taste what we just shared.

But kissing on the lips? I don't know if I can ever get that intimacy, that trust and tenderness back.

"Poison." His kiss skims my cheek instead. "Goddamn, I've never come so hard like that. Promise me, that's another secret we'll share."

"Can we do it again?"

He lifts, searching my eyes. "Does sucking me off really turn you on, too? Because going down on you is my new fetish."

I bite my lip. "Lick my pussy, Daddy, and taste how much I love choking on your cock."

"Fuck, yes," he huffs, aroused and returning the pleasure. It makes him hard again; I can tell by his deep moans into my cunt. They only make my lust more maddening.

I turn our bodies to lavish him with my mouth as well, but I'm too petite, straddling his face. So, I reach, stroking his screaming erection. It drips with my pussy on his face, his tongue worshipping my clit, his fingers taking me until I come. My orgasm makes his cock swell, and I move down his hard, inked abs to worship him, too. To take him in my mouth, his hand cupping my head.

"Fuck yes, poison," he groans. "The taste of your cum on my tongue makes me come so fucking hard." And I make him do it, hollowing my cheeks to suck every drop of him; his grunts are erotic music to my soul.

"God..." I finish him, rolling off and falling on the pillow, his taste tingling on my tongue as I flop my arm over my head, and he flips his body, returning to his place, lying beside me. "Too bad you really suck at cunnilingus."

He chuckles, still catching his breath. "Like you fail at fellatio."

I laugh, wrapping around him. "You know what they say; learning is fun."

"Is that what all your books taught you?" he asks. "How to piss off men, then rock their world?"

"Something like that."

He's quiet, playing with my hair before he asks, "When will you be Doctor Vale Monroe?"

"At this rate?" I sigh, "Never."

"What do you mean?"

"I'm ABD eternally."

He lifts my chin. "What does that mean? I don't speak PhD."

"It means I'm 'All But Dissertation.' I've passed all my classes, done all my research, and started and stopped writing my final dissertation about five times."

"Why?"

I rest my chin on my hand over his chest. With Nash, I feel like I can confess anything. Like he'd never judge.

"Because for so many years, I felt like a fraud. At Delta's, I teach everyone about sex and sexuality, but my sex life has sucked. I guess deep down, I doubted myself. I didn't feel qualified to have a PhD in something I actually failed at."

He brushes the hair from my face. "You're speaking in past tense."

"Yeah, because suddenly, I'm having orgasmic sex with you, and we haven't even fucked, so I'm feeling like an erotic goddess, but..." He raises a brow, waiting. "But I don't want to finish now. I don't want to be a professor. I don't want to do research and write about sexuality; I want to help people with it. I think I want to be a sex therapist instead."

Jealousy flashes across his eyes. "You'll have sex with patients?"

"No, never! Get your mind out of the porno gutter. As an accountant, do you fuck numbers to fix them?"

"No. I figure them out until they work, until they balance."

"That's what a sex therapist does. I'd help clients figure out their emotional and mental blocks regarding sex and intimacy. You have no idea how many people suffer with it." I pause. "But I do. I have. It feels like you're trapped in a cage with no key."

His gaze, usually so cold and stoic, fills with warmth. He cups my cheek, his thumb gently brushing over it. "Do you want to tell me about it?" Softly, he grins, making me feel so safe. "*You* might not listen, but I always will."

Even his cute joke fills me with warmth.

If there were a man I trusted to tell this to, it would be Nash. But trusting men after one hurt me and another abandoned me is not a place I'm in. Not yet.

I shake my head. "Not really. Not now. I've done a lot of work to heal. And yes, all my pussy power books have helped. But let's just say," my throat suddenly strangles, "it's why I don't kiss on the lips."

It makes me pause as I chew them, fighting back the tears and the memory, too. "My kiss was taken from me," I share, "and I'm still trying to get it back."

But I give Nash this; I let him see my tears about it.

He clenches his teeth, his nostrils flaring as the hinge of his jaw flexes. He swallows slowly like rocks fill his throat, but he won't look away from me.

Nash holds my truth with me, and I know how protective he is, so that was hard for him to hear. His eyes look full of love, yet like he wants to murder, too, but he's helpless to do anything about it now.

He cups my cheeks, his voice stirring with deep rage and care. "Will you let me help you get it back?"

"You already have," I answer, kissing the inked flesh above his pounding heart. My pain beats through his veins, too; I can feel it. Then I kiss his neck, my lips sensing the thunder of his furious, protective pulse; it matches mine. Gently, I kiss his scruffy, granite jaw before I find his ear and tenderly confess, "You're the beast who set me free."

CHAPTER SIXTEEN
VALE

"They're all sourced locally," Alena tells me on our video chat. "Magnolia leaves, eucalyptus, white roses. I want simple wildflower bouquets."

"They're beautiful," I tell her, admiring the sample bouquet she's showing me. The florist sent it to Alena's ranger office in Pisgah Forest.

"Let me see." Blair pops up from her chair. She's in a good mood. I don't know what's gotten into her today, but it's not Beau Bronson, so I'm not complaining. "Oh!" She claps when she sees it. "I high key love it!"

"I think they'll look great with your dresses, don't you?" Alena asks like I wouldn't wear a garbage bag for her while I proudly carry a bouquet of used tissues.

"It's going to be the perfect day," I tell her. "*Your* day."

"I agree," Blair answers. "And I promise, I'm getting out of my fuck funk. I got my dress fitted yesterday. It just needs more room for the girls, but it looks gorgeous. It made me feel human again. Thank you. I love the sage green you picked."

Alena beams. "Vale, did you get your dress, too?"

"Yes, I got a message from the shop. I'll go by in a day or so to get fitted."

"Perfect," she says. "Is my dad there?"

"Uh...," I stammer.

"I need to ask about his suit."

"Yes." I clear my throat, sitting up straight. "He's here. He's our accountant. He's just auditing the mess I made of the books because I suck at math, and the software confused me and—"

"Okay, well, can you put him on, please?"

Alena doesn't care as I overthink and overexplain, trying not to sound guilty.

"Sure. Here he is. We're just at my desk. We're just doing the accounting and—"

"Give me that," Nash mutters, gently taking my phone away.

"Hey, sweetpea." He smiles at Alena on the screen, telling her, "Don't worry. I have a tux. I have two actually and—"

"Dad, I don't want you wearing a tux. I don't do formal stuff. I want the men in navy suits."

"Navy?" He resists, "That's not my style."

So, I snap, "Uh. *Whose* wedding is it?"

Nash smiles at me, licking his lips before he tells her, "According to your maid-of-honor, I'll be wearing a navy suit with a smile."

"Dad," she laughs, "you know better than to fuck with Vale."

If I had coffee in my mouth, I'd spew the desk with it.

Instead, my eyes get wide and flooded with guilt as Nash sits up, clearing his throat. "Yes, well," he rushes. "Whatever you want. It's navy suits for all."

For all?

Suddenly, I'm curious. I haven't asked who the

groomsmen are. Alena said Loch has brothers. If it's them, okay, but I still haven't met them. And that's still sketch.

The wedding is in July. It's May. So, when Nash hands my phone back to me, I ask her, "So, who's the lucky man walking me down the aisle?"

I glance over to find Nash glaring at my question.

"Since I don't want anything big or fancy," Alena answers, "and I only want you and Blair in my bridal party; Loch said he can't pick between his five brothers, and he never knew his father, so my dad and godfather will be the groomsmen."

"Your *godfather?*" I'm puzzled. "When did you get one of those?"

"When she was nine," Nash answers for her. "When she was baptized. Her mom and I didn't do it when she was an infant, but Lainey wanted it done before she was deployed and..."

He trails off. I know the rest of the story.

"And the pastor who baptized me will marry us, too," Alena adds.

"Okay." I shrug. "Who's your godfather?"

"Michael Cummings," Alena answers. "He's my dad's best friend. I don't think you know him. Not yet, but the service will be simple and..."

She goes on about the ceremony as I fight so hard to keep my face straight when I'm dying to whip my glare at Nash and make laser beams shoot from my eyes until his head explodes.

Michael Cummings? Mr. Not-Mafia-Mafia, who has a forbidden meeting room on our third floor, is Alena's *godfather?*

Holy, I'm gonna kill him.

Who?

Yeah, him and Nash.

"That's nice." I stomp on Nash's foot under the table. He

doesn't flinch while I feel like a ticking bomb. "I guess we'll all meet and be one big happy family at your rehearsal dinner."

"Yeah," Alena adds. "We'll rehearse, then have dinner at the club. It's just family and the wedding party. You can meet Loch's brothers, too. Some will be there."

Good. Maybe Loch's brothers can beat the shit out of Michael Cummings and take his evil ego down a peg.

"Car fifteen to base," Alena's radio squawks, so she says, "Gotta go. Call ya tomorrow."

She ends our video chat, and I stare ahead, seething and wondering how I can kill Alena's groomsmen without ruining her wedding. It's impossible. As impossible as me not losing my shit over this.

But I don't get a chance to rip Nash's head off because a swarm of women burst into the store.

"We want penises!" One shouts while the others laugh.

"Let me guess." Blair laughs, too. "A bachelorette party?"

"Yes." Ms. Penis Lover laughs. She's about three mimosas into her day. "It's a pool party tonight, and we want dicks everywhere!" She turns to Jace. "Well, hey there, big, handsome fella. Aren't you hotter than blue blazes? Can we buy you and take you home, too?"

"Ma'am." I rise and politely protect him. "Let's not take advantage of my staff, please." Then I smile, gesturing upstairs, "But we have plenty of big toys you can take advantage of all night."

If I had a dollar for every time Jace gets propositioned, or me, or Blair, we wouldn't need this job.

"Come on, ladies." Blair leads them upstairs. "When you say, 'bachelorette pool party,' I say, 'six-foot penis float.'"

"Thanks, fox." Jace winks at me for rescuing him. It's cute. He always makes his flirt feel innocent, but...

Wait! The logic smacks me.

Jace is one of Nash's Bratva brothers. So is his brother Grant, and so is Michael Cummings. And last night, Nash revealed something about the room Cummings rents upstairs.

"What we do in that room sometimes … It makes me hard. It makes us hard. We're like animals…"

That's what Nash confessed last night. Then he said it was…

"Something I'll never allow to be done to you."

Oh, my god, what is it? And does that mean Jace does it, too? And of all the taboos that implies, the only stupid thing I can worry about is … *is Nash with other women?*

But it's impossible. He hasn't really left my side in almost a month.

But will he be?

When they have their first forbidden meeting upstairs, will Nash go? Will he be with other women just to keep his bond with other men? Is that what they do? And why? Why does desire flood my core, imagining their ritual?

Questions rage through me like a storm. Waves of jealousy, lust, fear, betrayal, and love drown my vision.

"Vale?" Jace asks. "Vale, are you okay?"

He's sitting on his stool. I'm staring right at him but my mind is swept away with no answers to anchor me.

"I… uh…"

Like my dark storm conjured the devil, the bell by the door rings, and Jace opens it. Two large looming silhouettes stand, backlit by the sun, but they don't look angelic.

"Good afternoon."

It's Michael Cummings. He's walking in with a man of equal size, of equal suspicion.

"Good afternoon." His shadow seeks me, introducing himself, "You must be Ms. Monroe." *Same dark hair. Same glacial eyes. He looks like Cummings, only a little older.* "Sire Rutledge, nice to meet you."

His big hand shaking mine is hot. Hot like he looks with dark tattoos peeking out from under his starched white collar. His touch, strong and controlling. His icy eyes intrigued, almost amused to meet me.

Like a lion leering at a mouse. At his meal.

I'm supposed to stammer and be shy and sweet. I'm supposed to listen and be spoken down to. I'm supposed to wilt in the presence of the ominous threat of Nash, Jace, Michael, and now Sire.

But remember what I said about listening to men?

"Cut the shit." I squeeze Sire Rutledge's hand so hard before dropping it. "You're one of them, Monkey & Co. I get it."

Jace tries to stifle his chuckle but sucks at it.

"Yes, Ms. Monroe. Mr. Rutledge is"—Michael Cummings starts to drone with what sounds like will be another legal brief—"my business associate and—"

"Why don't you go associate a 'fuck' with a 'you'?" I snarl. "I know who you are and what you do, and now I know you're Alena's godfather, too."

He slices his eyes to Nash, seated over my shoulder.

I glance back, and Nash has his feet on the desk, his head resting in his hands. "Go ahead, poison," he smirks. "Fire away."

Okay, that's kind of sweet, but I'm pissed as hell at him, too.

I whip back and step into Cumming's shadow.

"I swear, if you ever hurt Alena, I'll bite your dick off. The human bite has one hundred and sixty-two pounds of pressure per inch, and it takes half that to rip your little thing off, and I can. I will. I practice on jawbreakers daily."

Jace chuckles while Cummings glares down at me, seething, "I would never lay a hand on Alena, and anyone who does will have more than his dick ripped off. Are we clear, Ms. Monroe?"

"No, because you're all lying to her. She doesn't know who—"

"If we say we have no sin, we deceive ourselves, and the truth is not in us." This Sire guy sounds half-holy, half-hot.

"I'm sorry, what?" I look at him, lowering my voice. "What are you? A mafia minister?"

"We are all sinners, Ms. Monroe," Sire answers with a calm face. "You are. We are. And we all keep secrets so that our sins do no harm. Be assured we will never allow harm to come to Alena Allen. We've made our vows."

My head spins. Am I surrounded by mafia, ministers, monsters, or monks?

"We need to meet." Michael Cummings, literally the godfather present, signals to Nash to follow them. Jace, too.

"Don't open the door," Jace tells me, locking it. "Not to anyone until I'm back."

"But what about our customers?"

"Distract them with dildos," he says, not kidding, while the four men tread upstairs.

I'd be worried that this is one of their taboo meetings Nash mentioned, but I don't get that vibe. They're going in alone, so this is something else.

Over the den of horny women in the showroom on the second floor, I can't hear the men disappear into their new meeting room. But I can see them on the security screen, using the camera at the top of the third-floor landing.

They're silent. They're serious. They walk single file: Michael, Nash, Sire, then Jace until they disappear from the camera's view.

And I grin because Nash said I could never enter...

But he never said I couldn't eavesdrop.

CHAPTER SEVENTEEN
NASH

AXEL LOCKS THE DOOR BEHIND US, AND SIRE STARTS clapping.

Slowly.

Loudly.

Sarcastically.

"Well done, Nash." Sire laughs. "You've really picked an easy one."

"I haven't picked a fucking thing," I seethe. "She's *not* my queen."

"Nope." Jace plops in his king's chair. It's the fifth in a row of seven. "She's going to be one of *our* queens, and it's about time. If I have to hear you two fight instead of fuck for another week, I quit."

"No one's quitting." Axel swipes his fingertip over the center platform. It's new. It's made of pristine, tufted black leather, but of course, he checks for dust. "But Jasha is right."

"*Jace*," he rumbles his own American name. "Don't slip up. Not in this house."

Jasha, aka. Jace is right.

Their real names are their greatest liability.

Sire was born Sergei. Axel was born Aleksi. Grant, Grigori. Jace, Jasha. Nick, Nikifor. And the baby was named Lyov. And all six brothers have the most dangerous last name in Russia—Kholodov.

That's why they hide under American names and pseudonyms like Michael Cummings and more. And they do it in a city where their father would never think to look for them.

Me? I'm the money man. Of course, I prefer using our numbers. Axel is "One," I'm "Two," Sire is "Three," and so on.

"We're running out of time," Axel continues, dropping his dickhead Michael Cummings guise. "Alena's wedding is soon, and you know what you must do."

When it's just us, I get the real him, the man who's been my best friend since I was eighteen. I met Sire first, but he's always been a loner, while Axel and I became men together.

"Vows can't be broken," Sire adds, "even if the bond breaks you."

"Fuck you all," I snarl. "You don't have a daughter. You don't know what you're asking."

"But I will one day," Sire adds. "Wren and I want to try next year."

I shake my head. "That's like saying you know how it feels to cry when you never have. I'll never hurt my daughter, so I can't choose Vale."

"She can handle us," Jace argues. "Vale fits right in. Hell, she's already in. Sort of."

"She knows too much now," Axel adds. "You don't have a choice."

"The hell I don't." My steps eat the ground between us. I stand eye-to-eye with Axel. "We keep the secret. We keep her safe. We find Turner. We kill him, and then Vale's free. Done, or someone else dies. We clear?"

"We found him," Axel answers coldly. "More specifically, we know where he'll be next Wednesday."

"Where?"

"Our club." He smirks. "We're hosting a Vegas-style golf tournament that he can't resist."

"Turner is a notorious gambler," Sire adds, "and a mediocre golf player. We got the word out, invited some pros, and he took the bait. He's ponied up ten K to play."

"What's the plan?" I sit in my king's chair, the second one, envisioning how this could go down.

"He plays. He loses." Axel sits beside me in the first chair, tenting his fingers. "We wait for the after-party, he gets drunk, goes to take a piss, and then—"

"No one goes to an after-party if they lose," I argue. "He needs to win some."

"True," Jace adds. "Let him win a few holes."

"So, who's playing him?"

They look at me. "Fuck. No."

"You're the only one exposed," Sire points out. "It has to be you. He doesn't know that's our club and course. We'll secure it. You can play him, fuck with his mind a bit and maybe get some intel before we scoop him up."

"Admit it," Axel says. "After what he tried to do to you and Vale? You're dying to watch him squirm."

"It should be you," I tell Axel. "You're our best player. You live on the course."

"Yeah," he says, "I make the best deals out there, get the best intel, and trust me, I want to watch that fucker suffer after what he did to those girls, but it's too risky. He found you, followed you, and almost found us.

"So, I admit," Axel continues, "your idea of meeting here is genius. We look like random customers, Jace and Grant look like staff, and you look like the man he knows you to be:

Nash Allen, the accountant who moves dirty money like a shell game. He has no idea we're connected."

"He hasn't found Delta's yet," Jace adds. "Grant has the block surveilled. No one's been around. So far, we're covered."

"That's why we strike now," Axel continues. "We take him down before he can find another second in command and rebuild his network."

"Fine." I demand, "I'll play with one of our pros, and we'll let him win five holes, but you better cover my six. Don't let one of his men snipe me from the river and ruin my game."

"Grant's got it covered," Jace promises. "We'll establish a perimeter, and I'll cover Vale that day. I won't let her out of my sight until Turner's deep-six in the Atlantic."

"Sounds like Jace is already her second king."

Sire's joking, but red rage suddenly veils my vision. On instinct, I jump, pressing my forearm to his throat and shoving him against the wall.

"Fucking say it again!" I thunder. "Say someone's going to touch her when she's mine! Do it! Do it, goddammit, and I'll kill someone!"

"Brother," Sire soothes, holding his palms up. "Calm down. You love her, and I understand."

He could match me, punch for punch, bullet for bullet. We all can. If a brother goes after a brother, it would be a tragic mutual kill. We're that skilled and stubborn.

"Hey, man." Jace's hand lands on my shoulder, tugging me away. "We love you, and we'll love her. It'll be okay."

"It's not happening." I step away from Sire, pulling back from Jace, too. "You don't touch my daughter, and you don't touch my woman."

"Okay." Axel puts his hands up. "One deal at a time. We take down Turner. Everything else will be here when we're done."

Here?

He means our room, our bond, our history.

I've never questioned it before. Why would I? It's not like I can walk away. When a man and his family that's not yours save your baby girl and her mother from ruin, you don't walk away. You owe them your life.

"Just." I clench my teeth. I've never wavered like this. "Just... Fuck you, Axel! Give me time."

"Hey." He stands. "We don't do this to make the other suffer. We do this to survive. We do this because we believe in a bond, and we're brothers. *You're* our brother."

Silently, I turn. I need air. I need to calm down. I haven't raised my fist to a brother in years.

With a quick flip of the lock, I swing the door open ... and Vale falls into my arms.

CHAPTER EIGHTEEN
VALE

I fall into Nash's arms, and his grip is vicious. With gritted teeth, his eyes blaze, furious.

This can go a hundred ways, so I might as well make it go mine.

"Let's not make this weird." I find my footing. "Yes, I was listening, and yes, I'm playing in that tournament with you next week."

"Over my dead body," Nash growls.

"Well, that sounds like a real possibility, and I'd really hate it because you've grown on me like a yeast infection, so let me help."

"We need a motion sensor alert outside that door." I hear Michael Cummings snarl.

Scratch that: Axel. He's snarling and pissed about me snooping, and he can kiss my ass.

All's fair in mafia and sex shops.

I shuffle, my arms still held by Nash's hands. Hands that probably itch to strangle me, but let's save the kink for later.

"Jace is right," I say. "I'm in. I know who you are, what you do, and I know the plan, and I'm part of it. I can play any man under the table on that course, so let me. Let me control the game while you get what you want."

"It's not a bad idea," Jace adds. "She's a champion player and a champion's daughter. It'll distract him."

I glance around the angry wall of Nash to try and get a glimpse of the room, and *oh, my Bratva beast sex den, do I.*

Black ceiling and walls with the gilded wall trim painted gold. Tall, golden candelabras. Gold velvet curtains framing the windows to the sunny courtyard below. Seven black king's chairs. Seven white queen's chairs. A large, low leather platform, like a bed, between them.

It's elegant. Eerie. Enticing. The setting drips with opulence and orgasms. The implications of the arrangement erotic beyond my wildest fantasies.

Please tell me they do what I think they do in here.

Please tell me Nash won't do it again.

Jace stands beside his brothers. They tower with muscles and tattoos. *Damn, that's a helluva hot DNA pool.*

Clearly, my eyes work, but my heart and body belong to one man.

He's the one holding me, ripping my curious stare back to his as he fumes, "You and I are going to have a *long* talk."

"Is it about the birds and the bees?"

I hear Jace snort behind him, but Nash tightens his grip. "No, poison. It's about bruises and bullets."

He whips his glare around, barking at Jace, "I'm taking her home, and you're covering for her. Tell her sister she's going to get her dress fitted."

"For the record," I hear Sire add, "I vote yes. Test her and see if she wants to join us."

I don't get time to enthusiastically second his vote because Nash manhandles me. He practically lifts me by the arms and carries me out of the room.

The door slams behind us. The customers and Blair can

be heard downstairs, but I can only focus on Nash and what I did.

"I'm sorry that I'm *not* sorry," I press. "It's like you said, we're in this together, so let me be the Bonnie to your Clyde."

"They were killed in an ambush; you know that, right?" He seethes, his voice low, "And that's exactly what can happen to us. At any moment or on that golf course, we can be ambushed. I can protect you from one, two, maybe three men, but not a half dozen or more with you in their sights."

"But someone in there said it's covered. That you can secure the club and course."

"Nothing is ever truly secure. It's just degrees of safety you try to control."

"Well, I can control a golf game better than any of you could, and you know it's a good idea. I can be the ultimate distraction." I bat my lashes. "Imagine the sexy little golf dress I can wear."

Whoops! I pushed too far.

The beast roars, "Home! Now!"

If Nash could take me by the hair like a caveman and drag me home, he would. Not that I'd let him, but I appreciate the instinct. He wants to hide me away so no one can hurt me.

Too late.

Ironically, the more I'm around Nash and his menacing men, the less I'm afraid.

After he aims his gun, clearing my apartment, he slams the door behind us. Three times, he flips the locks, securing them. Then he pushes the loveseat in front of it before he takes a seat and ponders the gun in his hand.

I flop down, sitting on the edge of my bed, and wait. And wait. And wait. And wait.

"Wow, you really never shut up, do you?"

"You really have no idea what you're asking to do," he answers.

"I'm not asking; I'm telling you, I'm playing in that tournament. That man traffics girls and women, and probably boys, too, and hurts them in the most horrific ways. So long before you and your Bratva beasts get a hold of him, I just might take my 9-iron to his skull and yell, 'Fore,' before I smash it open."

I catch it; Nash tries not to smile. I grab my phone on my nightstand and start tapping.

"What are you doing?" he asks.

"I'm putting the tournament on my calendar, along with the days we're going to fight about it and the days we'll get kinky and make up. It's what we do, and who wants a scheduling conflict?"

"*This* is a conflict," he barks, "and it's one you won't win."

"Oh, come on," I coax. "You gotta admit that you like it. It kind of turns you on; me and you working together."

He licks his bottom lip.

"You kind of like that I'm not afraid," I add. "I'm not intimidated by you or your men. I know I can trust them. Yeah, that Axel one can be a royal dickhead, but I adore Jace and Grant, and I think that Sire dude is right. Test me and see if I want to join you."

Tensely, he sets his gun down on the loveseat. Glaring at me, he draws several deep breaths before he reaches down, adjusting himself, making a salacious shiver whip through me. *He's getting hard.*

He rises like a threat, and I'm thrilled.

"You want me to test you, Vale?" He jeers, "Do you want me to show you what we do if you're mine?"

"Yes," I sigh because I have a very taboo idea of what they do, how they bond, and how I will come to sit on one of their queen's chairs.

Nash stalks my way, ripping his shirt over his head, tossing it aside as my teeth catch my bottom lip. He makes fast work of losing his shoes, pants, and boxers. He's huge and raging hard, muscles and ink everywhere, and my body ignites.

Standing by the edge of my bed, just feet away, he demands, "Lift your skirt, pull your panties aside, and show me what you want me to test."

I obey.

"I'm clear," his voice strains, "but do you want me to use a condom?"

"No. I'm clear and protected, too." And I'm already wet with his command, and the naughty display I'm giving him, tugging my panties aside and showing him my pussy only makes me slick even more.

He stares like a starving animal at my exposed sex, so I clench it for him. I have Kegel's that can crack rocks. I practice with my yoni eggs and his eyelids hood, watching how I can make my pussy pulse for him. Around him. It stirs his cock, soaring thick and veiny, a pearly drop leaking at the sight.

"Take them off," he demands about my panties, "and give them to me."

I lift my hips, wedging my panties off, leaving my schoolgirl miniskirt on while I drop my soaked cotton in his outstretched hand. When he lifts them to his nose, taking a deep inhale of my musk, my teeth grab my bottom lip, my thighs opening for him again.

I love showing him my pussy, how I'm wet for him. The hunger in his eyes is addictive. It's my drug. He's fighting something inside, but I know how to win.

Teasing my fingertip over my excited clit, I beg, "Please, Mr. Allen, fuck me. I've fantasized about you for so long, and you know it. You know I want your cock." I slide a finger inside, slowly pumping it. "Please fuck this tight, little pussy like you wanted to that night by the pool."

He drops my panties and spits in his palm before wetting his shaft with it, stalking my way.

I scoot back on the bed, making room for him, but like an animal, he's faster. He's on me. His knees wedge my thighs apart before he rips my blouse open. Buttons fly as he tugs the lace cups of my bra down, making my breasts succulent and exposed. He leans down, sucking one, then biting it before he does the same to the other.

I moan, looking down to see Nash's spit trailing from my nipple to his lips while he demands, "Say it, Vale. Say it one more time so we have no doubt."

"Fuck me," I demand. "Fuck me hard and now and test me. Test how much I can take of you because I want you, Nash. I want all of you."

In one brutal thrust, he's inside me, and we both cry out. *Oh, my god, he's huge.* With the next pump of his cock, I scream, "Yes!" and I don't stop.

"Fuck, poison," he growls over my lips, wanting to kiss them, I know. So he takes my ear, letting me hear while he grabs my throat, his cock thrusting inside.

"You're so fucking wet for me," he says. "So fucking tight, Vale. That's it. Lift your hips. Yes, baby, fuck me back. Take me."

I do. I am. I will.

I'm feral and fighting to have Nash inside me as much as he's a savage and pounding to do it. Over and over and forever. He's a beast when he fucks, and it only thrills me, my desire making his thrusts smack, the sounds of our hunger filling the room.

"So good." His breath urges. "Fuck, you're so good, Vale."

I think I'm screaming. I think I'm gasping, loving his perfect strangle of my throat, loving the hard thrusts of his cock, his force lusciously shocking my clit. *I found it. I found him.* This is more than I ever imagined. This is more than anything I've ever felt. We've burned to do this for so long, and our flames are hot.

"Nash!" I can feel it building. My body has never done this. I've never felt like I could come, but I will.

I want to. I need to.

He lifts, hovering his lips over mine, almost biting my cheek when I grab his back and swivel my hips under his pumping cock. "*Fuucckk*, yes," he groans, his ripped muscles tensing, his body desperate and seeking like mine.

"Nash, please." He sees me, letting him take me to my edge. He sees my pleasure, what he's giving me that no one else has, and it makes him pump deeper as I meet his thrusts.

Lifting my hips, my fingernails mark his ass while I tightly clench my walls around him. It'll help my orgasm, if I ever will, making my sex seize him, milk him, pulling him deeper inside.

"Goddamn, what are you doing to me?" He marvels, feeling my grabbing need, my clit starting to ignite. "Fuck, Vale. That's good." His lips shake. "So good." His eyes begin to roll. *Yes, I'm getting there, too.* He delivers hard, pounding thrusts, deeper and deeper like I'm taking him. Like he can't get enough of me. Like he can't control it. "Fuck, Vale," he grunts. "Oh, fuck, baby, I'm coming. I'm sorry. *Fuucckk!*"

With three more thrusts of his cock, battering my sex, every muscle on his beautiful inked body tenses. Nash stills inside me while he grunts, clenching his jaw. The animal in his eyes is trapped by desire while he stares into mine and comes, spilling deep inside me.

"Fuck," he exhales. He fights for breath. "Fuck, I'm sorry." He kisses my huffing cheek. "I'm sorry, baby. You make me feel sixteen again, and I've wanted you too much for too long. I couldn't control it. You felt so good moving your hips like that, and I lost it."

"It's okay," I pant, wrapping my legs around his waist,

holding him inside. We feel natural. We feel right. "This feels good, too."

He traps my gaze while he brushes the hair from my face. He's still finding his breath, too. "No, my poison, I'm not settling for good enough with you. You know I do everything three times," he promises, "so the next two are for you."

I peck his nose. "Just tell me if I passed the first test."

"After all those books you've read? After all you've studied? Goddamn, woman, you know how to fuck," he praises. "What were you doing with your pussy?"

"This."

I clench tight around him again, and he shudders, groaning, "Fuck, that's it."

Gently, he puts his forehead to mine, nuzzling our noses. With another breath, he sighs, "You're the best I've ever had, and that's the only test you need to pass."

His praise lights up my heart. The way we feel together is pure. The way he's looking at me makes me believe in him, in us. I'm not afraid of this. I want everything with him.

I trace my fingertip over his thick brow and boldly ask, "What are the other tests?"

His face falls serious. He doesn't pause. He gets it over with. "I fuck you in front of the other kings. I prove to them you're my queen and that you want to be with me ... with ... *us*; that's the first test."

My breath deepens. My lust that ebbed after he came comes flooding right back. "Okay," I sigh.

"Okay?" He raises a brow. "You're okay with me fucking you in front of my brothers?"

"I've had sex in public before. I mean, at the club. Why would that be any different?"

"I know you've had sex at the club," he says. "I've watched you."

"What?" This is news. "I've never seen you there."

"There's a VIP room on the third level, the one above the main floor. It's one-way glass, and I've stood there, watching you."

Which question to ask next? My head's unsure, but my heart needs to know, "How did it make you feel?"

Because if I had to watch Nash with another woman, I'd want to die. He's not mine, but why does it feel like he is? Why does it feel like I can't bear to share him, to lose him?

"To watch you with other women?" He admits, "I got jealous, but it turned me on. To watch you with other men?" He confesses, "I wanted to kill them, so I had to leave. It made me sick and furious for days. Weeks, honestly. Hell, I still am."

"I never came," I rush. "Not once, and I never kissed anyone. It wasn't love or anything; I was just exploring, just desperate. I was trying to get out of this cage inside." I trace over his lips. "The one only you can open."

His eyes flutter like I'm touching his heart. Like I've found his soul. And I want to tell him everything. Why I flinch. Why I don't kiss.

But I don't want him to see me as a victim because I'm not. I'm a survivor. I'm strong, and no one has ever made me feel as safe and sexy as Nash. Only he makes me feel this free, too.

"Poison," he sighs, "you say you want to pass our tests, and I believe you. It's your body; you know what you want. But it's my heart, too. I don't know if I can take it."

"Can take what?"

He's propped up on his elbows, gazing down at me. He's softening inside me, like my heart.

"This. Me and you," he says. "It took me forty-four years to feel this way for a woman, and I swear to you, it's not a feeling I'll ever share with anyone else."

Same.

I bite my lip, letting my sudden tear escape, sliding down and wetting my hair. "And it took me almost thirty years to feel this." I smile. "To feel how it's supposed to feel. It's a feeling I'll only share with you, Nash. I promise."

He nuzzles his nose to mine before wrapping me in his arms and rolling us to lie side by side. Briefly, I sit up and take off what's left of my clothes before I return to his waiting arms, lying on his chest.

He kisses my hair before he unbraids it. He's done it several times like he's obsessed with freeing my strands until they're black waves tumbling down my back. Then, he presses my head to his chest and laces his fingers through, combing my hair as if it calms him. It must, because it soothes me, too.

For minutes, I swim in our silence, connected like this, and I have no doubt only with Nash will I ever feel this way. It makes me confident. It makes me brave.

"Can I confess something?"

He tickles my arm. "Yes."

"Scratch that: Can I ask a question?"

His chest softly shakes with laughter. "That's more like it."

"You said last night that whatever you do in that room with your *Bratva* brothers makes you hard. Then you said you'd never allow it to be done to me. And then that made us get so hot and horny that I sucked your cock and played with your ass and—"

"Is there a question in there somewhere?"

"Yes." I rise and confront his amused stare. "Is it your kink? Fucking in front of others?"

"Sometimes. Sometimes it's not."

"What makes it not?"

"Details," he warns.

I raise a brow.

"I'm serious," he answers. "That's what the tests are for. To see if it's what you really want."

"I *do* want it," I rush. "I want to be with you. I want you to make me yours. I think... I think I'll get off on it." I chew my lip. "That's my confession."

Something stirs in his eyes, then I see it stir his cock.

"You'll get off on it too, won't you?" I ask. "It's making you hard just thinking about it."

"What makes me hard and will get me off..." His voice is low. He rolls me over, pinning me down. "Is showing everyone you're mine and how I'll never share you."

CHAPTER NINETEEN
NASH

Vale Monroe makes me a very conflicted man.

At times, everything feels right with her. Like she's the moon and I'm the sea, I'm forever drawn to her. That's what my heart tells me.

But my head tells me it's wrong. This is a grave mistake, and I know damn well why.

Then there's my cock; it just wants her. It feels everything, too, like this primal urge to claim her, to live inside her forever. Like this demand to take her again.

"Your turn," I murmur down her neck.

"But..." she suddenly worries. "But don't stress it. If I don't come while we fuck, it's okay."

I glance up from her cleavage and grin. "Are you doubting me again?"

"No." She blushes. "I just... Even though I feel broken, I don't need to be fixed. I just want you to know you make me feel so good. Even if I don't come, I like it."

"You *like* it?"

"Yeah." She laces her fingers through my hair. "I *really* like it."

I rise and climb off the bed.

"Where are you going?" she asks, and I don't answer.

I grab her mirror, propped against the wall, and lay it on the floor, the top of the frame wedged against the wall, the reflection facing the ceiling. Then, I take her hand. "Come here."

She lets me pull her until she's standing beside me, dwarfed by my size. *I love how she's so petite.*

"What are you doing?" She blinks up at me.

"You said you look in the mirror, touch yourself, and make yourself come. That you have a beautiful pussy," I fist her hair, "and I agree."

Gently tugging her strands, I linger my other hand over her soft mound until I'm barely teasing her hard clit, making her gasp.

"So you're going to look in the mirror," I demand, "and watch me fuck you and see how beautiful it is when you come on my cock. Because *liking* my fuck, Vale, will never be good enough." I spank her clit. She gasps. "You're going to watch your pussy fucking love it."

I spin her around, still holding her hair. "Step your legs apart," I order, "and straddle the mirror. That's it." I take her hand, then her other. "Put these on the wall. Don't move them, and bend over for me."

She arches her back, sighing, "I like it when you're a beast, Nash."

"It's clear you do, my poison. Look down."

A milky drop of my cum has fallen from her pussy to the glass from our first time.

"Such a dirty girl," I taunt. "I need to clean you."

I kneel, straddling her mirror, too. It's only a foot or so. It's not hard, but goddamn I am. I get rock hard, pulling her cheeks apart, my tongue searching for our taste. When I dip it inside her opening, savoring our salty tang, she moans.

"Are you watching?" I ask before coaxing my tongue over her clit, making a show over pointing it, darting it over her little pearl so she can watch. "Are you watching me eat your beautiful pussy, Vale?"

"Yes," she sighs.

I keep going, fluttering my tongue over her clit before dragging it down to take another taste of us, then I lave it up to her little puckered hole and circle it, over and over and making her groan.

Oh, what I want to do with her.

And I will, but what gets me off the most is doing this for her now.

I tongue her puckered hole, then her pussy, then her clit. Eating her is becoming my greatest kink until her thighs quiver.

"Nash," she cries, "please, I'm ready. Please fuck me."

"Hmm." I rise, giving her plump peach a bite. "When you talk like that, poison, I never want you to shut up."

I stand behind her, dragging my swollen tip through her soaked lips, and she trembles. Then I rub it over her clit until she's arching and lifting on her toes for more.

"Are you ready for this?" I tease her entrance.

"Yes, Mr. Allen. Fuck me like a dirty girl and make me watch."

Goddammit.

Smack. I spank her ass, and she squeals.

"Keep talking to me like that, Vale Monroe, and I will fuck your dirty girl pussy so hard, I'll make you my woman forever."

"Promise?" she gasps, but then I slowly urge inside her, leaving her no choice but to moan at my stretch.

I know I'm big, and thankfully, I know how to use it. I grab her hips and go slow. The first time I was inside her, I lost my mind; I knew I would. But now, we're going to find this together.

I gaze down, staring at the stunning sight of my cock, sliding into her slick, hungry pussy. *Goddamn, she gets so wet and swollen for me.* Slowly, I pull out, admiring her milky lust coating my shaft.

Fuck, it drives me insane, urging my tip inside her again, getting ready to claim every inch, every breath of hers; her moans belong to me.

"What do you see, Vale?" I want her to have this. I want her to feel this because I need it, too. I need this with her and no one else. "Tell me, baby, what do you see in the mirror?"

She's looking down, her hair and breasts swaying with my thrusts. "I see your hard cock." Her voice trembles. "I see it parting my lips ... and ... oh god ... oh god, you're sliding into my pussy; I feel it so much, Nash. I feel you everywhere. My god, you're huge and get so hard for me. You stretch me open... *aaaaaa*," she moans as I drive in deeper.

"I love it," she gasps at my next thrust making my eyelids flutter, lust pumping through my veins, pumping through my cock.

She does this to me.

With my left hand, I hold her hip; I guide our tempo. With my right, I put my fingers in my mouth, wetting them with my spit until they drip before I reach around and start circling her clit.

"Oh god," her legs buckle a bit, so I bend mine and grab her hip harder, holding her up.

"That's it," I tell her. "This is how you deserve to be fucked, Vale. Take it. Watch your pretty pussy take it. It loves an older man with a big cock who knows how to use it." I spank her clit. "Don't you, dirty girl?"

"Yes," she cries out as I thrust slowly while my fingers

circle harder over her clit, her moans taunting my cock to do the same, to fuck her fast and furious, but I don't. I wait.

I'll wait forever to give this to her.

"Do you like it, Vale?" I change my rhythm, swaying my hips, moving in grinding circles deeper inside her swollen heat, her tight cunt making my teeth clench. "Or do you fucking *love* it?"

"I love it. I love it," she cries.

"Do you like watching yourself get fucked?" I pinch her clit. "Or do you *love* watching my cock fuck you?"

"Yes, Mr. Allen. Fuck me, Daddy. Fuck me with your big cock. Yes."

"I mean it," I growl, spanking her ass again. "You're a dirty girl when you talk like that."

"Yes, I am. Yes, I am."

I have her so close. She's surrendering to her kink, to her lust, and it's the same as mine. I wasn't supposed to lust for an eighteen year-old, and she wasn't supposed to want to fuck her best friend's father, but we did.

We do.

"You wanna come for daddy?" I rub her clit harder, faster. "You want to be a good girl and watch me make your tight little pussy come so hard on my thick cock?"

"Yes!" Vale wails. "Yes, Nash, yes. Harder. Harder."

I give her what she wants. It's what I want, too. I thrust hard, my fingers brutally strumming her clit. I'm unrelenting and committed to her pleasure, taking her over the edge. I know how. "You're such a good girl, Vale, coming on my cock while I fuck your sweet pussy."

She groans, her legs shaking against mine. "Oh god, Nash, I'm coming. I'm coming."

"Good girl, come hard," I demand, moving my hand from her hip to wrap around her waist, to hold her up as her knees buckle and she falls apart, convulsing and groaning. *Good god,*

I've never felt a woman with a pussy this strong. I feel her tightening, her orgasmic contractions milking my cock to come, too, but I clench my jaw, holding back.

She's panting, she's crying. Emotions hit me like a tidal wave, too, but I fight it. I fight for her. I need for her to feel this, to know how good it can be ... we *could* be.

I let the wave shake through her body until she stills before I gently pull her to stand. Holding her warm back against my pounding chest, I wrap my arms around her, putting my lips to her ear.

"You were never broken, Vale." Love strains my voice. "You were always *mine*."

A sob escapes her throat as I kiss the tears falling over her flushed cheek. Her cries—joy, relief, awe, gratitude, pleasure ... and something else—flood my heart.

I hold her while it rains through us. I didn't know I could feel this much for a woman. It's overwhelming and undeniable. It makes me confess everything I've hidden for years, "Poison, you take my breath away, and you can have it. I belong to you, too."

Tenderly, she smiles, leaning into me, reaching behind her to hold me. The way she leans on me, trusting me, her edges melting into mine. This is the feeling men die for.

"Nash," she's still out of breath, "I... I..." She pauses, her body writhing against mine. "You feel so good." My cock is still hard and inside her. "I think you can make me do it again. I think I really need to."

"You need to come again?"

"Please," she pants, "but let me do it. Let me ride you."

I leave her body and guide her to the bed.

Gently, she shoves me, and I fall on the mattress, almost laughing because, *hell yes, I've fallen for Vale Monroe.*

But when she climbs on top and straddles me, I'm not

laughing. I'm about to have my world rocked once again; I know it.

She fists my cock, gliding my swollen tip through her wet lips. "Mr. Allen," she teases, "do you feel how wet your cock makes my pussy? How you made me such a dirty girl, coming only for you?"

"Vale," I mutter, reaching to palm her tempting breasts. "Don't. You drive me insane talking like that."

"Why?" Slowly, she lowers, taking my length, inch by inch, and I groan as she taunts, "Did you want to fuck me? Did you want to pull my little black bikini aside and make my pussy take your hard cock like this?"

She starts gyrating her hips, rocking back and forth, making me feel how wet and swollen she is. How much she wants me. How she can take me.

"Yes," I confess. "You'd walk around in those little tanks with these luscious tits," I pinch her nipples, "and those little shorts making me obsess over your pussy. Such a dirty fucking girl. Making me want to yank them down and fuck the hell out of you."

"Oh god," she sighs, changing her tempo to slowly ride me up and down, stroking my cock inside her slick walls.

She gets off on this, our forbidden desire, and I do, too. For too long, I was ashamed of it. I hated myself for it, but it's not wrong. Not now. Not when she feels so goddamn good.

"Show me," I tell her. "Spread your lips open, and let me watch you fuck my cock like a good girl."

"*Yesss*," she shudders, reaching down to obey, opening her lips wide to let me see, see how she's glossed my shaft with her lust, see how hard her little pink clit is, see her taking every inch of me.

"Play with yourself, Vale. Fuck me while you tell me what you used to do, thinking about me."

Blood roars in my veins. My dick throbs to come, talking like this, watching her do this, but I don't. I growl it back, waiting for her.

"I used to finger myself," she confesses, gazing down at me, her fingertip circling her clit, her pussy riding my cock. "I used to imagine doing it for you, right in front of you like a good girl and making you come while I call you 'Daddy.'"

"Oh fuck." I arch my back, grabbing her hips.

"I used to want to be so bad for you." Her breath is changing. She's getting close. "I *do* want to be so bad for you, Nash. Let me. Make me do the dirtiest things for you, with you, because I want to. Please."

Goddamn, if she insists.

I lift my fingers to her mouth, pressing them to her lips, and she sucks them, moaning. Then I take them out and reach around. The moment my fingertip circles her ass while she's fucking my cock, she groans, her eyelids fluttering.

"That's it," I tease, pressing my finger inside her. "You want to be dirty for me, Vale? You want me to fuck you in front of my brothers?"

"Yes," she gasps, leaning forward to rub her clit on my shaft, bracing herself against my pecs as she rides me harder. "Please."

Fuck. Hang on.

I slide another finger into her ass, and she groans, shaking when my other fingers tug at her nipple. I want to suck it, but I can't, not while I'm taking her over the edge. Not while I give her this. *This will take her. It'll take me, too.*

"You want me to show them how I make you my dirty girl?" I pump my fingers. I pump my cock. "You want me to fuck your tight, virgin ass in front of the kings? You want to be my queen?"

"Yes, Nash. Yes," she cries out, bucking on top of me, her

orgasm locking her eyes to mine as it crashes down through her; she's beautiful.

Too beautiful and mine.

I grab her hair and pull her to me, my hips hammering, my cock pounding harder inside her. It makes her orgasm last, her eyelids fluttering, her lips shaking over mine. We don't kiss, but I swear to her, "You're mine, Vale. Always. Every inch of you is mine to have. No one else."

I keep pumping my fingers in her ass, my cock in her pussy, white heat building in my spine, the pressure about to explode. She keeps groaning and convulsing. "Say it," I growl.

"Yes, Nash," she stutters. "Oh god, yes."

I hold her tight and let go, making her take everything I have. It's hers. She's mine. *She makes me come so fucking hard.*

I'm an evil man for wanting her, a redeemed man for having her. I will burn in hell for this heaven, and *let's go.*

I was going to hell anyway.

CHAPTER TWENTY
VALE

"Not that."

I step out of the bathroom in my third golf dress, and Nash is fuming.

"What?" I twirl in the black racerback sporty mini. "It's what women wear to play golf."

"I said nothing sexy, nothing cute, nothing hot, and you heard me."

I sashay toward Nash, seated on my loveseat with his arms thrown over the back like a king, while I confess, "I didn't hear you."

"I said it right next to you in bed this morning."

"Yeah, but you were all like words, words, words, and my eyes were all like, 'Look at this orgasmic man with muscles and ink beside you,' so I wasn't listening."

"Well, then, hear me now; you're not wearing anything short."

"What?" I stomp my white golf sneaker. "You think I'm playing eighteen rounds in a hoop skirt? Shall I get the vapors and pass out for you, too?"

I press the back of my hand to my forehead, my eyes rolling while I drawl, "Oh, *Naassshh*. How can I play golf with all these sticks and balls you men are swinging? And then when you yell, 'get in the hole,' I'm overcome. What is a girl to do?"

He narrows his eyes. He wants to laugh. I can see it.

"You know," he seethes, "it's arousing for me to see you like this." He lowers his gaze before combing up my bare legs. "Because no one else sure as fuck will."

I flit my hand at him. "I like this whole jealous mafia man thing you have going for you. It really brings out your eyes."

"I'm about to bring something else out to make you shut up and listen."

I lift the hem of my dress. "Promise?"

"Vale!" he snaps. "We're going to be late."

"We'll be real damn late if you keep freaking out about what I'm wearing because I only have three dresses left from my tournament days, and you popped a blood vessel in your eye at each one, so pick the lesser poison and let's go."

His lip snarls.

Damn, is he related to Elvis?

"The white one," he insists.

"You don't want me wearing the white one. It's too thin, and my nipples get hard when I beat men, and then you'll have to murder them, and all that blood will ruin my dress."

He doesn't answer. I'm getting too close to the truth.

"This one." I smooth my dress. "I'll match you in all black, and we'll look cute together."

"Yeah. That's the look I'm going for."

He deadpans because with each minute, Nash is going all Bratva on me. His gun is strapped to his ankle. His stainless steel belt buckle hides two small knives. He'd hide brass knuckles under his golf gloves, too, if he could.

On the drive over the bridge to the golf course, my knee won't stop bouncing.

Three times, Nash glances over and sees it. "Ask."

He knows I'm dying to. "Are you going to kill him? It's killing me to know."

He doesn't answer. He's hiding the truth behind his non-polarized sunglasses. They're designed not to interfere with his depth perception and to turn me on at the same time.

Who knew I'd fall for a man so good at murder and my former favorite sport?

"Can I say something to him?"

He almost laughs. "Can I stop you?"

"Uh! I can control my mouth for a day."

"Is *it* aware of your ability to keep it shut?"

"Are you aware you're being a big dickhead?"

He turns onto the main road to the country club and course. When the guard at the gate sees him, he nods and quickly lets us drive through.

"Listen." Nash parks, turning the engine off. "I need to debrief you."

"You need to take my panties off?"

"Vale!" he barks. "Get serious."

I exhale, making my habit of snark when I'm nervous pass before I inhale and answer, "Okay. I'm serious now."

He turns to me. "This man we're about to play, Claude Olan Turner the Fourth, comes from a long line of violent men. His father was arrested for assaulting an officer. You know her, Cade Bryant."

"Cade? Yeah, I know her. She's a loyal Delta's customer."

"Well, you also know how Stacey, your boss, was formerly married to the piece of shit senator, Gentry Evans, who was secretly running a trafficking ring using golf tours for men to disguise it. Stacey and Cade helped to bring Evans and his operation down."

"Yeah," I reply slowly, my brain processing fast.

"Well, Turner the Third was second in charge under Evans. He secured the contraband."

"You mean the trafficking victims."

"Yes," Nash answers. "But with both men behind bars, it created a power vacuum, and the young Claude Olan Turner the Fourth filled it, and he's worse than his father. Too preppy to suspect. Too rich to stop. Too young to know when to."

My pulse doubles. "How do you know all of this?"

"We hear rumors that lead to sources who give us intel."

"So you and your brothers stopped him?"

"Not yet. I found the money trail. I figured out his last ... *shipment*," Nash uses the word with disgust, "but we were too late. They were already sold."

"Sold?"

"A dozen girls sold at Myrtle Beach."

My face bends. My heart breaks. "And the cops don't *stop* him?"

"They can't catch him. He's an evil fucking genius."

"So now what?"

"We were getting the intel to stop him, to uncover his entire ring and associates. I was on his money trail, in his online accounts, figuring out how he operates, and that's how he found me. He detected me hacking and found me through a VPN that wasn't so well encrypted after all."

"And that's who was following us that night? He's the man who tried to kill us?"

Nash reaches out, his fingertips brushing my cheek. "I'm sorry I got you into this. Bet you wish you took that Uber."

I lean my cheek into his touch. "Bet the driver wouldn't have made a minivan look as hot as you did."

He grins ... barely.

"This is serious, Vale. This is the hunter being hunted. He's aiming for me; he'll recognize you, but he won't blow his cover in front of his date. To the rest of Charleston, he's just a wealthy asshole, so he'll play along. He's a gambling addict and an average golf player. We need to play him until he's our pawn. I need him in the clubhouse after the tournament. I need him right where we can get him."

I nod. For all my snark and sass, I can set it aside and get damn smart. "What do I say?"

"Nothing about my brothers. Nothing about Alena. Nothing about yourself other than you're a beautiful woman who's about to beat the shit out of him in golf."

"Who is he playing with?"

"He registered to play with a woman. Daisy Lantry. We looked her up. She's a former debutante and Southern royalty. She has no idea who Turner really is."

I grin. "Oh, this will be fun."

"It's not fun, Vale, it's work."

"Oh, I'm gonna work him alright."

Finally, Nash smiles.

"BEST OF LUCK TODAY, AND WE LOOK FORWARD TO SEEING you at the after-party!" The course's golf pro finishes his welcome speech, kicking off the tournament as Nash and I turn for our golf carts.

"Here we go," he mutters because our cart is parked next to Turner's.

Together, our foursome is supposed to drive our two carts to the first hole and play like friendly competitors.

So much for that.

After we secure our bags to the back of the cart and turn

toward him, it's almost amusing watching furious recognition fire across Turner's blue eyes before he hides it.

"Hi!" His date offers her hand to shake. "I'm Daisy. This is Olan, and I guess we're a foursome today."

"Hi." I shake her hand. "I'm Vale, and this is Nash, and let me apologize in advance for today because I have a case of the shanks."

She smiles, tipping her head, confused.

"I'm overthinking my swing," I explain. "I've been shanking the ball into the rough for years."

"Oh, that's okay." She seems genuinely nice. "I'm not the best player, either."

But she is gorgeous, and Claude Olan Turner the Fourth looks like a tall, sandy-haired Abercrombie model who hides his evil under the navy sweater jauntily draped over his narrow shoulders.

He even reeks of fierce cologne and perversion, too. He doesn't shake our hands. He doesn't introduce himself. He's got to be wondering why Nash is here, covertly confronting him, but Turner's ego is too big to back down.

"Let's play," Nash offers coldly, so I take the passenger seat in our cart. Nash glares at Turner, then smirks, gesturing with his hand as he taunts, "We'll follow *you* this time."

Good god, Nash is so sexy when he's a smartass. Wonder who's the bad influence on him lately?

While we follow them down the cart path, he quietly asks, "So that's how you're playing this? That you suck at golf now?"

"You know me. I'll suck at it, then stick it in his ass."

He huffs, amused by my reference to the mind-blowing blowjob I gave him, "That stays between you and me, poison."

"Not today. Today, I'm going to make Turner think I suck

at golf until we take the turn to the back nine, and then I'll ram our win up his ass."

At the first hole, I play off the women's tee with Daisy.

"Whoops!" I shout after I shank my drive left, off the fairway, and into the rough, exactly where I wanted it.

Then I step away from the tee-box and Turner makes a production of helping Daisy with her first drive. He stands behind her, mounting her like a perv while he shows her how to "swing better."

I watch, rolling my eyes. Mansplaining is an epidemic nowadays.

Daisy doesn't need help. She hits a decent drive without him. Then Turner drives, hitting the ball two hundred and twenty yards. Not bad. It's average. So Nash does the same.

We let Turner win the first hole at one over par. "That's a thousand," he boasts at the green after putting his ball in. "At this rate, you'll owe me eighteen by the end."

Nash nods. He's an iceberg while I'm hot and tempting, "Let's make it interesting. Let's double it on the back nine."

Turner raises a brow. "Twenty-seven thousand? That's how much you want to lose today?"

Arrogant little prick.

I shrug. "Maybe I'll play better if I'm under pressure. Anything to cure these shanks. If not, I'm playing Army golf all day."

"Army golf?" Daisy asks.

"Yeah," I joke. "Left. Right. Left. Right. That's my game lately. I can't drive it down the middle to save my life."

"You need to adjust your hips when you swing." Turner ogles them.

No, shit.

"Oh, is that it?" I sound dumb while Nash clears his throat, fuming at Turner noticing my form.

"Yeah," Turner sneers, raking his glare up my bare legs

before boldly staring right at my cleavage. "Bet those get in the way of your swing, too."

"God, Olan, you're such a bad boy," Daisy giggles. "Keep your eyes where they belong."

"Your mouth, too," Nash warns.

Shit, we won't make it eighteen holes in four hours if Nash murders Turner on the first green. Thankfully, the attendant at the drink cart calls out, asking if we want anything, and Turner takes the rookie bait. He orders a John Daly—lemonade, iced tea, and vodka—and I turn, winking at Nash.

We're off to a good start.

During the next five holes, I get to know Daisy. We let our "stupid little gossip," as Turner calls it, annoy him and fill me with hopes that I can get some intel for Nash.

"So, where did you two meet?" I whisper to her while we watch the men take their swings. They're silently ignoring the other.

"Hemingway's Bistro down in Beaufort," Daisy whispers back. "I was there with my sister. She spotted Olan first, but once I saw him, I told her he's mine." She elbows me. "But I'm making him work for it. This is our third date. He won't get lucky until the seventh."

Beaufort. I note. *Maybe that's where Turner has been hiding.*

"Good for you," I tell her. "Don't show him the promised land until he's ready to worship it." She winks at me, sipping from her water bottle. "Where did he take you on your first date? That's how they prove themselves."

"The Ribault Social Club," she answers, and I nod approvingly.

"Did he top it with the second date?"

"Not really," she answers. "We met up with some of his friends at Ladys Island Dockside. The place is cute, but I swear some of his friends are slicker than owl shit. They were hitting on me like I'm fair game. I made Olan take me home. He was in the doghouse until this date, so we'll see how it goes."

Yep, Beaufort, South Carolina. That's where he and his crew were hiding.

"What about you and Nash?" she asks. "Where was your first date?"

Do murderous car chases followed by a quarter pounder with cheese qualify as a date?

I roll my lips. "It's complicated."

"Honey," she whispers, eyeing them, eyeing us. "That man of yours is so fine, bringing all those hot zaddy vibes when he looks at you. Girl, he could complicate me like a Sudoku puzzle."

Mental note: once Daisy's wicked date is dead, take her out for mint juleps and gift her with a *real* date—a Vibe from Maude vibrator.

At the seventh hole, I need a needle and thread to sew my lips shut. I'm dying to say something. I want to bust Turner in front of Daisy because he's eye-fucked me so many times Nash is gnashing his teeth.

Wonder if that's how he got his name?

"I'm going to kill him," he hisses under his breath while we drive to the eighth tee.

"Don't kill him yet," I whisper. "I want the satisfaction of beating him first. Oh, and check Beaufort. That's where he's been hiding."

Nash stops the cart and looks at me, questioning, "How do you know?"

"I asked Daisy where they met, where he's taken her on dates. He's going to all the trendy spots, so he's got to be local. It sounds like some of his assholes live there, too."

Nash cocks a grin. "Damn, my woman, you're getting hotter with every hole."

I wink. "If you're lucky."

As the four of us walk toward our tee-boxes, I call out, "Watch out for the water hazard on the left. It's a doozy."

"Thanks," Daisy calls back.

Turner stays silent, walking ahead of us.

"What was that?" Nash side-whispers while I clean my driver.

"A trick my dad taught me. Put it in their head, and their ball will follow."

"Good god," Nash mutters, grabbing my ass while no one's watching. "I'm going to thank you so hard tonight."

Minutes later, "Fucking bitch!" Olan spews after he shanks his drive ... and *plunk!* Right into the pond on the left of the green it lands.

Bullseye, Bridge Bastard.

Turner whips around, charging my way, poking the handle of his driver at me. "That was your fault. Keep your fucking mouth closed!"

"Me?" I mouth, smiling and pointing to myself.

But Nash growls, "Speak to her again that way," gripping his driver tight, "and I'll drive your fucking skull down the fairway."

I reach for Nash's bicep, tugging him back, just in time for a tournament marshal to pull up in his cart.

"Gentlemen? Do we have a problem?"

"No," I chirp. "We're just giving our balls a bath."

Daisy giggles, and Turner collects himself, not wanting to make an ass out of himself when he wants a piece of her ass tonight.

Good luck with that.

On the ninth hole, Turner tries my trick on me. "Watch out for the three sand bunkers on the right," he yells. "You little ladies have been shanking right all day." But I also hear the four vodka drinks he's pounded down too.

It was particularly delightful when he pissed in the hedgerow on the seventh hole. Dang, the dick jokes I wanted to make, but I'm making my man proud, so I told them to myself.

Your dick's so small you're pissing on your nuts.

Are you gonna get that wart lanced?

So you're *the expert on micropenises.*

Those got me through it. I didn't snark once. But now?

"Thanks for the advice," I tell him. "Maybe if I shoot from the men's tee, I'll do better."

He scoffs, "Women can dream, but they can't drive."

"Wanna bet?" I sound like Nash, standing behind me.

"Yeah," Turner jibes, "let's bet. One thousand says you can't shoot from the men's tee and outdrive him or me on this hole."

I twirl my braid. "Ten thousand says I can outdrive you on every last hole."

He laughs, and it's evil. Turner looks like every other preppy prick on this course, but it's in his eyes—he's sick and twisted. He hides his perversion behind power and privilege. It's not enough that he has so much; he wants to take what is never his to have. Evil entitlement is wired into his violent DNA.

God, I know his type so well.

Suddenly, a memory I fight to forget fires across my mind. *My ripped prom dress. My tears. My screams swallowed by Chad's forced kiss. Taken by Chad's brutal assault.*

The mind is a beautiful thing that way.

If you're a survivor, you can smell the next predator a mile away ... or look him dead in the eye and know it.

I'd warn Daisy about her bad boy Olan, but thankfully, he won't live that long, and I can't find guilt anywhere in my body about it.

"You're on." He takes the bait before leering at my cleavage for the umpteenth time.

Whatever.

I set up for my drive off the men's tee, adjusting my grip, checking my stance.

"Watch your hips," Turner taunts.

"Watch your mouth," Nash warns.

"Olan," Daisy chides, "you're not supposed to make a sound while someone swings."

"Yeah, Olan," I say, eyeing the ball. "Did you forget?"

He can't faze me. My dad trained me. He'd try to distract me all the time. Sometimes it worked. Sometimes it didn't.

Like now.

I drive the ball, watching it sail high and long as I smile. It lands dead center on the fairway, and Nash admires, "Huh. Almost three hundred yards. The men haven't hit that far all day."

I turn to see Turner's jaw on the ground.

"Oh, I forgot to tell you." I adjust my cleavage for him. "I don't have a bad case of the shanks; I have a big case of about-to-beat-your-ass."

"That's impossible," he seethes.

"Not when you're playing a Rolex Junior Player of the Year," I answer. "You know, like Tiger was, too?" I furrow my brow. "Did I forget to mention that?"

He clenches his teeth, his thin lips spitting, "You sharked me."

I shrug. "All's fair in golf and bridges."

I make a covert reference to our car chase, and Turner narrows his eyes, threatening about more than this golf game, "You're going to look pathetic when you lose."

I smile. "Then, finally, we'll have something in common."

I win the next five holes, outdriving him from the men's tee on each. Then I put cherries on top of his eat-shit-sandwich and eagle every hole. That's two under par for those who are bored by golf.

In other words, I'm damn good.

At first, I only played to have time with my father. The only hours I had his attention were when a golf club was in my hand. I hoped if I could win games, I could win my daddy's heart.

Maybe I was driven, maybe it was genetic, or maybe I just needed a father. I became a young champion, and it went to my dad's head.

He coached me, then bet on me, screamed at me when I rarely lost, and mocked me when he made me cry about it.

The worst day was the afternoon I was awarded the Junior Player of the Year trophy. At the banquet, I overheard my dad telling one of my teammates she could be better than me. That he could coach her and "show her a few things." She was nineteen, my dad was preying on her, and something broke inside me.

He loved golf more than me. He loved himself more than me. He loved any other woman more than me, his first daughter.

That day, I gave up on him, the game, and love and never looked back.

It gives me a lump in my throat now, but I play through it like the pro I could've been.

Before I take my next swing, I glance at Nash.

He keeps giving me *that* look. It's one no other man has given me. It's the one that admires me, respects me, cares for me, and desires me, too. It's the one that says, "I'm so goddamn turned on watching you beat this man's ass; I'm kissing yours tonight."

It also reminds me of the objective. Why we're really here.

So I pull back on the power in my swing. I let Turner

match my drives and shots. Nash? He's too amused to give a shit. But what's really amusing is Turner is so invested in our bets and game, that he's forgotten about Nash. All his focus is on me, and that's the plan.

"Tired now?" Turner mocks after the fifteenth hole—the one I let him tie. "You know women don't have stamina like men. It's proven."

"Yeah," I put my putter in my bag, "I read that too. It was on the cover of *Full Of Shit* magazine. But here..." I take out my 7-wood. "Let me break your hand so you can feel the pain of childbirth and show us how much stamina you have."

Daisy giggles.

You know, even if this fucker were going to live to see tomorrow, I think I've ruined his chances of ever getting lucky with her.

"Bitch," Turner mutters, and I can't stop him.

Nash charges toward him, his hand aiming for his throat, choking him as he lifts Turner's toes off the ground. "Say that again to her so I can choke you on your last word."

"Hey, hey, hey." Some guys on the cart path stop.

But Nash only squeezes Turner's throat harder, shaking his jugular in his grasp. "Is this what you want?" Nash sneers, "A piece of me? A glimpse into my eyes before I kill you right in front of her?"

"Do it," Turner coughs. "Show them who you really are."

"Guys, guys." One of the other players runs over. "It's just a game. Calm down."

"Nash," I soothe his name. "My king, I'm a proud bitch, so let him go."

Nash drops his hand and Turner. Angrily, he glances around, then at me. It's not like Nash to lose his shit, and now I see one of the reasons he didn't want me here.

He's too protective of me. He forgets his mission if I'm involved. So, I keep us focused.

"They're fine," I tell the man rushing over. "They're fine, upstanding gentlemen who just forgot themselves because the wagers are so high."

I direct my question at Turner. "Right? We have ten thousand that says I can eagle the last three holes." I cock a brow at him. "Each."

"Thirty thousand?" The other player is shocked. "That's too much. No wonder you guys are losing your shit out here. Who do you think you are? Duncan Monroe?"

"Better," I answer him and Turner. "I'm his daughter."

Turner's nostrils flare. I've sharked him again, and he's furious but also hooked. "You good for it?" he challenges.

"She is," Nash answers as if he'd bet millions to watch me win.

The other player walks away, shaking his head. Daisy's shaking hers, too. She looks half proud of my tactics, half betrayed that I lied about who I am.

Sorry, Daisy. We're playing by Bratva rules now.

That's who I feel loyal to—Nash and his brothers—not the legacy of my father, his name, or even my ego.

I eagle the sixteenth hole. That's two strokes under par.

For an extra fuck-you, I double-eagle the seventeenth hole at three strokes under par. Yes, a winning score that low is extremely rare, but I'm an extreme bitch today.

So much so that on the eighteenth hole, I shank my drive. I aim my ball for the water hazard by the green and give Turner his victory.

His *very* last victory.

He's mocking, laughing, loving that he's getting the applause from the crowd gathered around the final hole before they give him back-slaps and usher him into the after-party.

Nash grabs my hand as I drop my putter in my bag. I turn to find his eyes in a storm of heat and ice.

"Why did you call me your king?" he demands to know.

I lift my chin. "Because that's who I want you to be, my king. I want to be your queen. No matter what."

He steps to me, looming and lovely. "I've never been so aroused and irate at the same time," he says. "You earned your name today because you're definitely my poison, and you're about to be his."

CHAPTER TWENTY-ONE
NASH

"King."

That's what Vale called me. That's what brought me back to her, back to the moment and the mission.

Does she know what that word means in my world? Does she know what it means to be my queen?

Murder pumps through my veins over Turner, and the thought of Vale made into my queen only makes my rage pound harder.

Never. As if I wouldn't gouge out eyes for looking at her. As if I wouldn't gnash throats open for touching her.

There's a plan for Turner today, and as of right now, it involves me.

I weave through the boisterous crowd in the clubhouse. Drinks are raised. Toasts are made. Bragging rights and bets are being cashed in. Aiming down the hall to the men's room on the right, I turn left, opening the door to the manager's office.

"I want in," I say coldly to Axel, waiting there.

Jace took Vale to the kitchen. He's feeding her a club

sandwich and Arnold Palmer's while we have eyes on Turner. Select trusted waitstaff. Our loyal bartender. A tournament marshal. As soon as Turner aims for the men's room, he's ours.

"No, Turner is mine."

I can tell by Axel's tone my change in plan amuses him, but he's not buying it.

"Not anymore. After how he just spoke to Vale, I want blood."

"And I want intel," Axel orders. "We leave quietly, take him to the boat, and keep him until we get what we want. You can never end the demand for what Turner sells, but you can kill the suppliers. As many as we can."

Axel sits on the edge of the manager's desk. It's just him and me and the syringe in Axel's black leather-gloved hand.

This is standard operation for us. Stellar operation, actually. We've done this too many times.

"One day, you're going to care," I tell him. "You're going to have someone you'd kill for."

"I've killed for you. I've killed for my brothers. Don't lecture me about loyalty."

"Loyalty isn't love," I rage. "You *choose* to kill for loyalty. Love gives you *no choice*."

"So you love her?" Axel softens. "You love Vale."

"I do, and I can't."

He nods slowly. "Alena."

"Yes, my other love, the other woman I'll kill for." I stand, staring down at Axel. I love him, but over this, I'll kill him. He knows. "You will *never* have her. Alena will never be a queen like the others."

"Then, at least make Vale your queen. You know she is! Make her our queen so the kings will protect her."

Red rage threatens to veil my eyes again. When I get this mad, I fight to control it. I fight to remember what I said or did. Often, I don't. It's all instinct. It's all animal. The man in me falls away, and the beast inside kills.

"No. One. Touches. Vale."

"That's *not* the custom. That's *not* the bond." Axel stands. We're nose-to-nose. "That's not how we escaped. How we've survived. How we've lived this long and will live to see another day. I will NOT be my father's son! We will make our queens and our heirs, and we will protect them. We will serve them as much as they serve us."

"You're NOT your father's son, so you can change," I argue calmly. "*We* can change."

"If you want change," he raises a brow, "talk to The Queen."

"He's on the move." The radio behind Axel is barely audible, advising that our target is on the way.

"In honor of Vale, I'll give you this one," Axel says. "Have some fun with him, but don't break him. I need him to have teeth so he can talk." He sees the look on my face. "And a tongue and ears, too."

"You're no fun."

"You're in love, and I'm not aiming your loaded fist at an asset we need. I'll already have to make Jace clean up your mess."

Blood rushes through my veins. "You didn't say anything about eyes."

Axel shrugs. "They are an inconvenience in a lineup." Long pause. "Leave him one. I want him to see it."

CHAPTER TWENTY-TWO
VALE

"Why do you do that?"

Jace watches me surgically extract a tomato slice from my club sandwich.

"These things," I dangle it over my plate, "are gross. They've got seedy jelly in it and are not fit for human consumption."

"But you'll bury your face in a bowl of salsa?" He laughs. "Don't lie. I've seen you do it."

"One time, and it was super fresh, and I had too many margaritas."

I scarf down a big bite of my sandwich, then burp my compliments to the chef.

"Manners much?" Jace deadpans.

"I'm starving," I answer. "Whooping a man's ass builds an appetite."

Sitting on the stainless-steel table of the service area for the kitchen, I swing my legs while Jace leans, propped beside me, arms folded over his chest.

He's not in his usual dark suit. So, it's hard hiding all that muscle stuffed into grey golf pants and a white golf shirt. Like a tube of biscuits, I'm waiting for his biceps to explode.

"So what now?" I whisper.

"We wait."

"Wait for what? Gunfire? Those *POW*, *BIF*, *BLAM* cartoon fight onomatopoeias to appear out of thin air?"

Jace shakes his head. "God, you're gonna make this dangerously fun."

"Make what fun?"

He doesn't answer.

"So now you take a vow of silence?"

"We all did."

"Who's we?"

Again, I'm talking to a silent mountain of muscle.

"Can I tickle it out of you?"

"Don't," he advises. "Because one, I'm cursed with ticklish spots. Two, my brothers tortured me over it growing up. And three, Nash will kill me if you touch me."

"But it would be *me* touching *you*. It would be my fault."

"Again, Nash will kill *me*."

"How well do you know him?"

"Like a brother."

"How well do you know him..." I'm probing. I'm dying to know because if I can crack any nut, it's Jace. "As a *king*?"

"Vale, don't ask or use that word." His husky voice seethes, "Don't let your mouth dig your grave deeper."

"Uh! Don't tempt me with threats like that!" I rant. "Now I *really* want to know because I know it's something kinky, and I'm not opposed. Hell, we work in a sex shop. You give me sex toy reviews on the daily. You've been my wingman in a sex club. You've held my hair when I threw up, and I've smelled your neck, helping you pick colognes." Pause. "You smell yummy today, by the way." His brow twitches. "We've worked together for over two years, and I know you love me in a sweet way, so tell me, what does it mean to be a king?"

"It's not kinky; it's sacred," he scolds. "And fuck..." He shakes his head, "Quit trying to make me talk."

"Sacred? What do you me—"

"Vale," he warns, "I'm supposed to protect you, and that's about to involve me locking you in that pantry to protect you from your mouth."

"I..."

I'm interrupted by Jace's phone buzzing in his back pocket. He takes it out, checks it, and grabs my arm. "Let's go."

"Where are we going?"

"To see your king," he hisses while leading me down a hall.

With a tap-tap, tap, tap-tap-tap on the manager's office door, it swings open, and I gasp.

It's Nash. Shirtless. Sweat glistening off his muscles. Breath huffing from his lungs. Murder in his eyes. Blood dripping from his hands.

"Give her to me," he growls at Jace, who lets go of my arm, only to have Nash yank me by my other arm into the room.

"She's all yours," Jace says most tenderly as he closes the door behind him.

"What happ—"

I don't get to ask the question.

Nash presses a bloody finger to my lips. "King? Is that who you want me to be for you, poison? Your king? Or is that a cute nickname because you have no fucking idea what you're talking about?"

This is the beast. This is the side of Nash he warned me about. I can smell his victim in the air. Sweat. Blood. Tears. Piss.

It's in a puddle across the room on the floor.

Nash made Turner bleed and piss himself.

"I took his eye for looking at you and a piece of his lip for talking to you," he snarls. "No one disrespects my woman."

The backdoor to the manager's office is cracked open, a beam of sunlight streaming in. That's where they took what's left of Turner. It's the only light in the otherwise dark room.

And I know.

I'm in a room with a beast.

"I know what I'm talking about," I answer, proudly tasting the metallic blood on his finger. "I want you to be *my* king."

It's the beast in Nash who almost slams me against the door. It's the monster in him who smears the blood off his hands, framing my face with the evidence of his violence. It's the savage in him, lifting me, pinning my body against the door before he reaches, ripping his zipper down. He's an animal in heat, about to breed me, freeing his cock, before jerking my panties aside.

"Spit in it." He holds his hand under my lips, and proudly, I look into his merciless eyes and drool for him, letting it pool in his palm.

With anyone else, I'd be terrified. I'd be triggered. I'd be fighting back, but not with Nash. Faced with his force, I don't flinch. Deep down, all I feel is safe.

He's *my* monster. He's *my* beast.

He coats his cock with my spit before wedging his fat tip into my entrance. I know he wants to thrust brutally. But he doesn't. He growls, slowly driving into me, but it's me. I'm the one who feels like a beast, too.

"Fuck me like a king fucks." I wrap my legs around him, sinking my nails into his back. "Make me take it like a queen."

With his teeth, he holds my neck. He's marking me, bruising me, and I'll wear it with pride. Like an animal, he fucks me against the door, his hands gripping my thighs so hard, they'll be bruised, too.

He doesn't speak. His erotic mouth is gone, seized by the beast inside him. The only sounds are his grunts, my groans, and the force of his body slamming mine against the door.

"Whoa, dude." A voice in the hallway outside marvels. "You hear that?"

Our audible audience makes Nash thrust harder, stretching my tender sex so much I'm moaning for it.

"Fuck yeah." Another voice exclaims. "They're fucking like animals."

"Fuck off," Nash growls, and they listen. Their sounds retreat into the bathroom, the door slamming closed.

"You want this, Vale?" He pulls his length out before ramming it back inside me, making me cry out. "You want to be my queen?"

"Yes." I press my forehead to his, sweating and furrowed.

"Play with your clit," he growls. "Come on my cock, and prove you like it like this, too."

Once I reach down, gliding my fingertip over my sensitive hood, I shudder. I'm going to come. I know it. Nash knows it.

He lifts me higher, giving me another angle, his cock rubbing that sweetest spot inside me. "Oh fuck," I huff. "Oh fuck, that's it."

"Do it," he demands. "Fucking come so I can fill you with mine."

Pressing down on my nub, I rub hard, matching the maddening intensity of the tender spot Nash is claiming inside me, the dual sensations so intense. The urge is overwhelming. It's like I have to pee, but I won't. I'm coming.

"Oh fuck!" I praise, biting his shoulder while I shatter, and he buries himself to the hilt inside me, and we don't move. I feel his cock jerk, his bite sinking again into my neck. I feel my walls clenching to claim him, to make him growl with my flesh gnashed between his teeth. We let the violent release, the intense connection, the orgasmic pleasure take us together, our breaths and bodies fused.

"Nash," I sigh in awe, in love.

I expect him to say something like he always does. Something tender that sews the pieces of me back together. Only he can.

But he doesn't.

He pulls out, and I drip. He lowers my feet to the floor, and he kneels. Swinging my legs over his shoulders, he doesn't say a word. I'm braced against the door as he spreads me open, burying his face in my pulsing pussy as he groans, feasting on our fuck.

"Oh god," I moan. He's going to make me do it. He's going to make me come again. He's going to leave me no doubt he's an animal.

He jerks off to it. His cock is still hard. He's going to orgasm again. Yes, men can do it. He may not ejaculate, but he wants this. He's starving for it. It makes him come, eating my pussy out, so I sink my hands into his hair and force him to do it.

"Yes," I stammer. "Eat my pussy. Drink our cum. Treat me like a fucking queen."

He grazes his teeth over my clit, his fist pumping hard. Barely, he bites it, and I scream, my thighs shaking over his shoulders. I stare down, watching him glaring back at me like a feral dog, his muscles tense and twitching as he clasps his puckered lips around my clit and sucks so hard I have to come. I have no choice. I cry out, glossing his face with my lust, and it makes him grunt, rolling his eyes like he's coming again, too. His thighs quiver until he stops pumping his cock.

Shaking, my body sags. I slump against the door, and he catches me. He lays me on the floor where I know he just violently tortured an evil man.

"Open your mouth," he commands.

I part my lips for him. I let him mount over me, his cock still rigid while he drools the taste of us over my waiting tongue.

I stare back at his shadowed face and proudly swallow while he says, "That's what it would be like if you were my queen."

Wait.

Would? If? Were?

Not *will? When? Are?*

I see it in his solemn eyes. The beast is gone, and Nash is here.

He's telling me...

It's over.

CHAPTER TWENTY-THREE
NASH

Vale isn't talking. She's looking away from me and staring out the passenger window.

Three times, I glance over at her, inwardly hating myself. I've left a horrific, biting bruise on her neck. Bruises on her exposed thighs.

A bruise on her broken heart.

"It's for the best," I tell her.

She doesn't answer.

"You know it had to end. You're safe now."

Silence.

It's not like Vale. She's not snarking or snapping. She's not fighting back. She's retreating. She's hurting.

I *am hurting her*.

"You need to get tested," I demand. "I shouldn't have done that." We're driving over the Ravenel bridge while I regret the last hour. The last month. Though I'll never forget it. "That wasn't my blood, and you need to be tested now. You have to take care of yourself."

More silence. More pain.

Sunset flames across the sky. The wide river churns below.

My muscles ache after the violence, the sex. But it's my heart I'm listening to. I'm driving Vale home because I can't stop hurting her.

"I'm sorry I did that," I mutter.

Sorry, I did what? The list is so goddamn long.

Sorry, I've wanted Vale since she was eighteen.

Sorry, she's my daughter's best friend.

Sorry, I'd do anything to protect her.

Sorry, still, I put her in a deadly situation.

Sorry, I used her to trap a man I want to kill.

Sorry, I didn't kill him. Yet.

Sorry, I fucked her like an animal.

Sorry, I shared secrets with her.

Sorry, I shared my heart with her.

Sorry, she gave hers to me.

Sorry, I made her love me.

Sorry, I fell in love with her, too.

So sorry ... *I have to let her go now.*

"Vale, speak to me."

She doesn't. She won't look at me. She's frozen. Her body, I ravaged, sits silent and still in her seat except for her hands folded in her lap. *They're trembling.*

"I'll still see you at Delta's sometimes," I warn her. "I haven't finished auditing this year's transactions. I have about a month's worth of work left."

I take the exit, slowly driving toward the French Quarter. I wish I could turn this car around and bring her home with me, but that's Alena's home, too.

Though Vale is safe now, our secret isn't. It's the greatest risk.

"I'll see you at the wedding, too. All the events for it. Alena is going to look so beautiful." Pause. "So will you."

Quickly, she swipes a tear away, a tiny sob escaping with it before she chokes it down.

"Poison, don't cry." Rocks suddenly strangle my throat. "You know I don't want to do this."

"Then don't," her voice trembles with her whisper to the window.

"We can't..." I clench my teeth. I hate this, too. "We can't go on, Vale. We're going to get caught. We're going to hurt Alena."

I circle her block three times. It's not out of compulsion or safety. It's to delay the inevitable.

The pain. The goodbye.

It will never be the same. *I* won't be the same.

Yes, I can be an evil, violent man. Yes, I can be a loving, devoted father.

And now I know I can love a woman more than I love myself. I can break her heart because losing her best friend will break her even more. I can destroy her because it will kill her to hurt someone she loves.

I won't move on. I won't feel this way for anyone else. I won't sleep with anyone. I won't hold anyone so tight against my heart that it beats only for her. I won't wrap my body around someone and give them every part of me. I won't be with anyone else because I can't be with her.

"Vale, please. Talk to me." I swallow hard, parking my car and turning the engine off.

Her cute red bicycle stares back at me from the car's hood. It mocks me with the life Vale had before I ruined it.

She doesn't like to drive. Her mother was killed in a car accident. I went to her funeral with Alena. Vale was twenty-five, sobbing by her mother's grave as I held her in my arms.

I don't think she remembers it, but it was the first time I really touched her. The first time I held her. It killed me feeling her pain. I couldn't protect her from it. I couldn't fix it or end it.

So now Vale pedals her bike around, to the local market, to the bookstore, to work, to the park by the river.

I've watched her. I've followed her. I told myself it was to protect her. But really? I'd smile, and that's rare.

The way she only buys a day's worth of groceries. The way she puts them in the black basket on the front of her red bike. The way she buys two paperbacks a week. The cute way she dresses like she feels nothing when she feels everything. The way she feeds the pigeons at the park. She doesn't shoo them away. She knows what it feels like to not be wanted.

And now I hate myself for making her feel not wanted, too.

I'm making the damage left by her dad even worse. I'll murder any man who hurts her but him. That would only hurt Vale more.

Because I *do* want her. I want everything with her. If she had been mine, I'd never let her go.

But she belongs to my daughter. She belongs with her best friend.

It's what I love the most about Vale. She loves my daughter as much as I do.

"Vale, please," I plead to her raven braids. Gently, I touch them. "I won't leave until I know you're okay."

Slowly, she turns to me, and I have to close my eyes at her tears. They're silently streaming down her stunning face.

"I won't be okay," she says.

No snark. No sass. No smartass quip or cute banter.

"Nash?" She's asking for everything I can't give her. Everything we can't have.

I open my burning eyes to the tears pooling at the corners of her lush lips. Lips that are shaking, holding back her pain. It's the same as mine.

"I'm sorry," I choke, barely able to speak.

"Sorry doesn't fix it," she answers. "It doesn't fix me. It

doesn't fill this ache in my chest I've had since I was a child. It doesn't make me trust since I haven't after my prom night. It doesn't make me laugh ... or love." Her chin trembles. "You did." She bites her lip hard before whispering, "And you never even kissed me."

"Vale." I reach for her, but she turns too fast. She opens her door. She won't look back.

"Leave," she says. "I'm serious. I can't breathe as it is."

"I can't either," I confess. "I can't fucking breathe without you."

I'm suffocating in this, too, but it doesn't stop her. I don't stop her. I'm breaking her heart, but I won't take her pride.

She's shaking and shutting my car door. She's holding her wet chin high and walking away. She's grabbing the railing to her stairs like she'll collapse, but she doesn't. She's holding her stomach, hugging herself like she'll be sick, but she's not. She's opening her apartment door, then closing it behind her, like her heart.

And I sit here for an hour as the sun sets and night takes the sky, waiting for her to turn on her lamp. Waiting to see the warm glow of her light telling me she's reading or writing. Something.

Please, poison, be okay.

But she doesn't.

It's all dark.

For days.

CHAPTER TWENTY-FOUR
VALE

When I turned twenty, my father forgot my birthday.

He remembered all the years before. It was hard to forget because he had two daughters who shared the same day.

So, he sent a card with a hundred dollars, as if he could buy himself out of his guilt for not being around, and he'd call to wish me a happy birthday.

But he never said he loved me.

That year, Blair was away at Alabama, where she went to college. Alena was on a field trip with her senior class, and my mom was alive, but she had a work trip in Atlanta that she couldn't miss. Of course, she called, suggesting we video chat over pizza to celebrate.

But then there was a knock on my apartment door. I looked through the peephole and choked back tears.

It was Nash. He had a brown bag with cheeseburgers and a bouquet of red tulips. At the time, he said Alena sent him to check on me. I still think that's true.

But now I know he drove four hours just to see me.

We sat at my little kitchen table and ate burgers while he

asked about my classes. He smiled when I told him I had a 4.0 but turned to stone when I told him I didn't have many friends at Clemson.

I didn't fit in. I never fit in.

I had a roommate who tolerated me. Guys who fucked me but never asked me out. And a best friend and twin hours away, but the thought of them was good enough. It got me through.

So, Nash took me to the bookstore that night and spent over five hundred dollars on my wishlist. At the time, he said the books were for school.

Now I know he bought them to keep me company since he couldn't.

When he left that night, I got that hollow ache in my chest, the one you must get when someone breaks up with you. That's what I figured at the time. I was right.

But this ache doesn't end. I can't find the bottom of it. I just keep falling deeper into its darkness.

For four days, I call in sick to work. I blame it on my period, which I force to start by taking off my patch. I want to bleed it out of my body, every last pain over Nash.

It doesn't work. Forgetting him will be a slow death.

Blair and Stacey bring me food. I ask them to leave it at the door. I tell them I have a migraine, too. That I don't want to let in the light. It's not a lie.

I want to lie in darkness. I want my sheets to stop smelling like Nash, but I'll never wash them. I want him to stop texting to see if I'm okay, but I won't block his number. I want to answer him and say I'm fine without him. Go to hell.

But I don't.

This is hell. Love, you can't have. Love, you have to lie about. Love, you have to let go.

I'm avoiding Alena because she'll hear it in my voice. I'll

burst into tears the first time I hear her sweet voice; I know I will.

I need time to stop crying. But I don't get it. After five days, Alena's knocking on my door.

"Vale," she calls out, "you better be shacked up with some hottie in there. And you better get your ass up and open this door and let me see your fuck-hair and smile, telling me you're just getting railed and you're fine."

I don't answer. My stomach twists. She's too close to the truth.

"Vale, I'm serious." She whimpers, "You're scaring me."

"I'm coming." My voice cracks. I'm dizzy, opening the door to the blinding sunlight and her sweet face.

"Oh my god," she gasps. "What's wrong?"

"Nothing." I shield my crying eyes from the sun.

"Don't lie to me."

"Okay, fine." I let her step inside. "It's some hottie from the sex club. He railed me properly and gave me fuckhair, and now I'm having a pity party because it's over."

I'm not lying to her; I'm twisting the truth to protect her.

"Oh my god," she gasps again, horror hitting her face. "Your neck. Your legs. What did he do to you?"

"I asked him to do it." My bruises don't hurt as much as the truth.

"Vale!" she explodes. "Did this guy hurt you? Did he ra—"

"No." I stand, hanging my head. "I wanted him. I wanted everything he did to me, and now he's gone."

I turn, seeking my bed, and she follows.

"Why?" Alena sits while I lie down. She starts rubbing my back. "Why did he have to go if you wanted him so much? Why did he leave you wrecked like this?"

"Because... " I close my eyes, searching for a lie that feels like the truth. "Because he's committed to someone else, and I understand, even though it hurts so bad."

"So he was cheating?" she asks. "And he didn't tell you or something?"

Damn, this is hard. My pain is too deep and raw, and my lies are only digging my grave deeper.

"It's just over," I mutter, tears streaming down my face. "And... And I can't breathe."

"Oh, sweetie." Alena cries with me. She lies down, spooning and holding me. "I'm so sorry." She gives me minutes to sob. "Men suck," she mutters.

"Yours doesn't."

She's too silent.

"What's wrong?" I ask.

"Nothing. I'm here for you. My shit is stupid."

I turn around, worried. "Are you okay? Please tell me. Give me something else to think about."

"I'm fine." She rolls her eyes. "I'm just pissed because Loch isn't happy about my dad and godfather being his groomsmen, but who else can it be since he won't ask his brothers to do it."

"Does he not have friends to ask? Like you have me and Blair?"

Focusing on her makes this feel better—just a little.

"He said his brothers are his friends," she sighs. "That's why he can't pick between them."

"So then have like a hundred groomsmen on one side and me and Blair on the other. Girl, it's your wedding. If you want us doing cartwheels down the aisle, we will."

"But then that makes the service big, and I'll get nervous. You know me. I prefer wild animals over people."

"Clearly... " I can't help it. I have to make her smile. "I prefer people who are wild animals."

She laughs. I don't. But it's a start back to feeling like my broken-hearted self.

"Well," she says, "at least you didn't do your primal play

kink the week of my wedding because it looks like an animal attacked you. Clearly, he wasn't a beige flag." Pause. "More like a red flag. It might be for the best."

Her words echo her father's, and all I can feel is more pain. Pain over losing him. Pain over lying straight to her face.

It feels so wrong that Nash is right. We can't hide this, and we can't do this to her.

"Can I take you out today?" she asks. "You need air, sunshine, and five spicy margaritas."

I let her convince me to eat a little, shower, and put on my black mini with white polka dots and my Mary Janes. But I don't braid my hair. I can't. It reminds me of how Nash would unbraid it.

After a lunch of fish tacos and, yes, margaritas, Alena suggests we get my dress fitted.

"It will make you feel better," she says as we enter the wedding shop. "It worked wonders for curing Blair of her NFL dick disease."

"I don't know," I reply, aiming for the bridal side of the store. "She's still running a fuck fever over Beau Bronson. Apparently, he gave it to her so big and blue that she'll never be the same."

Alena laughs, and she's right. Standing on the platform, surrounded by mirrors, I do feel a little better. The sage green dresses she chose are stunning. They flow to the floor, cinch tight around the waist, but have a convertible top. You can twist and wear its two wide fabric straps in multiple ways.

"Blair is wearing hers twisted and over one shoulder," Alena says, admiring me. "So wear yours however you like, too."

"I like it this way," I reply. "It looks more traditional. Like a Grecian goddess style, twisted and tied behind my neck."

"Traditional?" She laughs. "Since when are you traditional?"

"Alena?" A deep voice calls. "Is that you, sweetpea?"

No. Please. No.

"Dad!" she shouts back. "We're in here."

I can't move. I can't breathe. I'm frozen, watching the horror in the reflection of the mirrors. *Mirrors.*

Nash sweeps the velvet curtain aside and does it again. He stops dead in his tracks, but this time, it's not over his daughter. It's over me.

"Doesn't she look beautiful?" Alena beams, rushing to hug him.

"Yes," Nash answers with his heated stare locked on mine. "Very beautiful."

Don't you dare cry.

You can't. You can't let Alena know.

It takes everything I have to hide the breaking inside. The crushing weight. The suffocating pain. I want to die, but I have to stay standing.

"Dad," Alena is focused on him, "you look so handsome." She adjusts his jacket collar. "See? You make a navy suit look good. Maybe now you can go on those dates you always hide from me because I know you're hiding something. A girlfriend, right?"

God, this is cruel.

"No. No girlfriend..." He swallows hard, still looking at me. "We were, uh, just here getting fitted. I didn't know you'd be here, too."

He's talking to me, not Alena, but thankfully, she's not aware.

"We?" she asks. "Is Michael here, too?"

Michael?

She means Axel, and this is so fucking brutal and cruel. Them, lying to her. Nash, looking at me. Alena, trusting us.

I can't do this.

"I'm done." I look down, lifting the hem of my dress to run to the changing room.

"But dear," the seamstress says, kneeling by my feet, "*I'm not done.*"

"But I..." I chew my lip. I fear the burn, the biting at my eyes, the tears threatening to fall.

"Hey." A voice calls out. "Where'd you go?"

"In here," Alena replies to Axel.

It gets worse. So much worse. I'm trapped as Axel enters the room, too. Yes, he looks as sexy as Nash in his navy suit, but it's ugly, the secret we hide. But they can't hide it from me.

I know.

That's how Axel looks at me. That's how Nash looks at me, too.

They know.

They know Nash has broken me, and I know their bond.

"You look stunning, Ms. Monroe," Axel says with no ire, sounding soft and sincere.

"Right?" Alena gushes. "Her twin looks equally gorgeous. You're walking with Blair. And, Dad, you'll walk with Vale down the aisle. Hell, you all will look so good; no one will look at me."

"Yes, they will." I force myself to speak up. For Alena, I always will. "No one can outshine you now or on your wedding day. You're going to be the queen."

Whoops.

I cringe. I didn't mean to use that word. It's the one Ms. Faye used when we saw Alena in her dress, and it just slipped out.

Nash clears his throat, looking away. Axel gives me a "Watch It" look, and Alena is still unaware.

I don't know the details of these men and their bonds as kings with queens, but I'm wearing the bruises of an idea.

Bruises Axel suddenly notes, his stare shocked, then masked. Bruises Nash won't confront. He's forcing his focus on Alena. Bruises I see in the mirror, and suddenly, I'm not proud. I'm embarrassed.

Mortified.

Degraded.

Abandoned.

"Please," I tell the seamstress. "I need to excuse myself."

She lets me rush away, aiming for the dressing rooms.

"Vale," Alena calls out. "You okay?"

I force my strangled throat to work. "Gotta pee."

But I don't. I hide in the ladies' room and cry, muffling my sobs with my fist, desperate for Alena not to hear me. But like every best friend, she does. She must sense it like I can feel her pain, too.

"Vale?" She swings the door open. "What's wrong?" She sees my tear-stained face. "Do you hate the dress or something?"

"No," I mutter. "I just hate seeing my broken heart and bruises in it."

She pulls me into a hug. "They'll fade. Just like this pain. I promise it'll go away."

Thankfully, when we emerge, she's right.

Nash is gone.

Axel is, too.

CHAPTER TWENTY-FIVE
NASH

"WHAT THE FUCK DID YOU DO TO HER?" AXEL BARKS, BUT I'm not in the mood for a cross-examination.

I'm not in the mood for anything.

"She's not our queen," I seethe, "so she's not your business."

"Fuck you," he hisses back.

We're in his opal black Jaguar E type. It makes me huff an ironic laugh. Vale would say it screams class and money, not crime and mafia, and she'd be right.

"It's *our* business," he says, "when what I just saw back there risks it all."

Axel saw the bite bruise I left on Vale's neck. It's darkened to a sickening purple with sallow yellow edges.

"You broke her heart," he fumes. "She ran away crying, and now she's a liability." He takes the interstate exit to the old Navy yard in North Charleston. "What if she tells Alena? What if she tells anyone?"

"That's exactly why I broke her heart; we won't be able to hide it from Alena." I confess, "Fuck, I could barely hide it back in that shop. Vale's so goddamn breathtaking, and it would kill my daughter if she saw how I'm looking at her best friend."

Axel silently seethes, but he doesn't argue.

We know I'm right. We know I'm fucked either way, but at least this way, only Vale and I suffer.

And trust me, goddammit, I'm suffering.

Thoughts of Vale own my mind, even in my sleep. I dream about our nights together. Then I spent the day wide awake, sick over how I left her. Every minute, I worry about her.

I left her crying and broken-hearted.

Does it make it any better that I feel the same? I'm sick over it, too.

I went to Delta's the next day, hoping I'd see her, hoping Vale would show up and tell me to go fuck myself. *Which I do, thinking about her.*

I'd rather her fight me than give up on herself.

On the fourth day, Jace told me, "You look like shit, and if she comes in here and sees you, it'll wreck her, too, and everyone will know. You need to leave."

I did, but not before I texted Alena, telling her I was worried about Vale's absence from work.

If I can't take care of her, at least my daughter can.

Axel parks his car outside of a nondescript three-story brick building. After the Navy left North Charleston, this former complex of buildings, officer's residences, barracks, warehouses, and more is becoming one of the trendiest spots.

It's the perfect place to hide an exclusive sex club. There's no sign above the lone black steel door we open, just a keypad beside it, ready for our code to enter. Once inside, we're greeted by a security team in a discreet front vestibule.

Here, you show your identification, surrender your phone, and get patted down as you hear the strict rules. If you break them, you'll leave with broken bones.

Nadine Faye, the owner, will make sure of it.

But Axel and I walk through security unchecked. We show no IDs. We keep our phones. We don't get patted down; of course, we're packing.

The sight, once we swing open the black, leather quilted door to the club that greets me, could almost stir my cock.

Two nude women are on the stage. They're side by side and riding their men. I recognize them. Silas and Eily Van de May are partnered with Redix Dean and his wife, Cade Bryant.

Yes, it's a small, kinky world we live in.

But they don't know me. Few here do.

Silently, Axel and I move through the large room of areas for lounging and others for sex and play, all opposite a long, sleek bar that serves no alcohol.

At the door at the end of a long hallway, Axel enters another code. It beeps open, and we take the stairs.

They lead to a large, elegant seating area at the top of the landing with plush, amethyst velvet sofas, and sapphire velvet curtains framing a large window of one-way glass overlooking the club below. Seated behind a gleaming walnut desk with ornate golden legs sits The Queen, Nadine Faye.

"Mom." Axel leans down, greeting her with a kiss on each cheek.

I do the same. She is like my mother. I haven't seen mine since I was four.

"What do we know?" She gestures for us to sit. I do, while Axel aims for the gold and glass bar cart.

He pours three neat shots of vodka and serves his mother first, then gives one to me before he takes his.

Silently, we toast before we toss it back in one shot. Russian is never spoken in this building, our meetings, or even our homes. We can't risk the exposure. Though inwardly, we say it, "Vashe zdorovie." *For your health.*

It's custom. It's how you show respect to your elders.

"He's been moving product through Beaufort." Axel settles on the sofa across from mine. "They're using I-95, the Intercoastal, and the rivers. We need to find his base there."

She nods. "How are we sure?"

"Nash got the lead from his asset, and my interrogations confirmed it."

Axel's interrogations usually involve the loss of fingernails. Then teeth. One. By. One.

In Turner's case, I took his eye first and made him look at it with his other while I sneered, "This is for looking at my woman with disrespect. Lucky, I'll take your lip and not your tongue for how you spoke to her, too."

"Asset?" Nadine raises her groomed brow at me. "You mean Ms. Monroe? Vale?"

"Yes, ma'am," I answer, shifting uncomfortably under her stunning stare.

Nadine Faye laughs at fifty-eight years old. She looks like timeless elegance, with her sable hair swept into a French twist and her bright blue eyes that could burn a hole through a glacier. She always wears Chanel, never indulges in the freedom of her establishment, and it's impossible to escape her scrutiny.

It's aimed at me.

"You and Vale," she chides, "are about as covert as a buzzing vibrator on a church pew." Axel chuckles while I clench my jaw. "What did I tell you about her?"

"To be careful," I answer.

"And yet," she scolds, "when we were at Alena's fitting, you had Vale Monore glowing like a Catholic nun in a Greek orgy."

Again, Axel chuckles, and I snort. I can't help it. If Nadine Faye doesn't shoot you with the Hellcat pistol she hides, strapped to her thigh, her Southern sayings will get you. She does everything to blend in.

You'd never know she used to be Nadia Kholodov, a Russian Bratva princess.

"We have a situation," Axel coughs, trying to collect himself. "Nash loves her. She loves him. And—"

"And you're *not* breaking my baby's heart before her wedding," Nadine fusses at me about Alena. It's a common occurrence. "But after the wedding, you'll tell her. Yes, Alena will be upset, but she's strong. We raised her that way. She'll learn to accept it because I've watched you deny your love for Vale Monroe for too long. You stand up here like a rabid wolf, watching her, so get it over with and make her your queen."

"He's fighting it," Axel interjects.

"I'm not fighting it," I answer, "because it's not happening. She's *not* my queen."

"Son," Nadine calls me, "you are one sandwich short of a picnic if you think there's any other woman who is."

I'm not sharing her.

It's my fight with Axel, but I won't say it aloud. It's disrespectful.

To Nadine, it's sacred. All queens have two kings. All wives have two husbands, a primary and a second. And all kings protect their queens, while the queens give us a future worth fighting for.

It's how Nadine escaped Moscow with her six sons—her primary husband, the head of the Russian Bratva, was sadistic and violent, but her second husband, one of his men, truly loved her. He got them out.

Nadine studies me. Axel, too. I keep my face stoic and my mouth shut. I may fight Axel, but not his mom. Not after everything she's done for me, Alena, and her mom, Lainey.

"It's only one night." Nadine reads my mind. "One night, one ceremony, and then she's all yours until the day you die, and when that happens, she will always be safe and provided for." She grins tenderly. "I can already see the pretty babies you two will make."

That punches my heart so hard I have to stifle my inhale.

To make a baby with Vale? To have a family with her? I've dared to dream about it.

Nadine points her brow so high. "That's what you want, isn't it? To grow your family with her?"

"Ahem." It hits too hard. "It's just a dream," I reply.

"Well, darlin'." She gestures to the window behind her, to the muffled music and moans below. "It's my business to make dreams come true; for my sons, it's my mandate."

Rising in her blush skirt and jacket trimmed in black with gold buttons, she's taller than the average woman and still more beautiful than most. You can see why, tragically, an evil man kidnapped her at age fourteen. He forced her to marry him and did every brutal thing to her, but she was tougher. Nadia Kholodov survived, and love made her Nadine Faye.

She tents her French-manicured fingertips over her desk and lowers her honey voice, aiming her tender glare at me.

This woman has given life and proudly taken it. She's raised her sons and me to do the same. We aren't evil. We kill evil.

I believe in her. I'm loyal to her.

"Hear me now," she commands me. "I gave you one of my sons. You know our bond. So you will make Vale Monroe your queen, and then you will tell Alena after her wedding. *That's my mandate.*"

Guilt crushes my bones, humility flooding my veins, loyalty pounding my chest. Nadine's family has given me everything, and we're about to be bound by blood even more.

It's the ultimate insult to her, what she endured, and what she fights for now if I break a vow my brothers have made to me.

Yes, one of her sons has given me the ultimate gift. I'm

lucky it's what he wanted, but still, he was willing, so why can't I be? Why can't I, for one night, form a bond that will protect Vale? Why can I see a future with her and a family, too, if I'm willing to do this?

Once.

For the first time, I can see how I can finally be happy. I can have the woman I've always wanted.

"Nash?" Axel gets my attention. He tents his tattooed fingers, like his mother, but his icy eyes glow warmly. It's rare. "You've always loved her, and now you can have her. Do it. Be happy. Make her yours. Trust me, Alena will understand."

Something softens his tone, his heart, too. Yes, he has one; he just hides it. It's all Axel has known: hiding.

But I've known him for too long. He's telling me something about Vale and me.

Or him

... and who?

I want to ask who has claimed his heart, too, but his phone chimes. It's Grant. I know his unique tone.

Axel reads the text from him, and I know the sudden look on his face.

Trouble.

CHAPTER TWENTY-SIX
VALE

"I'm fine," I assure Alena for the hundredth time. "I promise."

"I can stay." She stands in my doorway. "I can call in sick. Loch can, too."

"You're not wasting your sick days on me. Go back to North Carolina and save Smokey the Bear, and I'll see you in a few weeks."

"You sure?" Her face twists. "We have a guest room in our cabin. You can stay. Hike. Fish. Canoe."

"I can vacation in a Dick's Sporting Goods hell?" I wince. "That's a hard pass."

She laughs. "How are we best friends? My idea of heaven is roughing it, and your idea of heaven is rough sex?"

Memories of Nash eating my pussy like a feral dog flash in my mind, shooting heat to my core. "I'm fine," I pant.

She furrows her brow.

"I mean... " I stammer, "We're best friends because we're so damn different, but I promise, no primal play and heinous hickies until after your wedding, if ever again."

After Alena's wedding, I'll move. I don't want to stay in Charleston, where I might run into Nash or his Bratva brothers. I can move to Atlanta, finally finish my PhD, and start over. I can earn my license as a sex therapist and open a practice there.

Yeah, that's the plan.

Anything to escape this feeling.

"Okay." She gives me one last hug. "Then answer my texts and calls, and don't scare me again. Promise?" She flips the bird at me.

"Promise." I flip her back.

It's a middle-school tradition.

After Alena leaves, I take a shower. I force myself to eat a leftover cheeseburger, and that only reminds me of Nash and our nights at The Mercier Hotel.

Dammit! What's the shelf-life of heartbreak? How long does it last? I've never felt this way, and now I know why people do the most dysfunctional things over love. Because it really sucks losing it.

And when you lose the love of a not-mafia-mafia man, but you're sworn to secrecy? It sucks worse than math.

I can't talk to Alena about it. I can't dissect every emotion with my twin, either. Where are my amateur counselors when I need them?

For hours, I try to find answers. I start reading *The Pleasure Zone: Why We Resist Good Feelings & How To Let Go and Be Happy* because this bitch is skeptical. But then I'm informed and inspired and then tired. I rest my book on my bed, close my eyes, and fall asleep.

I don't hear the locks unlatch.

I don't hear the door open.

I don't hear the creak of the floorboard by my bed.

I awake to a giant silhouette and a massive hand over my screaming mouth, and terror rips the seams of my being apart. All thoughts are gone but survival as I kick and punch at the shadowy figure.

"It's me, poison."

"Fuck you!" I scream to no avail. Nash's palm is the size of a polar bear's.

"Calm down," he says. "I need to talk to you."

"Calm down!" I shout the second he removes his hand. "You fucking thundercunt! You scared the shit out of me! Literally." I check the sheets. "Talk about shitting the bed."

Oh no.

He does it. I make Nash smile so big and beautiful like he used to in this bed with me and...

The explosion of emotions makes me burst into tears. I cover my face because embarrassment fires through me next.

"Vale." He leans down to hold me, but I shove him away.

"Don't touch me. Talk. Leave. Then die."

"That's a real risk," he says, "and that's why I'm here."

"Of course, you are." I roll my teary eyes. "Of course, this is some Bratva bullshit and not you, on your knees, groveling to get me back."

"I..." He clenches his jaw, shaking his head. "We don't have time for this. We gotta go."

"I don't have to do *shit*." I swipe my tears away. "Because I'm not going anywhere with an assmunch, beaver trap, cock-sucker, dick demon, fuckwad, groin zit—"

"Wow, are you going through the dictionary?" he dead-pans, ripping my bedsheets away. "Grab some tampons, your laptop, a man-hater book, and let's go."

I sit up in my *Dr. Pepper Is A Woman* T-shirt and cross my arms. "Not happening."

"Oh, it's happening," he says, aiming for my dresser with an empty black duffel bag in his hand. Then I notice the gun holstered to his belt. His black tactical boots, pants, and tight-fitted shirt, too.

He's not dressed like a hot, geeky accountant. He's dressed like an assassin about to murder my lingerie drawer.

"Touch my drawers and die!"

"Indeed, poison, your pussy kills me every time."

He grabs a fist full of my panties, shoving them in the bag. Then he grabs bras, socks, T-shirts, and random shit that are not properly coordinated for my look.

"I'm not playing Mafia Monopoly with you again," I insist. "I'm not going from property to property believing I can win a goddamn thing with you, Nash, so put my shit down and leave."

He huffs a laugh. "Someone please give me a GET OUT OF VALE JAIL FREE card." Pause. "And by the way, I don't have a thundercunt, but I can be a storm of a big dick if you don't move your ass. Let's go."

"Nope."

I'm going for maximum resistance. I lean over, pulling open the bottom drawer of my nightstand. Fishing through toys, I find my Sunset Dreams dildo and lie back in bed.

He turns around, zipping the duffel closed. "What the fuck are you doing?"

"About to rain my storm on this pretty dildo."

"*Vaallee,*" he seethes.

"What? I masturbate when I'm stressed. You should try it because veins are popping on your forehead. Is that your brain finally working?"

"That's it." He drops the bag, stalking my way.

"Don't you dare." I shake my head. "You will never fuck me again."

"I'm not fucking you." He yanks my ankle toward the edge of the bed, and I squeal. "I'm telling you. Get up. Get dressed, and let's go. Turner escaped, Grant's been shot, and you and I are going into deep hiding."

"Grant?" I scramble to my feet. "Is he okay?"

"Hopefully. Turner grabbed Grant's gun from his chest holster and pulled the trigger. He had on a vest, but it was at close range. They're checking him for internal trauma."

"And Turner escaped? I thought you killed him."

"I should've," he says. "But we were getting intel, zeroing in on his base. You're right. It's in Beaufort, and we were trying to make him crack to tell us where."

"So where is Turner now?"

"He jumped off Axel's boat, and either he drowned in the Wando River, or his preppy swim team ass is on his way here or anywhere he or his men think they can find you or me."

"Dammit, this is deja-vu."

"I know." He grabs my arm. "And I'm sorry. *Again*. But I don't have time to feel anything, nor do you."

I jerk my arm out of his grasp and yank a pair of my black jean shorts from the duffel on the floor. Tugging them on, I toe on my Mary Janes, too. Then, I grab my laptop, a vibrator, some lube, and my copy of *How To Date Men When You Hate Men* and shove them in the duffel, all under Nash's irate glare.

"Take this book, too." He storms to my male genitalia stack, and he grabs the book off the top: *How To Live With A Big Penis*. He waves it in my face. "You're gonna be stuck with me again, so study this real hard, poison."

I swat it away. "It's romantasy, not reality."

"It's time to fucking go," he says.

Slinging the duffel over his shoulder, he taps it twice, and I roll my eyes, grabbing it, letting him lead the way, his gun held down and ready while we wind down two flights of stairs outside. My heart is pounding, my body sweating, and not because the threat of Turner has returned.

It's this threat: touching Nash again. His warmth and muscles too familiar and heart-breaking.

A new, white Dodge Charger is waiting where he usually

parks his Accord. He opens the passenger door and orders, "Get in. "

I do, noting aloud, "This screams I-Got-A-Little-Dick-So-I-Drive-A-Big-Engine, you know that, right?"

"My Mini Cooper's in the shop," he says, slamming my door.

But it settles in as Nash drives. We're silent. We feel the stress of the threat, the relief of being in it together, and the grief that this won't last. We'll have to say goodbye again.

I'm not afraid. The only concern I have is for Grant.

"When will we know about Grant?" I ask.

"I don't know," he answers, taking the bridge to Folly Island.

"Is someone with him at the hospital?"

"Yes."

"Who?"

"Can we play twenty questions later?"

"No," I snap. "Let's play a hundred questions right now." I turn toward him, his sexy profile making me so damn curious. "How do you make your queens?"

"Jesus." He rolls his eyes.

"Oh, is Jesus involved? Hallejulah." I narrow mine. "Answer me, or I'll start singing Bible hymns. I was a horrible Girl Scout who murdered them all."

His face falls, amused, relaxed, silent.

"Alright." I shrug. "You asked for Jesus, and here he comes." I start swaying and singing, "The Lord said to Noah there's gonna be a floody, floody. Get those children." Clap! "Out of the muddy, muddy! Children of the Lord. So rise and shine and give God your glory, glory..."

And the dickhead doesn't stop me.

He smiles, letting me sing *Rise and Shine* for him like a possessed scout selling mint cookies. Then, he says, "Can I put in a request for *You Are My Sunshine?*"

"You can go stick it where the sun doesn't shine," I snap. "Nash, answer me! Give me details. Where are we going, how long will it be, and what will I do about work? I can't miss more than I already have."

"You don't need money," he answers. "I got you covered."

"It's not about money. It's about pride. No man pays for me."

He gives a resigned exhale. "Once Delta's is secure again, I'll take you to work."

I slump in my seat. "This again?"

"Got any better ideas?"

"Books full," I answer. "But you're allergic to intelligence."

"Wrong," he huffs. "I missed the firehose of smartassery from your mouth every waking minute."

Was that a compliment?

Tough to say because this is tough, too. I can smell Nash's woodsy deodorant working overtime, the sexy aroma familiar. He looks way too hot in his felonious fashion. Even the way he drives this sportscar, like Lewis Hamilton, has me wandering down a very salacious memory lane. Too bad it's a dead end.

The sun is starting to rise, but the stormy summer sky chokes its light. The air is heavy and humid as he parks his car in the gravel lot of a marina.

My pulse skyrockets. "Where are we staying?"

"On my boat."

"But I can't swim."

He snarls, "*That's* why they make boats."

Warily, I follow him to the last slip at the marina and scoff, "Don't you have a bigger one?"

I'm talking boats.

Unfortunately, I know how big his everything else is: heart, dick, ego, rage, and his mind that reasons we can't be together.

He throws our duffels on a watercraft that's way too small to contain my immense fear of the water. Yes, I grew up in a city surrounded by it, but I was too busy playing golf to learn to be a good swimmer. Floating and fearing I'll die: that's the extent of my skills.

"It's fast, safe, and doesn't scream 'mafia in a superyacht.' Now," he barks, "get on board, and I'll find a pair of kids' floaties."

"Great, I get to cruise with Captain Asshole Ahab."

I know he'll savor my *Moby Dick* reference, but I can't savor this, letting him take my hand and guide me onboard. His warm touch makes my broken heart flinch.

I scan the boat, dreading this. It's fancy but small—like a mini yacht. It has a tiny gleaming kitchen, a little banquette table, and one cabin with one bed.

Wonderful. I'm drowning in sexual tension with him again.

For minutes, I stand silently, watching Nash store gear and provisions. Then he lifts the banquette bench, and my eyes get wide. "Wow. Sure you got enough guns?"

There are dozens and a whole bunch of lethal-looking stuff from the mafia Walmart.

"You know how to use one?" He picks up a gun, releases its clip, confirming it's full before reloading it.

"The only gun I have is my mouth."

He mutters, "Ain't that the gospel truth," before setting the gun on the table. "This is not a toy, so the safety's on. Don't play with it. I'll show you how to use it later."

While he stows food in the kitchen, I sit on the bench by the table, staring out the window. The sky is smeared with dark, ominous clouds, and the water is starting to crest with white caps.

"Please tell me we're not leaving the marina."

"We're safer anchored in the inlet than here," he answers, turning toward the helm outside.

"But it's going to storm."

"It's just rain," he replies over his shoulder. "It'll pass."

But it doesn't pass—this feeling I have around Nash now. This heavy heartbreak once the adrenaline rush is gone. Being near him has picked my wounds open again.

How else did I think this would end? How can I be mad at him when he warned me it would?

I knew he'd choose to protect Alena. I love that about Nash, which makes this hurt so much.

For a few stolen weeks, we were perfect together. Beyond perfect. It was passion beyond my wildest dreams. We can't deny it. I finally felt loved by a man, and on the edges of my pain, I can't find regret about it.

But it's as if he's ashamed of it now. Nash won't look me in the eye. He won't speak to me. He stays focused on his mission. Whipping the ropes free with the help of a dock-hand, he starts the boat's engine and aims the bow toward open water.

The rising white caps I see through the windows terrify me, and the boat rocking makes it worse. I try lying on the bed for hours, but the nausea rolls in. I try sitting at the banquette table, twirling the gun like a toy since he told me not to, and it's no relief.

The storm outside matches the one I feel inside.

When this ends, I'll have to say goodbye to Nash and fall into the darkness again. I'll have to figure out how to live without love, and I don't know what's worse.

Never having love or losing it.

Having no man love me, or having the one I love be the one I can't have.

My past bleeds into my present around him. Nash has always been there. He used to heal my pain, and now ... he *is* my pain.

The wind and waves outside make the boat pitch, swaying back and forth, but...

All I can feel is the girl inside, waiting for her father to pick her up and take her for cheeseburgers, but he never came. All I can remember is the sobbing teenager taking off her torn prom dress and throwing it in the trash can. All I want to be is the woman held in the arms of a man who kissed her hair and made that pain go away, but then he left me, too...

...and the pain came back.

It finds me running for the toilet. It retches everything out of me until I'm empty and lying on the floor, afraid this will never end. I close my eyes, helpless to make it stop. It's not the storm making me sick. It's the love—the loss.

Forever, it feels like I lie in it.

"Vale?"

I flutter my eyelids open to Nash squatting beside me.

"I can't do this."

"You don't have sea legs. It's okay." He brushes the hair off my face. "I'll take us back in."

"No, Nash. This." I touch his hand on my cheek. "I can't do *this*. Please, just let me go. I'll find someplace to hide alone. I just can't be near you and not feel like I'm broken all over again."

"Poison, I..." He swallows hard. "I can't let you go."

"I can stay with Stacey," I urge. "Ford will keep me safe and—"

"No," he says. "I mean this..." His thumb gently brushes my bottom lip. "You. I know it now. I can't let you go again. I lo—"

A sudden wave knocks the boat, tilting the vessel, making Nash fall over as I slide across the floor and slam against the wall.

"Fuck." He scrambles to his feet. "The anchor's dragging."

He steadies himself. "Vale, grab a life vest, put it on, and stay down here until I tell you it's safe."

"What about you?"

"I'm taking us back to the marina. Just hang on. It'll get bad before it gets better."

It is bad. It's the longest hour of my life. I'm not worried about mine; I'm worried about Nash. A violent squall rages outside, the waves pitching us high before we drop back down to their shadowy trough.

"Nash." I rush to the galley opening, poking my head out to the lashing rain, the howling wind making the drops feel like a thousand knives stabbing my face.

"Vale!" he barks, standing at the helm, his fists clutching the steering wheel. "Stay below!"

He aims the vessel into the waves, trying to avoid a capsize, but I don't listen. I sit on the floor by the opening. *I have to see him. I have to know he's okay.*

He's soaked, rain pelting his face, not fully protected by the windshield. He clenches his jaw, staying focused ahead, slamming the throttle down as he fights each swell, over and over. I stay focused on him, praying he won't be thrown overboard until finally ... it ebbs.

The squall passes into gentle rain, the wind and waves calming, too. We find sheltered water, but the sky is still grey, with no sun in sight. This system will last days as Nash slows the vessel, maneuvering the boat back into its slip.

A dockhand helps him tie off before Nash kills the engine. Then he glances down and sees me sitting at the bottom of the galley stairs, gazing back up at him. He grins. "You never listen, do you?"

"I was too busy ignoring you."

His grin grows. "Get busy finding the candied ginger chews in the kitchen. They'll settle your stomach, and then we'll talk."

He grabs a shammy to start wiping down the helm while I'm barely sick enough to obey.

I brush my teeth first, the mint paste helping to calm my nausea, before I rummage through cabinets, searching for the ginger candies and the meaning behind what Nash said.

I can't let you go again ... and I don't want to go.

So, does that mean he's changed his mind? He wants us to try? He wants us to be together?

Then what now? We can't hide forever, and I don't mean from Turner but from Alena.

We'll have to tell her. We'll have to break her heart and hope there's enough love for us there that it will heal. But then again, Alena will feel so betrayed by our secret.

So many secrets.

How many can someone forgive?

Unlatching the cabinet by the microwave, I peer in, pushing aside boxes with teabags, sugar, coffee, and filters. I can't find the damn candies, but then, behind an old bottle of honey, I find...

Aviator sunglasses?

I pick them up, my hand suddenly trembling with recognition, with brutal memories. I'd know these sunglasses anywhere.

Chad.

They belonged to Chad.

What are they doing on Nash's boat?

CHAPTER TWENTY-SEVEN
NASH

What the hell was I thinking? Not even in a sudden storm can I hide from this.

I'm soaking wet and absolutely sure ... *I won't let Vale go again.*

I can't see her suffer and not fight to fix it. I can't listen to her murder songs in my car and not fall even deeper in love with her. I can't feel her trembling hand on my shoulder, trusting me to protect her and not need it there for the rest of my life.

Even if it's a short one.

The Queen was right. It is a mandate, and it's not hers.

It's my heart telling me I have no choice. I can't deny it anymore. Even if I tried, there would be too many times I'd see Vale, probably with Alena, and our pain would be so overwhelming my daughter would see it. She has a big heart, just like her mom.

I've raised Alena with love, so she'll want me to have it, too. She'll accept me and Vale one day ... *I hope.*

I call Axel with my change of plans. "We'll stay at the

marina until this system passes. And yes, I've found my queen."

"Told you."

What the fuck? This asshole barely gloats?

It's not like him, and suddenly, I know it. "And you've found yours, too, you sneaky piece of shit."

Normally, Axel would run my admission up a flag pole and let his victory whip in the wind for weeks, but he hardly blows out a candle on his victory cake about Vale.

"Who is she?" I demand an answer because this is monumental. After all Axel suffered over his first queen, I didn't think he'd ever love again.

"Grant's in the clear." I hit a nerve, and he changes the subject. "No internal damage, just some wicked bruising." Wait for the rage. "We're going to rip the last pieces of that fucker apart when we find him."

"We did so much damage already," I reply, "he could've drowned."

"We don't operate on luck. *Clearly.* I can't believe Grant let his guard down."

"He feared we were losing our asset. We always check a pulse."

I can see how it happened; Turner's that sneaky, too. He acted like he was dying from his wounds, drawing Grant close enough to where he could go for his gun. Even with a bulletproof vest on, firing at close range will knock any man down. It was enough time for Turner to escape. But I doubt anyone who jumps in a river in Turner's condition could survive. The gators alone could kill him.

But Axel's right. We run on intel, not doubts and luck.

It's not luck that Turner doesn't know the identities of the men who abducted and interrogated him. The numbers on Axel's boat trace back to a bogus LLC; the same is true for mine. We wear masks. We use numbers, not names. I'm still the only one exposed—me and Vale.

If Turner is alive, we're the bait he'll come after.

"Alena?" Axel asks. "The other queens?"

"Secure. *The* Queen?"

"With Grant." Axel seethes, "And she wants blood."

"She'll get it," I promise before Axel ends our call.

Going after a man like Turner is personal for Nadine, so it's personal for us. Not killing him immediately was a strategic risk. His intel was too valuable. She doesn't just want the man in charge; she wants his entire network, including the buyers. The kind of men who kidnapped, sold, and bought her at fourteen.

They're the kind of men who, if they find Vale, will rip my heart from my chest if they hurt her. They'll—

"What are these?"

Her voice turns my gaze to see her standing at the top of the galley steps with sunglasses in her trembling hand.

Oh, fuck. She found my trophy.

Now, they're my judge and jury.

"Why do you have my ex-boyfriend's sunglasses on your boat?" she presses.

"Was he your ex-boyfriend," I ask calmly, "or your nightmare?"

"He... he," she stammers. She's adding it up. "I haven't seen him in years."

I answer with silence.

Her eyes flare, disbelieving, "Did you—"

"What have I always told you, Vale?"

"But I..." She backs away. "I just thought you—"

"You thought I wasn't a beast when I told you I was?" I approach her. "Believe it when someone shows you who they are."

She steps back, fumbling for the boat's edge. "So that means you... You killed—"

"He was a monster, Vale."

She stammers, dropping his glasses in the water like any piece of him still burns her. "So... so what are you?"

"I'm worse. I'm your beast who killed him."

The white fiberglass is slippery in the soft rain, but it doesn't stop her. She starts climbing over. "I don't... I don't want to think about him. I don't—"

"Vale, come back." I reach for her, but she jerks away, stumbling onto the dock.

"I... I don't know who you are," she huffs, turning to run.

"Yes, you do."

I jump out of the boat and chase after her. She can't escape me. She can't escape this truth. Not anymore. We need to talk about this. She doesn't make it twenty feet down the slick dock before I grab her arm and whip her around.

"You know what I'll do for you. You know who I am," I growl, "and I *know* who he was."

Her beautiful face twists with agony, fighting the memory, but the terrifying trauma fills her grey eyes. Gentle rain mists her alabaster cheeks, flushing with pain as her giant tears fall.

They fucking kill me.

Her pain is my poison.

"I know how he hurt you, Vale," I confess. "Alena told me years after, and god knows if I had known, I would've handled it the *day* after." I soften my grip and tone. "It was your prom night, wasn't it? I remember you coming to our house. I remember you crying to Alena. That's why I made you breakfast the next morning. I knew something was wrong, but I figured you got in a fight with him and broke up. I'm sorry. I should have known and..."

More tears spill down her wet cheeks, her lips trembling, holding back her truth.

"You acted different after that night." I'll never forget it. It breaks my soul to remember, "Like he stole your light."

"He stole my kiss," she weeps before lifting her quivering chin, "but I got everything else back."

I cup her cheeks, pressing my forehead to hers. "He was going to do it again. It was Alena's twenty-first birthday. I was at the bar that night. I knew he was stalking you, and I watched him roofie your drink. You weren't his only victim, we found out. But I swear to god I made sure there would be no more."

Her eyes search mine, remembering, "But I thought I got blackout drunk that night."

"You did. He made sure of it. But Axel made sure Alena got you home safely while I made sure Chad never hurt you or another woman again."

She blinks, her tears still falling and mixing with the rain.

I can't read the look in her stormy grey eyes. It frightens me, and that's rare. That's love. *I can't lose her. I can't let her go.*

"Do you hate me now?" I ask. "Do you really think I'm a monster, too?"

"No." She blinks, pausing way too long before answering softly, "Give it back to me."

"What?" I ask tenderly.

I'm confused.

"My kiss." She lifts her lips to mine. "Give it back to me, Nash. Only you can."

CHAPTER TWENTY-EIGHT
VALE

"A*re you sure?*"

I've never heard Nash sound so soft, and I've never been so brutally shocked.

He killed my rapist.

A rapist.

If I should feel guilt over it, I can't. If I should be repulsed, I'm not. If I should be afraid of Nash? Never.

I'm in love with him.

"Yes," I sigh. "I've never been so sure in my life."

"Before I kiss you, Vale," he searches my crying eyes, "you need to know something."

"Please," I stammer, "no more surprises."

Tenderly, he smiles, his lips brushing mine. "Is it a surprise that I love you? I love you, and I mean it—I'm never letting you go again. You're mine. I'll give *my* life for you, too."

A happy sob escapes before I smile. "Please don't because I love you, too." The emotions strangling my throat release with my plea, "Don't *ever* let me go, Nash. I've always belonged to you."

Those words lift a thousand pounds off my chest, my

heart lighter and beating fast as Nash slowly presses his lips to mine. They're supple and seeking, his beard soft, his touch warm, and making me stifle another sob because...

... I don't flinch with him.

I don't pull away.

I want this. I want him.

He holds my cheeks, fusing his lips to mine, and I melt into his kiss, parting my lips to let his tongue sweetly seek mine. The way he does it, lightly laving and licking, is how he's lavished me everywhere else, and my body trusts him. I respond. The heat of our kiss slowly exploring sends warm ripples of desire from my fingertips to my core. Love floods my heart, joining the sensuous dance of our mouths, and I can't help it.

I'm free.

I cry.

"Vale," he lifts away, "do you want me to—"

"Don't stop," I insist.

"But you're crying."

"They're happy tears. I like kissing you."

He gets that look. That sexy one I love to resist because I can't. "Do you like it or do you love it?" He smirks. "Like me?"

"I love it." I sink my hands into his wet hair, grinning. "Like I love *you*." I tug at his strands, yanking him into another kiss—a hot and hungry one.

Desire prowls through my body, seeking his. Tilting my head, I grab his lush bottom lip with my teeth, playing and coaxing.

It releases his deep moan as he cups my ass in his hands and lifts me. My legs wrap around his waist, my wet lips locked to his.

He pants, barely pulling away. His muscles tense against

me, like he's worried. "Are you okay with it now? With your kiss? Did I give it back to you?"

God, how can he be so terrorizing then tender?

"Yes." I clench my thighs wrapped around him. "Now, give me all of *you*."

He carries me back to the boat, sharing more of our kiss while he swings his leg over the edge. Carefully, he descends the steps below. Rain gently patters against the windows as he turns, locking the door and securing us in the galley.

We're soaked, so he sets me down by the edge of the bed before he peels off my T-shirt, and I tug at his. In quick movements, we toe off our shoes full of water before we strip off our wet clothes.

Shivers bloom over my skin, so Nash grabs towels from the small bathroom before wrapping one around my shoulders while hastily using the other.

But we're not cold. I'm hot with anticipation because he's hard for me. He sits on the edge of the bed and pulls me to straddle him, wrapping my legs around his waist again.

"Poison." He pulls my lips to his, "Fuck, baby; my chest aches in the best way. It's all this love for you. I've been holding it back for so long and—"

"I know." I'm drowning in his warmth, in his heat, too. "It's overwhelming. But I don't want to talk about it. I want to feel it with you."

My towel falls to the floor as I kiss him again, letting his tongue dance with mine, and I don't stop kissing him until I know ... with Nash ... I'll never flinch again.

His kiss only fills me with trust. Need. Desire.

I reach between our legs and grab his rigid shaft, pressing his swollen tip to my slick entrance. Without words, we do this. We moan, our lips fused as I take every inch of him. In circles, I start moving my hips over him, and Nash suddenly groans, fisting my wet hair, our bodies burning for this.

So, I thrill him. I take him. I show him, yes, we're meant to be together.

Switching my ride, I slowly move up and down, tightly clenching my walls around his swollen shaft with every outstroke.

"Fuck, Vale," he growls, nipping at my lips. "Baby, the way you move. The way your tight, little pussy grabs my hard cock drives me insane."

I give him a show, playing with my tits. I lock my eyes to his and lift my nipple to my lips, licking and sucking it.

His eyelids hood with lust. "Damn, I love my dirty girl."

I tease my other nipple, the erotic show making my pussy pulse, and he can't resist. I arch my back while he does it, too. Licking my nipple, circling and teasing it, Nash sucks it so hard; I cry out, my hips gyrating faster, my clit loving the friction.

I can come with him. I can do anything with him ... and I will.

"Nash." I tug at his hair, lifting his drooling lips from my nipple. "Fuck my ass."

He blinks slowly, his brows lowering like a predator. "Say it again, poison." He demands, "Say exactly what you want me to do to you because I'm about to be a beast again."

I brush my lips over his, loving how I can kiss him now. "Please fuck my virgin ass, Mr. Allen." He pants at my taboo taunt, "Remember our night by the pool? I've been waiting for you since then. I used to imagine you doing it, and now it's all yours."

There is no cage with Nash. I'm free. We can do everything we desire, and I've never wanted anyone like this. I never trusted anyone to do it.

But now?

"Get the lube out of the duffel," Nash orders, nodding to

it on the floor by the bed. "And that vibrator you brought, too."

I slowly climb off him, loving how his cock bobs heavy and slick with my lust. Before I obey, I kneel between his legs and fist his base. Staring into his eyes, I lick my milky desire off his shaft as he sinks his hands into my hair, and I take every hard inch of him I can until I let him hear that sweet, gagging choke he loves. *I love.*

"Fuck, poison," he groans. "I swear I'm going to fuck your virgin ass, then eat your sweet little pussy until you're begging me to fuck your ass again."

I lift my mouth off his length, letting him savor the salacious sight of me on my knees, my drool webbed to his cock. "Please do, my king."

Those words raise his eyebrow, but this time ... he doesn't resist me. *I will be his queen.* So, when I bend over for the lube and toy in the bag on the floor, I pause, pulling my cheeks apart to give him a royal show of what's his.

"Vale," he snarls. "Give me that ass now, goddammit."

He's fighting for his control, and I'm testing it. "Is this what you want to fuck, Mr. Allen?"

"When you're my queen," he fumes, "you'll bend over and take it like a good girl from me. Every hole. Every day."

I grin, rising to turn around as I set the lube and toy on the bed.

"Let me, okay?" I straddle him again. "You're big, and I'll have to go slow. When your coronal ring, you know, the widest part on the head of your penis, starts pushing against my internal sphincter, I'll have to exhale and bear down and—"

"Vale," he grabs my throat, "get out of your head and make room for me."

He uses the lube, coating his fingers with it before he

guides me to ride him again, wrapping my legs around his waist while he reaches around and starts stretching me open.

It feels so good; my clit throbs. He ruthlessly pumps his fingers in my ass, matching our tempo as I ride his cock, and he leans me back to suck my nipple. Perfectly, deliciously, loudly. "Oh god, Nash, you're gonna make me come."

Suddenly, he stops, lifting me off his hefty shaft. "Not yet," he says. "You have to be real fucking hungry to take this."

"How..." I pant. "How do you know?"

He smirks. "Shut up, Vale."

Okay, that means he's fucked a woman's ass before, and right now, I'm not mad about it. As big as he is, I'm thankful for his expertise.

Yes, I've read almost all the books. Yes, I know how to fuck and suck to an expert degree, but this is new. This is trust only he has. This is a part of me only Nash can claim first. And forever.

He picks up the vibrator. "Show me your favorite speed." I take it and click it twice.

Slowly, he presses it against my clit, letting the deep vibrations draw me to the edge again. My body aches with need over his waiting erection, and he gazes down, admiring how I'm dripping for him.

"Nash, please." I tremble. "Please, I need to come."

He lifts the toy away, and I groan, getting frustrated.

"Now..." he picks up the lube, generously pouring more over his waiting cock before he sets it down. Lacing his other hand through my hair, he pulls my stare to his. "Look me in the eye, Vale, while you slowly put my cock in your ass. Let me see how you're mine."

Good god, yes, I am.

I reach behind me, fisting his shaft, shifting my body to take him like this, to ease him inside slowly. Since his fingers opened me, the first part is easy, but like I've read, quickly, he hits that spot, and *holy huge dick*, I don't know how people can even take a small one.

"Oh." I wince.

"Do you want this?" He searches my eyes, his chest huffing with restraint.

"Yes," I pant. "Yes, I do."

Taking the vibrator from the bed, he presses it to my clit again. With two clicks, it starts its perfect hum, making that sweet, aching throb begin again.

"Now, be a good girl," he coaxes, "and relax so you can take all of my cock in your ass."

With pleasure radiating from my clit to my core, I take the burning stretch, the overwhelming pressure. I want it. I want him past the point inside, resisting him. Bearing down with a deep exhale, I tremble, letting him in.

"Stay right there." Control chokes his voice. "Breathe. Relax. Get used to the sensation." He kisses me, his tongue laving over mine before he taunts, "Get used to loving my cock fucking your ass, Vale."

He's lost in our forbidden desire, too, our fantasy denied for so long.

The sensation is everywhere. From my toes to my scalp to my lips, shaking to my walls, clenching, and needing more. "Oh my god," I gasp at the intensity, at the look in Nash's eyes. They're a storm of love and lust. They match mine.

It drives me to take more of him, to sink slowly until I'm quivering, stretched full, and sitting on his base.

"Fuck, poison." He lifts the toy away, spreading my lips open and gazing down with praise, "Look at you taking all of me, baby. Look at your swollen clit and pretty pussy, open and dripping for this. Oh, my baby girl," he groans, "you *do* love my cock in your ass."

My body pulses, needy and loving his kinky praise. I'm losing my mind to it.

"Nash," I sigh with a brave urge. It's driving me to rise on his shaft before I lower, needing him. "Please," I beg, staring into his wild eyes. "Please, Mr. Allen, make me come." I scratch his flexing pecs, pleading, "Daddy, I need to come with your cock in my ass."

"Goddamn, Vale, when you talk like that," he snarls like a beast, yanking my mouth to his. He makes me groan, loving his claim, his penetration, his tongue, his cock, *his kiss*.

Pressing the vibrator to my clit, he takes us together. I'm shaking for it. I'm kissing him for it. With another click of the vibrator against my clit, he sends me *soaring* for it.

A million bursts of light fill my eyes, my body uncontrollable as I convulse in his arms, clenching around him, my screams of pleasure swallowed by his domineering kiss. By only Nash's kiss, which tastes even sweeter as he comes, too.

CHAPTER TWENTY-NINE
NASH

"So," Vale traces her fingertip over the lion on my chest, "will I get to wear a crown?"

I laugh. "This again?"

It's still raining outside the boat's cabin while we lie in bed. I could stay like this forever, but we'll have to face it too soon.

"I'm sorry." I squeeze her tight. "I'm so sorry I hurt you. It's just for too long, I had to hide how I felt about you; it was instinct. But fuck, it felt so wrong, and I promise I'll make it right."

Her grey eyes gaze up at me. "Is this you groveling?"

"There's not a goddamn thing I won't do for you, poison. That's how much I love you. Always. So, if you want me on my knees for you—"

Her eyes dance with her dirty mind; I can read it.

"Yes," I answer. "I know where my mouth belongs when I kneel for you."

"Is that what it means to be your queen?"

"That's what it means to be my love ... if you'll take me back."

"Back? But we were never official."

"I'll make it official. But first..." My chest, with her resting on it, suddenly feels heavy. "Vale, you need to know what you're agreeing to."

"I do. I'll be your queen, and we'll tell Alena about it, about *us*."

"The first part, yes, but the second part, no."

Her face bends, hurt. "But I thought we were—"

"We are." I brush the hair off her shoulder. "We'll be together, and I'm never letting you go. This past week, I felt sick without you. It ripped my heart out to leave you, and I won't do it again. I promise."

She nods. "Once, I'll let you break my heart. Never twice." Pause for her pride. "Or I'll bite your dick off. You know I can."

I trace her nose. "I don't doubt it ... or us. We belong together, so we'll tell Alena about us, but she can't know the part about you being my queen."

"Can you please stop confusing the hell out of me?"

"It's not confusing," I answer. "It's survival. We'll wait until after her wedding and tell her about us as a couple. I hope she'll be okay with it in time, but she'll never be okay with who I really am."

"You mean the not-mafia-mafia part?"

"Yes. Once the threat of Turner is gone, there will always be another. It's the risk we take with what we do. But it gets even riskier if Alena knows, if she becomes an asset someone can torture for intel."

"But," Vale scoffs, "it's okay if they take and torture *me*?"

"Never." I cup her cheek. "That's why you'll be my queen. I'll protect you, and so will the other kings."

"Okay." She pops up, sitting like a kid ready for her lesson, and I'm the teacher. "Tell me everything. What is this whole king/queen thing, and how does it work? I know it's not like the British royalty. It's all Bratva and taboo, and I'm in."

I scrub my face, mentally parsing what I can and cannot tell her. Yes, Vale is in my world, but she can never know the depths of it, the depravity sometimes. Not everything.

It's too dangerous.

"The king and queen tradition goes way back," I explain. "It was done for survival, to protect an entire family. A king claims his queen, and the other kings agree to protect her, to provide for her and their kids should something happen to him, which it usually did." I pause. "It *does*. This is a dangerous world we live in, Vale, and if something happens to me, my brothers will protect you."

"Okay," she shrugs, "I get that part. Of course, I don't want anything to happen to you, but it's romantic as hell they'll protect me, so what's the problem?"

"The problem?" I sit up, too. "Vale, with me or my brothers, you'll be in danger for the rest of your life. Do you not get that?"

She blurts, "Do you not get women are always in danger? Hell, I can go to the grocery store and have some man grab me outside and ruin my life. Safety is not a reality for most women. But at least with you and your brothers, I have a fighting chance."

Fuck, she's right.

Again.

"Besides," she says. "I love you, I adore Jace and Grant, I can tolerate Axel, and as long as that Sire guy doesn't preach all the time, I think it'll be fun."

"Fun? There are other brothers, and they're not always fun."

Her eyes grow. "There are *more*?"

"Yes, there are seven of us. Seven kings and I'm the only

one who's not a brother. Well, not by blood. And we all answer to one woman, *The* Queen."

"Wait? What?" Can her pretty eyes get even bigger? "*The* Queen? Who is it?"

"Their mother. She's like my mother, too, and you know her."

It's beautiful watching how wickedly fast her smart brain works. "Ms. Faye!" She snaps her fingers. The CIA has nothing on my woman.

"She's Jace's mom? And Grant's? And Axel's?" She sighs, "Jeez, it makes so much sense now. God, they all have her blue eyes. Wait!" Yep, her eyes *can* get bigger. "You said your tests involve fucki—"

"God, no!" I interrupt her assumption. "We don't involve her like that. When the kings make their queens, The Queen isn't there. She's not involved, but it is her tradition. It's how she escaped Moscow with her six sons. Their father, her husband, was an evil man. He kidnapped and raped her and made her his wife at fourteen, but he did *one* thing that wound up saving her. He made her have a second husband, in the king and queen tradition, and that man, her second husband, loved her and got them out."

Vale shakes her head, taking it all in, *and there's more*, but I don't want her to run away screaming.

Not like she could escape me anyway.

"What do you mean?" she asks. "A *second* husband? First, are we getting mar—"

My heart drops. "This isn't how I wanted to ask you." I take her hand. "Let me do that part right. And later. And you fucking better say yes, but there's more you should know before you do."

She chews her lip, joy dancing in her smokey eyes. "Okay, I'll wait." Pause. "And I'll say yes."

I can't let myself be happy about it. Not until she knows everything. Because once she does, she'll change her answer.

"I won't share you, Vale. You'll be mine, and only mine, but to be my queen, you have to have a second king. We're supposed to do your ... *initiation*. Just once and never again."

Fuck, I still don't think I can do this.

I can't watch another man with her and not murder him.

"What's the initiation?" she asks, but by the curious look in her eyes ... *she knows.*

"I make you my queen in front of them," my heart starts pounding, the beast threatening to claw its way out just saying it, "and you accept a second king, too."

"Accept?" She raises a brow. "You mean *fuck*. I'll have sex with you and one of your brothers?"

"Goddamn," I groan, suddenly imagining it. It makes fury flood my veins. "I can't do it. I'll kill him."

"Who would it be?"

"You decide, and hell no, it's not happening."

We aren't tossed by a storm outside anymore, but the one inside me rages. One force says I should do this; the other says to fight it.

"But, it's the tradition," she argues. "I've studied polyandry: one wife with multiple husbands, sometimes brothers. It was done to protect inheritance and scarce resources and—"

"Traditions change," I argue back. "I won't make you do this."

"Nash." She squeezes my hand. "If I'm with you. If you're there and we'll be together ... you're not *making* me do it. I *want* to do it."

"You can't give consent, Vale." I sneer, "It's coercion, pressuring you to do this, and I won't."

"Okay, we need to make a few things clear." She sits ramrod straight, and I struggle with furor and sudden lust, trying not to stare at her tempting breasts. "I'm a survivor, I'm not a virgin, and I've been no prude. I've done things because I *wanted* to. I've been with women. I've been with men. Two men one time because I *really* wanted to come."

"Fuck!" I roar. "Don't tell me that!"

"Why not? You know it didn't work. I didn't come, but boy, did I try. It was my choice. The only thing coercing me was the search for my ever-elusive orgasm until, of course, *you* found it." She arches her brow. "And don't act like you haven't been with women. Lots of them, I'm sure, and probably two at a time."

Don't do it. Don't let her see she's right.

She smirks.

Too late.

"I didn't love them," I answer. "I've never loved any woman but you."

"Thank you," she huffs. "That's sweet because clearly, we can make the other jealous as hell, and that's what I mean. We have pasts, and we've made choices. And I *choose* to do this." She leans toward me. "And good luck making me do a goddamn thing I don't want to."

Damn, I love her.

"I won't allow it."

But some habits die hard.

"Oh, so it's only about what *you* want? How patriarchal, and please." She rolls her eyes. "I'll get what I want, too, and I want to be your queen."

"You want to fuck one of my brothers?" I'll kill them. All.

"I don't *not* want to." She twists her lips. "I mean... I only want you. I love you, too, and yes, you better ask me in the most romantic way to marry you one day and make it a big surprise. But if I *didn't* know you, it's not like your brothers aren't hot enough to fry eggs on a sidewalk. Except Axel.

He'd have to shut up because he's sexy, but that mouth of his limps my pickle."

I don't know whether to laugh or murder.

"And if I get to decide," she eases, "I choose Jace."

"Jace?" I clench my jaw, wanting to gnash a brother I love with my teeth.

"Yes," she chirps. "I trust him. He's not hard to look at, and I've known him for years. Well, not the whole Bratva brother part, but any man who holds my hair while I vomit strawberry daiquiris and nachos has earned the privilege to fuck me. *Once*."

"I'll kill him."

"Just beat him up for doing it, and then we can move on. How about that?"

"How about fuck no."

"Nash," she groans, annoyed. "You're confusing me. You say I'll be your queen, but then you say you won't do the thing that makes me your queen."

"You'll be my queen," I bark, "you just won't have a second king!"

"Will your brothers allow that?"

Suddenly, guilt steps on my chest like an elephant, denial kicks me in the balls, and resignation breaks my bones.

Everything my brothers and Nadine have done for me and Alena. We wouldn't be here without them, and soon, we'll be a real family together. They've never asked for anything but my loyalty, and I've never hated this tradition before. I got off on it, honestly ... until it was my turn.

I am many evil things, but I'm not a traitor. If I give someone my word, they have it for life.

"No."

"Because?"

"Because," I concede, "we already have queens, and they were initiated. They have second kings, and I'll break my vow if I don't do it, too. It would be the ultimate betrayal and insult."

Suddenly, it feels done. It feels like fate.

Again, Vale's brain works like a supersex computer. It's fascinating to watch. And slightly terrifying.

"Are you a second king to a queen?"

"I am. But we don't reveal second kings until the queens are initiated. We stay in the background where, hopefully, we're never needed."

She looks over her shoulder. Slices of the sunset break through the clouds outside, shards of golden light illuminating the boat's cabin. "Is there someone here who's going to bust us?" she asks. "Tell me. No one will know."

"It's *not* tradition."

"So *now* you'll follow it?"

Like a burning white flag of surrender, I see no choice. I fucking hate to admit it, but oddly, I'm relieved too. "I think we should."

"You think we should follow the traditions?" Her lips purse, fighting her smile. "*All* of them."

"Don't look so goddamn happy about it."

She leans over, naked with a smirk, crawling on top to straddle me. I grab her hips while she traces over my scowling lips.

"Let's recap our convo," she says before softly kissing me, giving me something no man has had. *Over dead bodies, will any man have her kiss but me.*

"I've loved you, Nash Allen, since I was eighteen, and you love me, too."

Fuck. Open the hatch and toss out all my resistance to her.

"You've always seen my heart," she says tenderly, "and I've always adored yours, even when you try to be a big, sexy dickhead."

See? Why do I bother saying no to her? She doesn't hear it.

Vale presses her forehead to mine as if she can will *her* will into me, and goddammit, it's starting to work. I'm beginning to accept this.

"And one day," she sighs, "you'll ask me to wear a fifteen-carat, black diamond ring for you." *Noted.* "And I'll be your proud queen, and in my heart, you'll be my only king. You'll let one of your brothers, aka. Jace, make it official, and we'll live happily ever after in not-mafia-mafia heaven and hell."

She kisses me again, taking my hungry erection and possessive lips as signs of my agreement. But of course, she has to be, "Right?"

"Shut up, Vale," I answer, flipping her over.

And for the next four days, I treat every sweet hole of hers like I'm a king.

Her only king.

CHAPTER THIRTY
VALE

"Are you sure Delta's is safe now?" I worry.

I know I should trust Nash and his brothers, but now I'm all in love and shit and worried I'll lose it.

Death would be really inconvenient right now. The universe owes me ten thousand orgasms ... or more ... with Nash before I'm ready for my next life.

"Yes," he answers, driving north of the city at night. "Jace staged a little break-in that motivated Stacey to accept more guards at the store."

"Uh!" I yelp, "That's not right! You can't deceive Stacey and make her pay for security she doesn't need."

Nash raises a brow. "You think Stacey Evans doesn't need extra security? I know her three husbands are beasts, too, and they'd kill for her. She's safe in her home, but her store is a target. When she turned her ex-husband into the Feds, she earned a lot of enemies. Evil men who wanted what her husband and Turner the Third sold, and now Turner the Fourth wants her, too." Pause. "But mostly you. He'd get off on seeking revenge."

"When you put it that way..."

My stomach twists, getting sick with my vivid imagination.

"You'll be fine." He reaches for my leg. "We'll make sure of it and—"

"Okay," I interrupt, still worried, "I trust you and Jace and even asshole Axel to protect me, but please tell me how Alena is safe, too. She doesn't have a team of Bratva brothers guarding her. You said she had one guard, but that doesn't sound like enough now."

He takes the exit to the Naval yard. I know exactly where we're going, and it's not Delta's.

"Alena's location keeps her safe, too," he answers. "She may be innocent about me, but she's wise about the mountains where she lives and works. She knows how to track animals and hunters. She has perfect aim and good instincts. If someone goes after her, she has a secret guard and an obvious advantage."

I beam. "She is a badass, isn't she?"

"Just like her best friend."

"I smell a lie."

"I'm not lying," he says. "Just aim your mouth at any man, and he'll find the nearest cliff."

"Why don't you go jump off one?" I snap.

"Already did, poison." Nash smirks. "I fell for you a long time ago."

I smile. "You're forgiven."

"You're here." He parks his Dodge Charger outside a building I know well.

"Aw, the sex club." I clap. "My favorite."

"Settle down, Dr. Sex." He orders, "Your days of exploring are over. You found me, and no one sees what's mine." Pause. "Except twice."

"Twice?" I like this news flash.

For years, I was too focused on having an orgasm with a

partner to ever be shy about public sex. I mean, in the club. I figured you should take the orgasmic gift where you can get it.

But after wanting Nash for so long—having sex with him in front of his brothers is so taboo and right up my naughty alley.

Having sex with Jace, too? Just once?

How weird is it to admit I'm not against it? Jace looks like a bad and beautiful man, and he's been good to me. I trust that for one night, he'd make it okay. He wouldn't treat me like trash; he'd treat me like a treasure. Nash's treasure. If anyone can make this work for me and Nash, it's Jace.

"What do you mean *twice*?" I ask again.

"Once as a test. Once for the initiation. Meet with The Queen," he answers, "and she'll explain."

It's weird entering the club without showing my ID or surrendering my phone. With Nash holding my hand, security lets us in unchecked.

It's a Saturday night, and the club is full. Scanning the crowd, I smile, realizing tonight's fetish theme is CFNM—clothed female, naked male.

The soaring cocks everywhere make Nash yank my hand. "Don't look," he barks.

"Okay." I keep my eyes wide open.

He turns around and catches me admiring a long, pierced one. And when I say admiring ... I mean drooling and unable to look away, stumbling right into him.

He growls, "Put your tongue back in your mouth."

"Will you pierce yours for me?"

"My cock?" He sounds appalled.

"No, your tongue." I bat my lashes. "I promise to keep my mouth shut if yours with a barbell piercing is licking my pussy every day."

He laughs. "Your pussy is making a promise *your* mouth can't keep."

"Uh!" I stomp. "I can shut up."

He turns around, still laughing and tugging my hand. "Search 'impossible' in the dictionary, and you, shutting up, is the example."

I want to snark back, but as we reach the end of the long corridor at the back of the club, Nash presses a code into a keypad, and I'm too curious.

A black door unlocks, and he holds it open, ushering me up the stairs. I guess I knew there were multiple levels, given that the building is three stories, but I was too busy searching for my orgasm on the first floor.

But up here? It looks like a parlor in a Russian palace. Jeweled-color velvets. Ornate gold and wooden furniture. The Czarina, The Queen, sitting behind her desk.

Ms. Faye waves us in while she talks on a hand-held radio. "Break his finger," she orders. "He knew the rules. No touching without asking."

The man on her radio asks, "Right hand or left?"

"Is he wearing a wedding ring?"

"He has a pale ring line where one should be."

"Good," she answers. "Break his wedding finger so his poor wife can know he's a cheating bastard. Then break two more because he's an orange shit stain who thinks he can grab a pussy and get away with sexual battery." She grins. "Not in my world."

"Yes, ma'am," he answers.

She puts her radio down and rushes to hug me. "Vale," she coos. "What a pleasure to finally meet you. For real, this time."

I hug her back. "Thank you, Ms. Faye."

Have I always admired her? Yes. Am I building a shrine to her now? Pour the concrete.

"Honey," she says. "Call me Nadine, and take a seat."

"Yes, ma'am," I answer, sitting on the amethyst sofa.

Before he sits, Nash pours three shots of clear liquor—vodka, I assume—and offers one to Nadine and then me.

They raise their glasses silently, so I offer my usual toast: "Here's to staying positive and testing negative."

Nash almost spews his shot while Nadine laughs before throwing hers back. I do the same, loving the smooth fire down my throat.

"I always knew you'd fit in," she says, pausing, "but only if you want to."

"I want to!" I blurt. "I want to be Nash's queen."

She nods. "Has he told you the tradition? How you'll have the protection of two kings? Him and one of my sons?"

"Yes, ma'am."

"You must know..." she says, sitting in a jade velvet chair, looking regal in her fuchsia Chanel suit. "It's an honor to be a second king and husband. Of course, Nash will be your first and only unless something happens."

"Yes, ma'am," I parrot. "I understand."

"A king can only take a queen if it's what she wants. She has to want him *and* her second king." She lowers her tone. "That was not a choice given to me, but it wound up saving my life and all my sons' lives. They were destined for violence and young death like I almost experienced had it not been for my second husband.

"Now, the tradition makes sense to me. Now, it's sacred to us. My sons choose to do it out of honor. That's how I raised them. They honor their queens. They never hurt them. Do you understand?"

"Yes, ma'am."

But now I'm wondering who the hero is—or was. Who was her second husband? How did they escape the clutches of an evil, powerful man? And how has he not found her?

I can't imagine a man that violent and tyrannical not coming after his six sons.

But I dare not ask. Nadine Faye could intimidate the salt out of the ocean.

But I do ask, "What's my test?" Nash said there was one, followed by the initiation.

She turns to him, chiding, "Is that what you boys call it? *A test?*"

He winces like a kid caught with his hand in the cookie jar. "Sorry, ma'am."

She *tsks* before turning to me. "It's not a *test*, but of course, men have to turn everything into a competition. It's a *ritual*, a way to be sure it's what all want, particularly the queens."

She twirls the large, opal sapphire ring on her wedding finger. It looks rare and worth thousands.

"I was inspired to open this club so that I could offer people a life very different than the one I endured," she explains. "Here, we enforce consent and celebrate pleasure. I told my sons they must do the same. They must make sure their queen knows their bond and tradition and that she gives her consent to join them."

She flits her hand toward Nash. It's funny. "They come up with the ritual, the way to do it." She lifts her chin. "I'm a very proud and sex-positive woman now, but I don't get involved in their *test* or the initiation. It's bad enough one of my sons can't control himself in my club. No mother wants to see that, and I don't. I roll my eyes and look away."

Grant. It has to be him.

Like a protective wingman, Jace would always accompany me and Blair here, but I never saw Jace hook up, not at the club.

Axel? If he were here, I never noticed him. Then again, you can't miss Axel. He's a dick, but he's a very big and smoking-hot one.

So it's not him, and I know it's not Nash. I had no idea he was watching me from up here all this time. That breaks my heart and turns me on at the same time.

Damn, these are some complicated feelings.

But I'm sure it's Grant. Women can't resist him, and he loves them on their knees. Clearly, they love it, too, because I've seen him and his groupies here, sharing him like a lollipop.

Told you. These Bratva brothers are hot.

It makes me brave enough to ask, "Who are your other sons? Nash said there are six, but I've only met four."

"Well," Nadine answers, "Nash is like my son, too, so in my heart, there are seven. Seven sons."

She exchanges a look with Nash. It's weighted. It's guarded. "Two of my sons, my youngest, stay hidden. Rarely do they reveal themselves, even to the queens."

Dammit! Just when I thought I was getting answers, I get more questions.

Why would two of her sons have to hide? And who are they?

She reads my mind. "In due time," she assures, "you'll know all. But first, you must convince me you truly want to be a queen, and we must agree that Alena cannot know."

"All this time?" I ask. "You've been protecting, Alena? You're like her grandmother?"

"Yes," she smiles warmly. "I never had a daughter, and her mother, Lainey, was like mine."

Nash clears his throat. I glance at him. It's not out of discomfort, it's the grief. I realize now how hard it would have been, how lonely, too if Nash had to raise Alena by himself. But as long as I've known Alena, Nadine has always been there.

"That's a story," she eases, "I'll let Nash tell you."

"Good," I blurt, "because you all have too many secrets."

I don't mean to be disrespectful, but I love Alena, too.

"I don't like lying to her," I tell Nadine. "Yes, we'll wait until after the wedding to tell her about me and Nash, but Alena can know *everything*. She's strong. She's smart. She can take it."

Again, Nadine and Nash exchange a look.

"No, she can't," Nash insists. "You have to trust us on this."

I'm about to protest with something snarky, but Nadine asserts, "If you want to be his queen, one of *our* queens, you *must* trust us. We keep some secrets because they keep Alena safe."

Trust is not an easy emotion for me. Too many times, I've been hurt or abandoned. Ironically, it was by men, and maybe that's why I want this so badly.

I want the man I love and the men he trusts to always be there for me, too. To never hurt me as I have been. I want a big family since I never had one. I want to fit in because I never did. I want to be loved for who I am.

With Nash, I always have been. He's always loved my gothic style, my stacks of books, my odd cheeseburger obsession, and my love for red tulips.

And now? I can have more.

I get Nadine, who's like a mother because I miss mine dearly. She always liked Nash. I get men like him fighting for something I believe in, too. They'll honor and protect me. But mostly, I get the one man I've always wanted if I'm willing to trust him, too.

The thought makes my lips tingle. They hitch with a soft smile, remembering...

He killed for my kiss.

"Okay," I say, meeting his brown eyes claiming mine. "I agree. I'll be his queen."

CHAPTER THIRTY-ONE
NASH

"I can't wait." Vale wiggles in her passenger seat, excited like I'm taking her to Chuck E. Cheese and not preparing for two nights of taboo sex. "Test and initiate me ... like tomorrow. Or the next day."

We just met with Nadine about it, but I have strong doubts I won't murder anyone who touches Vale. I can't always control my rage, especially over her.

"I appreciate your enthusiasm," I pull out of the parking lot of the club, "but can we pace ourselves on the orgy plans?"

"Orgy?" She perks up even more. "It's not a gangbang or a double peno-anal?"

"No one is *gangbanging* you," I clench my teeth, "and no double ... whatever the hell. And yes, technically, it's an orgy."

"You're aware that means other couples having sex, too?"

I huff a sarcastic laugh. *Fuck my life; I can't believe I've agreed to this.*

Have I?

"Yes, Dr. Sex," I answer, "I know what an orgy is."

"So ... that means other *women* will be there?"

I hear it in her voice. Suddenly, Vale sounds worried,

almost jealous. I'd give her hell about it, but I won't toy with her heart. Not about this. To her, I'll always be faithful.

"Yes, the other queens will be there, and no, I won't fuck them. I fulfilled my obligation. I'm a second king. That's it, and never again. I'll only be with you."

"Phew." Relief fills her sigh. "Fit of jealousy avoided."

"What about *my* jealousy?"

"Are you jealous? I mean ... *will* you be?"

"No, Vale. I'll be perfectly fine with it *after* I murder everyone."

She giggles. "You're cute when you're sociopathic."

"Yeah, I'm going to be *real* cute when someone touches you."

"Is that the test?" she asks. "Others touching me?"

I'm about to crack my molars. "If you consent."

"Only if you're there. Only if you're touching me, too."

"Oh, I'll be fucking you while I strangle necks, don't worry."

"Erotic asphyxiation is a big fetish for some."

"The way I do it ... it's big *murder* for all."

"Nash," she huffs, throwing her chin up. I catch it in my side-eye. "If you don't want to make me your queen, then don't. I've made it clear: I want to do it. From what I gather, it's going to turn me on, but not if you're suffering. That only limps my pickle and breaks my heart. I'll always annoy the shit out of you, but I'll never hurt you."

This is the part changing my mind. The part willing to do this.

I love Vale. I love her goddamn mouth and gothic heart. I need her in my life forever, which means I need her protected, too.

Would my brothers still protect her if she weren't my queen? Of course. They already have.

But I can't look in the mirror and see a traitor staring

back at me. I can't reconcile what one of the brothers has done for me if I'm not willing to do the same.

This isn't about sex. It's about a sacred bond, an unbreakable vow. In most worlds, they're easy to keep.

In ours, bonds can break when bullets fly. You need to trust your brother's vow to protect the one you love, even if that means sacrificing himself.

That's the oath.

We will die for a queen, any queen.

"I'll find a way to accept it," I tell her as I check the rearview mirror, noting the same LED headlights two cars back.

"I don't want your acceptance," she says. "I want your happiness. If you can't be happy about it, don't do it."

"Vale," my heart rate climbs, "I will never be happy about you, even for a ritual, with someone else. But I'll allow it, and that's as good as it gets." I change lanes. The car behind me does the same. "Now get ready. We have a tail."

"A what?" She turns around, glaring through the back windshield. "Are you sure?"

"Sure as shit." I call out to my Bluetooth, "Call One."

After one ring, Axel answers, "Did she approve?"

"Yes." I focus straight ahead. "But we were followed out of the club. Secure it and find out by whom."

"Fuck," he grumbles. "What about The Queen?"

"She's fine. No one spotted us with her. Turner must have eyes there." I smirk at my pun. "Or one."

I make Axel huff, amused. "Now what?"

"Is the captain on duty?"

"Yes. It's third shift."

"Tell him I'm headed his way."

"Copy." Axel ends the call.

"Captain?" Vale pipes up. "What captain? Please don't say it's another boat."

"It's the captain at the police station."

"The police!" Vale shrieks. "But you're mafia! They'll arrest you."

"For what?" I smirk. "Being devilishly handsome?"

"Nash!"

"I'm serious. I'm not wanted for any crimes. None of us are. A few captains in town love the services we secretly provide. You think they care if we take out men like Turner? It only saves them paperwork. And the last place Turner or his men want to be is pulling into a police station. They'll drive right by, and no one will stop us as we switch cars. We keep one parked there."

"My god," she sighs. "You're like the Bratva Boy Scouts: always prepared."

"Not always," I admit. "We're human. We make mistakes, and we've learned some tough lessons."

"Like?"

"Like Sire, Nadine's oldest, is the reason I joined their family. He made the mistake of breaking into a drug store at seventeen, and that's when I met him in juvie."

"So, he made the mistake of being an *addict*?" She sounds sympathetic.

"No. He made the mistake of trying to steal Epi-Pens for his best friend's little sister. Their family couldn't afford them, and she had a deathly allergy to bee stings. So Sire and his big, dark heart thought it was a smart idea to break into a pharmacy covered by cameras to get some."

I turn right, not increasing my speed; I don't want to lose this tail. I want them to know *I* know they're following me, and secretly, I have the law on my side. *Sometimes.*

"That's sweet," Vale sighs. "You all make the mafia sound moral."

"We're not moral," I correct her, "because we're *not* mafia. Think of us as ex-mafia. If you saw the scars on Nadine's back, as her sons have, you'd understand why they vowed never to be like their father." I turn left and left again. "But you can take the men out of the mafia, but not the mafia out of the men. The brothers just use their talent for brutality and blood for good, not harm." The memory of Turner's gaping eye hole makes me confess, "*Sometimes.*"

"So that's how you met Nadine? When you were in juvie?"

"Yes." I check the mirror three times. *There they are.* "Sire was my cellmate, and he told his mom I was about to lose Alena to the foster system. Lainey couldn't afford to take care of her alone, and my dumbass was in jail. So Nadine stepped in. She gave them free rent, groceries, everything. When I got out, she even paid for my college. She babysat. She—"

"And Lainey never knew how you knew Nadine? She was just 'Ms. Faye: the nice neighbor'?"

"She still is to Alena," I reply. "Nadine didn't force me to join them. I wanted to. I never knew my dad, and my mom bailed on me when I was four. I went through the system and don't wish it on kids. Some homes are safe. Many are not. So when I finally got to choose my family, I chose them."

I slow down, letting the tail catch up. They're right behind us.

"Hang on." I make a sudden right turn into the parking lot of the police station. My tires screech as the tail squeals its brakes, not anticipating my sudden move. Then it almost slows to a complete stop, watching as I pull up to the front door.

"Stay in the car," I order Vale, taking my gun from the console.

If those fuckers get out and come after her, there will *be a shootout in the parking lot; I don't give a fuck about the police.*

But they don't. Quickly, they speed away.

With my gun in hand, I command Vale, "Stay," praying for no snark. I bolt out of the driver's seat, grab our GO BAGs from the trunk, and rush to her passenger door, swinging it open. "Come." I reach for her hand, and shockingly, she obeys.

I guess we're getting good at this old game. I'm usually the hunter, not the hunted. It makes me clench my jaw; *this is fucking bullshit.*

Holding her hand, I tuck my gun into my waistband, reach into the bag with my other, and find the key fob to a black Chevy Tahoe parked amongst the unmarked cars in the lot.

All the cameras on the lot record us, but the captain owes us some favors. The footage will disappear.

Besides, the department can consider the Dodge Charger my yearly donation. They won't be able to trace the car, and soon, they'll add it to their unmarked fleet.

The lights beep as I unlock the doors. Vale races to get in on the passenger side while I open the driver's door, set my gun on the console, and toss our bags in the back.

Bonnie and Clyde would be proud.

"We can't go back to the boat," she says, thinking ahead. "What if it's been burned?"

"Look who's sounding like a queen already." I grin, pulling out of the back entrance of the lot, still scanning for those LED lights in my mirrors.

"Can this queen go back to The Mercier?" She puts her cute shoes on the dash. "I want a do-over on our nights there."

"I'm not watching *The Exorcist* again. You know I used to like pea soup." I check the mirror. "Besides, it's too late to book a room."

"Fine," she sighs. "Just take me where I can have a cheeseburger."

I take the ramp for the interstate. It's time we visit my eldest brother.

"Just what is it with you and cheeseburgers?" I ask to pass the time, checking my mirrors two more times.

"You'll laugh," she answers softly.

I glance at her. She looks sad.

"Poison, I won't laugh. I promise."

After a heavy sigh, she shares, "When I was little, I always ordered the cheeseburger Happy Meals because *I* wasn't happy. I missed my dad, and my young, naive heart believed if I ate them, I would magically get him back, and I'd be happy."

"Fuck," I mutter. "I want to kill him. You know that, right?"

"Please don't."

"I won't."

"I think that's why I want this so much. I want a big family with you."

My heart hitches. I can see it too. "A family?" I raise a brow at her. "You mean with me and my brothers? Or just me and you?"

"Both." She turns toward me, resting her cheek on the seat. "Nash, we can make it work. It won't be as bad as you think because I trust Jace to help us. And I think it's sweet. When you and I have a family, Jace will protect them, too."

A smile lifts my lips, hiding the goddamn fireworks bursting in my heart, imagining having a baby with Vale. Yes, it stirs my cock, too. "So, we're having a family together? Me and you?"

"Yep." She pops her lips. "It's not like we just met. It's not like we just fell in love. Remember? You've always been home for me." She rushes, "But not yet. I want lots of orgasmic sex with you first, and changing diapers may get in the way, but when we do, we'll name our daughter Wednesday and our son—"

"We are NOT naming our daughter Wednesday Allen."

But I'm laughing because Vale gets her way. *Sometimes.* "And no son of mine will be Pugsley or Lurch."

She bats her eyelashes. "Gomez?"

"Nope."

"Fine," she sighs. "To be negotiated."

We drive for minutes, swimming in happy silence, while I dream of diapers, bottles, and baby carriers.

I missed a lot with Alena.

But if I get my dream of a second chance? If Vale makes me a father again?

I'll carry our baby in a front carrier and holster my Beretta in the back.

CHAPTER THIRTY-TWO
VALE

"Where are we going?"

I'm finally curious. My surprising rush of baby fever has passed. I can see a future with Nash, so now I'm focused on staying alive.

"Sire's place." Nash aims this big SUV down a narrow alley off the popular King Street in historic Charleston.

Pressing an app on his phone, the gate to a parking area opens, and we pull in. He kills the engine, then grabs his gun and our bags.

I could get all snarky with comments, but this chase is starting to feel too real.

Too close.

Too dangerous.

Holding Nash's shoulder, my heart races as we enter a secure door using a code and climb a narrow stairwell. At the top, Nash presses a doorbell. After a minute, I hear a *click*, and the steel door opens.

"Well, let me be my brother's keeper." Sire fills the threshold, grinning at me. "Look at what his pretty cat is dragging in."

Dressed in grey cotton pajama pants and no shirt, Sire has more ink than Nash. From some on his handsome face to his thick neck, all the way down to his drawstring, he's covered in vivid tattoos and defined muscles. He looks menacing yet radiates calm, like a big, evil angel.

"Sorry for waking you," I state the obvious. With Sire's mussed hair and the late hour, he wasn't expecting us.

"It's fine!" A woman chirps from inside. "Stallion, let them in."

Stallion?

I smirk, intrigued by Sire's amorous nickname, as we brush past him.

Nash holds my hand, leading me into a modern, two-story penthouse loft atop an old brick mercantile building.

"Hi!" A stunning woman, much younger than me, rushes my way. "I'm Wren!"

Her gorgeous raven waves are piled on her head in a messy knot. She's wearing a man's white button-up that fits her like a gown, contrasting with her dark, glowing, tawny skin. Her eyes sparkle like she's thrilled to meet me as she yanks me into a hug. "You must be Vale."

"You must be burned if you're here," Sire adds.

"They spotted us at the club," Nash answers. "We lost their tail, and here we are."

Instantly, this connection warms me. "Nice to meet you, too," I sigh in Wren's long embrace.

"Please," she offers. "Have a seat. I'll pour some drinks. We have lots to share."

Share? I suddenly sense it. *Wren's a queen.*

Reverently, she lifts on her tip-toes, offering Nash a kiss on his right cheek. Nash respectfully pecks her back, and that's when I notice Wren's piercing on her left cheek. It's a diamond Monroe piercing just above her puckered top lip.

Sire watches their greeting as he sits, reaching his

tattooed hand out for Wren's. She takes it, and he kisses her fingers, lightly tonguing her interdigit with a knowing smirk on his lips before she giggles and pads past him in bare feet to their kitchen.

Nash pulls me to sit beside him on the sofa. "This chase is getting old," he seethes. "I want blood."

Sire sits like a king in his black leather chair, his arms covered in angels and crosses, draping over the sides. "Could be a blessing." The gold cross around his neck catches the lamplight.

Nash huffs, "This isn't divine."

"It isn't?" He lifts his chin. "If people do not believe the first sign, they will believe the second."

"Stop preaching." Nash wraps his arm over my shoulder. "You're not the ones being chased."

"No, you are." Sire nods at us. "And we'll use it to our advantage. We'll protect you while you draw them out of hiding, then we take them out. One by one."

"Yay," I murmur, "I've always wanted to be a target."

Nash hugs me tighter under his protective arm. "I got you, poison." His lips brush my hair as Wren joins us with four shots in hand—vodka, always.

I like this tradition.

She serves us before Sire pulls her to sit on his lap. "Thanks, Angel." He kisses her, way too long and hot, before taking the glass from her hand.

Then he raises it, we all do, and Nash whispers, "Don't say it," and I pout, loving my toast as we toss them back.

"So," Wren beams, "is it official? Did you get The Queen's approval?"

I pull away, turning to Nash. "Did *everyone* know about me *but* me?"

"We always knew about you." Sire chuckles. "It just took

Nash way too fucking long to add it up. Kind of sad for such a genius accountant."

Wren shrugs her dainty shoulders. "Don't feel bad. I just found out, too. As a new queen, there are a lot of secrets to tease out of them. It's not personal," she assures. "They were raised to hide, so it takes a while for them to come out."

"Oh, I *come*." Sire seeks her slender neck, biting it and letting us see his tongue lash her flesh.

It sparks my core, heat tingling my nerves, the recognition of another beast. It's the same way Nash devoured me at the country club that day.

Wren sighs, "We have guests."

"That's my brother and his future queen," Sire rumbles against her flesh, his hand cupping her pert breast, his tattooed fingers pinching her nipple under the shirt. "You know our bond."

Wren moans softly, and with the corner of my eye, I catch Nash licking his lips. His fingers clutch my shoulder tighter. He can't hide the slight roll of his hips beside mine, too.

He's getting aroused by their desire. I am, too.

I suddenly feel warm with Sire and Wren. I feel like we belong. Like together, we'll always be safe. More than safe.

Nash said the mafia life is a gilded, barbed, and bloody cage. I don't doubt it is. But now I know ... it can be an erotic one, too.

"We need to do this soon," Nash orders, icing the hot vibe. "If Vale and I agree to be hunted, to bait Turner's crew to find us, I need her protected. *Now*."

Sire lifts from Wren's neck, nodding. "Give us two nights to prepare her test."

"Wait," Wren blurts. "You kings aren't in charge. The queens are." She turns her topaz eyes to mine. "Woman to woman, is this a good week?"

"Yes." I grin, immediately loving Wren for understanding.

The first night on Nash's boat, I put on a birth control patch, along with a motion sickness one. My menstrual monster won't be here for a few weeks.

"Then it's perfect!" Wren bubbles. "We can use the new room. Right?"

She asks Sire, but Nash answers, "Let the kings handle the details. Delta's is our most secure location. It's crawling with our men, but we need to find the right night."

"Tuesday," I suggest. "It's one of the store's slowest. I could tell Stacey it was dead, so I closed the store early."

"Can everyone be there?" Wren asks like an eager party planner, and I can't lie.

The question rouses me in ways I never felt.

Everyone?

"You mean like Jace and Grant?" My pulse starts to thrum. "Axel and the other kings, too? *And* the queens?"

Wren rolls her lips, not saying a word.

Sire lowers his stare at Nash, making Nash thunder, throwing his chin up. "Fuck! Brother, you better stop me from murdering someone."

Sire laughs. It's deep, dark, and delicious. "This test is more for you, my brother, than our beautiful, new queen."

I turn to Nash, admiring his profile. Jealousy, passion, possession, protection, rage: they all strain his sexy, sadistic face and those lush, snarling lips.

Aw, he's capable of murder for me. Again.

Yes, I'm clearly fucked up, too, because I find it romantic.

I put my hand on his chest, swooning at how his heart hammers under his tight, black T-shirt. "We can do it," I ease. "We can pass the test together."

"Sire was the same way." Wren swings my eyes back in her direction. "It's cute how the kings don't want to share until they realize how much their queens like it." She winks, her youthful aura morphing into a very wanton one. "They made me *love* it," she confesses, "and that made my king crave sharing me even more."

"I think I'll love it, too," I confess.

"Goddamn," Nash mutters his favorite word, dragging his hand over his trimmed beard. But I hear it in his tone. His anger fights his arousal.

"Let's get this done," Sire demands, reading his brother's war. "We need to anoint a new queen before another gets married."

"Wait? What? Another gets *married?*" I turn, confronting Nash. "Does he mean Alena?"

I'm about to lose my shit, as Nash explains calmly, "By default, as my daughter, Alena is a queen. She'll never know it. She'll never be initiated, and she'll always be safe."

Once more, doubt smacks me. I don't like lying to Alena. It feels unnatural.

But now I understand what Nash means about being a valuable asset. Too valuable.

I know about The Queen at the club. I know about Axel's law office. I know what Nash has done to victims on his boat. Axel, too. And now I know where Sire lives. I've never visited Jace and Grant's homes, but they said they live on Sullivan's Island.

If Turner and his men were ever to kidnap, traffic, and torture me, how long could I keep secrets protecting my king? All of the kings?

"I haven't met Alena yet," Wren offers sweetly. "But Sire protects her, too. He's performing her service, and I can't wait. It's going to be a beautiful wedding."

"Hold on." I put my hand up to stop the race of logic mowing me down. "You?" I stare at Sire. "*You're* the one who baptized Alena?"

"It was my honor," he answers.

"So you're a... you're a *priest?*"

Sire laughs, throwing up his chin, exposing the winged warrior angel on his neck. "No priest is allowed to love as I do."

"He's a non-denominational pastor," Nash explains. "When I met him, he had a copy of the Holy Bible, the Torah, and the Quran open on his cell bed. He studies all religions."

I stare in awe because Sire doesn't look like a pastor, but now I can see how he can switch from a very sinister to a deeply soulful man.

It makes me feel safer, sleeping in Sire and Wren's guest bedroom with Nash wrapped around me, his Beretta ready on the nightstand. I have more than seven men protecting me. More than The Queen and other queens like me.

I have a future that feels like divine fate.

CHAPTER THIRTY-THREE
NASH

"What do we do with him?" Grant asks, standing over the man he just choked in the courtyard behind Delta's.

Grant still has wicked bruising from the shot he took in the vest. I catch him wincing from his effort, but like a raging bull, you can't keep him down.

He busted one of Turner's men, crawling over the back brick wall of Delta's, and now the man is passed out, but he'll awaken soon.

"Take him to the bunker," I fume. "They'll swarm like flies to this place, so let's use it. We'll collect dozens before this is over."

We've never used our warehouse in the Naval yard with an old underground bomb shelter.

That changes today.

We have two scouts on Delta's roof. A sniper, too. There's a man on each porch, along with our usual surveillance and guard by the front door.

It took less than forty-eight hours for Turner to send another butcher after me and Vale. This guy is armed with multiple hunting knives, and he looks jacked. It's as if he's been trained to fight his entire life. Something odd strikes me about him. I can't place it, but at least he was no match against Grant.

Like a beacon, Vale and I will draw Turner's men to Delta's or any place where we let ourselves be spotted, and our team will scoop them up.

"Pull a few fingernails," I order Grant. "Get him to confess where Turner's base is. If we collect more of Turner's men, one will turn with our torture."

Grant nods, motioning for the guard on the second-floor porch to help him while I turn to go inside.

I search for Vale and her twin, Blair, back at work, their loyal customers oblivious to the dark world outside. In the second-floor showroom, I find Blair helping two wives select a new strap-on while Vale adjusts a display on the shelf.

Her little black dress lifts, exposing her alabaster ass cheeks. *So cute. So tempting.* Vale's back to her gothic tease, and it warms my heart, firming my cock, too.

She isn't afraid of my life.

She's eagerly joining it.

Her signature black thigh-highs with white bows draw me near, but I keep my safe distance, knowing I'll lose control if I touch her.

She's adjusting two silver balls the size of peas on a realistic-looking silicone vaginal display.

"What are those?" I'm beyond intrigued.

"They're magnetic orbs. Their pinch is so painful, it's pleasurable to some," she explains, positioning them over the clitoris on the model. "You can use them like this, on nipples, on the frenulum of a penis, or the crus of one. You know … where your shaft meets your balls."

"I didn't know," I grin, feeling my crus suddenly swell, "but thanks for the lesson, Dr. Sex."

She whips around, winking. "You're my best student."

I lower my glare. "I'm your *only* student."

Seeing Vale's stunning smile makes me even more obsessed with protecting her. I nod to the glass display shelves. They wrap the large room. "What do you have in here that will *persuade* a penis to divulge the truth?"

I don't need to explain. Vale knows we just captured one of Turner's men. Jace is working downstairs to erase the surveillance footage so all Stacey, the owner, will see is a safe and empty courtyard.

"Persuade?" she asks. "Or thrill because careful—one man's interrogation is another man's kink."

"Either way, we'll have him begging for it to stop or for someone to finish him."

Her eyes gloss with desire. "Will that someone be you?"

It rouses my cock even more that Vale will embrace any dark kink I may have, but no, not this one. "That's Sire's domain."

"Sire?" Her eyes get wide.

Sire and Wren have been warm hosts. In two days, Wren and Vale have gotten close.

Not like sisters. Not like friends.

Like our queens.

It's beautiful, arousing even to watch. It's eroding my resistance to this. Since I've secretly loved Vale for so many years, my brothers always knew. Vale has always felt like mine. Like ours.

I don't answer her question about Sire's proclivities. I raise a brow. *She'll find out soon enough.*

"Oh!" She bounces her brows. "Male on male BDSM? Big fan."

"Who said anything about *only* male-on-male?"

"Is that an invitation?"

"You'll be my queen," I taunt. "It's a very firm possibility."

What in the hell am I doing? My cock swells under my

nerdy trousers. To the rest of the store and staff, I'm still the quiet accountant, hiding behind my usual glasses.

But now, I'm the king, imagining all the kinky ways I'll love my queen, all the bestial things I'll do with her, and all the brutal ways I'll protect her, too. It makes me rock hard.

"Show me," I demand. "Show me the ultimate submission for a male."

With a swish of her luscious hips, Vale aims for two cabinets down, pointing at the curved black bar on the top shelf. Two padded cuffs with chains are attached to each end.

"This is an extreme humbler with ankle restraints," she explains. "That wooden bar is actually two, screwed together. See the small opening at the center? You put a man on his hands and knees and pull his balls behind him, locking them between the two bars. Then, you screw the bars together, behind his thighs, before you attach the ankle restraints chained to the ends of the bar. It puts his ass in the air, and if he tries to fight, it pulls, torturing his scrotum."

My face twists with a "fuck no." It's not my kink, but it is our new tool.

Told you, I get creative with torture. Psychological is the best. You don't need extreme violence if you fuck with a man's mind. The bonus? It leaves no evidence.

"Give me four," I order.

Vale chews her lip, half aroused, half impressed.

"Every man who comes for us," I tell her, "gets put in one of those."

"But where are they—"

"Details," I growl. "Don't ask."

While she gathers four Humbler boxes, I search the store for more inspiration, making plans for Vale's test, too. I mean ... *her ritual*. Almost everyone will be here tonight.

I'm not worried about our security. It's tight.

It's me I worry about. I'm a cyclone of love, lust, rage, and primal possession. A different emotion storms my veins every hour.

When I watch Vale laughing with Wren in Sire's kitchen, I feel love. Vale looks happy and free.

When I hear Sire fucking Wren in their shower, his taboo taunts make lust scorch through my veins. Sire makes sure we hear them. It makes me fuck Vale for the second or third time in a night.

Then rage seizes me, watching Sire or Jace smile at Vale. How each brother silently adores my new queen.

Yes, they said this would happen a long time ago—the day I killed Chad. But they didn't have to wrestle with my guilt over my daughter finding out. It took time for me to confront it.

Hell, I still feel it. Not guilty for loving Vale. It's guilt for how she needs my protection now. I've made her the ultimate bait for Turner, as my daughter always has been. I'll do anything to keep them safe.

I climb to the third floor of Delta's, with the demonstration room on my right and our new meeting room on my left.

The juxtaposition of the open ivory door, where select customers are invited to watch how the sex furniture and toys can be enjoyed, is set against the closed door at the opposite end of the dark hall.

It only makes our locked, black door with its gold doorknob and keyhole more tempting, more forbidden.

Will Vale pass the test tonight?

Better question. Will I?

Past that gilded, black door, I can see my future with Vale. I just can't see the next week or the next month. With all the secrets I hide, I'm not sure we'll get there.

CHAPTER THIRTY-FOUR
VALE

I won't be lying to Stacey. Delta's really is dead tonight. A summer storm cracked the sky outside, sending people scurrying home.

Jace turns out the lights on the porches, indicating we're closed. Then he works on his laptop, switching the camera footage from live to pre-recorded.

If Stacey ever checks, she'll see that her beloved shop is empty and secure—which it sort of is with the team of men guarding it.

I should've known Nash and his brothers have a small army they employ. If they trust them, I do, too. Besides, I'm too excited about tonight.

Nash fed me an early dinner of cheeseburgers, then left. "I'll be back in a couple of hours," he promised before a long kiss. "Be ready for me."

Ready?

I make a thoroughbred in the starting gate at the Kentucky Derby look sedate.

I don't care what the test is tonight; I'll pass it.

I want a life and love like Sire and Wren have. Their love is as taboo as the love Nash and I share, and it makes them beautiful together. How they're too in love to care.

I'm not sure who the other kings and queens are, but I've never felt so powerful, so accepted, and so adored, and I'm not even officially a queen yet.

Eagerly, I get ready in the ensuite bathroom of a bedroom-turned-boudoir photography studio on the second floor. Drying my hair before braiding it, I swipe on my makeup, too.

When I emerge in my robe, I laugh, finding what Nash must have had Jace leave for me to wear on an ivory velvet chaise.

Of course, he did.

Nash chose a Fleur du Mal collared bodysuit for me tonight. With a white collar, a solid black bodice, a see-through black dotted tulle neckline and long sleeves, it's demure for lingerie. If you wear it as a bodysuit with pants, it's almost street fashion. I chose it for Delta's to sell.

But I roll my eyes, grinning, because Nash chose it to cover me. My Mary Janes are here, along with black, opaque thigh highs. All that will be exposed of me is all that's his.

Playing along, I get dressed and wrap myself in a plush white robe before venturing downstairs.

"Hey." Jace doesn't look up from his laptop.

I glance around the first floor. "Where is everyone?"

"Not here yet."

"Where's Nash?"

"With Grant. He'll be back soon."

I study Jace's profile. Black ink on his thick neck peeks from under his starched white collar. His inked fingers click and tap, securing the fake footage for tonight.

It's just him and me and a conversation we need to have.

"So, about you fucking me."

His thick fingers pause over the keys. He doesn't look up. "Yeah?"

"You okay with it? We'll be cool after?"

"Cool?" he chuckles. "Is this a John Hughes film? Are you giving me your diamond earring afterward?"

"Gah," I sigh. "I love that you're his biggest fan."

I know so much about Jace.

He loves Blair's paranormal romance books. He can max rep three hundred and seventy pounds on a deadlift—whatever the hell that means. I just hear him bragging to Grant about it. He loves peanut butter and hates bananas. He owns a Nikon and collects photography books. He's a hopeless romantic who, by my count, has broken nine noses outside the door of the sex club.

Now, I realize he did it for his mom, punishing the men who broke her rules.

But this? Me and him? I don't know how he feels.

"I'm fine with it," he answers, setting his laptop on the stool beside him.

"*Fine* with it?" I roll my eyes. "Jeez, I'm not a wallpaper pattern you have to live with."

He grins, finally meeting my eyes. "Have you seen yourself, fox? You are *fine*. Fine as fuck. Don't tell Nash. He'll kill me, and I wouldn't blame him."

"But me and you." I point between us. "Our friendship. I cherish it and don't want to lose it."

"You will lose it," he says stoically. "I'll be more than your friend. I'll be your second husband. That means if we lose Nash," the thought clenches my heart, "I'll protect you and take care of you ... if it's what you want."

I shuffle in my Mary Janes, worried. Not about my love for Nash. I'll always worry something will happen to him. But now, I worry I'll hurt Jace, too. "What if you get feelings for me?"

"I already got 'em." He cocks his thick brow. "I told you; I love you, but not like Nash. No man loves you as much as him. But I'll kill anyone to keep that smartass mouth of yours alive."

I bat my lashes. "It is pretty brilliant, isn't it?"

"Yeah," he huffs, amused. "You're brilliant, and you belong with Nash. He's so fucking in love with you, and we've known it for years. It's about time you're his queen."

"What about you? Who do you belong with?"

I've never seen Jace with anyone. I've seen him invite hotties home, but for all I know, he fed them Reese's peanut butter cups while they watched *The Breakfast Club*.

Jace spins the platinum ring on his pinky. "I belong with my family. I was seven when we got out. This scar," he points to the one down his cheek, "is courtesy of my father. It's what he gave me for picking up my baby brother when he was crying." Pain, tinged with rage, storms his blue eyes. "The only reason we survived him is because we did it together.

"When I got older, I was the first one who saw our mom's scars. She's a proud woman who hid them well. But one morning, I needed toothpaste and barged into her bathroom and saw her in the shower. I saw her back and what our father did to her," he swallows, "and I've never been the same."

"I'm so sorry," I murmur, feeling tears prick at my eyes. With each passing day, I'm growing to love Nadine, too. Any girl, woman, or mother who's survived what she has would make you drop to your knees in veneration.

I survived a night.

Nadine survived a decade.

"So," Jace reaches for my fingers, holding them lightly like a gentleman, not a lover. "It will be an honor to be your second king. Yes, we can be beasts; I won't lie and say we don't relish that part. But other times, we're men honoring where we came from. We honor our queens."

"Aw, shucks." I punch his arm. "Ouch!" I shake my shocked hand. "What are you packing under that suit? Teflon muscles?"

"All the better to fuck someone up with," he teases.

"Fuck *who* up?" A voice calls down the hallway to the back door.

It's Nash.

How long has he been standing there?

He's stoic except for his huffing bare chest, his abs flexing with ire. The blood splatters on his creased khaki pants are an odd contrast as I realize it's not me and Jace making him seethe. It's whatever he and Grant just did to Turner's man.

"Poison," he snarls. "Take your robe off."

With a yank of the knot, I let it fall from my shoulders, pooling at my feet. I'm not afraid to be exposed to Jace, too.

"Come here," Nash beckons with a finger caked in dry blood.

I don't hesitate. I don't snark. "Yes, my king," I answer.

Standing in Nash's shadow, I smell his sexy deodorant, wafts of coppery blood hitting my senses, too.

Without a word, Nash reaches into his pocket, pulling out a wide strip of fabric. It looks like a piece of a grey T-shirt, splatters of blood adorning it, too.

"This is from the man who thought he could take you from me today," Nash glowers. "I carved your nickname on his back and left his balls in a very humbling position."

With his bloody finger, he lifts my chin. The man I love is in his eyes, but the beast has taken his body. It's covered in the evidence of the violence he'll commit protecting me, protecting anyone he loves.

"Vale, do you want this life?" he tempts. "Do you want this man and beast because you have to love both?"

I'm shocked and aroused by what Nash did for me ... again ... because if that man had taken *me*, I'd be the one bound and bloody.

"Yes, my king."

CHAPTER THIRTY-FIVE
VALE

NASH TIES THE STRIP IN A BLINDFOLD OVER MY EYES. I CAN smell his victim's sweat on it.

I gasp as Nash lifts me in his arms. Draped over them, I wrap mine around his neck as he carries me up two flights. At the top of the stairs, I sense him turning right toward the demonstration room, and I stifle my disappointment we didn't turn left toward the secret meeting room.

"That's for your initiation." He reads my mind. "Tonight? We test you in here."

In a fast movement, Nash shifts me, his hands cupping my ass, as I sense him walking me back before carefully setting me down. The surface is cool and pillowy, sagging a bit at my weight.

The sex swing.

It's not a cheap one made of thin straps. It's a high-end swing made for ultimate comfort. It has a small black swinging bed, fluffy loops for feet or thighs, and a trapeze bar to grab, all dangling from the ceiling on a suspension chain.

I've never used it. But Stacey and her husbands crave showing customers how much they love it and each other.

"Stay here," Nash orders. "I need to wash my hands."

I hear his footfalls and trust he'll return. Unlike the father who abandoned me, Nash comes back. Unlike the man who hurt me, Nash never will.

For all the books I've read about sex and love, my emotions can't be contained in words. You have to *feel* this, not just define it, to believe it.

After a few minutes, I melt into the soft swing, hearing Nash's return.

"What now?" I ask, sensing his approach, thrill skittering through my veins.

"First." His clean, cool fingertips brush my heated cheek. "Tell me again you want this."

"Nash," I rush, "I love you. If you need proof, I want this; the fact that I'm not kicking you in the balls right now is it."

"On that note, poison." He secures my legs in the straps. "Let's get these ball kickers out of the way."

I'm splayed open and curious. "Just tell me who's coming tonight."

"*You.*"

I can hear his smirk.

"No, who's going to be here? Who will touch me and ... what else will they do?"

"No one kisses you," he insists. "They won't fuck you, either. They won't go anywhere near your mouth or pussy or—"

"What's left?" I chuckle.

"Touch," he growls. "That's what I told them I'll allow." His lip curls. "If you consent."

"Will you be touching me, too?" I reach, trying to find him in my darkness, and his hand wraps around mine.

His lips kiss my palm, his words promising, "I'll make sure you love it and pass the test. I want you as my queen and wife, Vale, whatever it takes."

He snaps open the crotch on my bodysuit, tucking the ends out of the way. With my legs hoisted high in straps, I'm vulnerable and exposed to him, and I love it.

I can sense we're alone in the room, but then I hear the din of deep voices entering the home two floors below. Heavy footsteps and clicks of high-heels ascend the stairs as a sudden wet tongue licks my exposed cunt.

"Oh god," I cry out.

"They're going to watch..." Nash bites the inside of my thighs. He must be kneeling between them. "How hard I make you come." He barely licks my slit. "How many times I make you do it." And licks again. "How you belong to me." Then licks harder. "Don't you, poison?"

He spanks my sensitive clit, making me jump, crying out, "Yes!"

Nash works his magic mouth. With five licks over my sensitive hood, he gets me ready, anticipating. He stops and blows cool air over my clit before hotly kissing it, over and over, making the tension build, making it hard and ache for more, his slick slurps driving me mad.

The sounds of heavy feet enter the room with voices hushed.

Nash pulls my little lips apart, the hood of my clit retreating, exposing it, making it rouse to the air. Deep sighs of admiration excite me even more as Nash shows our audience my screaming wet cunt.

"Look at what's mine," he demands.

His possession lifts my hips in this shameless display. I moan, adding to my submissive show. "Yes, my king, I'm yours." I clench my walls, making my sex pulse for anyone watching.

"Damn, her pussy is pretty." I hear a deep voice admiring my powerful cunt. I think it's Sire.

"Show them again," Nash orders with husky control.

"Show them how your tight, little pussy milks my cock fucking dry."

I do it again, clenching and moaning, needing Nash's mouth, his cock, his anything as he taunts, "See how she's such a good girl for me? Always so wet and ready."

He rewards me. Sliding two fingers inside my cunt, his tongue licks my clit in every direction I can't anticipate, making me beg with a sudden urge, "Nash, please. I need to come."

"Let her come." It's a woman's voice in a sexy accent I don't recognize.

Nash curls his fingers inside my walls, his devotion to my clit unrelenting while the heat of bodies surrounds me, heavy breaths of huge men admiring my pussy.

"Oh god," I cry out. Loving and needing. Lusting and demanding. "Please, Daddy. Please show them what a good girl I am for you."

"My, my." I hear another deep voice praise. "She *is* a good girl for you, Nash."

It's Axel, and suddenly, his annoying tone is arousing and smoky with desire. What he must see—Nash on his knees, his mouth feasting on my pussy—gets me off even more.

"Show them, my poison." Nash's fingers start pounding hard into my sex, making my walls clench tight to release. "Show them you're mine."

With a brutal, puckering suck of my clit, Nash makes me scream, fisting the pillow of the swing as my orgasm crashes through me, his fingers and mouth not stopping as I cry out, shuddering and twisting on the suspended platform with another sweet spasm.

"She's beautiful." I hear Wren whisper.

"*You're* beautiful." I hear Sire reply before the sound of a zipper being dragged down adds to their lustful exchange.

"This is your test, Vale." Axel's now arousing voice tempts

my left ear. "You'll be loved by Nash, but you'll belong to us. If you want our protection, you must prove you trust us." Fingertips, they must be Axel's, linger down my shoulder, toward my breast. "Starting tonight."

"Get your—" Nash snarls before, "Brother, you have to trust us, too," Jace calms him.

"We'd never hurt her."

That's Grant. Relief fills me that he's here; a little shyness, too.

Let's face it. You can't go from sharing friendship to a naughty fuckshow overnight without a little dose of awkwardness.

But it's cured as Nash caresses my thigh, his voice strained with ire. "How are we doing, poison?"

"Good," I huff happily, "and very horny for you."

Wren sighs, "Same."

The sound of shuffling bodies and shifting clothes fills the air while I feel Nash stand and settle between my thighs. The seductive sound of him dragging his zipper down makes me softly gasp. The knowledge his pants are splattered with blood shed over me makes me ache for him.

If that's fucked up, I'm too in love to care.

Nash teases his velvet tip over my sensitive clit, making all my shyness evaporate, leaving nothing but my hunger for him. "Please, Nash," I beg. "Do it. Fuck me. Show them I want to be your queen."

"*You* show us, too," Axel corrects, "not just him."

The brush of Axel's fingertip over the swell of my breast makes Nash drive inside me. "She's mine," he growls, holding my hips, swinging me toward him as he buries himself so deep, his claim is undeniable.

I arch, moaning at his penetration.

I love it as Axel argues, "No, brother, she's *ours*, too." He swings me back toward him, his fingers tugging at my bodice. "Isn't that right, Vale? You want to be his *and* ours?"

"Yes," I groan at Nash's next brutal thrust, yanking me toward him, his hands gripping my hips so hard, I'll earn the bruises I love, too.

"Do you *consent?*" Axel urges, his touch waiting above my breast, and he doesn't sound dirty, degrading, or even demeaning.

No, it sounds like consent is Axel's highest value. His one true law. The principle he fights and kills for.

Consent: it's not where Axel comes from; none of his brothers do. What a haunting legacy to be born with, so now they give it to others. It's what they need from me, too.

"Yes." I heard it in his voice. I trust it. I want it. "You can touch me, but only Nash can love me."

"I *can*," Axel presses, "or do you *want* us to touch you? Tell us. We'll honor it."

Nash is silent, letting the smacks of his cock pumping in and out of my open cunt, fill the room. What he must see from where he stands between my thighs, claiming what's his but asking me to trust his brothers, allowing them to pleasure me, too? He must be wrestling with his demons and desire for this.

The urge to ask for Nash's consent fills my mouth, too, but then he moves his hand off my hip, his thumb circling my clit, pleasure sparking through my nerves, and I know it. I feel it. He's telling me...

I want this. I need this for us.

The admission will never fall from his possessive and panting mouth, so I answer for us, "Yes, I want it. I command you all to touch me."

"Yes, our queen," Axel praises before I feel the yanking tear of the tissue-thin fabric connecting my sleeves to my bodice. Axel tugs it down, revealing my ample breasts. My nipples are immediately aroused to be exposed to the others.

"Fuck," Nash growls, his powerful thrusts matching the tempo of his thumb circling harder over my sensitive nub. The rousing pleasure he's giving me reveals it's his too.

This is his kink. This is the part he didn't want to admit to me. It's taboo and everything he desires, and I want it, too.

"Touch them," I demand with an ache in my nipples, my breasts bouncing in cadence with Nash's thrusts. "Touch what belongs to my king."

A warm, calloused hand surprises me on my right. Axel's on my left. Nash is between my thighs. I don't know where the others are in the room, but someone else obeys me. He gently cups my breast, making Nash groan. I swear I can feel his cock swelling even more.

"Beautiful." It's Sire, his pontificating voice distinct. "She's so beautiful, Nash."

"Yes, she is." It's Wren, her voice panting in concert with Sire's.

"Do you like this, my queen?" Sire fondles my breast as he taunts Wren, "Do you like me touching her breast for you? Do you like us getting her off for you?"

"Yes, my king." Wren's tiny voice resonates with undeniable lust. The swing shakes like Wren is grabbing its side, too.

Oh my god, Sire is fucking her. After the nights we've spent in their guestroom, I know the sounds of their lust.

"Yes, touch her," Wren urges. "Pinch her nipple while you pinch mine, too."

"Oh, my filthy angel." I hear Sire before he obeys her. With his gentle pinch, clamping down on my bouncing nipple, I groan.

"Goddamn," Nash snarls, slowing his thrusts.

He's too aroused by what he sees. He's fighting for control. I know his body too well now.

"She likes it," Sire taunts Wren, "just like you. You're so wet watching a king fuck his queen. Stand with your little legs together. Good girl. Make that little pussy even tighter for me to fuck."

"Damn, my queen." I hear another deep groan. It's Grant. I've heard his carnal lust too many times at the club not to know his grizzly growl. "Yes, fuck that pussy with your fingers while you suck my cock. You were a good doll for me this week. You've earned it."

I don't know who Grant's with, but it must be the other queen.

"Yes, my king." It's Wren sighing near my ear while Sire pinches my nipple, and Nash fills me with his cock, his fingers taunting my clit.

I don't know the rules; I just know I love this. I don't need to see it to want it. To feel like I belong to something forbidden and fiercely defended. To sense its history and bond. There's a reason this is an ancient ritual. It transcends time and taboo. It's how we survive. It's how love survives.

"They all approve." I hear Axel on my left, praising as Nash drags his length out, leaving me open and dripping, streams of my lust puddling on the soft leather beneath me.

Axel still hasn't touched me; my left breast aches for his praise and pinch, too.

"But does *he* approve?" Nash asks and...

Who? Who is he asking about?

"Yes." Jace's voice sounds on my left. He must be standing beside Axel. "We'd be honored if she became our queen."

"Prove it," Nash orders, pressing his swollen tip against my waiting entrance. I moan at his tease. "Prove to us you can be her second."

Nash's tone isn't taunting; it's flooded with doubt.

Why? Why would he doubt Jace?

"You'll fucking kill me." Jace doesn't sound scared. He sounds sure.

"Do it, and I won't." Nash urges inside me. "Help make her my queen. I need her. I fucking love her."

I'm right here, and I'm not. I'm everywhere else with Nash, too. I'm in our past when he felt ashamed of his desire for me. I'm in the years and all the sweet, infuriating ways he proved his secret love for me. Love we couldn't have. Love we've had to deny. Love that left us lonely too many times.

Now, we can have this, but we can't do it alone.

We need Jace.

"Here." A big, warm hand gently lifts my left one. It's Jace. I know his caring touch. With the sound of another zipper being dragged down, Nash thrusts inside me, moans escaping my throat as my hand is wrapped around the stiff shaft of Jace's erection. *Fuck, he's thick.* He guides my hand, stroking it over his cock. "This is your hard proof," he boasts. "If I need to, I can take care of her, too."

"Oh, my god," I sigh at the trust and taboo. What's forbidden falls away as Jace pumps my hand over his cock, and Nash claims my pussy with his.

"Suck her nipple." I hear Wren beg Sire, "Please, suck her nipple and make me come."

"Fuck." Nash is thrusting harder, faster.

"Shit." The gravel tenor of Jace's voice trembles, his hefty cock swelling in my grasp.

Sire's mouth clamps down, his weight shifting with Wren's, straining the swing, too. He must be fucking her from behind, letting her watch his mouth suck my nipple.

"Fuck," Nash huffs again. "Fuck." He strums my clit harder. "You love this, don't you, poison? You're so fucking wet and swollen. You love being so goddamn dirty for me, for us, don't you?"

Nash is taking me there. He knows it. I'm shaking for it,

arching for it, gasping for it. "Yes, Mr. Allen. Yes, Daddy, I'm your dirty girl."

"Hmm," Sire moans at our kink with my nipple in his mouth.

"Shit!" Jace grunts as I grip his cock so tight. "Shit, I'm coming." His hot seed spills over my hand, thick streams running down my wrist and splattering my breast.

"Vale, do you want to be Mr. Allen's queen?" Axel taunts my ear. "Do you want to be *our* queen, too?" He's not judging our kink; he's indulging it.

For years, Axel has known about our love and wants it. He wants my ultimate consent for Nash. My past and present collide as I scream for our future, "Yes! Yes!"

"Then be my good girl." It's Nash, dragging me over my edge. "Let them watch your pretty pussy come on my cock." He pinches my clit, and I fall into my deep orgasm, convulsing with a shameless groan as Nash pounds his cock inside me, making it last and last.

He grunts, "Fuck yes, baby, milk me," as my walls pulse and clench, claiming his orgasm, too.

"Fuck. Fuck. Fuck." Wren is going, too. She's yanking the swing so hard. I feel Sire tugging it too, all while Nash grunts, his final hard thrusts primal, bestial, and brutal and...

"Oh shit!"

It's so sudden, and I'm blind. I don't know what's happening as I fall even more. Not into my orgasm but onto the floor with Nash collapsing over me with a loud clank.

"Oh shit!" Jace shouts again. "We broke the swing."

"You okay?" Nash huffs.

"Yeah."

Axel laughs. It's an odd sound from his voice. "Guess I lost my deposit."

"What the hell?" I struggle with Nash on top of me.

"How did we—" I move to take off my blindfold, but Nash stops me.

"Wait, poison. You can't see us yet."

He holds it over my eyes while I protest, "I don't need my sight to see how I'm about to get fired for breaking the swing."

"Everyone, go." Jace assures, "We got this."

"You sure you're okay?" Wren's voice on my right sounds worried but about to giggle.

"Yes." Okay, it's funny. "I'm fine and fucked and fired."

"Stacey will never fire you." It's Grant. "You and Blair are like her little sisters. Just tell some lie, and you'll be fine." He mumbles, "Come on, my chérie."

Chérie? Who the hell is his queen, and since when is Grant French? I'm just barely coming to terms with the fact that he's ex-Russian mafia.

Footsteps scurry by as Axel orders, "You and Jace come up with something."

Axel must be speaking to me, so I shout at the ceiling. "I'm going to slap you so hard, even Google won't be able to find you! Take off my blindfold!"

"Seriously," Nash worries, "Are you okay? Are you hurt?"

I push against his sweaty pecs. "I'm fine." He's left me dripping, empty, and about to laugh. Or cry. Or both. "Just let me see the damage."

Slowly, Nash peels off the blindfold, and I blink until I can focus, glancing from side to side.

On my right, everyone is gone. Sire. Wren. Grant and his chérie and what other members of Congress heard my slutty testimony. I have no idea.

On my left, my gaze climbs from Axel's polished black shoes to his dark pants, his starched white shirt, open and revealing lots of hot ink, and his ... evil smirk.

So, I stick my tongue out at him.

Then my stare bounces over to Jace, dressed similarly, his cock deflated and tucked back in, while his smile is warm. I'm not even shy that his cum is on my tit, so I blow him a kiss.

Then my gaze lands on Nash, who's slinging his sunshine with his stunning smile. His eyes sparkle with mischief and love—love only for me.

Laughter bubbles through my declaration. "We *crushed* the test!"

CHAPTER THIRTY-SIX
NASH

"How did that go?" I mutter to Vale as she flops into her chair beside me.

I heard the shouts and raised voices from two floors above.

"Well," she sighs. "I'm not fired, we're busted, and my sister is a bestseller. Jace saw on his phone how her NFL Beau is back in town and reading her book in public. It's going viral and breaking her heart. That's one drama. The second is..." she leans closer, "your brothers just threw us under the bus."

I chuckle. "Of course they did."

"But Nash," she whispers, "they all know about us now, so that means—"

"*That* means they know I'm their accountant, you're my daughter's best friend, but we're adults in love. That's all they'll ever know."

"But they weren't convinced," she stresses. "All the sex Stacey and her husbands have had on that swing never ripped it from the ceiling. They don't believe it was just me and you."

"It wasn't." I feel my pulse rise again. "It was me, you, and my beast because that's who I am, watching someone else touch you."

We left the swing on the floor, knowing Vale would explain it in the morning, but I wanted her to myself after the test.

I booked us a suite at The Mercier, where I made us take a shower, watching the rivulets of my brothers' touch wash away. Then, I wanted to soak in the tub and hold her. I wanted to lie on the bed and eat popcorn with her head on my chest while I made her watch the classic *Married To The Mob* as a joke—sort of. I wanted Vale under the bed sheets and only mine to love and claim again. The sounds she makes coming on my cock are the only thing that satisfy me.

It took a while to settle the beast inside me, especially when I know he'll only return when she's initiated soon.

Speaking of...

Jace and Grant bound downstairs. They give us an amused "Have fun with that" nod while Jace takes his post by the door, and Grant excuses himself.

He says he's going for sushi, aka—another raw beating of our captive.

We still don't know where Turner's base is, but it must be in a remote location where prying eyes won't ask questions, and those places are rare in the South. If we can find Turner soon, we can scoop up his crew and their phones and laptops with contact names for his buyers.

But the guy we caught yesterday is a tough nut to crack— literally. We're still working on him while I focus on the desktop screen, making sure the second quarter reconciles for the third time as Stacey and her husbands, Ford and Mateo, appear downstairs.

Stacey stands in the parlor, studying me as I sit beside Vale at her desk. She smiles warmly, as if I have her approval, while she rubs her swelling baby bump. "Mr. Allen," she coos, "do take your time with that audit. It appears my staff appreciates your expertise."

Vale blushes, and if I could, I would, too, while Mateo winks at me, but Ford glares. He didn't appreciate having to patch the plaster ceiling.

"Apologies." I raise my palms. "Seems I got carried away. I'll pay whatever price you think is fair."

Stacey shrugs. "Just make a generous donation to the women's shelter, and all is forgiven."

"And stay off our swing," Ford seethes.

Vale twirls her braid. "But it's an adult playground we can't resist."

Ford opens his mouth to bark something back, but Blair steals all the oxygen from the room. She shuffles her slippered feet, trudging down the stairs before flopping into her chair with a loud huff. "Beau's here ... and he's ghosting me."

The entire afternoon, Blair pouts about it, and we avoid her. Finally, I get my work reconciled before I gently rub Vale's thigh under the desk.

"Tonight," I murmur, "let's go shopping."

"For what?" she whispers. "We've got room service and sex toys in a luxurious Mercier suite. What else could we need?"

Yes, I booked the suite for as long as it takes to initiate Vale. Even though Sire and Wren welcome us at their place, I want a place that's our own.

I take her hand. "Let's shop for our home."

I spoil her with quarterpounders with cheese, and Dr. Peppers before I drive her past beach homes for sale on Sullivan's Island.

After a proud burp, she asks, "But what about your Isle of Palms house?"

"It's burned. Besides, I want to start over. I want a place that's ours."

"Can we get something that screams 'gothic chic meets air-conditioning'?"

I laugh, parking in front of a property my agent told me about. "Gothic chic means dangerous streets. I can't secure a home in the historic district. Too many eyes are there. But out here," I point to the house nestled behind groves of palms and oaks, "I can give you security, a library, a nursery, a pool, *and* air conditioning."

She tilts her head, considering the home. "Can we paint it black?"

"Can you sell your soul to the devil to pay the electric bill if we do?"

"I've already sold you my pussy." She turns to me, winking. "Now you want my soul?"

I lean over the console, yanking her greasy, sassy lips into a kiss. "You can paint the interior black. Even Wednesday's room."

She beams. "Gomez's, too?"

"*Vaallee...*" Should I seethe or smile? "Woman, I give you an inch, and you take a million miles."

"No, my king." She hikes her black miniskirt to crawl over the console and straddle me. It's awkward and cute. I turn off the engine, kill the headlights, and let her unzip my tenting pants as she pulls her white cotton panties aside, arguing, "You give me these thick eight inches and make me moan for a million years."

And I do.

We fuck on the side of the road in this SUV parked on an exclusive street of multi-million dollar beach homes while all I feel with Vale is overwhelmed by how there's no one else I want this dream with.

No one.

I was lying to myself all these years, saying the reason I

never loved or married was because my life was too dangerous.

That's not true.

Years ago, I gave my heart to Vale, then resigned myself to die alone. That's why I never loved or married.

But now, the forbidden love of my life gives *me* life. She's right here, taking everything that belongs to her because she wants our life together, too ... and I'll crack any skull to make it happen.

Sisterly love. I wouldn't know anything about it. I've been surrounded by six brothers most of my life.

But now I'm watching it, front row and center. Pass the popcorn.

"Beau made you a bestseller," Vale yells, frustrated with Blair, "but he didn't show up today. He hasn't called or texted or dropped into your DMs, and I swear to god, if you sigh like a pining romance heroine about it one more time, I'm cramming an alien cock sheath down your throat."

I'm leaning back in my chair, admiring these two. They're like identical black jaguars in a catfight of clawing truths.

"Go suck a bag of daddy dicks," Blair half laughs, half snarls at Vale, and I confess that makes my daddy dick stir because that's precisely what Vale did last night in the shower after our house shopping.

"Proudly!" Vale shouts back, "I suck dick almost every night."

See?

Guilty.

"And so did you!" She keeps pushing Blair. "Where is my

shameless sister? The one no man could break? Since when do you crumble for cock?"

"You got as much room to talk as a cheap Vegas honeymoon hotel," Blair snaps.

Vale narrows her eyes. *Uh-oh.* "At least I don't have a dead fish city between my thighs."

"No, you got a hot Daddy treating your puss like it's his Disneyland." *Yep, that did it.* She points at me. "How many times have you ridden Mr. Allen's Space Mountain?"

While I appreciate the reference to my galactically entertaining girth, I'm concerned one of these sisterly brawls could break out in front of Alena.

Her wedding is in a few weeks. Sometime before, I'm supposed to initiate Vale. Of course, she wants it done tomorrow, but Axel wants everyone there, and I don't. It's too risky as I watch in disbelief when their fight turns into Vale and Jace convincing Blair to get over Beau Bronson and go to the club tonight—the sex club where Turner's men last spotted us.

"What the fuck are you thinking?" An hour later, I confront Vale in the bathroom at Delta's. Hissing low, I demand, "You clear your plans with me, and this one isn't happening."

She gives me a PhD-worthy eye roll. "Can we not take a tour through Dickhead town right now? I have a twin in crisis, and I'm going to help her."

"You have your little neck on the line, too." I snarl, grabbing it. "Remember that whole not-mafia-mafia thing? It doesn't stop because you want a girls' night out."

"If you want to choke me," she hisses, "you better be fucking me hard while you do it. Otherwise, slow your Bratva roll."

I relax my grip. "Poison, this is dangerous—me and you,

going back to the club. We haven't prepped security for it," I nuzzle my forehead to hers, "and I won't lose you. *Ever.*"

"Your mom has her club on lock twenty-four-seven. We'll be safe there."

Technically, she's right, but my instincts tell me it's the wrong call.

"We'll go separately," she urges. "You can watch from the VIP room, post extra security on the exit, and when I leave, if one of Turner's men tries to follow me... Boom! You got him dead on target."

I wince. "Bad metaphor."

"You know what I mean." She caresses my hand on her neck. "I'm not afraid. You and Nadine would never let anything happen to me." Her mouth seeks mine. "Okay?"

"You can't bribe me with these lips." I nip her plush bottom one, totally fucking lying. Her kiss could convince me to name our son Lurch.

Don't tell her.

So, Blair drives Vale, and Grant rides with Jace to the club. Of course, Grant doesn't miss a chance to go. His queen awaits him there.

I follow the convoy of Blair's car and Jace's truck, not loving how, for miles, all I can see is Vale jerking off Jace and making him come all over her tits at our kinky daddy taboo. Nirvana's "Come As You Are" streaming through my speakers doesn't help.

They park and enter through the front while I drive around back and use the fire escape stairwell to enter the second floor. We rarely use this door to one of Nadine's private residences.

But she's not here. I find her in the office on the third floor, gazing down over her erotic dominion.

"Let me guess," she says, "the kittens want to play, and there's nothing the big, bad wolf can do about it."

"I told her I'd allow it."

"Uh-huh." She turns to me standing beside her, her blue eyes dancing with delight. "Son, you look very handsome pussy-whipped. I'm so proud."

I fight the urge to snarl. Instead, I give her a guilty grin. Nadine's never seen me in love. Well, finally, having the love I've always wanted. I think it's all she wants for her sons: love and family.

Sipping a whisky she serves me, I note Blair sulking to Jace at the bar. Those two are best friends.

I must admit Vale's right; Jace is the perfect brother for us. He's a skull crusher with the softest heart. I've never seen him with someone else unless it's a test or an initiation, and it made me doubt during Vale's test if he could *perform* as her second king. *Once.*

Now, I'm sure he can because I damn well know the other brothers are too beastial like me. No way I'd let one claim Vale, too.

I watch her talking with Silas and Eily Van de May at the bar below. They're her loyal customers and friends.

Then I spot Grant and Delphine, with two of her friends, going at it again.

How Grant wound up with a French queen whose kink is the French sex—fellatio—and why she loves giving it with her friends, too? I don't know. But she's perfect for him, and I'm not jealous.

I'm a one-woman kind of man.

Scratch that: I'm Vale's man. Always have been.

Yes, I get off at an orgy. Who doesn't?

Vale told me it's scientifically proven. Scientists have wired people's genitals to monitors, and even though their subjects insisted they didn't get aroused watching sex, the blood flow to their happy zones revealed otherwise.

No, you can't wire my dick for such an experiment, but

yep, it proves we're animals. Maybe it's a survival thing, like mating season for all; it keeps us alive.

God knows I feel like an animal during our tests and initiations. So, why deny it? Why be ashamed of it? It's natural.

It's the sharing part that feels unnatural to me, but clearly, not to my brothers.

Though Grant and Delphine take it to the next level, and I'm not judging. I have my kinks, too. Clearly, because Vale's bikinis aren't safe around me.

"Lawd, that boy," but Nadine huffs, turning away from Grant's spectacle. "I'm gonna smack him into next week. Why must he have his little pecker licked daily?"

I snort. *Little pecker.* Hardly.

"His queen sure likes sharing it," I observe, humor filling my voice.

"His queen barely escaped with her life from a VIP Paris nightclub. She was part of a sex scandal that blew up the tabloids." Nadine pours herself a shot. "Delphine knows the darkest secrets of some of Europe's most powerful men. She could destroy them, so she hides here to stay alive. Lucky for my son, she hides in his sheets, too. I swear they're wilder than an acre of snakes for each other; they lose their damn minds."

I watch Vale innocently chatting with her friends while guilt suddenly crushes my chest.

Have we lost our minds, too? Have Vale and I fallen so deeply in love, we're fooling ourselves?

Yes, we've gotten used to being hunted. We're using it to our advantage. This feud with Turner will end one day soon, but then...

What about Alena? Even if she approves of my love for Vale, I know one day Alena will find out what I did so that she would be loved, too. Vale will find out, as well.

I'm no fool. Secrets can't stay hidden forever. I'll have to tell Vale, and she'll have to understand; love left me no choice.

"My son," Nadine reads my silence, "when will you tell her?"

She's not asking about Alena.

"Before her initiation. I should tell her and—"

"No." The Queen insists, "We made the vow over my second wedding ring in this room, and it won't be broken. Alena will be my family and have the wedding she deserves. She will be married and protected forever ... *then* we tell them."

In the past, a queen wore two rings: one from her first husband on her right wedding finger, according to Russian Orthodox tradition, and the other from her second husband on her left.

Now, The Queen demands we blend in. We follow local traditions. Wives wear their first husband's ring on their left wedding finger while wearing a piercing that proudly marks them as our queen, too.

Wren and Delphine chose Monroe piercings.

No, the irony that Vale *Monroe* will be my queen isn't lost on me.

Our other queen? He chose something less visible but equally proud, and we understand. He can't be out in some circles.

I'm trapped in my dream of putting a black diamond on Vale's finger and my nightmare of losing her when she knows the whole truth.

It leaves me watching the floor below, feeling like a hero and villain to the woman I love.

Suddenly, Jace confronts a man who's harassing Blair. He towers over him before snapping his fingers, siccing Nadine's security on him before Jace escorts Blair safely outside.

That leaves Grant and Vale in the club, and I shake my head.

Grant's lost in triple blowjob heaven.

He doesn't know Vale's standing alone at the bar. He doesn't see her glance up, searching behind the glass where I'm standing, as she smirks with pride before ... "Goddamnit, poison!"

She disobeys me.

Proudly, Vale swishes her ass toward the door. She's supposed to tell Grant she's leaving but doesn't. Alone, she lures a man dressed in navy pants and a plaid button-up shirt to follow her outside. But I clock it—the knife he's hiding cupped in the palm of his hand.

"She's on the move," I bark at Nadine, who joins me at the glass, reaching for her radio.

"Grab that preppy bastard," she commands her security, "and secure her. I want him in the bunker, and I want her to see this."

CHAPTER THIRTY-SEVEN
VALE

D R A W I N G   A   R A G G E D   B R E A T H,   I   W A T C H   N A S H'S   B R U T A L   F I S T collide with the man's defiant face. The snap of bone distinct. The gush of blood immediate. His nose broken and bleeding.

Nadine's security snatched this man up outside the club. Then they grabbed me, too. Quickly, we were tossed in the back of a white van while her men slapped him into cuffs, and I screamed, "Let me go, you pencil dicks, or I'll curse you with anejaculation until your cocks explode with your pathetic, pent-up cum!"

One of her men looked at me, aghast. "Is that a thing?"

"Yes!" I shouted. "Open a book instead of Pornhub and read all about it. It can be caused by stress, and I'm about to give you a fuck-ton of it!"

The men were silent until the van stopped, its doors ripped open.

"Let's kick this off," Nash snarled, standing there. "Go ahead. Ways I'm going to spank your ass for disobeying me."

At the sight of his rage, I relaxed. "If you want to worship me, all you have to do is ask."

But ... he wasn't laughing.

He took my arm, stifling his anger. I knew he wanted to yank a knot in me, but instead, he quickly escorted me, the building a blur as we rushed through double metal doors and down a long, concrete hallway with dusty light fixtures barely illuminating our path. It smelled of pluff mud, meaty mold, and Nash's sexy deodorant that really deserves a vacation from this.

Behind us, I heard clicking heels and turned around.

Nadine elegantly stalked down the long hallway, flanked by four guards, with two more dragging their new captive behind her.

"What's going on?" I muttered to Nash.

"You're about to see the dark side of being a queen," Nash replied.

And here we are...

Me, watching Nash interrogate the man who was about to nab me and Nadine, standing beside me, smoking a cigar that smells like berries and vanilla.

"Where is he?" Nash holds a pair of pliers poised over the man's front tooth.

He's cuffed to a metal chair, spitting through the blood pouring over his thin lips. "Fuck you. We'll get her one day. You know it, and you know what we've done to the others, we'll do to *her*."

Who? Me? Alena?

It doesn't matter to Nash. Evilly, he sneers. "Oh, I think *you're* the one about to be fucked." He turns to Nadine's guards. "Strip him!"

I stand by the closed, heavy metal door with Nadine. Beige paint peels off the concrete walls of the room. This must be an old underground bunker in the Naval yard. I can smell the river nearby and the bucket the first man, the one who crawled over the wall at Delta's, is using for his toilet.

It's foul. It's disgusting. But god, their first captive isn't.

He kneels on a soiled mattress, his chiseled cheek and full lips pressed against it. He's a hot, muscular brute, sculpted and naked and covered in ink. He's bound in one of the Humiliators I sold to Nash with his ass in the air, his scrotum stretched taut and squeezed between the bars bound to his inked ankles.

But I grin.

Because, as I warned Nash, the man's dick hangs huge and hard for his humiliating torture. *This isn't his first time submitting.* His ass is too groomed. His eyes are too trained. He's staring at Nadine with murderous lust in his eyes.

No wonder they can't break him. He loves this.

But the second man? He must be one of Turner's preppy golf buddies, all money and perversion, no mass and real power. As soon as he realizes what Nash and the men are about to bind him in?

He fights like a cat getting a bath. "No! No! No!" he shrieks, clawing at his captors.

"Oh, so you don't *like* this?" Nash taunts, mashing the man's bloody cheek against the concrete. "You don't like being forced? You don't like being made my bitch?"

Nadine's guards cuff the man's kicking ankles. One of them grabs his balls, jerking them as another traps them between two wooden bars, screwing the bars tightly together.

"Fuck you! Fuck you!" The man swears, realizing when he fights, it only tortures his scrotum more.

"Read the room." Nash laughs. "Who's the one about to be fucked if he doesn't tell me where Turner is?"

The man's penis shrivels, his body sweating, his eyes frantic and scared.

He doesn't like this. This is his worst nightmare.

Just like the nightmare he's been to so many children and women. They've suffered far worse than the humiliation he's enduring now.

A little part of me feels sympathy, though I know Nash or any of Nadine's men would never sexually violate someone.

But the bigger part of me, the future queen in me, wants this intel, too. As a survivor like Nadine ... I don't give a damn. Sacrifice this evil man to save innocent people. We just need a location.

To my point, Nadine approaches one of her guards with her hand outstretched. Quickly, he puts his phone in her palm.

She stands with Nash over the man whimpering with his naked ass presented to her. "You pigs like to take pictures," she says. "You're too pathetic to have someone desire you, so you take pictures of people forced to endure your stench. And trust me, you stink."

Urine puddles beneath him. I suspect he's about to shit himself, too.

"So what if we take pictures now," Nadine smiles, "and send them to all of your country club, good ol' boys? My, my, how they'll laugh at pictures of your pancake ass in the air and your saggy balls drawn tight. Your picture will spread like a prairie fire in high wind. And don't you worry a thinning hair on your greasy little head about it. I'll make sure you barely live to endure the humiliation. Or..."

Nash squats by the man, pressing two fingers against the bridge of his broken nose. The man howls in pain while Nadine roars, "Tell us where he is!"

"County Shed Road," the man snivels, "the Deliverance Chapel."

"Of course, he fucking did," Nash sneers. "Turner's hiding the most immoral sin in a church."

NASH UNBRAIDS MY HAIR WHILE CALMING LAVENDER bubbles surround us. I sit between his legs, admiring his muscles and soaking in his love while my bottom still stings from his punishment.

I earned a helluva spanking for my stunt tonight. *Whoops.* Then I got the most luscious, brutal fuck against the window of The Mercier as Nash fisted my braids like reins, loving how a man watched our silhouettes from the sidewalk below, knowing I was a woman getting railed to orgasmic delight.

Now, the beast is gone, and Nash is quiet.

Too quiet.

"All your talking sounds like white noise." I joke.

Still, no answer.

"Do we need Jesus to make you talk?" I warn, "I can screech *This Little Light of Mine* and crack mirrors for you."

He finishes with my hair, pulling me back to rest my head on his chest. My dark strands fan through the bubbles, falling over his arms that wrap around me.

"If I lose you," he murmurs, "I'll die inside. I'll live for Alena; she's my soul, but you're my heart, Vale. If you pull another stunt like that again and get hurt or worse, my heart will die with you, too."

"But I'm okay." I reach for his hand.

"But you don't know everything. There's more. So much more. Some I can't even tell you; you have to see it to understand."

"I understand what you have to do sometimes. I know you don't want to; you have to. It's one of the things I love about you. Nash, all you do is fight for the ones you love."

"Just promise me," his lips press to my ear, "when you're my queen, you'll remember what you saw tonight. You'll understand the threats we face, the work we do, and the decisions we've made. Promise that you won't hate me for it."

"I won't hate you." I turn around in his arms. I kneel, cupping his clenched jaw. "I promise I'll understand."

He takes my promise with a kiss, the kiss he killed for. Then he takes me in the tub with such passion I swear a tear falls from his wet cheek along with our sloshing bath water.

All I can feel is our love.

All I can wonder is...

...what else is he hiding?

CHAPTER THIRTY-EIGHT
VALE

Funny how a few days can change your life.

For me?

I'm dressed in the couture fashion Nadine brought to our suite at The Mercier. A glam team just finished my makeup and hair while a piercer waits to give me the final touch.

In the mirror's reflection over the dining table, I look like a different version of myself and love it.

I'll always have a gothic heart, but I can drip with some boujee French fashion, too.

But my twin?

Her life changed on an NFL dime. In a matter of days, Beau Bronson and his teammate Colton Hawke whisked Blair away to a Caribbean island. But now she's blowing up my phone, and instinctually, I know something's wrong.

I answer her FaceTime call. With one glimpse at my new look, Blair's pressing her face to the screen. "You look like a New York City socialite. What is that? Chanel?"

"How do you know Chanel?"

"Because," she scoffs, "I got champagne taste on a box of wine budget. That's a couture bouclé Chanel jacket, and it's pink! What the hell? I'm gone for three days, and you've moved to the Upper East Side. I swear, if you have an ankle-biter yipping dog in your Birkin bag, too, I'm having you committed."

I tell her my glow-up is for a meeting with Nash, and she's all shook.

"*Vaaallleee,*" she drawls suspiciously. "What's going on? You're not eloping with your best friend's dad or some shit like that. Because I'm your maid of honor no matter how fucked up the union."

"We're not eloping, you naked nosy ho." I caress my hair, twisted into an elegant chignon. "It's a meeting. That's it. Quit asking questions I won't answer."

"Quit saying you have a meeting with Mr. Allen when I know you're fucking him and someone else tonight. Probably Tarzan with the way y'all ripped the sex swing from the ceiling at Delta's."

Meeting? No, it's my initiation.

And Tarzan? Try Jace. He'll be the someone else tonight, and only tonight.

I'm dying to tell Blair about it. Keeping this from Alena is bad enough, but usually, I tell my twin everything. Hell, we share the same DNA. When she fucks too much, I get the yeast infection.

But I'm thankful to have Wren now. She's here with Nadine, sitting on the sofas in the living area, sipping champagne and looking highly amused as Blair and I resolve her NFL double-dick dilemma and get to the bottom of all of Blair's pain. It's the same as mine.

Our dad.

Blair has a different relationship with him. I think my dad sees himself in me and our mom in Blair, which makes him kinder to her. But still, he's broken our hearts too many times.

Blair fears she's repeating the same cycle, going from being the daughter of a famous athlete to the girlfriend of one.

Or maybe two?

She worries she'll get hurt again. She stresses about Beau, saying he'd never treat her like a distraction, but "What if I am," she frets, "and he loses and resents me for it? Like Dad did?"

"Look..." My heart softens. Yes, I fight with my sister. It's only because I love her with a ferocity I can't control. "Think for yourself, not for someone else."

Tears brim in her eyes. "That's what Mom used to say."

"Exactly, and that's what she'd say now," I sigh, knowing we miss her. Then I see Nadine sipping champagne. She's another strong woman blessing my life, so I tell Blair, "I never thought I'd say this to my boss-bitch bookish twin, but just do it. Be a WAG."

Her face twists. "A WAG?"

"A wife and girlfriend of a high-profile athlete."

Because I'm about to be a queen, a Belle to the Beast I love, so I hope my sister can follow her heart, too. No matter the risks.

But she scoffs at my advice, so I tell her, "Then be the girlfriend in love with that cute guy from college that you write all your alien porno love books about. The guy who really loves them and loves *you*, too."

That's who Beau is to Blair, and Blair is to him—the one who got away.

And that's what Nash is to me.

The sweet man who brought me red tulips and cheeseburgers. The brutal man who ended my nightmare with Chad. The tender man who held me by my mom's grave, and I cried even harder in his arms, holding me for the first time ... because I couldn't have his love then.

But now, I can. I will.

I end our call knowing I'm far more than some man's daughter he neglected or some boy's victim. I'm a woman, born for this.

I'm not afraid to sit beside Nadine as the piercer, working with gloved hands, carefully marks me as a queen with a gold and diamond bezel-set Monroe stud.

Yes, it hurts.

Yes, I'm proud.

"This diamond is my gift to you." Nadine pulls me into a tight hug. "I've always wanted daughters, too, and now you're like mine. You have my love forever, *moya doch.*"

It's the first time I've heard her speak Russian, and I don't know the language, but I know from her warmth it means *my daughter*.

But to me, it means more because I can feel the scars on Nadine's back, the welts of tortured flesh under her soft, silk Chanel wrap dress.

"Thank you." I squeeze her tighter.

She leaves with a kiss on my cheek and one on Wren's. We're left in the suite to share one more glass of champagne and a secret I'm dying to know.

"Can I ask who your second king is?"

Wren twists her petal lips. "I'm not supposed to say yet," she whispers as if we're not alone, "but I think you can guess."

I search her eyes, and her brows raise.

"Nash?" I gasp.

Quickly, she nods, worried like I'll be mad. "Just once," she rushes, "and he didn't *finish* like the others. He held back. We didn't even kiss. He didn't even look me in the eye. It's like part of him was there, but the rest wasn't."

How do I feel about this?

I search my shocked heart, and all I can find is ... *love.*

Nash kept his honor to his family, but he didn't give his heart away. That's what Wren's telling me. Woman to woman, I know what she means. I've had so many men fuck me who never gave me their heart. We were there for a reason, and I could never find mine.

Until I found Nash. With him, I find my heart; I find my reason.

That man has waited over twelve years for me and did what he had to do with Wren. He helped Sire, and as Wren's second king, it's all Nash will ever do with her. If he ever needs to, he'll protect her, as he should.

"Nash was sweet," she explains, "because I wasn't that night. It's like the animal in me came out, and I wanted all of them; I'm not ashamed to admit it."

"You shouldn't be. I get it. They're hot."

"They are," she licks her lips, "and when I told them to take me like beasts, they did. Sire likes it like that. I do, too. He's my pastor and twenty years older than me, and I guess our love is so taboo; why not? All I feel is loved and safe with Sire. And then you add in his hot brothers—"

"*All* of them?" Yes, I'm digging. "You mean all seven?"

"No." She shakes her head. "Only five, including Nash. To Sire, Nash is his brother, probably his closest. But one of his brothers isn't into women, and the youngest? The one who should sit in the seventh king's chair? I've never seen him."

"He wasn't there?"

"Like you, I was blindfolded for some of it, so maybe he was, but when I could see, no, he wasn't there."

"Who is he?"

She shrugs.

"Who's the gay brother?"

She smiles. "You'll find out tonight, and I love his queen. You will, too. I swear, if you close your eyes, our fellow queen sounds like Matthew McConaughey."

Paint me so goddamn curious, I'm dying.

"Listen," Wren reaches for my hand, "there's more to know that's not my place to tell you. But please," her eyes beg, "don't leave us. Be a queen with me, and let's raise our babies together. Then one day, we'll be sixty like Nadine and badass, hot grandmothers like her, too."

I laugh, nodding because I can see it. It's a vision beyond my wildest dreams.

STANDING BY THE FLOOR-TO-CEILING WINDOW IN OUR hotel suite, I watch the day melt into dusk. Wren left an hour ago, and anticipation claws inside me.

All the questions, too.

In a normal life, I'd be a fool to agree to this initiation, to consider marriage and children with a man who's told me he hides secrets.

But clearly, I don't want a normal life. I want this one.

Because what I *do* know about Nash is more than anything I've ever seen from another man. He's fiercely loyal and deeply loving, and yes, he's a little homicidal and a real dickhead when he's grumpy, but I kind of love that about him, too. He lets me fire the snark right back.

Happy, horny, in love, and fearless: this pretty much sums up my current state when a heavy knock startles me.

"Poison!" Nash barks, "Let's go! We're late!"

This murderous meat dagger.

I storm toward the door, my mouth about to fire as I swing it open, "That's not my fau—" but a bouquet of red tulips greets me.

They lower, and that damn, sexy smile slings its sunshine. "You never did tell me why you love these so much."

Don't cry. Don't cry. Don't mess up your eyeliner.

"They were my mom's favorite."

Nash softens his smirk.

"Symbolically, they're supposed to evoke passion, love, and romance."

"Oh," he grabs my waist, crushing the bouquet between us, "they do." His eyes take in my face, hair, and Chanel suit before they land on my new piercing. "Damn, poison. You truly do kill me with your beauty."

"You like my new look?"

"I love your other look, too. But now you look like every dream I've had of us together except..."

His face twists, scrutinizing mine.

"What?" I drop my chin. "It's a mod look with a smokey eye and nude lip." My dramatic lashes blink with insecurity. "You hate it, don't you? It's my hair." I reach for the two gold combs in it. "I can take it down. I can braid it or—"

"Don't you fucking dare; I'll get that privilege later." He sets the bouquet on the table in the foyer. "You're just missing something."

"My Mary Janes?" I glance down. "I wasn't vibing them tonight. Nadine gave me these." I click my nude, high-heeled Louboutins. "I feel like a sexy Dorothy in them." I close my eyes, mimicking her in *The Wizard of Oz*. "There's no place like an orgy. There's no place like an orgy."

I make Nash laugh so hard, he hugs me, smushing my face against his quaking chest.

Tonight, he's not wearing his usual, either.

He's in a fitted black suit, a white starched shirt, and hallelujah, he left it unbuttoned, his ink on proud display, and his deep brown eyes. No glasses tonight. No disguise, either.

It's just Nash, smelling like sweet leather and looking like a Tom Ford mafia lollipop my mouth waters to lick.

"I bought something for you. It's why I'm late." He reaches into his jacket pocket. "I don't know if they go with your new look, but they screamed, 'Vale meets seventeen thousand dollar earrings.'"

My savage man is joking ... my hot accountant is not.

He cracks the jewelry box open, and I gasp. They're black diamond earrings shaped like little, coiled snakes with long, dangling tails. "Oh my god," I sigh. "They're too expensive. I can't accept them."

"The hell you won't. I'll spoil you into being an even sexier brat."

"Nash, I can't wea—"

"Vale," he looms over me, "my queen wears my jewels. Always." Tenderly, he kisses the new diamond above my lip. It's sore, but...

Okay, if he insists.

While he removes the arrangement from the flower vase left by the hotel and sets my tulips inside it, I put on my new earrings. They dangle, tickling my neck.

They have me smiling to Delta's while one of Nash's guards drives us in a black Mercedes—the symbolism not lost on me. When we arrive, I clock armed security lurking in every dark corner. Silently, I hold Nash's hand while he leads me inside. Jace isn't at his usual post. Some random guard sits there instead as we stride upstairs.

"Is everyone already here?" I whisper.

"Almost," he answers. "I've warned you." We stop at the top of the landing on the third floor. Gently, Nash lifts my stare to his. "You know what happens tonight. You know what I have to do."

Of course, we fuss about it one last time before I insist, "I *want* you to do it." Then I kiss him as passionately as I can.

How else can I shut his sexy mouth? How else can I convince him I'm in a make-me-your-queen-in-an-orgy kinda mood?

The door at the end of the hallway slowly opens, stopping us. I glance at the ominous sight and stifle a gasp.

It looks like a scene from that hot, soft porno mafia movie. You know, the one with a year of kinky kidnapping and sexy spit?

The doorknob, keyhole, and hinges on the black door gleam in gold. The Acanthus carvings on the black columns and molding around the door glimmer in gold leaf, too. They glow in the sconce light illuminating the dark hallway while large silhouettes loom in the doorway, candlelight flickering behind them.

It's Axel ... with five men shadowing him and one petite woman standing by his side.

She's dressed like me in a Chanel skirt suit, but hers is navy. What thrills me is that she's wearing a black silk blindfold over a black lace bondage hood, with her hair, eyes, and face concealed except for her ruby lips.

Around her neck is a dainty, black collar; its gold chain attached to the handle Axel gently tugs. She smirks at his control as classical music, Tchaikovsky, the Russian composer, gently lulls in the background.

With a snarl, Axel taunts Nash, "Is your princess ready to be a queen?"

But, you know ... I don't buy Axel's extra asshole act anymore.

Yes, he looks like a sinister son of a proud bitch (who I love), but there's more to him; I'm beginning to give the asshat a lot of credit now.

So he can take a seat, asking Nash because it's for me to answer, "Yes. I. Am."

Our steps aim for the room.

The silhouette of the kings blocking my view is eerie and

erotic. All the while, I feel like someone's watching us. Tingles crawl up my spine, so I whip around and see an empty hallway and the ivory-paneled door to the demonstration room cracked open. The room is dark as usual.

I know we're safe here, so why do I sense we're not alone?

Fuck it. I roll my eyes. This old house is haunted, I know.

So I grin, silently inviting the ghosts to join my initiation, too.

CHAPTER THIRTY-NINE
NASH

I should've known seeing Vale like this would be my undoing ... in the best way.

She looks like a queen tonight, rich with power and grace. Yes, she looks like my future wife and mother to my children.

Possessively, I hold her hand. It starts trembling as I proudly guide her past the wall of my brothers dressed in black suits.

Well ... most of them. One better not join us tonight. He could ruin everything.

Sire gently bows to Vale, the heart tattoo under his eye crinkling with his smile. Grant gives her an approving wink. Jace softly smiles at her while Axel surprises me.

Who's the woman he brought to Vale's initiation?

Axel initiated our first queen years ago, but then he lost her. She vanished without a trace, and it's as if she took Axel's noble soul with her and left him with a cold, angry heart.

Yes, he fucks other women. He has very dark, primal urges he can't fight, but I've never seen him share his heart again. Until now.

Axel would never bring a woman into our sanctuary unless

she means something to him. Unless he's testing her to make sure, she won't run this time.

It leaves me full of questions watching Vale meet our sixth king.

Nick wraps his hulking arms around her, gently kissing her blushing cheek. "Finally, Nash gets his beauty, his Belle. He's been suffering a long time without you."

Of course, Vale recognizes him. Nick is the NFL's leading defensive end and a local hero. Of all the brothers, he leads the most public life, though ironically, he hides the most.

No one but us knows he was once Nikofor Kholodov. Only a few trusted friends and we know Nick is gay and proudly in love with his queen, *our* queen.

It's an odd label for the man Nick loves. But Zar Rollins wears his title with pride. His Texas swagger and billionaire clout are not threatened by any role. They only prove his love for Nick. It only proves the power of being one of our queens. We worship him, too.

"But you're..." Vale stammers, unsure if she should reveal how else she knows Nick. "You're with—"

"Zar?" Nick grins. "And Luca and Scarlett Mercier, your loyal customers? Yes. But this, my queen, is our big secret."

Vale promises, "I'll protect it."

"I know." Nick hugs her again.

I lead Vale past the row of white velvet queens' chairs with ornately carved legs and backs painted gold. They sit opposite our black velvet kings' chairs, with a large, black leather-tufted platform between them and a sapphire velvet bench at the top.

Guiding Vale to the bench, I hold her hand as she sits gracefully, scanning the room like she's never seen it before.

It's the former owner's suite, with a high black ceiling meeting black walls trimmed in ornate molding gilded in gold leaf. The tall windows at one end are covered by gold velvet curtains, billowing over the original parquet floors. The view outside overlooks the guarded courtyard.

I'm sure Vale saw this room before Axel claimed it. But she's never seen it transformed like this.

Around the room stand tall, golden candelabras, holding flickering tapered candles. Their ivory wax drips in romantic rivulets onto the glass squares beneath them.

In one corner stands a princely, antique mahogany table with gold trays brimming with treats for the night, a crystal decanter of vodka, and over a dozen crystal glasses.

At the top of the room, centered on the wall, stands a lone red velvet throne. Black, gold, white, and red: they're the colors of Russian royalty reflected in this room, and that's clearly The Queen's unoccupied throne.

More gold candelabras hold ivory tapered candles on a matching table in the opposite corner as each king silently lights one. It's an orthodox tradition as I offer a prayer—to who, I'm not sure—but all I can do is hope for Vale to be mine from tonight and always.

And please, God. The devil? Anyone? Don't let me murder Jace.

I blow out my match.

Sire pours our shots in perfect timing with a coded knock at the door.

Grant smiles, turning to open it for our queens.

Wren, our newest, enters wearing a black velvet corseted minidress. Every time I see her dainty face and lithe body, I have to remind myself ... *she's of age. She's twenty.*

Hell, she's more. Wren fought to be Sire's queen. No one can deny her fierce desire to be here.

Delphine, who's much taller with proud, feminine curves, strides behind her in a similar black satin corseted mini dress, but hers has a long, sheer, black chiffon skirt. That woman is French, through and through. Even Delphine's blonde hair, twisted in a messy bun, and her long bangs, skimming her smoky eyes, reveal it.

Last but never least, Nick's queen saunters into the room. *Damn, I love his style.* Zar chose a black velvet tuxedo tonight, his dark waves styled like a handsome devil.

My stare slides to Vale, who's stunned silent. Each queen greets her next with kisses on her cheeks, their smiles warm and welcoming.

With a round of vodka shots served by Sire, we stand, circling Vale. She sits proudly as we hold our crystal glasses high in a silent toast to her, and for a moment, I don't believe I'm here.

Guess this is the feeling of a dream coming true. Guess this is love because each time I think Vale can't look any more beautiful, I'm so wrong.

I toss my shot back before noting the goosebumps blooming over her alabaster calves.

Vale feels it, too.

The kings escort their queens to their thrones before taking their thrones across from them. I stand before Vale with my hands clasped, my eyes anchored to hers as Axel drones on about tradition, honor, and vows.

The whole time, his mystery woman kneels on a golden velvet pillow, her masked face submitting to his lap, his hand caressing her head.

Vale's grey eyes grow wide, taking in the story Axel shares of their escape from Moscow, why their mother hid them here, how we chose this tradition years later, and why we fight for what we do now.

Yes, it's sacred to us. It's our history and bond, but I've heard it all before.

I want my queen.

I've waited too damn long for her.

I'm impatient to begin, my heart pounding to claim her. She's always been mine.

Finally, Axel concludes, "Do you, Nash Allen, with a free and unconstrained will, claim Vale Monroe as your queen?"

I nod, reaching for Vale's right hand. Lifting it to my lips, I kiss her third finger and vow, "I do."

"Will you guard her, above all, with your life? Will you love her, above all, with your heart? Will you die for her, with no hesitation, leaving her your soul?"

I swallow, lost in the tears welling in Vale's eyes. "Always."

"Will you, Vale Monroe," Sire begins, "with a free and unconstrained will, accept our brother, Nash Allen, as your king?"

Vale chews her trembling lip.

Don't cry, poison.

I kneel, cupping her cheeks, feeling all the years I couldn't have her rush through my veins until finally, my fingertips tingle, holding her before me now.

The years she suffered alone, waiting for me, swim in her eyes, too. They make her tears fall, wetting my palms, her beautiful, silent emotions strangling my throat. Her lips tremble as if, for the first time ... *Vale can't speak.*

I nuzzle my forehead to hers. "Time to use all those words you love, poison."

"I will..." She stammers, smiling, "I mean ... I do. I take Nash as my king."

"Will you love him, above all, with your heart? Will you give him, more than any other, a life worth fighting for? Will you honor him, even in death, as his queen?"

"Forever," she promises.

"Deliver them, safe from wrath and danger," Sire prays aloud as I pull Vale's lips to mine. "Preserve their bed and fill their home." Our lips part, her tongue and breath meeting mine. "Let them see their children's children." I deepen our kiss, my heart hitching and wanting nothing more. "Unite them into one flesh, one family with us." I taste Vale's tears. They make me fight mine. "Crown them, king and queen together, tonight, and in the stars forever."

"I love you, my poison," I murmur over our lips.

"I love you, too," she whispers, "you sexy dickhead."

She makes me chuckle into our kiss as Wren softly sighs, "Aw, they belong together."

FOR AN HOUR, WE CELEBRATE.

Kings and queens laugh and catch up, though I don't miss how Axel remains seated with the mystery woman's covered head in his lap.

Vale and I light a candle together, and I grin, knowing her prayer. It's the same as mine—*little Wednesday Allen.*

We raise another round of shots. Caviar on canapes is passed before Sire blesses the Korovai, the traditional Russian wedding bread, hand-braided and prepared by Nadine. I serve Vale a bite before she does the same to me.

Later, I'll give Vale the wedding of her dreams. I'm sure it will be gothic and glamorous, and I won't be surprised if she walks down the aisle to the Addams Family theme song.

But now?

Christ, I want this woman.

"It's time," I tell my brothers.

Silently, they nod, settling onto their thrones while Axel and his woman remain on his.

I whisper to Vale, "Go refresh in the restroom down the hall. We'll wait for you."

Wren joins her. Delphine, too.

While they're gone, Zar takes his place on Nick's lap, as Nick jokes with me, "Damn, Nash. It's about time. You've been a very patient man."

"It only took... What?" Grant asks, "Ten years?"

"Twelve," I answer. "And fuck patience. I was protecting Alena, but she's old enough to accept it now. One day, I hope."

Silence falls over us before Nick jerks his chin left toward the seventh throne. The empty one. "Is he coming?"

"I ordered him to join us," Axel answers.

He makes Sire scoff, "Like he listens to anyone but Nash."

"He better obey me," Axel seethes before I snarl, "He better not—"

"He knows what to do!" Axel barks. "It's fine."

Flaring my nostrils, I'm about to fight him on this. *Seven should NOT be here.* But Wren and Delphine bound into the room with Vale. "She's very ready!" They giggle, guilty as fuck.

"Come here!" I command Vale, lust and fury thrumming through my veins.

Swishing my way, Vale smiles from ear to black diamond ear, but I pull her toward me, whipping her around, all humor escaping when I crush her petite back against my chest. Grabbing her delicate throat, I feel her excited pulse as Wren sits with Sire and Delphine drapes over Grant.

Jace is the only king with no queen, no one kneeling before him either.

Suddenly, it evaporates my rage.

I love Jace. I love that he taught Alena how to ride a bicycle; I was too protective to see her fall. I taught her how to shoot, but Jace taught her how to dress her first kill: a deer. She cried some, and Jace never chided her. He patiently talked her through it.

He looks like an alluring devil, just like his father, but he's a good man.

Maybe he's more like me than I realize. Maybe, like me, tonight he'll keep his vow to his family while he waits for the love of his life, too.

It's not Vale. No man loves Vale as I do.

But I know Jace cares for her. And once I tell my massive ego to shut the fuck up, my humanity reminds me; Vale may need him to protect her. So, I give Jace this.

I stand, holding Vale before him while I reach around, unbuttoning her pink jacket, one gold button at a time, before sliding it off her milky shoulders and letting it fall to the floor.

Underneath, she's wearing a black lace bra, the contrast to her creamy skin, breathtaking.

I unzip her skirt, noting her ribs softly heaving in anticipation. All watch as it falls, revealing her matching black lace thong.

Without my command, she proudly kicks her skirt away, staring at my brothers in her lingerie and heels.

Peering over her shoulder, I lick my lips at her aroused nipples under her sheer lace. Claiming her neck, I bite it, marking her as mine, making her gasp before I command, "Tell me to stop at any point, and I will."

"Don't you dare," she sighs. "You know what I want."

"My pretty little poison." I press my lips to her ear, grinding my hard cock against her ass. Pulling her lace cups down, I expose her breasts, tickling her nipples until she moans, and I taunt, "Let's show my brothers how you torture me with these."

Playing with Vale's luscious tits, I make Axel lick his lips, too, his fist reaching for the mystery woman's hand, guiding it to stroke his hard cock, covered by his black pants.

Sire's inked fingers snake under Wren's dress. He starts playing with her pussy; it's obvious by how she leans back and spreads her legs for him. "Yes, my lord," she gasps for him.

Vale pants at their adoration, their amorous reaction as Delphine proudly unzips Grant's pants, freeing his pierced cock.

Nick does the same to Zar. Nick may not be attracted to women, but Zar is. He's hard and attracted to all.

It's only Jace who remains stoic.

He doesn't free himself, but he can't deny the thick erection strangled under his pants. With slanted eyes, he watches her writhe against me as I roll her nipples between my fingers, making her moan when I gently tug them.

"Tell them how long you've wanted me," I demand while sliding my hand under Vale's panties, tickling her hard clit, and making her pant, "Since I was eighteen."

"Tell them how you want me now." I plunge my fingers inside her tight cunt. Her slick lust coats my pumping digits as she grinds against my cock, confessing, "Every way, my king."

"Shall I make you my queen?" I coax, biting her neck again, leaving another exquisite bruise.

"Yes," she pants.

"Then get on your knees on the bench, bend over, and spread your cheeks." I relish the command, "Show my brothers what's mine to fuck."

CHAPTER FORTY
VALE

IF I THOUGHT I KNEW DESIRE, I WAS WRONG. WE WERE strangers. At least, I've never met desire like this. One that finds me proudly obeying Nash.

Released from his controlling grip, I kneel on the sapphire bench, my back to our court, proudly assuming my position as a new queen.

Earlier in the bathroom, with Wren and Delphine waiting in the hall, I snuck a diamond butt plug in. Before I did it, I asked them if I should, and they nodded eagerly.

"Trust me," Wren insisted. "If they initiate you as I asked them to initiate me, you'll need it tonight."

Pressing my cheek to the velvet, I pull my thong down, leaving it around my thighs before spreading myself open. It makes me so wet, being on royal display, showing how I belong to Nash ... or skulls will crack.

He sees it now. "What's in your ass?"

"Your jewel, my king," I tease and...

Smack. "You dirty." *Smack.* "Little." *Smack.* "Naughty girl."

His spanks are so sweet. My bedazzled ass stings with delight.

He steps in front of me, lifting my chin. "You want to choke on your king's jewels?"

"Yes, my king. Please." I stare into his wild eyes. I've never felt so beautiful, my tingling sex exposed to his brothers as Nash steps back and strips before me.

As a silent promise, he turns away, draping his discarded garments over the second queen's throne.

My throne to earn tonight.

Turning to face me, lust rips my breath away at the sight of Nash. He's nude, covered in ink and shredded muscles, his erection jutting hard and exposed for me, for his brothers and their queens to relish it, too.

I part my lips for his tip, peering up at him.

He pulls the gold combs from my hair, dropping them on the floor, my raven waves tumbling free before he sinks a hand into my strands, his other fisting the base of his cock.

Slapping his tip against my waiting lips, he demands, "Open those lips wider for me. Yes, stick that naughty tongue out, too. That's it. Now, show them what a thirsty little girl you are for this cock."

In one ruthless thrust, Nash claims my waiting mouth, choking my throat. I gape up at him, my eyes suddenly tearing, loving the beast fucking my face.

It makes my exposed pussy leak, my muscles clenching around the steel plug, thrilling my ass, too.

I love that he's doing it like this.

Nash is proud of our lust. He's not hiding it anymore. He's going to fuck me like an animal because his brothers already know how long he's loved me.

Tonight, he proves how much he's wanted me, too.

Fisting my hair into a ponytail, he guides me, making me take as much of him as I can, my proud chokes filling the air. Then, lewdly, he taps my head, like he's petting me, as he thrusts his thick cock into my mouth. "That's it. Good girl. Suck it. Take it all the way, poison."

I can't. It's impossible. He's too long, but I try. I drool. I cry, moaning and wanting every inch of him, tasting his teasing, salty drops on my tongue that only drive me to gag on him.

Nash pulls out at my struggling sound, dragging out my spit and letting it drool from my lips. I weep and smile up at him before he guides me to turn around.

Fisting my hair as I kneel on the bench, Nash declares to his brothers, "This is my beautiful queen. She's always belonged to me, and I'll always choose her. Don't touch her. You know I'll kill for her."

In a violent rip, he tears my thong off, tossing it at Axel, who barely grins.

"But you've known how much I love her, too, haven't you?" He challenges them, and every head nods except Jace.

I want to cry tender tears at how long Nash has loved me, at all he's done for me, at how long he's waited for this, for us.

I can't believe we're finally here, but I keep searching Jace's stare. It's not angry, jealous, or lecherous. Jace's erection is obvious. We arouse him, but I've known Jace for some time, too. I know ... *he's doing this for Nash*.

He's not letting the beast inside him come out, too. That would be a bloody fight to the death over me, and Nash wouldn't lose. Nash *will* kill for me.

So Jace finds the man inside him, the one who'll keep his vow and protect his queens.

But Nash?

He's here to claim me. He has to be a beast to initiate me. One whose overwhelming instinct is to fuck me for all to see his primacy and property.

It's so primitive and barbaric. It's so beautiful, too, how Nash gently turns me to face him. Wiping away my smeared mascara and tears, he asks, "Do you want to show them everything? Every way you're mine?"

I answer with every cell in my body, "Yes, my king."

With a smirk I didn't expect, Nash unclasps my bra, letting it fall to the floor before he aims for his jacket on the second queen's throne—my throne. Reaching into the inside pocket, he pulls out a small white box.

No way that's an engagement ring.

Nash may be kinky, but he's romantic, too. He'll save that for later, and I'm right. Opening the box, he lifts three pairs of magnetic orbs.

Sneaky, sexy, dickhead. He's been shopping in my store without me.

Pulling them apart, he orders, "Face your kings and queens."

Proudly, I do. I'm nude except for my heels. Desire licks through me when I feel Nash's erection, wet from my spit, pressing into my crevice.

"My queen likes to be a very dirty girl for me," he taunts, reaching around, letting his hand hover over my breast before the pull of the magnetic balls snaps together, pinching my nipple so hard, I cry out.

"Don't you love it, poison?"

"Yes," I huff at the searing pain, edging into slick pleasure.

"Did you teach me about these? Do you know every kink that makes your king wild for you?"

"Yes," I answer before the muffled *click* of Nash pinching my other nipple between magnetic orbs, pain ripping to my fingertips, pleasure rushing my core.

I'm fighting to stand at the explosion of sensations radiating from the sweetest torture while he turns my chin, seeking my kiss. I gasp into his mouth while he rubs the last cold, metal pair over my mound.

"Do you want this, my poison?" Lust owns his voice. "Do you want every pleasure I can give my queen?"

"Please," I beg over his lips.

"I want those." I hear Wren sigh to Sire.

"Same, mon amour," Delphine tells Grant in her raspy accent.

"They feel great on your cock, too," Zar adds.

The queens approve of the pleasure our kings give us. It makes me wonder about their initiations. Who is Zar's second king? Who is Delphine's? Who is the woman kneeling for Axel? And why is the seventh throne sitting empty?

But my logic won't work. It's too pummeled by the electric shocks of pleasure radiating from my throbbing nipples.

"Kneel, my queen." Nash lifts my hand like a lady as he guides me.

My knees sink into the soft platform. Then, Nash gently pushes my head down, making my cheek rest on the black leather, my sex once again exposed to the others, but this time ... he kneels, too.

Like he's praying at my altar, Nash kisses my clit, over and over, letting all watch his maddening skill of eating my pussy like a starving animal, to the point I'm willing to die just like this. Nash rules my cunt with his wet, velvet tongue; his slurping sounds proud and potent.

I'm moaning, relishing how he proudly fucks me with his tongue, too. The approving sighs of the women in the room are audible before a sudden, searing pinch of my clit makes me scream.

He uses the last set of orbs on me, the stinging pinch blinding. I can't breathe until he laves his tongue over the magnets and my clit, soothing its pain into the most excruciating pleasure.

My thighs shake. My lips, too. "Oh, my god. Nash, please. Let me come."

"My queen needs to come?" He licks my clasped nub, nerves I didn't know I had lighting up my center. Tugging at my butt plug, too, he makes me groan, desperate and wild for him. I feel my pussy dripping over his lapping tongue. My body is clenching tight, ready to explode in release. "Does my queen want to come with my cock in her ass?"

"Yes," I beg. "Please."

But then he abandons me, leaving me panting before I realize he's lifting the bench. Its top half opens, revealing it's a lid—*clever, Bratva brothers.* From the hidden storage, he gets a condom and some lube before he returns, standing behind me.

"Say it again, my queen." Reverently, his warm fingertips linger down my spine. "Say what you want me to do to you in front of my brothers."

Jeez, don't make me say it.

That was in the heat of pornographic passion. Yes, I want it, but Nash making me confess it to everyone makes me suddenly and ridiculously shy.

"Please," I beg. "Please just do it."

"No, my queen." Nash lifts me by the throat, pulling my ear to his lips. "Always say what you demand of your king, and say it proud. You're mine, and you're powerful. Your desire knows no shame with us. We worship it. You have my love forever, Vale, so demand what you want from me."

Lusciously, he slaps my pinched breasts, sending fiery shocks to my clit; the white-hot thrill making the command storm over my lips, "Fuck my ass, Nash. Now."

Oh, my god, I said it.

Oh, my goddess, thank you; he does it.

Bending me back into my prone position, he rolls a condom on before shamelessly pouring lube over my sex. Gently, he tugs my plug out, his fingertips tickling my clit while he does it. I almost come at the salacious sensations, at the gaping ache before Nash rises to fill it slowly.

Oh.

My.

King.

I moan at his burning entry, at the exposed position he puts us in, our backsides and feral union on display for all.

It's primal and proud how Nash mounts me, crouching over my hips and grabbing them. His hulking legs squat, straddling me while he claims what's his alone. Slowly, he drives his sheathed, lubed cock inside, burying himself to the hilt in my most vulnerable place, my heart and body trusting him, taking him.

"Who's ass is this?" he groans.

"Yours, my king." I reach for his hands, bruising my hips.

With no shame and urged on by my moans, Nash fucks me like an animal. My cunt aches and drips, pulsing empty and loving this while he dominates my ass.

"Dear God." I hear Sire praise our performance.

"He's always wanted her," Nick marvels.

Grant agrees, "Hell, yes, he has."

"She needs to come like that," Axel commands. "If she doesn't like it, stop."

"No, I love it. I love Nash," I argue. I demand, "Don't stop. I want it. I want him like this."

"Show them," Nash strains, lifting my hips and thrusting harder. "Show them you belong to me. That you're my good girl who comes with my cock in your ass."

"Yes, Mr. Allen." I reach between my legs, rubbing my pinched clit, and taking us there. "Yes, Daddy, fill my ass with your cum."

"Goddammit, Vale." He spanks me. When I talk like that, I make him come, but he doesn't want to yet. He wants this for me. "Show them how you've always been mine."

I was. I am. Strumming my clit so hard, I come, letting his brothers watch as only Nash can make me do it. My thighs quake. My stinging nipples rub against the leather, adding to my convulsions, to my shattering, orgasmic screams.

The ache for him in my empty cunt is almost painful; the pleasure he gives me divine. The taboo thrill of it all, of tonight and forever letting his brothers watch him mark me as his. "Nash," I sigh. "I love it. I love you."

"Yes." Zar's approving drawl fills the room. "Treat her like the beautiful queen she is."

"Come here, baby." Carefully, Nash pulls out before lifting my shaking body and wrapping his arms around me until I catch my breath. "You okay?" he asks tenderly.

"More than," I answer. "Finish serving me now."

He grips my chin, turning my lips to find his, and I feel his smile in our deep kiss. I feel him let go of me with one arm before the *snap* of him tugging his condom off tells me he's not done.

With my back to his chest, he turns us around to kneel, facing the others. He wedges my legs apart enough for all to watch him surge inside my waiting cunt, for him to fill what only he can. Only Nash claims the most tender places inside me.

Thrusting into me, he does it slowly, his fingertips playing with my keening clit, his other hand not letting go of my neck; my new Monroe piercing barely stings while his lips won't let go of our kiss, either.

Nash always fucks me like this; with so much passion and possession, the world falls away. It's only us, and it's all I feel now. Him. Me. My sweet, panting shudder at the next orgasm he gives me before he finally gives me his.

Before he proudly makes me his queen for all to see.

CHAPTER FORTY-ONE
NASH

All await the second part of Vale's initiation when she accepts her second king.

Arousal fills the room, its musk distinct. The anticipation is thick and tense because I'm the only brother who's ever resisted this.

Axel was eager to initiate our first queen. Too eager, we've since learned. Grant charged like a bull with Delphine. Nick was proud of his love for Zar. And Sire? Sire turned Wren's initiation into a dark, holy ceremony.

Fuck, I think I meant that pun.

But me?

I wrap Vale in my arms, protecting her. Our breath and bodies recover as we lie intertwined on the platform while the others take another round of shots.

Dresses have been discarded. Pants and suits, too. All are nude, their bodies either erect or aroused, except for Jace, Axel, and his mystery woman. How she's knelt silently for this long, I don't know.

But still, it's Jace, dressed in his suit and sitting uncharacteristically quiet, who traps my attention until the coded knock raps at the door.

Shit. No.

Sire smirks, rising to unlock it. When it swings open, a large, masculine figure enters, shrouded in all black and a black balaclava. Even Seven's dark sunglasses disguise his distinct eyes.

Axel was right; you can't tell who he is.

Axel was a dumbass; his sudden appearance shocks Vale.

I feel her tense in my arms, almost wincing as Seven's heavy steps aim first for the altar. He lights a candle. Even his hands are covered by black leather gloves.

"Is that...?" Vale whispers.

"Seven." I want to spit bullets.

"Why is he...?" she presses.

"He's like Nick. He's too public to be seen, even coming here."

I try to keep our voices down while the others share greetings. Like it's not awkward as fuck greeting their youngest brother, who's dressed like a street-styled ninja.

"But Nick shows his face to me. He can trust me. Why can't Seven?"

Of course, Vale asks the obvious questions.

Of course, I want to throat-punch Axel for thinking this was a good idea. But that man and his rituals...

Though Sire was destined for the Russian Orthodox clergy at one time, it's Axel who might as well be the Patriarch of Moscow. He's so committed to traditions, he ignores logic.

All kings are supposed to be present for a queen's initiation. It's an honor to watch. The intimacy binds us.

Alena is the only exception Axel has allowed. Not like the brothers wouldn't rebel if he insisted otherwise, but we agreed. Her throne will always be empty. Her feet will never enter this room.

Alena will never be initiated, though deep down, rage plucks at my nerves, knowing Axel has such a compulsion for it. And deep down, way past six feet, is where I'll bury him if he ever does it.

Silently, Seven approaches us.

From where Vale and I lie like naked lovers, he looms large, reaching into his front pocket. Vale grabs my chest, watching Seven pull out a purple velvet drawstring bag, silently signaling Vale to approach him.

Cautiously, she leaves my arms, crawling closer to the plat-form's edge as Seven kneels before her. From the bag, he presents her with a gold bracelet: seven gold lions, each with tiny jeweled eyes.

Every queen receives a jeweled gift with gold lions. Each gift is different, but the meaning is the same: honor, loyalty, bravery, and dignity. Lions are sacred icons and the only symbols from the Kholodov crest that The Queen and her sons kept.

With suspicious eyes, Vale watches Seven carefully clasp the bracelet around her slender wrist. "Thank you," she murmurs, admiring it. "It's beautiful."

He bows slightly before rising to back away.

Vale doesn't take her eyes off him as he takes his seat on his seventh throne. Even Wren leans forward, studying Seven with equal awe and scrutiny.

"Ahem." Sire clears his throat. "Now that all are present, let us continue."

Vale slides her stare back to me, worried I'll resist, but suddenly, I'm too concerned about Seven being here to protest what's next.

I feel adrift at sea in this initiation, and the only way to shore, the only way to have Vale forever, is to finish this.

"Kneel, our king and queen," Sire commands, so Vale mimics me, kneeling by the platform's edge. I reach for Vale's right hand while he continues, "Which brother here will vouchsafe as a second king, declaring this union honorable and protected? Who here is pleased to join their bed, mercifully granting that they may live long and bountiful lives but pledging, should her first king perish, he shall guard our queen and their children in his stead?"

"I do."

Jace stands, speaking for the first time tonight.

With hands clasped before him, he approaches the platform. He keeps his eyes on me, avoiding Vale's nude beauty, and I know it's to keep me from losing it.

I feel the beast threatening, clawing to emerge. I still don't know if I can do this, but there are enough brothers here to hold me back should rage overwhelm me.

"Will you, Nash, allow Jace to honor your queen?"

I squeeze her hand. Painfully, the words choke my throat. "I will."

It's not rage. It's raw emotion.

"Will you, Jace, honor Nash's queen?"

"I will," his voice strains with it, too.

It's this next part that grabs my soul every time.

"Will you, her kings, be subject to her as she is subject to you?" Sire evokes the sacred orthodox text and the scars on our mother's back. "Will you love your queen as you love your own bodies?"

This is the vow her first husband defiled.

This is the vow her second husband honored.

"For he who loves his queen loves himself." Sire exalts. "For no noble man ever hated his own flesh. He nourishes and cherishes it, as every king shall nourish and cherish his queen. Every king shall protect his queen, *all* queens, for they fill our lives with children, prosperity, and all good things.

This is the love you will give her. State your vow if you agree."

This is the reason for our bond. For all that we risk and fight.

I'm trapped by Vale's gaze, holding her hand while I promise, "I vow to my queen."

"I vow to my queen," Jace echoes me.

Vale blinks back tears, the magnitude of our tradition settling in her eyes.

"May those present declare this union sacred," Sire concludes. "Have mercy on us and save us. Protect and preserve us for many years to come."

"Here, here." Nick knocks on the wooden arm of his chair. The brothers join him.

"Each queen decides how to receive a second king." Axel takes over the ceremony. "A queen may receive more than two kings if that is her or his desire, for we are here to honor our queen's flesh. Be it tonight or any other, we always serve our queens."

Deference and desire crawl through Axel's deep voice. Slowly, our ceremony shifts from the exalted to the erotic, too.

No brother here would ever harm a queen, but most desire to please more than one. Even Nick has allowed Sire to please Zar. Even Seven has honored Delphine's flesh as her second king.

I'm Wren's second king, a fact I'm confident Vale has figured out, or I'll tell her tonight. There are so many secrets I need to tell her.

But me sharing Vale with Jace?

Us doing this right now?

The red veil starts to bleed over my stare, my nostrils flaring, my pulse climbing.

"Tell me how you want to do this." Jace kneels before

Vale. "I don't want to hurt you. I want to respect you. I want to respect my brother, too; just tell me how."

My fury ebbs with Jace's humility.

Fuck, he's trying hard.

Fuck, I'm a dickhead if I don't try, too.

Vale smiles tenderly, brushing Jace's dark hair from his face. "Wear a condom," she insists. "If you go slow, you won't hurt me. And no offense, but don't kiss me. You're hot, and I trust and adore you ... but only Nash can kiss me without triggering me."

The strangle over my throat is sudden, just as I lethally strangled Chad. I watch Jace swallow hard, understanding what she just shared.

"Okay." Emotions fill his voice. "I'll never hurt you, I promise. But I'll stand in line, right behind Nash, and kill anyone who fucking does. You have my vow."

"I know." Playfully, she punches his arm, and Jace rubs it, grinning like it hurt.

It didn't.

"Fuck, this is awkward." Grant chuckles. "Are we in middle school?"

"And who beat your ass in middle school?" Jace suddenly barks at him. "Yeah. Me. That's right, so shut the fuck up."

Aw, brotherly love.

"Do not kill the mood," Delphine chides. "This is about your queen. You need to get her ready again. This can be an amazing night for her, but only if you beasts behave."

"I like it when they're beasts," Wren sighs.

"Hmm."

We all turn, shocked by the first sound from the woman kneeling for Axel. He's still caressing her lace-covered hair. She's still stroking his covered cock.

"Will you lift that sweet woman off of her goddamn

knees?" But I can't take it anymore. "Let her sit on your lap," I demand. "She's at least passed *this* test."

Axel sneers at me, so I raise a brow. *Really, motherfucker? Want to get into this now?*

So, he fights the urge to brawl, gently tugging at her arm and patting his thigh for her to sit.

There. She's comfortable.

Now, it's Vale's turn.

"Poison, come here." I guide her to lie back. One last time, I have to ask, "Are you sure?"

Whoops. That yanked the cat's tail. The feral look Vale gives me is one second away from clawing my eyes out.

"Okay, okay." I chuckle. "Let me get you ready."

"I'm very ready."

"Not enough," I fear, speaking for myself, not her.

I need to worship her more. I need her to want me, not Jace. I start with our kiss. *If she flinches, this is off. No one touches my queen.*

But she responds to my lips, her body rising for my mouth, our tongues teasing, before I claim her neck, kissing, biting, and marking her even more until her moans beg for more.

Kneading her breasts, I lower my mouth and suck her pinched nipple. It's so raw and ready, she bows her back, crying out, "Oh god!"

"Do you want these off?" I ask about the magnets. Maybe she's done with this kink, but "No," she rasps. "Leave them on. They feel good. *You* feel good."

I devote my attention to her nipples, licking and sucking them, the metal orbs clicking against my teeth until my woman is a writhing mess. Then I kiss her belly, sighing over her flesh, at how I can make her quiver with my kiss. How I can smell her lust and mine as I tease my way to her sweet pussy.

Spreading her thighs apart, I lick my lips at what I see. My creamy cum drips from Vale's pink entrance, so I scoop the drop up with my fingertip and plunge it back inside her.

"Oh god," she cries again.

Proudly, I drool over her clasped clit before I warn, "You're going to drip with every drop of me before he's allowed inside you." I crouch between her legs, lowering my tongue. "Watch me, Vale," I order. "Watch me eat what's mine."

She props on her elbows, her stare heavy, her breath, too. I lock my eyes on hers, fluttering my tongue over her clit. "Oh fuck!" she jumps. "Oh fuck, Nash. I'm going to come."

I don't stop with this singular pleasure until she does. Until she's panting, shaking, and pulsing, her entrance leaking with my cum again, so I shove it back in.

"Now," I command, crawling over her before I roll her on top of me, "straddle my cock, and rub your clit on it while you look me in the eye."

She obeys, surrendering her body to me and presenting herself to Jace, waiting at the platform's edge.

"Do it," I tell him, "and don't hurt her. Make it feel good, or I'll fucking kill you."

The sound of his zipper lowering makes me snarl. The rip of the condom foil before he rolls one on coils my muscles. The heat of his body, brushing his concrete legs against mine and taking his position behind Vale, makes my pulse skyrocket.

Fuck, I'm losing it.

I'm going to lose it.

I'm going to kill him.

I hold Vale so tight, fisting her hair and grabbing her hip. *I'll never let her go.* I feel myself slipping into a rage. It's a familiar descent. It's served me well until now. Until the man in me wants this woman so much, I'll sacrifice all for her. *Just once.*

Her clit and its hard, teasing magnets rub over my swollen shaft. Her lust glosses my length. She's braced over me, straddling me and staring into my eyes, obeying me on this rarest occasion...

Until she gasps. Until I feel a hard cock rub over mine. Until I feel Jace slowly urging into her pussy, hovering and rubbing over my cock, too, making her leak over my tip. Until I feel Jace's massive hand hold her ass, his fingers brushing mine on her hip.

"Fuck!" I roar.

My vision blurs, my brain tunnels, my ears ring. The beast inside me wants blood. *Kill for her*—a million souls I'll take for this one in my arms.

I tense to flip her over, to punch him off of her, to gnash my teeth into his neck and rip his goddamn jugular out, his blood dripping from my chin, but ... Vale kisses me.

As if it was never stolen from her before, she gives me every breath she has, so I'll survive this, so I'll allow this. Her tongue takes mine, her hands caressing my jaw. She rubs her little, hard clit over my angry, swollen tip, smoothing my razor edges and calming my fury. She suddenly floods my veins with my favorite poison: *I love her.*

She holds me bound to our kiss while she accepts another man.

Jace isn't a beast about it. He tries to go fast without hurting her. He tries not to grunt and make a show of it. He tries not to rub his cock against mine, but we can't avoid it.

She's our queen.

She deserves pleasure.

I would never make Vale suffer, but I can make her come.

"Come on, poison." I grab her neck. I keep taking her

kiss, my tongue lashing hers. "Rub that clit on me and move those hips."

"Nash, I..."

She's afraid. If she moves her hips like she does for me, she'd be taking Jace even more.

She doesn't want to hurt me. She doesn't want to make me mad. She doesn't know how much this makes me love her even more.

Die for her? No.

Even in death, I'll be devoted to her.

"Do it." I grip her neck harder. "Grind those sweet hips and smear that wet pussy all over my cock."

She obeys, rubbing her clit over my tip, and circling her hips with her maddening moves, making Jace grunt, "Shit. Holy fucking shit, she's good."

Jealousy, pride, rage, raunch: it all ignites my blood. With my free hand, I slap Vale's peaked nipple. "You're going to be a good girl and come for me like you always do."

I do it again and again until she shudders, moaning, "Yes, Daddy."

Her pleasure makes Jace drive harder. His sheathed shaft, wet with Vale's desire and slick with my cum, rubs my bare cock, gliding over my length while Vale's pinched clit thrills my sensitive slit.

I've never felt this before, and I don't know how to feel about it now ... *because it feels so fucking good.*

"Goddamn," I groan.

Yes, I've doubled inside a woman before. Dutifully, I fucked Wren's pussy while Sire claimed her ass. I did the same with Axel and his first queen.

But it was never this close, this intimate. It was never with my love, my queen, and with a brother who cares for her, too. It's suddenly warm and right. It's carnal and taboo, as well, and it takes my eyes; Vale sees it. She feels it, too.

"Yes, Nash," she sighs at our pleasure. "Feel it. Love it. You like it."

I do. I moan my confession.

"Shit," Jace huffs, letting his balls brush over mine, making me feel his hard dick glossed with Vale's lust, grind against my cock. *He's pleasing me so I won't kill him; I won't hate him.* "Shit," he grunts, "I need her to come so I can."

The initiation isn't complete without it, and that's my secret with Wren. I couldn't come inside her, even though I wore a condom. She could see it in my eyes, so we faked it for the others. I know Wren realized then that I belonged to someone else.

I belong to Vale.

I glance around, and all eyes are on our union. Axel's icy stare burns for this. Like he knows my ruse with Wren, he won't let me get away with it again, and I don't want to. Vale deserves everything real with me, and I know how to give it to her.

"That's it," I coax her ride, my hand gently strangling her neck, her stare locked to mine. "Be a good girl and rub that wet pussy and little clit all over my hard dick. Be my horny little queen while he fucks you, too." Her eyelids hood. Her lips tremble. Her alabaster body blushes with sudden heat. "Say it, Vale. Say what you've always wanted with me."

"Yes, Mr. Allen. Yes, my king." Her thighs shake. "Make me yours."

"You are, Vale." I suck two of my fingers, drenching them in my spit. "Oh, my pretty little poison, you fucking are."

I reach around, brushing Jace's hand aside before I slowly plunge my fingers in her ass, and that does it. Vale shatters in my grasp, her stare breaking over mine as her body bucks, her shoulders convulsing, her groans my goddamn symphony.

"Mine." I grab her, pulling her gasping mouth to my lips. I kiss her, my heart soaring at how she doesn't flinch with me, *only me.* She gives me her kiss while Jace grunts, his legs shaking. I can feel his cock pulsing against mine while Vale's orgasm makes him come.

"Fuck." He groans, marveling, "Fuck, her pussy is strong."

"Goddammit." I can't take any more. I wrap around Vale, barely kicking Jace off of her, before I flip her over and bury myself so deep inside her. I fuck her so hard, she cries elated tears while they bite at my eyes, too.

I don't care who sees, who protests, who I offend, or who I have to kill.

I will *never* share her again.

CHAPTER FORTY-TWO
VALE

"I have a bad feeling about this." I rub Nash's concrete chest hidden under his black tactical shirt. "I'm afraid something bad is going to happen to you."

"Just so we're clear, I never want you to feel good about my job."

"Yeah, I hate math."

"That job, too." He grins. "But my money is about to be yours, so I'm getting you activity books on basic arithmetic."

"Not interested. My erotic coloring books teach me all I need to know."

"They're a waste of time." He cups my cheeks. "You already know your sweet pussy, plus my hard cock equals what I live for every day."

I fist his shirt. "Just promise me that you'll *live*."

I've had the best week of my life as Nash's new queen. We work side by side at Delta's. I love how he rubs my thigh under the desk while seriously auditing my abysmal use of percentages.

"Tamayto, tomahto."

That's all I hear when he lectures me on county versus state taxes.

Jace is there, too. He joked about me giving him my diamond earring and leaving him with a smile. It's a nod to *The Breakfast Club*, so we're good—more than good. Jace and Nash act relaxed about it, too.

Every evening after work, Nash and I drive to the islands and house shop. I think we've found one we like. It's on the wide creek overlooking the tranquil marsh. It has a dock house Nash wants for his boat, for our rapid escape if needed.

Every night, I introduce Nash to new adult toys, and our play turns into passion until I'm lying in his arms, and we're dreaming aloud about our future—about that house.

After Alena's wedding next weekend, we'll schedule a showing because Nash says it's too risky until they get Turner.

So, I hate this. Maybe it's natural to fear the worst. Maybe it's a premonition.

Nash, his brothers, and their small army will ambush Turner and his crew tonight. For a week, they've surveilled the church where Turner hides. They've reviewed their ops. Their tactical approach. Their weapons. Their extraction. Their...

I forget the rest. That's just what I've overheard, filling me with dread.

"I'll be back," he promises me about tonight.

"Okay, Arnold Schwarzenegger. Not helping."

"Be good for Zar." He peppers my lips with kisses.

"I'm not a puppy who'll piss on the carpet."

"No," he smirks, "you're my poison who can kill a man with your snark, especially when you're nervous, so behave while I'm gone."

Nash holds me in the kitchen of Zar's suite at The Mercier while Zar and Nick recline with Wren, Sire, Delphine, and Grant in his living room.

Not only is Zar the CFO of this luxury hotel chain, but he also serves as the loyal sub to Luca Mercier.

Though Nick and Zar will marry one day, Zar will always serve Luca and Luca's wife, Scarlett. Nick knows. Nick joins them. He loves them, too. And for his beloved sub, Luca Mercier will deploy all of his security at Zar's request, no questions asked.

"So…" I press my cheek against Nash's chest. His heart rate is too calm. "We're just supposed to stay locked in this tower like your Rapunzels until you return?"

"No," he kisses my hair, "you stay secure in this vetted location with a security team we trust until we complete the mission."

Part of me wants to grab a gun and help Nash. Part of me knows that's ridiculous. Once I start shooting evil men, I won't stop, and that can be really dangerous for my morally grey kings. I may, *whoops*, pop a cap in Axel's ass, too.

Just kidding. Sort of. Like vinegar, Axel's a taste I'm slowly acquiring. Excuse me while I gag a little, too.

"How long will you be gone?"

"Don't know."

"Are all the kings going with you?"

"All but one." He rubs my arms. "One always stays behind in case…"

"Who?"

He shakes his head.

"What will you do with Turner?"

"Can't say."

"Can I at least whack him with my nine-iron?"

He kisses me before, "Shut up, Vale," steams over our lips.

Two hours after our kings leave, I'm losing my mind.

Wren falls asleep on the sofa while I join Zar and Delphine for cigars on his balcony. They smoke, I cough, and don't get the appeal.

"So this whole not-mafia-mafia thing?" I stub out my stogie. "How can you stand it? I won't sleep until Nash is back."

Delphine shrugs a shoulder. "I've been traded amongst evil men my whole life. I've always known danger; I'm used to it. But I've never known love until Grant. At least his evil is the good kind, and I support it. He and his mother saved me, so here I am." She flits her cigar. "*C'est la vie.*"

I like Delphine. She's so flippant; she's dead serious.

"I don't get all het up about it," Zar drawls. "It's not like the NFL is without its risks, now or later for Nick. But what I worry most about is him being gay in a sport where everyone is closeted. That's the real risk, and the only ones who can protect him are his brothers." A puff escapes his lips. "Especially Axel."

"Axel?"

Zar chuckles. "When it comes to his brothers? Axel's horns hold up his halo."

"Why is Axel on the first throne if Sire is the oldest?" I hope my queens will give me some answers.

Nash gets quiet every time I ask questions, so Zar reveals, "From a young age, Sire said he wanted to be a priest. For his father, it was an honor and—"

"And it was strategic," Delphine interjects, "because then his evil father could infiltrate the Russian Orthodox church, too."

"So, Axel, as the second son," Zar continues, "became the heir apparent to his father's wicked empire."

"Okay, so why is Nash before Sire as second on the throne?"

Zar raises his thick brow. "He never told you?"

"I suspect there's so much to tell me; he's pacing himself."

Delphine nods, puffing her cigar.

"One night, years ago," Zar taps his ashes, "Nadine was babysitting Nash's girl."

"Alena."

"Yes," Zar continues, "and some man invaded Nadine's home. He tried to take Alena, but Nadine stood guard at her bedroom door. She fought him off and took a helluva beating for it until Nash got there and lived up to his name." Pause. "He gnashed the man's neck open before he choked him to death. So, in Nash's honor for defending their mother, who was protecting his daughter, the brothers put him second in charge. When he needs to be, Nash is the most ruthless."

I shiver. "Who was the man?"

Zar puffs. "Dead men tell no tales."

The cigars and night-blooming jasmine on Zar's trellis perfume the humid air. Tourists bustle on the summer streets below. A ship on the river blasts its horn in the distance. And I'm beginning to realize there's far more to being a queen in this world than I ever imagined.

"Who is Seven?"

It's been haunting me since my initiation. Nash will tell me in time, but I want to know *now*. Something compels me. It's like a clock is ticking down, and I fear it's to a bomb.

"I don't know," Zar answers truthfully. "He's a lion in bear's clothing—that's all Nick has told me."

I turn to Delphine, whose stare is trapped on the view of the church spires and glowing city below.

"You know. Don't you?"

Silently, she nods.

"Will you tell me?"

Silently, she shakes her head.

"But... But..." I stammer. "Why do I feel like I need to know? Like, I'm okay with so many secrets, but not this one?"

Delphine rolls her lips, slowly stubbing her cigar out in a white marble ashtray on the coffee table of Zar's balcony.

"Please understand," her French accent soothes, "as my fellow queen, you will always have my love. But as Grant's queen, he has my loyalty, too. He swore me to secrecy. Seven is my second king, and I cannot betray him."

For the rest of the night, I fake reading while I sit beside Wren, sleeping on the sofa. We share a white, knitted blanket Zar gently drapes over me, then her, but while she sleeps peacefully, something troubles me until I doze off and awake to Zar making us breakfast. The smell of biscuits, bacon, and coffee makes my stomach growl, but I can't eat.

Not until I see Nash. Not until he holds me. Not until I cling to him in this desperate need to feel like everything will be okay.

But I can't fight this maddening feeling like it won't.

It's like something is about to explode.

CHAPTER FORTY-THREE
NASH

Through my night-vision goggles, I see green bodies carpeting the pine wood floors between the pews of the old church.

Turner's men lie dead everywhere.

The sobs and whimpers of the five teenage girls and two teen boys we found held captive disturb my soul. They huddle in the corner of the sanctuary, where Jace stands guard over them while the others clear the auxiliary spaces of the church.

One of the girls cradles a newborn swaddled in a blanket. She breastfeeds, trying to silence and protect her baby while terror fills her eyes, staring up at our lethal forms.

They murmur desperate prayers in Spanish, so I squat down and take off my goggles. I let her see my face and sincere eyes. I don't speak the language well, but I try. "*Esta bein.*" I tell her it's okay. "*Soy padre. Estas seguro.*" I pause. "*Lo siento. Estas segura.*"

I struggle with the language I learned in college, but I need her to know I'm a father, too. That she's safe, and I'd never let anyone hurt her or them.

Axel storms into the sanctuary. "Turner's in the wind."

"You sure?" Jace asks.

"It's none of these bodies." Axel points his AK-47 with a Wolverine suppressor at the carnage we created. The suppressor is best at silencing any Kalashnikov weapon. No one heard us coming, killing, and they won't hear us leaving, either. "They all have two eyes."

"You think he knew we were coming?" Sire asks.

"I think he bet on it," Grant answers.

"What if he was never here?" Jace wonders. "Our surveillance never saw him enter or leave. So, what if he jumped off the boat and never made it to shore, and his men have been sitting here with their thumbs up their asses, not sure what to do?"

"We know he's alive," Axel assures. "Yesterday, Two perfected the art of BDSM interrogation."

"What the—" Nick looks at me. He stops his task of loading all the tech into duffels. In his off-season, Nick treats our missions like training camp. "What does he mean you perfected 'BDSM interrogation'?"

"Why so curious, Six?" Sire laughs. "Would've guessed you and your Texas queen would be experts at it by now."

"Jealous much?" Nick chuckles.

"No." Sire winks. "Divinely inspired."

Leave it to Sire to joke at the worst time. So I cut the shit. "The first guy we caught climbing over the fence at the Bonneau mansion has a torture kink. My queen warned me he would, so yesterday, I asked her what we should do. Apparently, hours of stimulation and orgasm denial with a large prostate massager will make any man cry to come ... and confess Turner is alive."

"Damn." Nick nods. "Sure helps having a PhD in sex on our team."

Sire laughs. "Two ain't complaining."

"Enough!" Axel booms before turning my way. His goggles are still on, but I swear I see the ice in his stare. "Call Seven and warn him. Turner's still out there, and you're still the bait."

Carefully, we gather the latest group of Turner's trafficking victims. In broken Spanish, I assure them it's okay. I ride with them in the van, calling Nadine, who prepares for their arrival. Medical care. Food. A counselor fluent in Spanish. An immigration lawyer. Even diapers will be waiting for them.

Tragically, we're pros at this.

As dawn rises, Axel and I secure the victims, leaving them safe in Nadine's hands, while the others dump Turner's men in the Atlantic, and I begin this fucking game all over again.

"I need to call off Alena's wedding."

Numbly, I stare out the window of Axel's Jaguar. He's driving me back to The Mercier. All I want is to see Vale and hold her in my arms. All I need is for my daughter to be safe, too.

"Don't." Axel's tone is sincere. "Alena's too excited, and I don't know what bullshit excuse you can give that won't break her heart. Just..." He starts to reason quickly because I can't.

Something about those victims, that young mother, and her newborn, brought it all back to me.

Lainey and Alena.

It freaked me out at sixteen when Lainey breastfed her. I wince, remembering how I pressured her to bottle-feed. Not like it was my body or business. I was just an uptight fuckwad who wasn't used to seeing what was perfectly natural.

No, it was beautiful.

But now I know what a good father will do for his daughter.

And what a real man will do for the woman he loves.

It makes me tell Axel to take the next exit. Before I see Vale, there's someone I need to talk to.

"Just get Alena to one of the villas at the club," Axel strategizes, obeying my order. "Her wedding is this weekend, so tell her it's so she can be pampered. We'll put the other queens in the villas and lock it down."

"Secure Alena in a villa at the country club with her guard? Alright," I agree, pointing left for him to turn toward the Daniel Island Golf Club. "Leave Vale alone without me protecting her? Fuck no."

"We'll all be there, protecting them," he counters. "We'll put you in an unlocked villa and parade your ass around the course, placing bets and winning. Make an obnoxious show of it, and Turner will come for you."

I suck my teeth. *It's a bad idea. It's the best idea.*

It's an idea I easily sell to Vale.

When I return to Zar's suite at The Mercier, she runs toward me, leaping into my arms and wrapping her legs around me.

My poison doesn't care she's in a black minidress, thigh-highs, Mary Janes, and showing off her white cotton panties to all while I proudly cup handfuls of her ass.

"My sexy dickhead." She kisses me, crying. "When can you retire from the mafia?"

"I'm not *old*."

"I am." She won't stop kissing me. "I got my first grey hairs waiting on you."

"How about we wait this week at the golf resort? *Our* resort. You stay with Alena in her bridal villa and take a break from all this."

I don't tell her Turner is still alive. I don't tell her about the victims. I don't tell her the dozens of secrets I've kept over the years because they keep everyone I love safe.

Even if they eat me alive from the inside out.

My third shot of vodka takes the edge off of a long day.

We've secured the queens in the villas at our resort. Even The Queen is bunking with Alena and Vale. Nadine is like the mother of the bride who's no longer with us, so I left them putting some shit on their feet that will peel their skin off in a day or two.

Far be it from me to question bridal beauty rituals.

The other kings are in their villas with their queens. I suspect Axel has his mystery woman with him, too. But once again, Jace sleeps alone. He's like me, devoted to securing our queens.

Security holds a perimeter around the vast golf course, palatial clubhouse, and luxury resort housing, but I still don't like it.

There are too many shadows. Too many risks. Too many ways someone can slip through.

And too many secrets.

I sit on my deck overlooking the tenth hole. Like a beacon, I left the porch light on while I wait, hoping I draw Turner my way. When he comes around, I won't use my Beretta on him. I'll use my teeth on his neck for what he did to those kids.

Searching the darkness, I try to find a way to tell Vale about all of it. I want to. I need to. I won't put a ring on her finger until I reveal my secrets.

As my wife, she deserves to know everything.

As my queen, she'll need to.

I just need more time. I need her to understand threats

like Turner and believe as I do—that it was the right thing to do.

Once, I abandoned Lainey. I left her and Alena without my protection and never did it again.

Twice, still, Alena was almost taken from me by the system and then by some stranger. We found out that the man who invaded Nadine's home was a convicted pedophile, but we never found out why he targeted Alena.

So, three times, I got into brutal fights with Axel about the best way to protect Alena. His love for her was relentless, too—it still is.

So, his suggestion was unthinkable until it made sense. I raged over it, and Axel took my beatings until I relented.

Until I saw no other way.

Until I saw it his way.

CHAPTER FORTY-FOUR
VALE

"Come on." Alena straddles Loch on the sofa. "They help with puffy eyes."

"I don't have puffy eyes." He laughs, not resisting as she sticks gold patches under his icy blues, blinking at the intrusion. "I only have eyes for you."

"Aw." She tilts her head, planting a sickeningly sweet kiss on his grinning lips. "Will you put that in our vows?"

"Babygirl, I will say, 'Yeehaw,' and do a line dance down the aisle for you."

"Promise?"

"I've already practiced."

My smile tugs at my under-eye patches, too. Snuggled in a side chair, I relax in my pink satin bridesmaid pajama top and shorts, my heart glowing at how hopelessly happy Alena is.

Nadine smiles at them, too. Sipping wine, she sits in the chair opposite mine, looking as elegant as ever in gold eye patches and black silk pajamas while she tries to text discreetly.

In her covert line of work, I guess you never get a break.

Tender moments like this make me miss Nash. But it's a

small sacrifice of a few days without him while Alena gets the wedding she deserves.

Tomorrow, Alena wants me to teach her and Loch how to play golf. My clubs are polished and propped in their bag by the front door. When I know, really, we'll just get drunk on spicy margaritas and zoom around the course in a golf cart.

Blair is supposed to return from her Caribbean three-way in two more days and join our slumber party and the wedding.

Then, ship this: she's moving to Atlanta to be a double WAG. Who saw that coming? Me.

"Now, about your eyebrows." Alena twists her lips.

"What about them?" Loch raises one.

"Can I just—"

"Nope." Gently, he grabs her fingertips about to pluck an errant hair. "A man's gotta draw the line somewhere."

"But it's for our wedding," Alena protests.

"I like them," I chime in. "They're all masculine and thick. Leave him some hair and dignity."

"Thank you, her bestie." Loch smiles at me, bowing his head slightly, and...

Why did that look familiar?

Alena tries to tickle her fiancé into compliance. It's an amusing sight because Loch looms so large he doesn't have to submit to anyone, but he does to her.

In a few days, he'll stay in another villa as the groom, waiting for his blushing bride, but tonight, he lets her win. He lets her lift his T-shirt to tickle his flinching abs, their laughter booming across the open living room, with its windows to the golf course outside.

They're cute and rolling around on the sofa. Even Nadine laughs, watching them, until...

...I clock it.

A lion on Loch's chiseled oblique? And another? And another?

What the...? I count seven of them, roaring in distinct black ink, flexing over his muscles, his deep laughter booming at Alena's torture and...

Oh.

My.

King.

Shock rips my breath away so quickly, I'm dizzy. It's not the wine I'm drinking. It's the recognition. The secret. The lie. The betrayal. It's the pieces of my heart breaking at the weight of my logic falling into place.

"Excuse me." I force myself to speak. "I need to call Blair."

I lie, too, and grab my phone. Rushing outside to the deck, I close the glass door behind me and glance over my shoulder. Nadine watches me while Alena and Loch are oblivious to my departure.

Acting like I'm calling my twin, I pace across the deck, not sure what to do next. Then I see Nash sitting on his deck, four villas down, and I don't know whether to scream, cry, or both.

Quietly, I descend the wooden steps. Immediately, an armed guard steps out of the shadows.

"Shit!" I hiss at him.

"Sorry, ma'am."

"Out of my way." I shoulder past him.

"But ma'am." He tries to stop me.

"Balls are about to be ripped off," I sneer. "You want in on my eunuch party?"

With one hand on a rifle, he holds up his other. "No, ma'am."

He doesn't stop me as I storm across the neat patches of Bermuda grass, each marking a villa's backyard, until I stand at the edge of Nash's deck. Stomping up his wooden stairs, he stands to greet me.

"Poison, what are you—" He slings sunshine, pausing at the sight of me.

Fuck, my eye patches.

I rip them off and throw them at him. "Don't fucking call me that!" My heart pounds at his betrayal.

He reaches for me. "What's wro—"

But I jerk away, clenching my teeth. "I *know*."

He pauses, his eyes glaring down at me while he lifts his chin, adding up the damage done. "I was going to tell you."

"Me? I don't give a fuck about me. I mean, I do. I won't love a liar. But what about your daughter? What about Alena? How can you do this to her?"

"Let's go inside and talk like adults." He motions for me to comply.

"Why? So you can lie again?"

His nostrils flare. "So I can explain."

"I'm sure whatever you have to say can wait until I give a shit."

"Now, Vale!" He booms, yanking me into his grasp and throwing me over his shoulder.

I punch and fight as hard as I can. I want to hurt him as much as I hurt, but it's useless. Nash is too strong and getting pissed.

He throws the door open before slamming it behind us, glass reverberating and threatening to break.

Tossing me on the sofa, I don't get a chance to scream before he roars, "It's for Alena! It keeps her safe. I'm her father, so don't you ever question what I do to protect her!"

"Oh, yeah? Well, I didn't mean to offend ye olde patriarch, but it's a huge bonus because I'm her best friend who's full of facts she deserves to know!"

"Know what?" He shouts. "That Loch loves her? That he'll always protect her? What else does she need to know?"

"That he's Seven!" I jump to my feet. "That somehow, I

know it; you, Axel, and all of your Bratva ballsacks arranged this marriage. She thinks..." Tears bite at my eyes. "Alena thinks she met Loch at a gas station. That he fell in love with her at first sight over Coca-Cola Slurpies."

I hate this for her. I hate that her meet-cute is a lie.

"You know how shy she is," I grieve for her. "You know how she got teased. You know no one asked her out. The cruel boys called her 'hips' in high school, and I could only beat so many asses and love her so much as her best friend until she finally met Loch, and he made it okay. He made her feel beautiful and loved, and she believes he adores every-thing about her, but it's a lie!"

My tears fall, and they threaten Nash's eyes, too. For Alena, he has a deadly soft spot.

"It's not a lie." He swallows. "My daughter *is* beautiful and loved. *Loch* loves her. So, don't take it away from her." He swallows again. "Please."

"Tell her," I seethe. "Tell her the truth before they get married, or I will."

"It will break her heart."

"You broke her heart the moment you bargained it away! You had no right. She deserves true love. Not one built on a lie." I pause, tears streaming down my cheeks. "Not one like ours."

"Vale," he shakes his head, "our love is *NOT* a lie, and you know it."

"No, I don't. I know a thousand facts from books, but I never knew the facts from you, Nash. Since the day we met, you've been lying to me."

"I never lied about how I love you." He steps toward me. "I proved it but never said it. I didn't say it for so long to protect you. I'll always protect you."

"Yeah," I lift my wet chin, "well, who's protecting Alena from her father now?" I throw up my hands. "Oh, look, it's me, and another thing we have in common. Our fathers chose their jobs over their daughters."

"Don't you ever compare me to your father!" Rage threatens his voice. "Every time I could, I was there for you. After you gave up your golf scholarship, you didn't win an academic one. I was the anonymous benefactor who paid to make one for you. That nice old lady in your building? She didn't give you her vintage bike. I paid her to give you the red bike I bought for you. Your mother's headstone with tulips engraved on it? It was me, not her coworkers, who had it made for her. I have *always* loved you, Vale. I will always *choose* you!"

Sobs burst up my burning throat. *He's so kind. He's so cunning.* "But don't you see, Nash? Even when you love me, you lie. You're lying to Alena, too."

"No," he snarls, "I'll do anything. Anything! For someone I love. I'll lie. Kill. Sacrifice. I'll do it for you and my daughter, too. So you can hate me, Vale, but I will never stop loving you."

I can't breathe under the weight of his vow. I can't find words that don't hurt. I can't find a truth that doesn't break my heart.

"But I can't love a father who lies to his daughter." Tears pool over my lips. "You know all those Happy Meals I ate as a girl? They only made me cry because I saved all my toys from them to play with my father, but he never did. Every time, he was too busy. Every time, he left me waiting and never showed up. His love was a lie. And sometimes, I hate to admit, I wished he were dead because then he wouldn't have a choice. But no. He's alive, and he never chooses me. But you can choose Alena. You can choose to tell her the truth."

Pain bends his face. It mirrors mine. Every emotion Nash feels drowns me, too.

"Vale, please." His tone softens. "I love you, and Loch loves Alena. You have to believe me."

"You have to tell her." I wrap my arms around my clenching stomach. "Or I will."

Right now.

I turn for his backdoor.

"Where are you going?"

"Every moment you wait only hurts her more." *And me.*

Nash doesn't stop me. He follows me. Too quickly, I'm at the steps to Alena's villa. Too easily, the guard lets us by. He knows better than to try and stop me.

Rocks fill my throat. My cheeks burn hot with tears. My bare feet weigh a ton under this burden as I climb the stairs and open the glass door.

Nadine lifts her stare from her phone and immediately reads the situation.

Me, crying.

Nash, seething.

Secrets, unraveling.

She sets her wine down, and Alena lifts her head, reclining on Loch's chest. They're cuddled on the sofa, but she pops up once she sees my tears.

"What's wrong?" Alena's eyes flit from mine, pouring pain to Nash's, flooded with rage. "Dad?" Dread fills her voice. "What happened? Why is Vale cr—"

"We need to talk, sweet ... pea."

I've never heard Nash's voice break with pain like it just did.

I glance at Loch, and his chest heaves, realizing *this is it.* He moves to rise, to stop Nash. "Let me—"

"No." But Nash stops him. "She's my daughter. This is my doing, and it's my fault, so let me tell her."

"Tell me what?" Alena glances from Loch to her Dad and

then to me. "Vale, what's going on? Oh, sweetie, why are you crying so much?"

She starts to cry, too, and I can't stop the words. I can't hide it. I can't lie to my best friend anymore.

"I love your dad." It rushes over my lips. "I've been in love with him since I was eighteen, and I'm so sorry. I really am. I hid it for so long so you wouldn't get hurt. And now, we've been together and hiding it from you, but we were going to tell you after the wedding. I thought we were in love, and it would be okay, but then I found out he's been lying to you and—"

"We *are* in love," Nash fumes. "Don't you ever put us in the past tense, poison. I won't fucking allow it."

"Wait." Alena shakes her head. "What do you mean you're lying and in love?"

Nash whips his passionate fury from me to Alena. "I love her. I love Vale and never acted on it all these years because I never wanted to hurt you. *Ever.* I was willing to die alone, without her, to keep you happy and safe until—"

"Until it stopped being safe," Loch interjects. "Until I came around."

Alena turns to him. "What? You? What do you have to do with..." She stammers, gesturing to me and Nash, "Them and..." She looks at me. "And you love my dad? Like *love*, love him?"

I nod, streams pouring down my face. "I'm so sorry, but I do ... I mean, I did." I want to throw up. "But he lied to you. To me. And now I don't know what to feel."

"Lied to us? About what?" Alena jumps up, waving her finger our way. "If you two are ... whatever ... then yeah, it freaks me out. A lot. It's weird. I never saw it coming, but..."

She's on a roll. You can't stop her.

"But it's not a lie that you're *adults*. You can do what you want," she reasons. "Dad, you've acted like a goddamn monk my whole life, but I knew it was a lie. I just figured you kept your sex life away from me. And Vale, you've been miserable and lonely. It kind of makes sense. And now half of me wants to vomit, and half of me is relieved you're not alone." She balls her fists. "So, am I pissed? Yes! Will I get over it? Give me a goddamn chance to breathe, and maybe I will!"

This is the Alena I love—the strong one, the one who will yell down a grizzly bear and send it running away. She gets this from her dad.

"So why the hell are you freaking me out?" She shouts. "Days before I get married, and what does this have to do with Loch?" She turns to him. "What's going on?"

"Alena, I..." Loch stands, reaching for her hand. His eyes burn so blue with his plea, "Babygirl, I love you. Please believe it. You have to."

I stand in our tornado of lies and love and can see the eye of Loch's storm—*he's not lying. He loves her.*

"Nash." Nadine finally speaks. Calmy. Warmly. Like a matriarch who could quell any fight. "Go speak with Alena, and we'll wait here. Then, she can speak with my son."

Alena's brown eyes shock wide open. "Your *son?*"

Nadine nods. Loch bows his head in shame, and Nash takes over.

"Come on, sweetpea." He steps toward her. "Just, please, let me tell you everything, and then you can hate me as Vale does."

He's trying to joke to calm us, but it doesn't work.

The bomb has exploded, I'm furious, and Alena's in shock. She lets him wrap an arm over her shoulder and lead her down the hallway to her bedroom, closing the door behind them.

The silence is deafening until I hear her muffled cries. Then my glare slices from Loch to Nadine. "How could you do this to her?" I shake my head, not believing of all people; Nadine lied to her, too.

"Because I love her, Vale." Loch addresses me for the first time. "Just like I saw with my own eyes how much Nash loves you. And I *will* fight for her." He clenches his teeth. "So, don't get in my way and regret it."

"Lyov," Nadine arches her brow at him, "that is *not* how you speak to a queen."

"My apologies," he fumes, "but Vale, you read this all wrong. Does it matter how we fall in love with someone? Or does it matter more how we'll love them until the day we die?"

Suddenly, I see Axel's fury in Loch. I see Sire's conviction, Jace's warmth, Grant's steel, and Nick's wisdom. Suddenly, I see the man who's been standing right in front of me for over a year.

He's a beast, too.

And he's in love with Alena.

"Then, if you truly love her, it starts today." I lift my chin. "You'll stop lying to her and fight to win her love again."

"Will you keep that promise, too?" Nadine asks. "For you, *moya doch*, are no different. Nash has revealed his greatest secret. There are no more lies, so will you let him fight for you, too?"

I chew my lip because I don't know the answer.

No man has ever fought for me. No man has ever made a mistake, then dropped to his knees and begged for my forgiveness.

Sure, Nash almost destroyed me last time, but he didn't fall to his knees, groveling to get me back. Though I know he would've.

No, he did more.

He brought my soul to *its* knees.

I couldn't believe a man loved me so much he'd do more

than grovel for me or fight for me. Nash killed for me. And he'd do it all over again.

"It's my fault," Nadine laments. "Please don't hate my boys, and I mean Nash, too. Yes, they're grown men now. They're responsible for their actions, but it started with me. Their father never loved me, so they were born into the violent lie of our marriage. Then, I hid the lie of loving my second husband, and he lied to help us escape. I raised my boys to survive, to lie and hide, and once Nash joined us, I taught him the same. My dear, all they've ever known is lying to protect the ones they love, and I think you might know a little about that, too."

I nod, letting my last tears escape.

I lied to myself for so long, refusing to admit I was in love with Nash.

Then I lied to him, denying it and being a snarky brat about it.

Though that last part was fun.

But then, I looked into Alena's loving eyes and lied to protect her from the truth; that's how I justified it.

Yeah, the worst liars are the ones who say they never lie.

CHAPTER FORTY-FIVE
NASH

"So, Mom never knew?"

"No." I kneel before Alena, sitting on the bed. "She never knew about Nadine, her sons, or what we do. It was too dangerous. It's all I've ever cared about: protecting you from danger. But..."

My daughter's tears kill me, and there's only one way to stop them—*tell the truth*.

"But I'm not ashamed of what we do." I confess, taking her hands, "We're the beasts who kill the monsters, and we do it to keep girls like you ... I mean, women, too ... We risk it all to save them."

"So Michael, my godfather, is really named Axel, and he's Loch's *brother*?" Disbelief fills her eyes. "And Sire, my pastor, is his brother, too? And there are three others? They're Loch's five brothers, whom I've never met? And you're telling me you're sort of the Russian mafia, but you're not? You're like *good* mafia?"

I nod.

"Is that the lie Vale is so mad about?"

"No, and it's not a lie."

"Dad." Her brows pinch. She looks just like her mother when she's mad. "Quit being so cryptic and spit it out."

Here it goes.

My soul lights a million candles now, praying I won't lose my daughter over this.

"I told Loch to befriend you. To meet you and keep an eye on you to keep you safe. You moved up there to those goddamn mountains, and we have too many enemies who can come after you. So, I needed to find a guard to protect you."

"You told Loch to *befriend* me?" She pulls her hands away.

"Yes. But I never told him to fall in love with you or ask you to marry him. In fact, I wanted to beat his ass for it."

She tilts her head, searching my gaze. I'm staring down the Spanish Inquisition, but she's my mirror. Alena has my eyes.

"You're lying."

I clench my jaw. "A little."

"God. Fucking. Dammit. Dad!" See? She sounds like me, too. "Give it to me straight, and quit bullshitting."

"Once I found out he fell in love with you and wasn't backing down, I—"

"You told him to marry me." Tears spill over her dark lashes. She looks away, her chin quivering. "So it's a lie. This wedding. Our marriage. Our love. It's a lie."

"No, Alena, it's not. Loch loves you. He fought for you. Literally. He and Axel almost killed each other over you."

Her glance darts to the floor. It's odd, but I don't know how to read her right now. I've never hurt her like this before. I'm just thankful she's hearing me out.

"Axel told Loch if he loved you, he had to commit to you. He wouldn't let him walk away and break your heart, and I..." I swallow, confessing, "I agreed. Nadine, too. I didn't want your heart broken, and even more, I wanted you safe, and no one else, other than me, can protect you like Loch."

Solemnly, she nods. "So he lied and became a ranger because you told him to."

"No," I shake my head, "he's into all that nature shit, too. I mean it; he loves you. You're a perfect match. And trust me, as your father, who still sees you as a little girl in animal pajamas crawling into my bed during every lightning storm, and not because they scared you, but because you wanted me to listen to them with you ... I hate to admit it ... but Loch loves you as much as I do."

"No, he doesn't," she chokes. "Love is a choice, Dad, and you didn't give him one."

"A choice?" I huff. "I'm sorry, sweetpea, but you're wrong. I don't choose to love Vale. I can't fight it; I just do and always will. And you don't choose to love Loch; you just feel it. Right?"

"I can't believe this." She closes her eyes. Tears drip from her jaw. "I've lost my best friend and my fiancé in the same night."

"Don't say that," I murmur, reaching for her hands again. "Vale loves you. She'll always love you and..." Fucking tears. I blink them back. "It's what I love about her most. And Loch, too. That goddamn shithead loves you, too."

"Do you really love her, Dad?" She slants her eyes at me. "Like this isn't some age-gap kink that's going to run its course, and then I have to choose between my dad and my best friend? Because right now? I don't like your chances."

A grin tugs at my lips. I fight it. "Yes, I love her, and you're not losing her as your best friend. I just need her, too. I need Vale in my life. I need to finally be free to love her. I want to marry her and give you a little sister with her and—"

"Ewww." She cringes. "One revolting image at a time." Pause. "I mean ... I love babies, but just..." Her shoulders sag with her sigh. "I want you to be happy. I hated how you were always alone, and Vale's been so alone, too. Ever since her ex-boyfriend, Chad, and—"

"Yeah, about Chad."

She stops and reads my eyes.

"No," she gawps.

I raise a brow.

"Dad," she mutters. "You didn't."

"I did, and I'll do the same for you. Even your precious Loch. If he ever hurts you, he's fucking dead." I brush a tear off her cheek. "But he wouldn't, and that's what I mean. Give him a chance. Hear him out. Nadine, too. There's a lot to tell you, but start with him. Let him tell you his side of the story."

"The wedding's off." A stern look takes her eyes. I've seen it in the mirror before. She's not joking. "I'll hear him out. And Nadine. But there's no way I'm getting married this Saturday. Not like this."

"But what about the pounds of shrimp I just paid for?"

She narrows her eyes. "*Daaaddd.*"

"Kidding." I just wanted my baby to smile. "Loch's brothers will eat it all in an hour flat."

Again, her gaze drops to the floor. "What did you mean about Michael ... I mean *Axel* ... fighting with Loch over me?"

"As much as I fight with Axel," I explain, "I've always been the closest to him. Sire is like my big brother, but Axel's like my twin. Like Vale and Blair, I guess. And so, Axel always took a shine to you."

"A shine?"

"He always cared. He's usually a dick to everyone but never to you. So, I asked him to be your godfather, and he takes it seriously. He almost beat the shit out of Loch when we found out about you two. Part of me knows he did it, so I wouldn't. And he did it because he couldn't help himself. He loves you, too."

She nods, and more tears fall. "I need to talk to him."

"He's waiting right outside for you."

She startles, then stammers, "Yeah. Loch. Send him in to talk to me."

"Give him a chance."

Silence.

"And please forgive me."

She raises a brow.

"Okay. In time. I hope." I cup my hands over hers. "Just please know, Alena, how much I love you. From the moment I held you in my arms, I knew why men wage wars. I will always fight for you. You're my greatest gift and the reason I live. So please, try to forgive me one day."

She chews her lip, staring me down. I see her fury, but I feel her love.

Goddamn, she's my soul.

I kiss her hands. "You just have a fucked up dad who fucked up. And I'm sorry for hurting you. I really am. But I'll never apologize for loving you and keeping you safe."

Her big brown eyes are almost the same size as when she touched my cheek and first called me "Dada."

They're still the center of my world.

"Just get her back, Dad," she insists. "So at least one thing will be right in my world again."

CHAPTER FORTY-SIX
VALE

"You're being stubborn." Jace tosses a shrimp up, proudly catching it and chomping it down. "It's not a good look on you."

I roll my eyes.

He catches that, too. "Keep doing that," he says, "and maybe you'll find that big brain of yours back there and start using it again."

"He's your king." Axel drums his inked fingers on the arm of the side chair. "You owe him an audience."

I laugh. "Are you always such an idiot or just showing off for me today?"

Jace laughs at that, too.

I'm holding court on the sofa in Alena's villa, where I've camped for three days, while she's finally in her bedroom, trying to sleep.

Blair was supposed to come, but I told her not to. It only reminds Alena of her destroyed dream.

Alena talked to Loch, called off the wedding, made him leave, and then sobbed for hours about it. Nadine tried to comfort her, but Alena said she needed space, so Nadine quietly left, too. Then, I tried to comfort her, but I started sobbing with Alena the next day because she said she forgave me about Nash.

But what kills me is that the only reason she does is because she's too heartbroken over Loch.

Me, screwing her dad, is the lesser of two betrayals, and that's not the kind of best friend redemption I deserve.

No books. No vibrators. Swim lessons. A glowing tan. I'll take any punishment to feel like I genuinely deserve her forgiveness.

And me?

Well, I told Nash to leave, too. I don't forgive him.

Sure, he finally told Alena the truth, but only because I forced his hand.

How long was he going to lie to her? To me? And if he does it out of love like Nadine says, then I guess Nash loved me so much I would've never known the truth.

"He lied to protect Alena." Sire's here, too. He's reading my mind, preaching, "Forgive him so that you may be forgiven, too."

Yep, that's my scarlet letter sin. A big *S* for *"Slut, who was DTF her best friend's dad many times and lied about it."*

"He was going to tell you after the wedding," Grant adds.

"Nash is an honorable man," Nick assures. "Once he's your husband, there will be no secrets."

The kings circle me like lions around a tigress.

They say, one-on-one, a tiger would defeat a lion. But five lions against one tigress?

Well, it depends on how pissed she is.

"What language are you all speaking because it sounds like Bullshit?" I lean forward, not intimidated by them. "Tell us *after* the wedding? So, Alena would have been heartbroken, betrayed, *and* divorced? And me and Nash, getting married, too? Uh-huh. I see the 'Fuck That' fairy just arrived."

Jace keeps laughing, but Axel sneers with evil confidence. "You *will* be his wife."

I slant my glare at his glacial eyes. "I'm glad you're not letting your law degree get in the way of your stupidity."

He jeers, "I don't know what's making *you* so stupid, but it really works."

I fire, "You talk so much shit, I don't know whether to give you a breath mint or toilet paper."

Sire snorts, amused. "Come on, Vale. We're sorry we didn't tell you, but we thought it was best for Alena. Loch genuinely loves her. Even when Axel tried to beat it out of him."

"They'll work it out," Grant says. "They have to because I've never seen our baby brother so brokenhearted."

Every day, Loch sits on the front steps of Alena's villa, holding a fresh bouquet of wildflowers because Alena likes nothing cultivated. I peer out our kitchen window and see the crumpled envelope in his hand, too. It's a letter he insists on handing to her.

But she won't see him.

So, he's staying with Nash.

Like two beasts sharing the doghouse.

But Nash doesn't sit on our porch. No, he sits on his and texts me pictures of the books he's reading. Two a day from the bestsellers list on marriage.

It makes me roll my eyes, furious, because it's so goddamn sweet. How many men crack a book open about love for their women?

Only the best ones.

"Just play eighteen holes with him." Jace catches another shrimp. "Stab Nash with snark, beat his ass, and then make him drop to his knees and beg for you. Or," he catches another, "stay mad at him because it's hilarious when you are."

"It's not funny," I mumble because it hurts.

I feel like a three-day-old bruise. Worse and aching. Even if I give Nash a chance, what about Alena? I won't swoon off into the sunset with her father and leave her alone in this hot mafia mess.

"I'm sorry." Jace sits on the sofa beside me, wrapping his arm over my shoulder and tugging me near. Not like a lover. Not like a friend. I can't describe our bond. "I know it hurts. It hurts like hell when love lets us down."

My lips smush against his pec. *God, does he eat steel Cheerios for breakfast?* "Who let you down?" I ask. "Because I'll kill a bitch for you."

Grant chuckles. "Spoken like one of our true queens."

But Jace doesn't answer, and usually, I'd dig to know his secret, but I don't have it in me.

"Can we just have some time?" I sigh. "Just leave me and Alena alone tonight. She was supposed to get married tomorrow, and having you all here makes it worse."

"Okay." Sire rises. "Let's give them some peace."

The other kings rise, turning to leave. I close my eyes and fall back on the sofa, hearing their heavy footsteps before the front door closes, and I set a mental timer for when I'll go check on Alena.

"You know, the other morning..." But a deep voice shocks my eyes open. It's Axel standing over me. "After our mission. Before I drove Nash back to The Mercier. He told me to make a stop."

Slowly, he sits beside me, tenting his inked fingers. Malice is written all over Axel's skin, but it's not in his eyes. They're suddenly kind when he tells me, "Nash paid a visit to your father. He confronted him at his golf club and told him he's a deadbeat dad. That he should be grateful to have an amazing daughter like you."

"What?" Shock grabs my heart. "What did my father say?"

"That he agreed. That he fucked up and doesn't know how to fix it with you. That he's always been proud of you and ashamed of himself."

Easily, I can imagine Nash fighting for me, but I can't imagine my father. I can't see his bloated ego submitting to any man.

"Did Nash punch him or something?"

Axel grins. *God, he's so beautiful when he's not a dick.*

"Never. Nash would never disrespect you like that. Instead, he told your father it's his choice to have a future with you. But for Nash? He told him that he was going to ask you to be his wife. That he would be honored to have a future and a family with you, and it was up to your father if he wanted to be a part of it."

I chew my lip so hard, I want to bite it. I want to bleed with the overwhelming rush of love I feel. This doesn't erase my childhood wounds, but now, because of Nash ... they can start to heal.

All we need is one person who will fight for our love.

Maybe my father will start fighting for mine.

But Nash never stopped.

I don't know what to say. I don't know what to do.

Axel's wintery eyes glow warm while he teases, "I love the sound you make when you finally shut up."

I punch his arm, and he rubs it, grinning, before his face falls, casting his stare down the hall. "Is she okay?" he asks about Alena.

"Would you be?"

"No. I know what it feels like to lose love."

Axel loved someone? Someone not blindfolded and forced to kneel on a pillow for him? "Who?"

"That's a story for another day. Just..." he answers, rubbing his hands together. "Just tell Alena I asked about her. Tell her we love her, and it will be okay."

I nod, expecting Axel to leave, but he surprises me. Tenderly, he cups my cheek, brushing his thumb over my new piercing. It's not sexy or disrespectful. I can feel the reverence in his touch.

"For so long," he says, "Nash has loved you from afar while I watched him suffer alone. I always knew you were his queen. So please, don't throw away your love because he loved his daughter, too."

With a chaste kiss on my cheek, he rises and silently leaves.

He leaves my world spinning. My head, too. I flop back again and close my eyes, processing all Axel shared about Nash and my father, too. And all Axel made me feel as well. Like I belong with Nash, with all of the kings and queens.

They're my family now.

I MUST'VE FALLEN ASLEEP, OVERWHELMED BY IT, BECAUSE I awake to a crash. It startles me, and I sit up, glancing through the windows to the deck.

A violent summer storm rages outside. The extreme afternoon heat finally bursts the evening sky open with thunder, lightning, wind, rain, and then hail. The lights flicker off, and we lose power.

These storms are normal around here. It'll pass in an hour, but it's time to check on Alena. She loves lightning, anyway.

Barefooted, I aim down the hall. The bedrooms face the side of the house, leaving the dusk light and view to the living area. The shadows grow darker as I approach her bedroom door, but I won't knock. I won't wake her in case she's sleeping through the storm.

Quietly, I nudge her door open and...

Terror seizes my heart.

A man straddles Alena, his silhouette narrow and tall. Her screams are muffled by thunder, and the sock shoved in her mouth. He's tied her wrists to the headboard. He's ripped her pajama top open and torn her shorts apart. The window to her bedroom gapes wide open. He crawled through it; don't ask me how with the guard outside.

It doesn't matter.

Hell is here.

"Daddy's not going to like how I'll fuck his pretty daughter up." He holds a bloody hunting knife to her nipple. "I bet you were even prettier when you were ten."

Lightning slashes the air, its light illuminating his face.

It's Turner.

It's on.

"Hey, Cyclops!" I yell. "Want another ass beating?"

He whips around, confirming my insult. The mutilated hole where his eye used to be stares me down. His flaccid eyelid is swollen and raw, like the scars that mar his face. A piece of his bottom lip is missing, too—all courtesy of Nash's wrath for me.

"You fucking bitch," he hisses.

"Yeah, I am. So you want another round?" *Just get away from Alena.* Tied up like that, she doesn't have a fighting chance. But I do. "Why don't you show me all your little dick stamina while you mansplain a micropenis to me?"

That's all it takes.

Turner climbs off of Alena's bed and stalks toward me. Instinctively, I want to run, but I wait for a heartbeat. I wait until he'll follow me and not hurt her.

"You cheating fucking bitch," he hisses, his lone blue eye glaring. "I'm going to carve off eighteen pieces of your flesh and then fuck them into every hole you have."

"You couldn't fuck a hole if you stood in one." I whip around, running down the hall, taunting him to chase me.

Knives. In the kitchen. Go!

I race that way, sensing his heat behind me. It's not a big house. There's not much room to escape.

My pulse rockets to heights never known. My vision tunnels, focused on my goal. *On a weapon. On a knife.* The only thing I hear is his grunt as he grabs my long braid so hard, I scream. The flame of my torn flesh, of my ripped scalp, is instant.

In a whirl, I'm spun around, crashing into the wall, breath exploding from my ribs, pain ripping my vision away.

"You little, fucking bitch." His scalding slap to my face shocks my eyes open. My world rings in my ear. "Where's your mobster now, you cheating cunt?"

Turner grabs my chin, crushing it and forcing me to face him. His one eye is crazed as he squeezes my lips, his hot mustard breath, and Chiclet teeth nearing. The smell of his preppy cologne is repugnant, too, reminding me of...

My prom.

My nightmare.

My survival.

"Fuck you!" I scream, fighting back.

He can't take my kiss, but he can take my goddamn knee in his balls. It's enough to buy me a second as he stumbles back, cupping his groin.

My heart hammers. My blood seeps from my torn scalp in warm rivulets down my neck. My logic struggles. *The knives? The knives?*

But he's blocking the doorway to the kitchen now. And if I escape? He'll go back and murder Alena before he's murdered, too.

So I circle the living room furniture, putting the sofas and chairs between us.

He stalks around, his knife waving low, as I circle right, and he tracks left to catch me.

"You watching my hips now?" I taunt, and he sneers, slowing.

He craves this chase, this hunt. He's a true predator.

All humanity leaves his eye, and he's a vacant animal. He can't take his rabid stare off his prey as I dart one way, and he prowls after me. Like an evil dance, we slowly circle the room.

He licks his lips, his bloody knife dripping in one hand, and suddenly, I know it's blood from the sweet guard at the bottom of the steps. *Turner snuck up on him and sliced his throat.* That's the only way he got in.

"You pathetic two-incher," I snarl. "Your mother should've swallowed you."

"Swallowed me?" He leans one way, so I dash the other while he unzips his navy shorts. "Yeah, you'll swallow me while you choke to death on my inches."

It's vile. It's gross. It's not sexual, it's depraved how he pulls his dick out. It's not big, but it's hard. Violence arouses him, so he exposes his erection, proudly, lewdly showing me how he gets off on hunting me, brandishing his bloody knife while his fiendish eye ogles my tank top and shorts.

"Choke on you?" I jeer, "Your baby penis could barely sneeze a wad of cock snot."

His dick stabs the air, angry and red like his snarl, but it doesn't soften. No, it hardens at my insult, bouncing when he suddenly lunges my way, and I race around, putting my back to the front door and his toward the golf course.

His ego hungers for my fight. He'd get off on my resistance. But me? I notice his dick drip, waiting and begging, and I've read too many books. I have an educated guess.

"You want to fuck me with that little thing?"

His mutilated lips part with a gasp, his hand instinctively returning to fist his erection.

Now, I have a solid theory, and I test it. "You know, I've heard excessive masturbation shortens the penis."

His chest heaves. He starts jerking himself off.

One more test of my hypothesis. *My professors would be so proud.* "Would it squeal if I squeeze it?"

"Yes, bitch," he hisses.

Yep, SPH. Small penis humiliation. It's a legit fetish, and many men have it, even if they aren't small.

Turner's a textbook case. Born into so much power and entitlement, he craves humiliation, the emotional sadism of it. It's cathartic for him. He doesn't even realize it; he just gets off on it.

But I know how to use it.

The violent storm outside has muted to evening rain. The yellow flag to the tenth hole flaps in the waning wind, grabbing my quick attention, reminding me…

My golf clubs.

They're behind me, down in the foyer by the front door.

I just need a chance to get to them.

So, I lick my lips and let him relish my singular focus on his penis while I fire my over-educated snark.

"Is it cold in here, or does that little thing run in your family?" Slowly, I step back while I cuckold him, "Lucky for you, it'll clearly be a short race. It obviously won't take long." Another step back. "But your little helmet does explain your huge car. A Tesla Truck, right? I bet your little man fits easily inside it." I laugh, backing into the foyer. "But who are we kidding? Your puny prick will fit in Ken Barbie clothes."

I could almost be wildly amused by this, but I'm not.

He's stroking and stalking my way, clutching the blood-stained knife in his other hand. God, this explains some of his violence, too. This isn't a fetish for him. It's sociopathic.

A fetish respects consent. It's harmless when all parties are respected, when it has no negative impact.

But Turner thrives on harming innocent people, on violating the most vulnerable. He has no remorse, no empathy. It's terrifying, disturbing, and vile what he does to children, women, and others.

My educated mind labels it Antisocial Personality Disorder. But my instinct, my memory, tells me to fight, to survive.

I hope he rots in hell with Chad.

"But is it supposed to drip like that?" I point at his tip. "Careful, green semen means it's infected."

He falls for it, glancing down while I spin around, racing for my clubs. They stand in my black golf bag, and it's training. It's years of reaching blindly. I know the heavy weight in my hand. The cold forged steel. The titanium-plated front. The distinct design made for accuracy, trajectory, and control.

My nine iron.

In a fast jerk, I whip it out of my bag, my skilled hands wrapping around it. They know the grip. My shoulders know the rotation. My hips torque for maximum strength, ready to unleash pure power.

Turner charges my way, his teeth gritted, his dick raging. But his head? It's a much larger target than any golf ball, and I swing at it with all my might, never losing focus, watching my club make full contact as it smashes his temple.

No, I don't shout, "Fore!"

I let the sickening crack of his skull be the only sound. Instantly, my stomach lurches at it while he grunts, "Bitch."

It's the only word he can say, falling against the wall. But I didn't knock him out. The permanent damage takes too long to start. It gives him too much time. He staggers, dizzy, as a crimson drop falls from his nose. His lips snarl, his eye blinking while he raises his knife.

I'm not at a good angle.

He's too close, and this foyer is too small for me to backswing to strike again as his knife lifts with his evil, scarred smile.

Oh, god. This is it.

I raise my arms, holding my club as I duck my head to protect my neck while he sneers, "Told you." His words slur, "Men have more—"

BANG! It explodes out of nowhere.

I'm startled, yelping and jumping back as blood spews from Turner's head and...

Oh my god, he's been shot. He's shot!

I still clutch my club as a weapon, watching as Turner collapses before me, his body almost knocking me down, so I jump back.

"Vale! Are you hurt?"

In a shocked haze, I lift my focus from Turner's dead body at my feet, blood pooling around his shattered skull.

It takes a moment for me to focus. For me to see ... Nash ... with a gun in his hand.

CHAPTER FORTY-SEVEN
NASH

After what happened with Turner, the instinct to hold my daughter was overwhelming. Thankfully, she let me.

I went there to check on Alena and grovel for Vale. I was ready to beg for forgiveness, but I found the guard slain at the bottom of the villa steps. Then I caught Turner raising his bloody knife to Vale ... so I killed for them instead.

Afterward, all the kings stormed the condo while Alena and Vale huddled together. I got them out of there before Axel and Sire took care of the body and Jace cleaned the scene. Loch, Nick, and Grant swept the resort for more of Turner's men and found none.

And me?

The need to comfort Vale was overpowering, too, but furiously, she pushed me away.

"I don't know how I feel about all this," she hissed, shaking her head, reluctant to get in my car. "About this life. About you."

"Sometimes you have to think, not feel." I fought back, explaining, "You survive in the moment and feel later. That's the life we lead. We protect each other. We kill for each other. You're in shock. You'll know how to feel about it later."

Then I raised a brow. I wasn't leaving her. "Now get in my fucking car," I snarled.

We had come full circle to the night this all started.

Alena said she wanted the solace of her apartment on Folly Island, and I wouldn't leave her side, either.

It's been a week, and Vale has stayed with her, too, but her silent treatment is killing me. I need Vale's smart-ass snark. That's when I'll know she's okay.

And my daughter? A hundred times, Alena's told me she's fine. Turner didn't hurt her; he only enraged her. Lucky for him, he's at the bottom of the Atlantic, where she can't shoot him.

That was my job.

Thinking about how Turner touched my daughter. How he almost assaulted and killed her. How I can see the raw scab healing at the base of Vale's scalp, where that fucker grabbed my woman, too...

I want to retrieve Turner's corpse and gnash his fucking neck open, killing him all over again. Fifty times wouldn't be enough.

Loch shares my rage. He's here, too. He sits by Alena's front door. She won't speak to him, and he won't leave.

It's a stalemate of stubborn love, and part of me enjoys the irony; Alena and Loch are just like me and Vale. The more our women resist our love, the more we fight for it.

I don't regret ordering Loch to protect Alena.

Yeah, I was furious when he fell in love with her, too. And don't get me started on him calling her "babygirl." I want to crack his skull every time he says it. No father wants to hear that shit.

But now? I'm thankful that he loves her, that he's fighting for her.

I knew this secret would explode in our faces one day, but we're so used to keeping them. We're so used to protecting each other.

Sure, the truth will set you free in most worlds, but not in this one. The truth is lethal in our world. Sometimes, you have to hide it so it won't hurt the ones you love.

It's the only thing I regret—hurting Alena and Vale. But I'm man enough to wait for their forgiveness.

With my daughter, it won't take long.

With my poison? Well ... she *is* breathtaking when she's pissed as hell. It turns me on when she rolls her eyes.

This life is a lot to take. I get it.

People think it's like what you see on the screen or read in a book. But once you see it, smell it, feel it? You cross over. There's no return to innocence. Turner's violence was a bloody wake-up call for Vale. It's what I warned her about, so I'll wait for her to come around.

Because I meant it; like hell if I'll ever leave her.

NADINE VISITS. THE OTHER QUEENS DON'T.

Alena doesn't know about them yet. That whole side of our story feels too cruel to tell her right now. She has enough to process, but the other kings come by. They check on her from afar, but she doesn't want to see them, either. She needs time; we understand.

And Vale? She talks with Jace and no other king. I watch them on Alena's balcony. Jace wraps his arm over Vale's shoulder, and I'm shocked because I'm not jealous. I'm grateful.

Now, I understand our tradition. Jace is truly her second

king. He's fighting for us. He's fighting to keep me and Vale together.

"That's it!" But it's the eighth day, and Alena storms out of her bedroom where she's hidden with Vale, her camping backpack slung over her shoulder. "Peace out, everyone. I'm going back to work."

I rise from the sofa, and Loch jolts from his chair. "I'm going with you," he insists, and she shrugs.

"Go to hell. Go to work. Your choice."

"Alena!" I bark. "He's here, fighting for you."

"No, he's here because you command it."

"My brothers can't command me to do a damn thing I don't want to," Loch seethes, grabbing his keys. "You go. I go. Always."

Alena struggles, her eyes welling with tears. "But I can't breathe when I see you," she chokes. "You make me remember everything, but it was all a lie. And I don't want the guys at work to know, to see me cry, and if you're there, you make it too hard."

"But what about our cabin?" He pleads, "Alena, I love you. It's not a lie. Just give us a chance."

"It became *my* cabin when you decided to lie," she answers furiously. "Go find your own."

I shrug at Loch and let him read my eyes. *"Put on your big boy boxers. She's going to give you a helluva fight."*

She turns back, rushing to hug Vale, standing by her packed luggage. They whisper, and I'd pay anything to know what they share because Vale sadly shakes her head before Alena softly pecks her cheek.

Then, she crosses the room toward me. "See ya, Dad." Her arms snare my waist.

Kissing her russet waves, I wrap around her and beg, "Please let Loch go with you. He needs to protect you."

"I can protect myself," she mutters. "I don't need him."

"But he needs *you*."

She rises on her toes, whispering in my ear, "Like you need Vale, and I need a little sister. Get her back, Dad, then I'll forgive you."

It's the hardest thing, letting my daughter go. It's the warmest thing, watching Loch follow her.

After they leave, the apartment door yawns open. The sunlight spilling in illuminates the awkward silence between Vale and me.

Without a word, she collects her phone and handbag.

"Where are you going?" Because I'll follow her, too.

"Atlanta." Her tone is dead. "I'm going with Stacey. We're helping my sister move."

"I'll go with you."

She whips my way. "You'll give me space. You'll leave me alone."

"Space? Yes. Leave you?" I vow, "Never."

"Great." She rolls her eyes, grabbing her suitcase. "You're going to be a hemorrhoid. Like a giant pain in my ass."

Oh, what I want to say about loving her ass, but I like breathing.

So, I trail behind her, admiring it while she storms down the stairs, clunking her suitcase behind her.

I FOLLOW VALE AND LET HER SEE I MEAN IT. FOR DAYS, I shadow her from Charleston to Atlanta and back. And for days, she flips me off every time she sees me.

I give her space for another week while she returns to work.

I know my poison. She's processing. She's all up in her

head. It's warring with her heart, and only a stupid man steps into that line of fire.

So I sit in my car, parked across from Delta's, watching Vale's silhouette through the window when Jace calls, worried.

"She's being nice and quiet," he whispers, "and it's all wrong. You have to do something."

"I will." Or a fearless man. Or one in love. Yep, here I go, stepping into Vale's war—*okay, because I started it*—while I answer him using my Bluetooth.

I see Jace pacing the porch outside, his phone pressed to his ear.

"Just answer me something."

"What?" he grunts.

I've been wanting to ask him. Ever since Vale's initiation, I feel connected to Jace. Like he's in pain, and I can feel it, too.

"What about you? What's wrong with you and don't bull-shit me. I know it's something."

"What's wrong with any man?" He huffs, "Love."

It's not Vale. I know it. Jace doesn't burn with furious passion and insane urges like I do for her. Yes, Jace would kill for her, too, but he doesn't live for Vale as I do.

It's someone else.

"Who?"

"She's married," he answers. "End of story."

No, it's not.

Marriage is when many stories begin.

CHAPTER FORTY-EIGHT
VALE

I lock my vintage red bike to the iron gate by my apartment and think of Nash. The fact that he's following me everywhere makes it impossible not to. I swear I can feel him parked across the street somewhere, protecting me.

It makes this hollow ache I've had in my heart since childhood feel open and vulnerable. One man was supposed to fill it, but another man did.

People joke about "daddy issues," but they're not funny. They're real. They hurt deeply and to the bone.

Anytime someone who was supposed to love and protect you hurts you instead? It marks your soul.

And sure, it affects the love you seek from others until you learn to love yourself.

I do. I love myself enough to admit Nash isn't my father figure. He's more. He's my soulmate.

He's my Happy Meal.

I just need my heart to catch up to my head. It doesn't happen overnight. It takes time to figure out what's normal in our relationship and what's trauma left over from my dad and everything else. I get it. I read the books.

Ironically, my dad called me this week. He wants to talk and mend things with Blair and me. He deserves a chance, and I deserve to forgive him. It's for me, not for him. I deserve to heal.

So, can I forgive Nash, too?

Or is it acceptance?

The catch is there's nothing normal about our not-mafia-mafia relationship. I can't find those answers in a book.

Turner was my first dead body, and me and my nine iron had a lot to do with it.

Is something wrong with me because I don't feel guilty about it? I've given myself weeks, and all I feel is... Relief. Justice. *Revenge.*

Or does that make me a boss-bitch mafia queen like the others? Like I was meant for this?

I can hear it in Alena's voice when we talk. She's starting to accept this life. She forgives her father. Nash has proven his love for her too many times for Alena to let one colossal mafia mistake erase everything he's devoted to her.

And when she complains about Loch sticking around? How he moved out of their cabin but still goes to their work? How he acts like nothing's wrong in front of their colleagues, but he leaves wildflowers by her door every morning? I can hear it, too. He has a fighting chance with her.

Trudging up my porch stairs, I smile.

The kings and queens are fighting for me, too.

Jace has been ... well, *Jace* ... bribing me with Reese's peanut butter cups while sweet-talking me about how I belong with Nash. Sire and Wren invite me to dinner, and we talk about everyone *but* Nash. They make me feel like I belong with them, too. Axel comes by, claiming he's buying naughty toys for his mystery woman, but I know he's checking on me.

All urge me to forgive Nash's lie about Loch and Alena,

especially Nadine. She won't stop blaming herself, and I know there's so much more to her story, to the story of all her sons, that would explain some of my resistance away, but right now?

I'm not the little girl waiting for her dad, who never showed up. I'm not the teen survivor who's free of her tormentor.

So, who am I?

Who are you when you let your past go and face your future?

I huff, sweating as I round the final rung of stairs to my apartment and stop dead in my tracks. "What are you doing here?"

Nash looks too sexy, kneeling by my door with a wilted red tulip in hand, slinging his smiling sunshine everywhere. "I came for my poison."

The fight in me is instant. My nostrils flare. "I'm not in the mood."

"Too bad," he answers. "Because I am."

"Fine," I snark. "Stay there and stink. The trash gets picked up tomorrow."

Maybe that's who I am now—a fighter.

He smirks. "You'll get a spanking for that sass."

"And you'll get a middle finger. You're why god created them."

His smirk only grows. "God knows where I crave *your* middle finger."

"I have one nerve left, and you're dry-humping it." I march his way, fishing for my keys in my bag. "Get out of my way, or I won't be responsible for what my knee does to your balls."

"I love it when my balls are the center of your attention, too."

"Nash!" I stomp my Mary Jane. "I'm serious. If you think I'm short, you should see my patience."

"I can't." He's still on his knees. "You have none, just like me, and I'm tired of waiting, Vale. Time to talk."

"Oh yeah?" I stick my key in the doorknob. "Then, on your mark, get set, go fuck yourself."

Yep, I'm a fighter...

...and something else.

Because he grabs my shaking hands, gently tugging them away, leaving my keys dangling in the doorknob. He holds my heart, too. It's hanging by a thread with him touching me again.

I'm his.

"I'm sorry." He sounds so warm. "I truly am. Alena can forgive me, but it won't be right. *I* won't be right until I earn your forgiveness, too."

"Why should I forgive you? If I had a dollar for every time you lied to me," I tremble, "I'd be rich."

"You *are* rich. You have a life of me giving you everything I have: heart, body, and soul." Slowly, he rises. "I'm a flawed man living a dangerous life. I warned you, Vale, but you said you wanted it, so I need you to understand it, too. Understand *me*. I'll do whatever it takes to protect you and Alena. So, let me inside, and we'll talk about it."

I don't know if I can talk because I already understand him. Nash is a beautiful beast who protects the ones he loves.

But me? I'm a storm of emotions I don't understand, so I rely on my lonely habit. It's gotten me this far. "I wanna be alone."

"No, you don't." He cups my flushed cheek. "You're not alone, and you never were. I've been here all along, and I'm not leaving. If I have to kneel, watching a tulip wilt in my hand while I fight for you every day, I will."

I mutter, "No, you won't."

No man's ever fought for me.
Well ... Nash did. He killed for me.
Twice.

"Wanna bet, poison?" he asks, letting my hand go so I can swing my door open.

He waits at my threshold while I blink, my pupils adjusting from the bright sun outside to the muted shadows of my apartment. It takes a moment to look around. To realize...

They're everywhere.

Dozens of red tulips in glass vases circle my apartment. They're nestled between my stacks of books. They're on my dresser. They're in baskets on my loveseat. On my bed, there's a blanket of their red petals, and on my laptop stands a sculpture of hand-blown glass tulips, two intertwined.

"Oh my god," I sigh, knowing Nash did this and not believing it.

Then, I glance left to my kitchenette, to the bistro table, and I choke down my sob. My happy sob.

Two Happy Meals.

They sit in their red boxes on gold trays.

When I don't understand my emotions. When they flood me with pain and memories ... Nash anchors me. He's strong enough to feel them with me. Lust, love, or loss; it doesn't matter. He holds me until my storm passes. He slings his sunshine and makes it all okay.

He's right.

He's always been here.

He's always fought for me.

He's always loved me.

And me?

I'm the queen who belongs beside him.

"Bet on us, Vale." His lips press to my ear. "Let me love you. Let me inside forever, and I promise I'll never leave."

How do you start forgiving someone when, deep down, you always will? You'll always love them? You'll always give them a chance because they're the only one you're willing to take?

I turn around and give him my kiss. He's the only man who gets it, as Nash gives me his, too, tender and slow at first. Like he'll always understand my past while he kills for our future. While his tongue finds mine, claiming even more of me.

"You have so much groveling to do," I warn over our heating lips.

"Poison, I'll fall to my knees for you." And he does.

At first, I think it's to lift my miniskirt and rip my panties aside. He has such a fetish for eating me out, and, *god, I've missed him*.

But Nash surprises me.

Reaching into his disguise, his creased khakis, he lifts a black velvet bag and tugs its gold drawstring open. Grinning, he pulls something out. "If I tried to hide a ring box in my pants, you'd snark about my huge size, so I hope this is too big for you, too."

"It's not too big." I shake my head at the enormous black, pear-shaped diamond surrounded by a halo of clear ones on a gold band. "It's perfect."

"Perfect for my beautiful wife." He lifts my left hand to his lips. "Poison, will you marry me and vow to kill me with that mouth every day?"

I nod, tears salting my smile. "On one condition."

"Only one?" He smirks.

"Okay, three."

"Should've shut up at one."

I wink. "You'll learn."

"Name them."

"Okay, five, now."

"*Vale.*"

"Okay, one: You dress like Gomez Addams at our wedding. Pinstripe suit. Pencil mustache and—"

"Fuck, no." He laughs on bended knee. "Try again."

"We get married at night by the river." His brown eyes sparkle, imaging it, too. "In the backyard of our new house."

"Done."

"I want all the kings and queens there. That means Alena and Loch, too. So we have to wait until they're back together, or she's moved on."

He nods. "Of course."

"And three, but I'm saving the last two for later. That's part of your groveling punishment..."

He holds the ring poised over my shaking black fingernail. "Yes, we can serve Happy Meals at our wedding."

How did he know?

"Okay, then, four: We invite my father to our wedding. I want to give him a chance to make it right."

"Whatever you want, poison, it's yours." He still holds my ring, waiting, asking, "Now, will you finally let me make *us* right? Will you marry me?"

"Only if you vow to stay big and hard like my ring."

That's my sweet, snarky answer, and he smirks, sliding it on. "This diamond, my heart, and my dick are yours forever."

He rises with my smile. After a kiss that rips my breath away, he scoops me up and tosses me on the bed, red tulip petals bouncing around me.

He tugs off my shoes, leaving my thigh-highs on. "Show me what's mine," he orders. "Only mine, or I'll kill someone. Do you understand me now?"

"Yes, Daddy," I tease because I *do* understand him, and he understands me, too, as I lift my black mini-skirt and tug my white panties aside. He licks his lips, staring at my pussy, so I clench it for him. His heated glare and hard cock in his pants are making me wet. I need him so much…

"But Nash," I nod toward my door, "go lock it. I know we're safe and all now, but—"

He arches a brow, "Yeah, about that…" and I roll my eyes, grinning.

Great.

More Bratva bullshit.

CHAPTER FORTY-NINE
VALE

I love the humming whir of a label maker. Usually, I use this thing to label our inventory. Trust me; you better know the difference between clear bottles of water-based versus anal-numbing lube.

Amirite? Who wants a numb pussy?

Not this bitch. All I feel is pure satisfaction, labeling what's mine.

QUEEN VALE MONROE ALLEN

I smile, peeling off the adhesive strip with glee and—

"What are you doing?"

A deep voice startles me. I glance over my shoulder, and Nash grins, looming in the doorway of our throne room. I'm not supposed to be in here alone, but I love a good spanking.

"Labeling my throne." I've tipped it over. Its gold back rests on the parquet floor while I carefully center my label on the underside of my white velvet seat.

"We don't need labels." He steps inside, closing the door behind him. "Everyone knows you're my queen, and that's your throne. They watched you earn it."

"Yeah, but what if we play musical chairs one night?" It

thrills me, pressing the label on. "I'm sure there's more kink to come, and we're always prepared, right? I'll want my throne back where it belongs."

He chuckles. "You say that because we anointed it last week."

Yeah, we did.

Nash wanted to celebrate our engagement, so we invited the kings and queens to join us.

And, oh, my Bratva beasts, how they *joined* us.

First, we had a lot to discuss. Nadine was here for that part.

We discussed Turner and his crew. Or the lack thereof. But now the task begins of hunting down his buyers. Our queen won't rest until she has all of them by the balls. Literally.

Then we talked about Alena, Loch, and their limbo and decided to give them some time. Everyone is giving them space while Nash and I plan our gothic wedding.

My queens loved the idea of my black wedding gown. As my bridesmaids, they'll wear something similar. Zar said he'd even find a black lace gentlemen's cravat to tie around his neck. He already has a black brocade suit.

Of course, Blair and Alena will be my maids of honor. Who knows? Maybe Blair will have an NFL newborn by then, while Alena's future is still in the air.

I just want her to be happy again. I won't get married until she is.

After our wedding talk, Sire reclined on his throne, offhandedly mentioning how he and Wren are trying to get pregnant. And with his name that screams "breeding kink," it won't take long.

But I was surprised. I thought Wren really wanted to wait, but clearly, Sire has another agenda. It was odd. He sounded too aloof. His casual tone didn't match the blazing blue intensity of his eyes.

Maybe it was just Sire's usual fervor, all zealous and believing his life depends upon his future child's. Maybe it was just me, shocked at how they had changed their plans, but something was going on there.

Grant and Delphine, however, are in no rush to start a family, though Delphine said she wanted to go home to Paris to visit hers.

But Nadine sat on her red velvet throne, smoking her cigar and flatly refusing, "No. It's too risky." She warned her, "It's an election year for the European Union, and you could bring down their conservative party. You won't leave France alive, so I won't allow it."

"Our queen is right, *chérie*," Grant agreed, nodding toward Delphine, who sat across from him. "I need you here where I can keep you safe."

"Where *we* keep her safe," Axel seethed as usual, but it was sad. He didn't have his mystery woman kneeling before him, and he seemed destroyed by it. Dark circles rimmed his stunning glacial eyes.

"Speaking of safe," Nick cut in. "What's the plan? Because I don't give a damn about the NFL; I want to crush skulls."

"I'm right beside you," Zar snarled, his gaze locked on the man he loves.

"What's going on?" I had no idea what they were talking about, but Nash gave me a measured look from across the room. It said, "Trust us," and I was. I am. I'm trusting our life together.

The kings sat on their thrones. The queens sat on ours. Nadine sat at the head of the room as Axel read her warning eyes. Then he swung his focus my way.

"Your twin," he asked me, "she's partnered with two NFL players?"

"Yeah," I worried. "Why?"

"But they're not out," Nick asked, "as a throuple, right? They're closeted?"

I didn't know what I could share about my twin's love life. And I mean *LOVE*. Blair, Beau, and Colton are neck-deep in it together.

Nash read my protective silence. "That's my queen's sister. You can't ask her to betray her privacy."

"I'm not," Axel answered. "There's a way we can protect her, too."

I wanted to ask more. I needed to, but Nadine ruled the room. "Enough. We have a plan in action, but it's too soon to discuss it." A plan? For what, I wondered while Nadine, wearing a black leather Chanel sheath dress, rose to her stunning glory. Stubbing out her cigar, she proclaimed, "I have a captive to interrogate, and y'all have an engagement to celebrate."

A captive?

She meant that hot one in the bunker, bound, hard, and on his knees for her and *good for Nadine*, I thought. *I know a dominatrix when I spot one.* Yes, mix more concrete for another shrine to our queen.

Once she left, Nash took over.

He'd been waiting for me. "It's time to celebrate my future wife." He lowered his gaze. "Turn around on your throne, my queen. Kneel, lift your skirt, and pull your panties down."

I thought he would put me on display again, and I wasn't opposed. But that's not my beast. He's done sharing me.

No, he was on me.

While I grabbed my throne's golden frame, Nash kneeled before it and feasted on my cunt in front of everyone until I came so hard to his pounding fingers and brutal tongue. He made me drip over my white velvet seat before he stood, dragging his zipper down. Grabbing my hips, he started fucking me like an animal, and I loved it.

I cried out, our passion inspiring Nick and Zar. Nick claimed Zar on Nick's throne, while Grant took Delphine on the platform. Sire took Wren right beside me on her throne. They matched our position. Sire was definitely breeding her before I glanced over my shoulder.

Half of me grieved, worried, and wondering why Axel had mysteriously left. He wasn't there.

Half of me moaned, witnessing Jace, who stayed. He sat alone, fisting his cock, pumping it in cadence to Nash's thrusts inside me.

I know Jace doesn't love me as Nash does. It's different. It's sweet and a little sexy between us, and it breaks my heart because I know Jace is brokenhearted over someone else.

But he won't tell us who, and it was like watching Nash's love for me gave Jace hope that he'll love again. It gets him through. At least, I hoped it did.

I still do.

"Can I ask a question?" I rise before reaching to tip my throne back up, but Nash leans over and beats me to it.

"Poison," he grins, "does your mouth ever stop asking questions?"

"Nope. So go ahead and tell me what's going on with Jace and Axel. Separately and in great detail."

Nash reaches for my hand, the one wearing his black diamond. It may be months before we wed, but I believe we were already married in this room.

I'm eternally his.

He guides me across the room and settles on his throne, pulling me to sit on his lap. Axel's throne is empty beside us. The other five are empty, too.

It's just Nash and me learning to talk through this instead

of him going into beast mode and me storming off like an angry belle.

This is love. This is acceptance.

This is the not-mafia-mafia life.

"Jace is in love with a married woman." Nash reaches for my braid. He starts unraveling it. "That's all I know. I swear."

"Who? And are they having an affair or something?"

He chuckles at my interrogation. "No. I haven't asked him, but Jace wouldn't do that. That man is all about honor and vows. He loves her from afar, and I know how he feels." His face softens. "How much it hurts and for so many years."

I nuzzle my nose to his. "Like us."

"Yes, like us, but not anymore." Nash brushes his bearded lips over mine. "You *will* be my wife soon. I won't wait long, Vale. I'll elope with you if I have to."

"I know. I want to marry you tomorrow, but then I feel guilty because Alena's going through so much, and Jace is hurting."

"Alena will be okay," he assures. "I underestimated her, and I should've known better. She's strong like her mother was." He winces. "But yes, Jace is hurting. He vowed to protect you, and he will. But I feel like we should protect him, too."

My heart warms. I love this about Nash—he can sense someone else's pain. "I feel the same way. I want to help him."

"He's too proud to let us help him."

"Then what do we do? Because I can hunt this woman down and bitch-slap some sense into her. She'd be lucky to have Jace."

His lips near mine. "Let me think about it while I kiss *my* woman."

I let him kiss me. I let the heat rise between us before I realize his ruse. *This sexy dickhead thinks he can make me forget my second question?*

"What about Axel?" I nip his lip. "What's going on with him?"

"I can't tell you."

I lift from our kiss. "You're supposed to tell me everything."

"No," he answers, unraveling my other braid. "I'm supposed to love and protect you, and over dead bodies, I will. But I can't tell you everything. Not on your timeline. That's for your protection."

"But Axel was asking about my sister."

His eyes narrow. "You think I'd let someone harm your sister? Or her partners? And do you honestly think Axel would, too?"

I twist my lips. "You? No. Axel?" I pause before huffing, "Okay, fine. I trust that arrogant asshole with my life."

"So trust us. Trust me. That's how we work." He lifts my gorgeous black diamond to his lips. "Because I'll trust you. You'll be Doctor Vale Monroe Allen, licensed sex therapist, and I'll be your possessively protective husband who'll trust his wife to help others have the best sex like we do."

"God, you're so sexy when you're right."

"I'll be *damn* sexy when I kill any of your clients who cross a line."

"Nash," I roll my eyes, "you can't kill my clients. That will ruin my Google reviews."

"Speaking of crossing lines." His hand slides up my bare thigh, snaking under my skirt. The man is damn lucky I have a fashion fetish for schoolgirl uniforms. "I heard dirty girls love crossing lines."

"Slow your kinky roll, my king." I grab his hand on my hip. "Finish answering my question."

"Which question?" His eyes hood with lust, his cock hard as I sit on his lap.

"The one about Axel."

He laces his hands through my wavy hair. "Poison, I answered you."

"No, you're horny and half-listening. I trust you about Axel asking about Blair. He won't hurt her, but what about Axel's mystery woman? Who is she, why wasn't she here, and why did he leave the other night?"

Softly, he bangs his forehead against mine. "Goddamn, I can't wait for you to be a therapist so you can ask everyone else questions and leave your husband in peace."

Okay, I kinda love that. A lot. *Nash, my husband. Me, a therapist.* I can see it.

"Then just answer me," I smirk, "and end this session so we can anoint your throne, too."

I know how to get what I want. Every queen does. I shift, turning to straddle my king on his throne before I reach down and unzip his pants. "Tell me what *I* want," I tug my panties aside, "and I'll give my king what *he* wants."

He gazes down at his swollen cock in my grasp. How I'm teasing his tip over my slick entrance. "You're driving a very hard bargain."

"Exactly. So, tell me who Axel's mystery woman is."

"I honestly don't know."

Nash lets me search his heated brown eyes. They're a deep storm of lust and love. *So much love.* Every day, he proves it. Every night, I feel it. This is my beast, my man. He is honest. He's telling me what he can, and when he can't ... I trust it's to protect me.

Nash will always protect me.

"But let me tell you something right now, my queen." He fists my raven hair, vowing, "You *will* be my wife. We *will* have a little Wednesday Allen. And I'll carry her in one of those baby things with my Beretta tucked in a holster while I *will* hold your hand. And you're going to—"

Suddenly, I sink down his thick shaft. He moans while I

demand, "And I *will* be pregnant with our son, too. He *will* be our little Gomez Allen and—"

"Goddamnit, poison," he growls ... then smiles, taking my kiss. "I love you."

Thank you so much for reading NASH!
Please leave your review. It's such a gift.

Find out what happens next in AXEL,
where more shocking secrets are revealed.

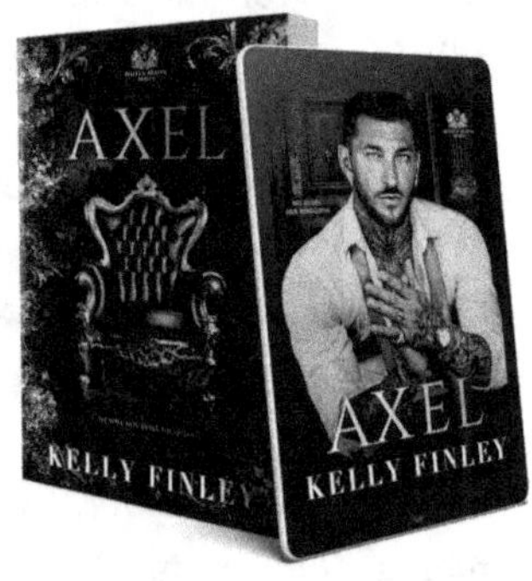

If you want to be ready for even more stunning secrets, spice,
and twists, order SIRE and LOCH today.
With more brothers coming soon.

Enjoy Axel's shocking teaser next, where you'll also find a link
for a free bonus scene
revealing Jace's love.

TEASER - AXEL

YOU KNOW THE SAYING, **"T**HE **D**EVIL TAKES CARE OF HIS **own."**

Oh, I care for her.

I own her.

I stalk her.

Hell, Ruby Jones works for me and has no idea who I really am. She just hates me with a white-hot intensity. I make sure of it.

"Ms. *Jones*," I seethe, stalking toward her desk. She sits

right outside my office so I can watch her. So I can torture her hourly. Okay, every minute if I please. "I just spoke with Ms. Alonso. She thanked me for the legal advice that you gave without my supervision. She said—"

"Shh, Mr. Cummings." Ruby flits her hand. "The adults are talking."

The adults? Talking?

No, she's not even looking at me. She's wearing a shit-eating grin and scrolling on her phone.

I glance and see hot men on book covers filling her screen. One shirtless fucker after another.

Ruby lives to torture me, too.

I lick my bottom lip. "Oh, I'll get very adult with your next paycheck, Ms. Jones, unless you put your phone away. They're forbidden in my office."

Phones are a considerable risk. I don't want my picture taken. All obey my rules about them except Ruby.

Yes, I trust her. Yes, she knows it. And yes, she does every little thing she can to tap dance on my last fucking nerve.

"Yeah, this chat?" She rolls her sapphire eyes, aiming them at me. "We're done. I need coffee."

She shifts in her chair to go to the breakroom, but I lower my glare. "Move an inch, and you'll need a new job."

I tower over Ruby, locking my glare on her stupefying eyes, not her mesmerizing auburn hair or her mouth-watering cleavage. She's dressed like a polished paralegal in a fitted navy dress, and it makes me feral. Literally, she's a runner, and I chase her every morning.

As usual, she has no idea.

"Look," she huffs, a sexy tendril falling free from her ponytail, "Ms. Alonso has a pervert for a landlord, so I just told her to buy a hidden camera to prove it."

"Uh-huh, and where did you tell her to put the camera?"

"I don't know where she'll put it," Ruby scoffs. "Why? Is

she going for a Golden Globe nomination in the 'Best Performance By A Son-Of-A-Bitch' category for her landlord? Because don't worry. You got that one on lock."

I clench my molars. Fighting my snarl. My smirk. My truth.

You know that other saying about karma being a bitch?

She is. She's my mom. And I'm a proud son-of-a-beautiful-bitch. For my mother, my kind of karma kills, too.

That's why I hone my hunting skills with Ruby. She's my practice. My prey. Though, when I finally feel like catching her, it's not murder I want.

It's marriage.

She hates me; she's perfect for me.

"I advise our clients, Ms. Jones. Do you understand?"

I tent my fingers on her desk. Instantly, her gaze drops to the cryptic symbols inked on them, and her cherry lips part, fixated. Inwardly, I smirk. *My tattoos get her every time.*

"When I have to represent Ms. Alonso in court," I lecture, "she needs legally obtained camera footage." Besides, I don't need cameras recording what I plan to do to Ms. Alonso's landlord. I know all about him. Any man who preys on single moms will be my slow, murderous entertainment for days. "Did you consider that, Ms. Jones, when you played lawyer for a day?"

Ruby snaps, "Did you consider the color of the lipstick you can wear when you kiss my ass, Mr. Cummings?" Then ... she winces.

Getting fired or fired up? Yep, Ruby flirts with it daily.

Fuck, I love our games. I love our chase. I love that she detests me. She should. I'm not a good man.

I arch my brow.

"I mean..." She exhales calmly, setting her phone down. "She's a young, single mom, and that man is extorting her. I'm trying to help her."

Ruby's desk is organized, her work impeccable. The only thing that gets Ruby in big, bad trouble with a wolf like me is her fiery, stubborn streak.

She's a fighter like her sister, Scarlett Mercier, so I hired her. I wanted Ruby's research skills and close access to Charleston's most powerful people. Her sister is married to one of them: Luca Mercier, the billionaire hotelier. That's a resource I plan to exploit.

The fact that Ruby makes me sweat like a rabid wolf is just icing on my bloody cake.

I didn't think I'd fall for a woman again. The last two almost killed me.

But Ruby?

I've never felt this alive. This obsessed. This hungry. This perfect fighting match between me and a woman.

"Then help yourself and pick up my dry cleaning," I say, smirking at her.

"That's harassment." Her gaze narrows. I relish how it crinkles her button nose, too. "Fetching your tiny little suits is not in my job description."

Tiny? Hardly. I'm six-four and only swell larger around her.

"How cute." I wink. "Lecturing me on the law when you're the paralegal who engaged in the unauthorized practice of it with my client. Let's tell that to the judge, too. Now..." I reach into my jacket and toss the claim ticket on her desk. "Fetch my suits. I have court first thing in the morning."

Fuck me, it's hot how she grinds her teeth, the hinge of her dainty jaw flexing and making my teeth snag my bottom lip.

I love a good fight. I'm anticipating it. Waiting. Wanting. Needing her to say something feisty while my cock twitches for it, too.

Ruby crosses her legs every time I approach. Yes, I've noticed. Instinctually, she's an animal, too. Her body knows what I hunt. I'm just curious if her whip-smart mind is aware of her arousal as she snarls, "Mr. Cummings, why don't you—"

My smirk slides into a grin, craving her next insult, but...

The elevator *ding* lifts my glare from Ruby to the vintage brass doors as they slide open.

Across my law office, with its gleaming wooden floors, large arched windows, and stately antique desks I collect in this refurbished historic brick building on Meeting Street, stands...

... my goddaughter?

Alena Allen steps out of the elevator, her big brown eyes frantically searching the room until they find mine, and *something's wrong*.

I've known Alena for too long, from when she was a toddler to a young woman now. *Very much a woman*, I made sure of it.

And I shouldn't have. It was the most taboo and tempting and traitorous thing I've ever done, but I couldn't say no to her. I couldn't resist her tears.

"Michael..." Alena marches my way, using my pseudonym. The one that hides my American name—Axel. It's one of my many lies, hiding the name I was born with—Aleksi Kholodov. "We need to talk, please."

Yes, lies. They hunt *me* when I'm around Alena.

"Ahem." I clear the sudden strangle over my throat. Turning to Ruby, I fight like hell to hide this from her. From everyone. "Ms. Jones, clear my afternoon."

"But," Ruby debates me, "Helen's getting lunch. She's your assistant. I don't know what your schedule is."

Yes, I make sure of it. Until now...

I grab a pen from Ruby's desk, quickly scrawling the password to my schedule, kept on Helen's computer while the dangerously familiar aroma of Alena's perfume nears. It's powdery and innocent. Just as she was ... before me.

"Do it," I order Ruby. "Ms. Allen is family, and I need to meet with her." My pulse triples. "*Please.*"

Ruby arches a brow at my pleasantry. At my plea.

I want to say something shitty and mean to her—something so characteristically me because if Ruby really hated our fights, she'd quit. Any law firm would kill to have her. But no, that's my instinct. I'll kill to *keep* her. Ruby's mine. She loves our fights, too, but not around Alena.

I'm a different man with her. Indeed, Alena has no idea who I am, either.

Yes, I'm the most respected property lawyer in South Carolina. Yes, I've been her godfather since Alena was ten. Yes, her father is my best friend; he's like my brother. So yes, I'm a dead man if Nash Allen ever finds out about me and his daughter.

Sure, Alena knows to hide our secret from her father, but she doesn't know she's engaged to my baby brother now.

Their engagement party is tonight.

Hell, that's probably why she's here because I won't let Alena tell her fiancé about us. *No one can know about us.*

But Alena's too honest. Too innocent. It's killing her to lie while I live for it. Lies keep me alive. They keep my brothers alive. I have six ex-Bratva brothers, counting Nash, and if they find out about me and Alena, it *will* kill us. Our secret will kill my family.

To Alena, I'm her biggest secret.

To me, she's my sweetest shame.

To Ruby?

Politely, I hold my office door open for Alena. She brushes past me, fully trusting and familiar. It's instinct. I barely touch Alena's back, always protecting her, before I glance over my shoulder, catching the look in Ruby's eyes.

They're searching. They're suspicious. They're ... *oh, fuck* ... jealous?

Get Jace's bonus scene and more on KellyFinley.com

DEAR READER,

THERE'S MUCH MORE TO COME WITH THE BELLES & BRATVA BEASTS. AXEL. SIRE. LOCH. JACE. THE QUEEN AND SOME SURPRISES. MORE SECRETS WILL BE REVEALED. MORE SPICE WILL BE SHARED. MORE SNARK WILL FIRE. OH, AND SOME HOT, CRAZY, CONTRACT-KILLER, COWBOY COUSINS ARE COMING, TOO. JOIN MY NEWSLETTER FOR FREE BONUS SCENES, TEASERS, AND MORE.

ALSO BY KELLY FINLEY

-Interconnected Books & Audiobooks

Available in Kindle Unlimited and Audible-

BELLES & BRATVA BEASTS

NASH

AXEL

SIRE

LOCH

JACE

A Not-Mafia-Mafia, Dark RomCom Series

SHAMELESS PLAY

SHAMELESS GAME

featuring Blair, Beau & Colton

A Frenemies to Lovers, Why Choose, Football romance

MAKE HIM

featuring Luca & Scarlett with Zar and Nick

A Billionaire Dom, MMF, Why Choose Romance & Audiobook

TEMPT HER

featuring Stacey & her husbands

MMMF, Why Choose Revenge Romance & Audiobook

HOLIDAY FOR SIX

HALLOWEEN FOR SIX

with cameos of MCs from characters above and below!

VERY SPICY, LOTS OF FRIENDS TO LOVERS ROMCOMS &
AUDIOBOOKS

ALL FOR HIM

featuring Silas & Eily Van de May with Cade and Redix

A FORBIDDEN CINDERELLA RETELLING POLY ROMANCE

AFTER HIM

WITH HIM

AN ANGSTY SECOND CHANCE TO AN MMF, WHY CHOOSE DUET

PROTECT HER

PIERCE HER

HUNT HER

CHASE HER

A SPICY, ROMANTIC SUSPENSE, BODYGUARD/CELEBRITY TRILOGY

JOIN MY NEWSLETTER.

I SHARE SNEAK PEEKS, GIVEAWAYS, AND MORE.

KELLYFINLEY.COM

ACKNOWLEDGMENTS

My husband and silver fox: As long as you keep me in coffee and kisses, I promise to take you to paradise to read my books.

My Book Team: Deborah and Lizzie, my proofreaders! It takes two to find my typos. Thank you so much. Thank you, Lori, for another stunning cover design. All hail, Wander Aguiar and his gorgeous photo of Aaron. As always ... big hugs to my BTS team: Ange, Ashley, Brit, Erica, Kenzie, and more.

My Beta Team: Brittany, Heather, Jay, Katelyn, Marie, Pana, Rachel, and Thorunn. I love y'all! Your comments gave me giggles, ideas, and inspo.

Kelly's Spicy Team & ARC Team: I love our sweet, smutty group! Your posts, reviews, and support melt my heart, while our DMs and chats kick my feet. I truly can't do it without you all. Like. Legit. Thank you!

#Bookstagram, #BookTok, and FB Spicy Book Babes: You truly keep me going. I love hearing from you! I get all teary at your edits and comments. Thanks for your love.

Romance bookstores! I found you! I love supporting you or just popping by. Here's to filling shelves and hearts with smut.

Author Friends & Mentors: Particularly Eva, Maggie, Rachel, and Trisha! You listen, and you only judge others (lol). I am not alone with book besties like you.

Best for last - You, my readers: Thank you for giving

your time to share this story with me. I welcome your messages, posts, and emails and promise to keep giving you more spice.

Please leave your honest review. It's the greatest gift to an author.

Xoxo,
Kelly

ABOUT THE AUTHOR

Kelly Finley lives in the Carolinas with her sexy husband and sweet family.

A rebel with many causes, she fancies black leather, dirty jokes, big hearts, and smart mouths.

She believes in shameless love, so much so that her readers started calling her **"The Queen of Spice,"** and she wears her crown with pride.

Dedicated to writing swoony, spicy books, she's most likely at her keyboard putting the next hot story on the page for you.

Want to connect with Kelly and her readers?

Website: KellyFinley.com

for free bonus scenes, her newsletter, special editions & more

instagram.com/kellyfinleybooks

threads.com/@kellyfinleybooks

tiktok.com/@kellyfinleybooks

facebook.com/KellyFinleyBooks

bookbub.com/authors/kelly-finley

goodreads.com/goodreads_kelly_finley

amazon.com/author/kellyfinley